Born in Carlisle in the surroundings of Roman antiquities, Thelma became fascinated by history at an early age. The past as well as the present has always enthralled her, particularly the interweaving of both together. She always wanted to share more of her love of history, and especially the quiet corner of her heart that still lives in Hadrian's country.

Marrying a sailor meant a nomadic lifestyle, something she still embraces. Her occupations have ranged from teaching in Derbyshire, to a steam-engine fireman in Wales, to nursing gunshot wounds in New Zealand. North Wales is her current home.

Also by the same author

Relative Dating
ISBN: 978 184386 456 1 (Vanguard Press)

Tree Dimensional
ISBN: 978 184386 512 4 (Vanguard Press)

Grave Doubts
ISBN: 978 184386 557 5 (Vanguard Press)

Diverse Distress

Thelma Hancock

Diverse Distress

Vanguard Press

VANGUARD PAPERBACK

© Copyright 2009
Thelma Hancock

The right of Thelma Hancock to be identified as author of
this work has been asserted by her in accordance with the
Copyright, Designs and Patents Act 1988.

A CIP catalogue record for this title is
available from the British Library.

ISBN 978 184386 558 2

Vanguard Press is an imprint of
Pegasus Elliot MacKenzie Publishers Ltd.
www.pegasuspublishers.com

First Published in 2009

Vanguard Press
Sheraton House Castle Park
Cambridge England

Printed and bound in Great Britain

Disclaimer

While historical details are believed to be accurate all the characters in this book have no existence outside the imagination of the author, and have no relation whatsoever to anyone bearing the same name or names. They are not even distinctly inspired by any individual known or unknown to the author and all the incidents are pure invention.

1

"Poor Bastard!" The comment was accompanied by a puff of condensation as the speaker breathed out into the cold, wet atmosphere.

Detective Inspector Sandy Bell, holding a powerful police torch steady on the water in front of them, looked at the speaker and then across to his partner. He wasn't sure if Mark Forester was referring to the top of the corpse's head, the hair a strange silver weed swaying gently on the outgoing tide; or to the much stiller head of Bob McInnis as it viewed the corpse, but he agreed anyway. Either man, he felt, deserved the comment.

He blinked the rain out of his eyes and flicked his cowlick of grey-brown hair off his forehead. "Yeah." He gave an infinitesimal shiver and then turned to the young forensics man. "What time can we expect the divers?"

DS Mark Forester, warmly wrapped against the late September rain, stood on the side of the Senhouse Dock at Maryport, and looked down into the inky water as he absently tucked his mobile away in a back pocket. "They're sending a team down from Ayr. Should be here in a couple of hours. I vote we get tea in the incident van and wait for them, sir. Not much in the way of forensics I can do yet, or anyone else for that matter."

Sandy nodded. He couldn't see much sense in standing around at one thirty in the morning in rain which wasn't so much a sheet as a badly sliced shroud, and with the strong odour of decaying vegetable matter and oil infiltrating his nostrils and cosying down at the back of his throat. He could think of better things to do. He'd lay his last pound he'd be tasting eau de school cabbage for the next twenty-four hours.

"OK, go and put the kettle on, lad." He turned back to his partner as he removed the torch beam from the scene and Mark moved off. "Bob?" He took a couple of steps nearer the dockside and gently touched the younger man's arm. "Bob, let's get out of the wet, lad. Nothing we can do here."

Detective Inspector Robert McInnis gave a shrug, in resignation rather than to dislodge the hand, but moved away from the greasy stone edge. He turned and walked beside the older man, skirting the pools of pitch black and oily water, through the rain with its soft patter a funereal drum beat on their shoulders.

They headed to the big white van on the far side of the dock, the lights beckoning them towards warmth and a spurious comfort. McInnis offered no comment until they were both inside the well lit space. He stood blinking; allowing his eyes to adjust to the brightness as he pulled off his heavy, waxed, Burberry and dropped it on the nearest bench. He dropped down beside it and behind a small Formica table. "Rain's going to make our job harder."

Sandy nodded and took the seat opposite, shuffling his fifty-year-old body into the corner and resting his arms on the table top.

The inside of the van was in stark contrast to the cold autumn night outside. The whole presented a slightly clinical atmosphere under the glare of strong overhead lighting. The far end was occupied with banks of screens above small desks. All the screens grey and empty as yet, the small lights and dials surrounding them, shuttered and silent. One side of the van had a row of computers humming quietly on standby, like virtuosos warming up for the big solo.

The other side had a long low board area jutting out from the wall, with pieces of technical equipment and a couple of landlines, their spaghetti-like wires wriggling across the surface to disappear into wormholes at the back.

Sandy sighed, relaxing, "This is going to be a difficult one, lad. I don't know who's in that water but it doesn't look like a suicide to me."

"No, Sandy, it doesn't," said McInnis, watching absently as Forester stood making tea in the corner behind the driver's seat, the one real concession to humanity in the sea of technical equipment.

Mark came over with mugs of the hot, sweet tea. Sandy Bell accepted his mug and wrapped his hands around the pottery, seeking some warmth for chilled appendages, then pulled a face as the hot aches crept up, in his fingers. McInnis looked up, nodding his thanks as the younger man set a mug in front of him.

"This is your home town isn't it, Mark?"

"Yeah, I moved to Carlisle after university, when I joined the force, sir."

"You know anything about boats and tides and such?" McInnis took a tiny sip of tea, breathing in the steam more than drinking the liquid, and looked the younger man over. Forester looked like a fashion plate, even at this ungodly hour. The guinea-gold curls shone in the overhead lights as they clung to his scalp like so much lambs wool; the jeans might be stonewash, but they carried a brand name; the polo-neck had a Calvin Klein logo on the pocket. The man, Bob thought, smelled of expensive aftershave, he'd also shaved; something neither Sandy nor Bob had bothered to do.

"My dad used to run a fishing smack out of here, sir."

Bob sighed. "Mark, it's too early in the day, or maybe too late in the night, to be calling me 'sir'. Do you think you could bring yourself to call me Bob when we aren't in company?"

Mark gave him a quick surprised look. "Yes, of course... Bob."

"OK. I know damn all about boats and the sea, so I'm going to be picking your brains a bit on this one."

Sandy settled back against the van side, allowing Mark to sit down next to him. "How deep does this harbour get?"

"About twenty-seven feet at high spring tide, maybe only twenty at neap."

Sandy pushed back a still damp cowlick of grey-brown hair. "And already I'm out of my depth, lad. Again, and in English, for us landlubbers."

Mark flashed a grin. "Sorry, sir. Every month the tide range, high to low, varies. The maximum range is called a spring tide and the minimum range is called a neap tide." He looked at his two superiors, checking they were with him; they seemed to be.

"But there is also a variation throughout the year. The highest variations are in spring and autumn, the lowest in summer and winter, all about the time of the equinoxes. I don't know the exact parameters of the harbour off the top of my head, sir, but I can contact the Harbour Master or my dad, they'd know." He lifted a buttock to pull his mobile out again.

"No, lad, let them sleep, for now." Sandy laid a hand on his arm. "We'll be disturbing enough people before this case is over." He sipped more tea. "I asked the wrong question before; what I should have said is, how high up the wall does it go and how near the mud at the bottom does it get?"

"Ah!" Mark mentally stepped back and reassessed his audience. "Er! Maximum height about twenty-five feet, with about three foot of freeboard." He caught the look on Sandy's face, as of a man with acute toothache. "Three foot to the top of the wall above the water." He paused for thought, "Probably about four foot of water over the mud, but more in the central channel and less where it's silted up."

"Let's not worry about the channel lad, he ain't in the channel." Sandy rubbed a hand over his face; he was tired and this young man was trying to be helpful. "The height or do I mean depth?" A puzzled frown flitted across his face, barely wrinkling the surface, then he waved a hand, brushing the words aside as if they were a silken cobweb touching and obscuring his thoughts. "Whatever. Would it be common knowledge to anyone working around the harbour then?"

Mark wrinkled his brow. "I should think so, but more in relation to how much their boat draws and what state of the tide they could enter and leave the harbour."

"Hmm." Bob McInnis frowned down into his mug. "Are we looking at someone who didn't want the corpse found but didn't know how shallow the water got?"

"That's a damn good question, Bob. How long before the tide is out, Mark?"

"About another two hours, maybe two and a half, Inspector Bell."

Sandy cocked his head on one side, "It's a pity we can't stop it coming back in."

"Harbour Master can shut the gates, sir."

"Right, I knew that!" Sandy grinned wryly. "Arrange that will you, Mark, as soon as it's a decent hour to rouse the man."

The men sat silently listening to the patter of the rain on the roof of the van. Bob was remembering holidays that smelled and sounded like this, holidays in small caravans at the seaside, where he'd drawn pictures and waited for the sun to come out. He allowed the sounds to seep and soothe.

They'd all been summoned from their beds in Carlisle at midnight, at the request of the Maryport constabulary who had been

17

disturbed shortly before that by the apparent ravings of a couple of drunken teenagers.

Sandy Bell stirred on the seat at the quiet entry of a burly young constable. "Gareth, got the lighting arranged, lad?"

"Yes, chief. The local lads say they'll have the place as floodlit as an international game in another half hour." He came over to the table as he spoke; his tired voice had a slight sing-song quality, betraying his Welsh roots. He stood, forming a small puddle around his number ten, police-issue boots as he waited for orders, like a small tree come to rest inside the van.

Bell looked up at him. "Don't stand there dripping and looming, lad! Get a hot drink and then tell us what the locals make of it all."

Gareth turned away, flicked the switch on the kettle, and then swung back, wiping his hand over his face. They all heard the rasp of his five o'clock shadow. "Jason Meeks, the Sergeant, Scene of Crime Officer, isn't sure what to make of it, sir. But he's got several ideas."

"Let's hear some of them, Gareth." Bob McInnis tipped back his sleek brown head and leaned it against the white paint of the bulkhead of the van, looking at the young man's dark, serious, twenty-something face.

"When they got the first call, they thought it was a couple of drunken teenagers, messing about. He says it's an ongoing war to keep them from drowning themselves or breaking their necks jumping into the harbour!" Gareth swung round at the quiet click of the kettle, and poured water onto a spoonful of instant coffee. He slopped in a good dollop of milk and turned back, holding the pottery between his large hands.

"They sent the constable down to see what was going on, because you have to check these things out don't you?" He sipped and an expression of bliss flitted across his face as the warm liquid stole down his throat and settled into his stomach, like a cat settling on a cushion.

"Anyway, he found a couple of youths who might have been drunk some time last night, but who seemed sober when the copper got to them. Apparently no amount of alcopop or lager can withstand finding a dead body." Gareth leaned back comfortably against the small jutting surface of the service centre, crossing his legs at the ankles and warming his hands on the mug.

Neither of the police inspectors present passed a comment at this flagrant lack of discipline. Mark glanced at them both in surprise. He'd been the recipient of Sandy Bell's cutting castigations once or twice, when he'd forgotten to give Bell the respect his rank merited.

"The Sarge' said the constable had called it in as a genuine find and checked the area, but there were only the two teenagers so he secured them in the police car and waited for reinforcements." Gareth sipped more coffee.

"Sergeant Meeks thought at first the man had fallen in. It's pretty close to the side of the harbour. The teenagers say he's fastened down though."

"What exactly were they doing?"

"We…ll, they claim they were just daring each other to jump in, but it seems more likely they were planning on, or maybe had already, nicked a boat for some other nefarious purpose. Since both of them are relatively dry and they claim to have tried to pull the body out, I don't think they did much jumping in the water." His lips twitched. "They know they're in enough trouble already, one's fourteen and the other's just turned sixteen. They've both been sick as dogs already, part booze and part their first sight of death probably."

A knock on the door heralded the arrival of the local Detective Sergeant for Maryport. Gareth ap Rhys was standing upright, coffee mug behind him, at parade rest, before the man had swung around from closing the door.

"This is Detective Sergeant Oakes, sir." Gareth introduced the black haired, fifty something, thickset man who'd just entered.

Oakes nodded at the three seated men.

"Get him a drink, Constable, and then perhaps you could check to see how the SOCO is getting on."

Gareth nodded his head. Turning he flicked the switch on the kettle again at the man's quiet "Coffee, black, no sugar, Constable." It was obvious to everyone present that he had the makings of a world-class cold. His voice rasped out as thick as porridge. He also seemed to be in a time-share deal with 'Rudolph the reindeer' for the nose. Sandy found himself thinking, uncharitably, that the man could have stayed in bed, instead of spreading his germs about and creating more problems for them.

Gareth handed over the mug of hot liquid and left the van, causing it to rock slightly as he shut the door behind himself and jumped down outside.

"I understand you've sent for some police divers from Ayr?"

Mark nodded at Oakes.

"Kendal's nearer."

"They've been searching Ullswater for a missing walker, sir, couldn't come over the mountain yet."

Detective Oakes nodded an understanding that Bell and McInnis didn't have. They exchanged a look; Sandy would find out what that meant when the locals weren't around.

"They said they could send a team tomorrow if we needed them."

"I'm hoping we won't, and this is just some fool falling over and getting his foot hooked in something on the floor of the basin." He sipped the hot coffee. "But I'm very much afraid it isn't." He set the mug down and pulled out a hanky, wiping his nose before blowing it vigorously.

"I'm not going to be much use to you, I'm afraid. My head feels as though it's stuffed with sheep's wool. Even worse, you're all coming at me through a foggy haze." He shook his head in disgust and pocked a finger in one ear, wiggling it about. "Grandkids came to visit last weekend and this is the result. The wife is even worse!" Bell now felt guilty at his previous thoughts; the man was obviously ill.

Oakes stowed the handkerchief in a side pocket of his Mac. "We're checking the missing persons list for the area, but until we get a visual of the face it's not a lot of help. I arranged for a fifty-metre perimeter, but that body looks as though it's been there awhile. On its second three, from the brief look I got from the harbour wall just now, and the boy's accounts. Your clues will have been trampled and washed away long since."

"Second three?"

Mark glanced across at McInnis' quiet words. "Roughly, sir, bodies sink for three days, surface for three days, and then sink for three weeks, sir, though wrapping and water temperature and place affect all that, but second three. Detective Oakes means it's been in the water for about a week, sir."

"Ah! Right, thank you, Forester." He looked at the local man, "We hadn't fully heard the report of the original finding."

"The lads state they were messing about on the harbour wall, and spotted something in the water. They couldn't have seen it from

21

the wall, it's too dark, so they must have been in the water themselves, physically, or in a boat, but we won't worry about that for now." Like a cow clearing its throat, Oakes sniffed prodigiously, whether as a result of his cold, or as an addendum to his previous comment, his listeners couldn't tell.

"They say they borrowed one of the dinghies to go and investigate, and saw what they thought was a seal bobbing in the water. When they got up close they realised it was a human head, and tried to pull him onboard without success." He pulled out his handkerchief and blew. It sounded to McInnis like a greylag goose calling to its mate.

"Give them their due," Oakes spoke round the white cloth, his bushy eyebrows moving independently like denuded hedgerows blown by a gale, "they did contact the coppers even though they knew they were going to be in trouble with us and their parents."

Sandy grunted an acknowledgement, "So what's the plan of action?"

Oakes sniffed again. "Now you're here I'm going home to my bed. If you need me you can contact me, but I've arranged with Sergeant Meeks to cooperate with you fully. I'll tell you straight I've never dealt with a murder, nor do I want to start now. I've got six months to retirement and I can hardly wait."

Sandy looked more closely at the man; his hair was still thick and black and his face cherubic; he must be older than he looked if he was old enough to retire, or... Sandy looked again while McInnis spoke, early retirement? He wondered if or why?

"That's fine by us, sir, if you're sure. As it happens we've brought our own local knowledge across with us."

Oakes looked across, nodding at Mark Forester again, "Say hi to your father, Mark. I haven't seen him for weeks. He keeping OK?"

22

"Not so bad. He took Mum away for a cruise this summer, thought it might improve her asthma."

"That's a good one, a fisherman going for a holiday on a ship!" Oakes sniggered slightly, and then stopped as he had to cough.

Mark grinned, "Well the Lotto win last year was a great help for both of them. He couldn't have run the boat much longer, between rising diesel prices and EU quotas, and she was getting worse every winter."

And that, Bob McInnis thought, explained the clothes and some of the attitude to them, like a small child with a new pair of shoes.

After a little more housekeeping information about the local staff Oakes took his departure and the three men settled down to await the diving team and the dawn. Both were going to take some time to arrive.

Three thirty found the crime scene ready for processing. The harbour area, and especially the area the police were interested in, lent itself rather well to cordoning having two basins, one in front of the other, with a road that circumnavigated both in a capital E shape. The centre of the E was a high wall and the openings of the E gave access to the harbour channel. These openings could be closed to sea traffic, and the sea itself, with gates.

Gareth had arranged for the gates to be closed as soon as the tide was at slack water, around, four o'clock. He'd contacted the Harbour Master, a surprisingly young man for such a responsible post. Hugh Pheby had a moustache and a shrewd pair of blue eyes. He'd taken in the situation very quickly when he arrived and was busy arranging for the fishing boats that were out to find berths further down the coast in Whitehaven.

Gareth was standing in his office, while Pheby used the RT to speak to captains and masters. The Harbour Master's office had a commanding view of most of the area. Gareth was planning on asking the man a few general questions as soon as Pheby had dealt with the shipping problems. He absently noted that Pheby didn't give a reason over the RT, just a command which apparently he expected to be obeyed without explanation.

The constable looked through rain-bespattered glass out over the water, and took careful note of the area where the body should now be visible under the large halogen lights the local police had erected. He moved his position and again looked through the glass, then moved to yet another area of window. Moving away he came into the middle of the room, standing at ease, and waited patiently for the man to finish speaking, then spoke before Pheby could call yet another mariner. "I'll go and report to my DI. Is it alright if they come up to your office for a few minutes?"

"Sure, be my guest. The sooner you see and do what you have to, the sooner we get back to normal."

Gareth nodded his thanks and left the room as he heard the man calling yet another boat. He walked round the commercial dock and made for the incident van. It was crammed with large male bodies all apparently expressing some opinion divergent from everyone else. He winced at the wall of noise battering his eardrums, and the smell of wet rainwear permeating the inside of the van. He decided not to add his voice and body to the throng, but looked rather pleadingly across the room at Inspector Bell.

Sandy grabbed his coat and squeezed his way past the multitude of policemen now filling the space. He managed to tag Bob on the way and the pair left, shrugging into their coats as they went.

The three stood outside the closed door in the relative quiet of the rainy night. "Diving team, sir?"

"Yeah, they got here ten minutes ago," McInnis said, with a quiet hiss of his zip, fastening his coat and hunching his shoulders, swinging his back to the worst of the rain and wind. "How are we doing? Are we nearly ready for them?" He finished pressing down poppers as he spoke to Gareth.

"Another hour to slack water, sir. The Harbour Master, name of Pheby, says he'll shut the gates then. The local lads have got the whole area cordoned off." The constable swung his bulk around, looking past the van at the cordoned section of pier. "The press were like moths round a flame as soon as we'd got the lights up, but they won't see much from there and hopefully we can keep them away for a while." Gareth sniffed and looked back to the inspectors' faces.

"The café owners grumbled a bit and so did the crazy golf people, especially ringing them up in the middle of the night. But when we said it was a murder scene they got all excited, and there hasn't been any more trouble from them."

Sandy gave a muted grunt of laughter; he recognised cynicism when he met it.

Gareth ignored the interruption. "I think it's being able to say you know what the police are doing that pleases them so much." Gareth shrugged his shoulders in his heavy police issue rainwear, reminding Bell of a tarpaulin tent lifting in the wind. "Not many locals about yet, too cold and wet. We're lucky it's the tail of the season; the marina's all but empty of boats by October, and that's the end of next week."

Sandy looked at Bob. "So where do you want to start, Bob?"

Bob glanced at the closed door of the van. "The ME on call is due in an hour, she's going to go out in a dinghy and then we can set the divers on to getting the body out. I think we'd better leave that bit to Mark; he seems to know what we need and he talks their jargon."

"When we have a timeline I'll see if the locals can find any witnesses." Sandy blinked rain away. "There won't be much in the way of clues on the ground what with rain and sea water, so we might as well keep the lads occupied as you say, Bob."

"Sir?" Gareth looked across at Bob. "I had an idea while I was talking to the Harbour Master. I'm not sure, but I think it might be best if you went up to his office."

Bob cocked his head on one side. "OK, lead the way." He caught the flash of surprise on Gareth's face. "We might as well go now before it gets busy."

They followed the roadway down one side of the commercial basin, the orange lighting wavering on the wind-whipped waves. As they reached the first corner of the oblong of water, a block of flats faced them. Going past the closed curtains of these, Bob reflected that the residents would have a bird's eye view of the police activities for the next few days. It ought to give them fuel for gossip for months.

Approaching the second corner they were confronted by a brick wall running parallel to the quayside, which formed the third side of the rectangle, the fourth being filled with the dock gates facing out to the sea and the channel for the river Ellen. Sandy rubbed a wet nose and looked at the young constable striding ahead of them into the gloom. "If he'd said, I would have brought the squad car, Bob. I'm not as young as I was and it's raining harder than ever!"

Bob offered the first smile of the day, a gentle curve of lips that failed to reach his fine brown eyes. "The exercise is good for us, Sandy." He stuck his hands into his pockets and walked steadily through the downpour. Ahead he could see a small building on the top of the wall; it reminded him of a school trip down the Rhine he'd once taken, where small medieval forts had guarded the river banks. The building was outlined against the sky by the strong halogen lighting that the police team had placed over the second basin.

The Harbour Master's office overlooked both basins and the entrance from the sea. Bob nodded at the building. "Our destination I take it?"

He was rewarded by a grunt of acknowledgement. Sandy said he needed a full eight hours' sleep these days; his wife said that sometimes she woke grumpy, and sometimes she let him sleep. But she'd said it with a very affectionate look at her husband.

The three police officers went up the wooden steps which climbed the outside of the building, and entered the brightly lit, glass-sided room. The smell of a schoolroom was the first thing that Bob noticed: a smell compounded of pencil graphite and wet socks.

Odd, he thought as Gareth introduced them, how situations and smells unlocked memories; he was definitely back in his school years this morning, where bullies and rivals and class clowns proliferated. He wondered how many of each he was going to encounter on this case.

"This is my Detective Inspector and his partner, Mr Pheby. DI Bell and DI McInnis."

Sandy and Bob shook the rain from their heads and shook hands with the Harbour Master like a couple of terriers coming in from a swim in the briny. "Good morning, sir, not that it is good between the rain and a murder. We're grateful for your assistance." While Sandy spoke, Bob filed away Gareth's introduction. Which, he wondered, was that young man's 'detective' and which 'his' partner? He swung his mind away from the irrelevance and looked Pheby over.

Pheby was doing a little looking on his own account. He addressed Bell, "I can't say it's a pleasure, gentleman, but we all have our jobs to do. You only have to ask and I'll do my best to oblige you. I want this business dealt with too."

Underneath the pleasantries Bob caught a hint of something else, impatience perhaps.

Gareth spoke up, "The body is down in that direction, sir." He pointed downwards and both detectives looked towards the window.

"Where?"

"That's what I wanted you to see, sir. It's the one bit of water you can't see clearly from here. I thought it might be relevant."

Sandy moved closer to the window, all but pressing his nose to the glass like a small boy peering into a toyshop. He looked down into the marina through the steamy and rainwashed window. He polished his exhaled breath away with a damp hand. He could see minions of the law moving about in the brilliantly lit area, their bodies silhouetted by the halogens. However, the corner directly under the office where the detectives stood was obscured by the very nearness to the wall the building was sitting on. "Well spotted, Gareth. I wonder if our murderer knew this was a blind spot?"

- Bob was watching the Harbour Master; now the man appeared to be angry. Bob filed away the reaction for future thought and maybe, investigation.

"Who has access to your office, sir?"

"Quite a few people, Inspector." Pheby took his attention from Sandy and his antics with the window pane and looked at McInnis quietly observing everyone. "People come in for charts, or to have cargo manifests checked. They come asking permission to berth, or use the landing areas, for weather reports, to pay dues, all sorts of reasons. I know them all."

"I'll need a list, sir."

"What, all of them?"

"Yes, sir."

Pheby raised an eyebrow, a slightly appalled look sidling into his eyes on a recce. "That could take some time. What time frame are you talking about here, Inspector?"

Bob paused, scratching his head and flicking the wet hair back yet again. "I should think over the last six months."

He registered the slight gasp but ignored it, swinging round to look at Sandy. "Anything else we need for now?"

Sandy looked from one man to the other. "Not at the moment. When we have a bit more information we'll probably have to interview you formally, sir."

"Thank you, sir." Bob gave Pheby a nod and turned to go, the others following him out. They clattered down the wooden stairs and stood at the bottom forming a huddle in a puddle.

"Gareth, go and see if the On-Call Doctor is here yet and bring her along when she arrives. You've arranged a boat?"

"Yes, sir."

The detectives watched him stride off. "He's going for detective as soon as he gets his stripes up, did you know?"

"He'll make a good detective. Do you suppose I'm your partner, or vice versa?"

"What?"

"Doesn't matter, Sandy." Bob turned away, walking around the corner and coming to a halt at the hidden corner next to the marina gates. He looked about in the artificial light. It was a rather surreal picture. "It's a good spot, Sandy. The high wall shields anyone from the land side. The Harbour Master can't see down and the other side is seaward. The only places you could get a good view are the north and south, from over there or the marina itself."

He pointed across the harbour entrance at the long mole on the far side, a dark concrete shadow pointing out to sea and forming one side of the harbour entrance. "Not much lighting over there, just widely spaced sodium lights. You'd need good eyesight, on a dark night, to see what was going on over here."

Sandy nodded agreement. "We'll need tide tables and a lunar calendar to see what the moon was doing. Once we've determined how long the poor man has been in the water that is!" He ran a finger around his collar where easing rain was sneaking down, searching out the warmth of his body with cold fingers, and a malignant desire to chill him physically and mentally.

Bob McInnis seemed indifferent to his own physical discomfort. Sandy tried not to let it worry him. McInnis hadn't been the same since his wife had died five months before. He knew the man hadn't got over grieving yet.

Bob, oblivious both to his partner's thoughts and the slackening rain, moved to the side of the basin. He looked down into the water at the head and torso that the tide had now revealed for his inspection.

The body was no longer apparently standing up at attention, but leaning over, unsupported by the water, so that he looked down on the back of a head and suited torso, as if the corpse had decided to do a bit of snorkelling in the harbour and observe the sea life, and generally drift lazily on the tide. "I wonder why no one else saw him before this, Sandy? You can hardly miss him floating about there, and we haven't got to low tide yet according to Mark."

Sandy stood slightly back from the wall. He didn't care for heights that beckoned you into cold water, and it must be over twenty foot down to the surface now. He shook his head. "Hm, I dunno, Bob."

Sandy looked sideways at Bob; he could see the resemblance to his old partner, Bob's father. He had been a handsome man too. The lighting caused Bob's features to have harsher lines than one might expect to find on a man of thirty-five. The hair had just a hint of grey at the sides. The boy had had his fair share of grief over the last few years. The strong patrician nose was flaring at the increasing reek of seaweed and the flotsam and jetsam crowding behind the harbour gate and the corner of the harbour wall.

Sandy peered down cautiously at the body; it now had its own small corona of detritus, cans, bits of paper, broken net, and one inquisitive seagull.

"We'll have to move soon or some of our evidence will become breakfast, Sandy." Bob scooped up and threw a handy pebble at a herring gull, which flapped lazily away and upwards, coming to rest on a handy bollard from where it proceeded to proclaim its right to the territory. It threw back its head and emitted harsh shrieks of protest at the milling constabulary.

Sandy nodded. "It looks like some of the gentleman has already been nibbled by the fish anyway, Bob."

"Yeah." McInnis pulled a face of mild disgust. "I hope that Doctor gets here soon. It's not as if we don't know the poor man is dead after all."

Bell shrugged, "Rules, lad. Rain's easing." He shrugged deeper into his raincoat as he looked up at the dark sky made darker by the pools of lighting they stood under. "Have you heard from Mary this week?" It was asked oh-so casually, but Sandy Bell almost held his breath as he waited for the answer.

McInnis nodded. "Hector has his posting through. He flies to Germany in three days; she'll take the kids out next weekend. He goes to Afghanistan in a fortnight."

Sandy desperately wanted to ask what Bob was going to do about his baby, a daughter, Mary, his sister had been caring for, for the past five months, but hadn't quite got the nerve against that clipped delivery. Before he could think of a way to frame the question, the moment was lost as they both heard the approach of a heavy vehicle.

"Doctor?"

"Maybe."

However the vehicle that pulled up on the solid tarmac between the two basins was obviously part of the diving crew's equipment. Mark hopped out of the seven-and-a-half-ton Iveco diesel lorry and came towards them. It might be a murder investigation but he was enjoying himself.

"Sir, the team are getting kitted out now. I partly came to show them the way and partly to bring you the preliminary missing persons report. There's only about seven on it so far." He looked over the edge. "And we can wipe off the four women by the looks of it." He stepped back and looked at the two senior men, "The Doctor should be here in about five minutes. She phoned to say she was on her way. It's a locum doctor from down Penrith way, but she's working at Greystone just now."

Sandy Bell nodded acknowledgement. "Thank God for that. Maybe we can start to do our job then."

He turned to Mark. "Why Scottish divers, Mark? What was that about coming over the mountain?"

"Decompression, sir."

Sandy exchanged a look with Bob and raised an eyebrow. Mark caught the look.

"When you dive you have to decompress as you surface." He waited for their nod. "If you surface and then go higher than sea level the blood can fizz. Even going up over the fells can create problems, sir."

32

"OK got that." Sandy nodded, "Have the local boys got any likely suspects and witnesses for us?"

"There's an elderly man been missing a fortnight, wandered away from home. He's a little absent minded, but perfectly able to care for himself. His daughter reported him missing, but they think it's more a case of him having had enough of nagging than foul play. The locals have been searching, but nobody has seen anything. Couple of local drunks might have seen something, one's under lock and key even as we speak, the other hasn't been seen for a week." He paused. "That might be him, bit hard to tell at the moment."

McInnis spoke. "Wouldn't that make life easy? Here's our Doctor, I hope."

A small blue car pulled up behind the police diving van. The rather stunning figure of a thirty-something emerged; she wore a bright red, three-quarter-length, duffel coat and dark blue jeans. Mark noted that these were filled to perfection when she bent over to speak to a small indeterminate breed of dog just visible on the back seat. Mark's "Very nice!" earned him a sharp look from Bob McInnis.

McInnis offered a hand as she approached. "DI McInnis, this is DI Bell, and this is DS Mark Forester, who I believe you've spoken to already."

The accent was barely perceptible when she spoke, but both McInnis and Mark pegged her as Penrith-born by the accent, which had distinctions from the general Cumbrian one which Bob, spoke. "Doctor Jennifer Lowther, your on-call doctor. So gentlemen, where's my body?"

Sandy's lips twitched; he suppressed the quick aside which would formerly have been made to Bob, about their young colleague having no trouble locating her body. Bob seemed to have lost his sense of humour along with his wife.

33

McInnis pointed down into the dock to where the body was now illuminated by yet more powerful spotlights supplementing the other harbour lighting.

"Ah, well, I should say, from this viewpoint, that he was very dead, but you know what they say, a body ain't dead until it's warm and dead." She gave them all the pleasure of admiring a small dimple in her left cheek as she smiled. "Boat?" She raised an eyebrow.

Mark, who appeared to be modelling for Madam Tussauds, came to life, nearly joining the corpse as he stumbled slightly. "I borrowed an R.I.B. It's down the steps over there."

Bob and Sandy exchanged a slightly wry smile as the younger man led the way to a set of steep, and very greasy, stone steps, leading down into the basin.

"R.I.B?"

"Don't ask me." McInnis shrugged.

They watched Mark hand her into the rigid inflatable with all the courtesy of a knight attending his lady. "Oh dear! I hope the boy isn't going to be trouble, it was bad enough when you and Beth..." Sandy stopped abruptly; cars hitting brick walls didn't cover it. "Damn! I'm sorry, Bob." The voice was full of compassion and the face full of contrition.

McInnis said nothing, but his face took on the shuttered look it had worn so much lately. Sandy didn't know how to get through to the man when his face had that expression: as if the owner had left the premises and the house had been boarded up.

They waited in silence for the doctor and Mark Forester to return. Sandy watched as Mark expertly sculled the dingy across the short distance and held it steady while the doctor leaned out and looked closely at the corpse. She stretched out a gloved hand and moved the head slightly, turning the face sideways out of the water.

She spoke softly to Mark, and set the body free again. Mark unshipped the oars and rowed against the slight swell back to the steps.

Sandy glanced at Bob McInnis; he was also watching the couple. "Perhaps we can get this job under way now." It was spoken quietly but Sandy heard the echo of his own words.

Mark had a hand on the doctor's arm. He led her up to the two other men. "Well, Doc, did you guess right? Dead." Sandy offered a weak smile.

"Very dead. I'm not absolutely positive, the face is badly decomposed, and the fish have been busy." They watched as she visibly swallowed. "But I'd say he's been in the water six to eight days. But the coroner will be able to tell you better." She stripped off and stowed the blue vinyl gloves, placing them in an evidence bag as she spoke.

The three men exchanged glances, and then Bob spoke. "Do you need to sit down, Doctor? You look rather pale."

"No. Just give me a minute." She turned her back on them, and looked out over the harbour entrance to the black line of the horizon. Sandy and Bob stood still, waiting patiently for her to recover. Mark swapped from foot to foot looking at her back. It was clear he was bursting to ask questions, or maybe he just wanted the toilet Sandy thought, sourly.

"Right. Thank you." Jennifer Lowther took a deep breath. She looked at the handsome profile and the fine brown eyes of Bob McInnis examining her with quiet sympathy. "I'll be fine, Inspector."

Sandy nodded and addressed her however. "OK, we'll get him out and then you can do whatever it is you need to do."

2

A police diver dressed in a dry suit, but without flippers or buoyancy wings, approached, splashing through physical puddles and the metaphorical puddle of silence which had followed. "Can we start now, sir? I've got the crew kitted out."

Bell turned to face him. "Yes, Constable...?"

"Sergeant Jeff Lyell, sir."

Sandy raised an eyebrow, "Lyell, family live down Seaview Crescent?"

Lyell raised an eyebrow in his turn. "Yes, sir."

"Say hi to your dad from Sandy Bell. Your dad is Senior Sergeant Ian Lyell isn't he?"

"Yes, sir."

"Went to school with him. Always had scabby knees. How's he doing?" Sandy looked at the sergeant with a smile.

"He's fine, sir." Lyell hid the grin. So his dad had scabby knees.

The gentle cough from Bob McInnis recalled Sandy to the present. He glanced across at Bob and then transferred the gaze to Jeff Lyell.

"Yes, well, Sergeant. Go ahead and get the team in the water. I want the body out and then the area searched for anything you think might be relevant. DS Forester will liaise with you." Bell nodded dismissal to the man and then turned to Mark. "Over to you, Mark, quicker the better." He stopped speaking as the huge metal gates began to move ponderously and creakily across the entrance to the marina, Transylvanian chateau wasn't in it.

"Slack water, sir. The Harbour Master said he'd close the basin off for us."

"Yes, I remember. OK, lad, go and do what you do."

Bell and McInnis stood back as the seven man team gathered at the steps and spoke to Mark Foster. There seemed some debate about an ROV, whatever that was, but otherwise the men carried out checks in an orderly fashion.

Two of their number carried a large and serviceable black dingy down the steps, with a third man following. After launching the dingy into the water they all climbed aboard. They rowed over to the body and waited for two others to step into the water off the bottom stone step and submerge, their nitrox tanks showing briefly as they flipped under the waves, and then with a flick of flippers they were under the corpse and boat with barely a ripple.

Bob McInnis turned back to the silent woman. "Right, Doctor Lowther, we'll have the body sent to the coroner, thank you."

"Thank you, Inspector. That poor man must have fallen into the dock."

She opened her mouth to speak again but Bob swung away, looking down into the water, watching the divers. One of them surfaced, making some sort of sign to the men in the boat who appeared to be occupied setting up a vertical line of lights in red, white and red at one end of the boat.

Sandy looked from her to the back of his silent partner. "Is there anything else you need to know, Doctor?"

Jennifer Lowther looked at the older man; Inspector Bell looked at her kindly. "No, no I don't think so." She glanced back at

McInnis; she wasn't vain but she did know that she rated a second glance, and the man had dismissed her. She wondered what she'd done wrong to offend him.

McInnis turned back as he heard the car driving away. "They seem rather excited down there, Sandy." He looked across at the top of the steps where Mark was talking to two divers. "Hi, Mark, what's going on?" Bob began to stroll towards the steps himself; Sandy went with him, taking care to keep away from the edge of the basin.

Mark came a few steps to meet him. "Don't know, sir." He looked across the expanse of water to where the boat was coming back with the corpse on board. "I'll see if they need a hand to bring him up, sir."

McInnis nodded and watched from near the top of the steps, absently noting that a couple of local constables had arrived with a stretcher which they carried down the steps to await the boat's arrival.

The sodden corpse was lifted from the boat and transferred to the stretcher, draining water as it moved from one position to the next. Even from the top he could see it was badly swollen, the clothes taut against the flesh of the neck and chest. The features grossly distorted, the skin grey and partially missing, so that the dermis, and even some bone, was visible across one cheekbone. He watched as they manoeuvred the remains upwards, and caught the rank stench before it arrived at the top along with the corpse.

McInnis looked impassively at the skeleton-like head; one of the eyes had sunk into the flesh of the face whilst the other appeared to be missing; the lips stretched into a grimace of apparent horror, revealing a protruding tongue through teeth. He skimmed down the body seeing the bound hands and feet, then backtracked as his brain registered that which his eyes had already noted, a thick cord attached around the neck and back to his feet. He heard Mark Forester mutter, "Poor bastard!" as that man also observed the rope.

Mark donned a pair of blue latex gloves and gingerly went through the suit pockets, coming up with a sodden handkerchief and a hearing aid in one trouser pocket but nothing in the jacket. "The hearing aid might help, sir, maybe get a serial number off it, if it's National Health-issue, but there's no wallet or card book, nothing to help us with identification." He stood back to allow the corpse to be covered with thick black plastic, mercifully shutting the sight from their eyes.

Mark turned to one of the men who'd come ashore and nodded. "The rope?"

"Yes, sir, the corpse was tied down. We cut it to get him out. He was fastened to a stone of some sorts attached to his feet, with the line running up to the neck rope. The lads will bring the stone up along with anything else. It's going to be slow work, sir. The bottom is silty and the wind's getting up."

"Divers can't work if it gets too windy, sir, disturbs the bottom mud too much, you can't see even with a full face mask and a rebreather. It can be dangerous in water that has this much pollutant in it." Mark supplied the information matter of factly and Bob accepted it as such.

"Definitely murder though, Constable?"

"No doubt about that, sir. Tied and thrown in would be my guess."

"Right, thank you."

The man turned away and Bob looked from Sandy to Mark. "You'd better go with him and see what you can glean from the clothes and such." He glanced up at the thick grey cloud scudding overhead, from which a few drops still fell, and obscuring a moon fighting to take its place in the galaxy of artificial lights.

Mark moved off in the wake of the stretcher and Sandy looked at McInnis. "What do you want me to do, Bob?"

"Do you want to check out the list of missing men to see if any of them fits the bill? I'd say that body was about five eight or nine, can't estimate the weight, but I'd put him in his fifties maybe."

"OK, I'll go to the Station House and see what they've got. What you going to do?"

"I'm going back up to that Harbour Master, then I want a chat with the teenagers. It's definitely a murder investigation now, Sandy!"

After one final glance back into the water at the divers, who had taken the boat back out to the area where the corpse had lately been floating, McInnis turned away. He and Sandy walked the few paces to the bottom of the wooden steps then Sandy continued, wending his way along the path between fishing boat lines and crates stacked at the side of the quay. The older man's shoulders were hunched against the chilly wind, but also against the rejection he'd felt from Bob.

Bob McInnis, watching him, felt a bit guilty. He knew Sandy was worried about him but he just couldn't bear to talk about Beth, not yet. God knows what he was going to do about the baby. Mary had been a darling, offering to feed the child, and he couldn't expect her to take her niece abroad when her husband, Hector, went to Afghanistan; six of her own were more than enough, but he didn't know how he was going to cope and do his job too.

He went slowly up the steps, stopping outside the door while he carefully and mentally laid aside his memories and worries and concentrated on the job in hand.

Hugh Pheby raised his head; he appeared to have been carefully examining a chart unrolled on the central table, and at McInnis' entrance laid aside a pencil and ruler. "Inspector, back again so soon?"

"Just one or two more questions, sir, which occurred to me. Why has the body not been seen in the harbour before last night? Any suggestions?"

Pheby frowned. "It's been pretty bad weather this last week, not many folks wanting to take their boats out. Not many people about in the Marina. Plenty of men over in the commercial dock, but they don't go round there if they don't need to."

"Who would go round?"

"Owners of the yachts, I suppose. But they don't need to walk all the way round, Inspector; there's a path over the back, the other end of this wall. Leads directly to the other end of the marina and they'd sail on the high tide. They haven't reported anything in the water this end, but then they wouldn't have seen it at high tide."

"Do you know who has been in and out, sir? We need to check them out."

Pheby scratched among his tight brown curls. "Sure, I'll get the log book."

He turned aside to another desk and pulled forward a big black ledger and ran a finger down the page. "Charlie went out Thursday, he was sailing into Liverpool, for the weekend." Pheby glanced up. "Charles Watts that would be, Inspector. He lives locally; he and his wife keep a ketch for leisure trips." Pheby looked back at the book. "Andrew Hamilton, he left on the early tide, Saturday last week, going across to Ireland; he runs a charter, does a bit of deep-sea fishing with private parties."

"Anyone else, sir?"

"Stephen Low and Martin Bassington. They have small boats for pottering about in. They've been in and out a bit over the week.

It's end of season, Inspector; most of the yachts are laid up for the winter. Do you want phone numbers?"

McInnis nodded, snapping his notebook open. "Thank you, sir, that would be helpful."

"Mr Hamilton is due back on Tuesday. I wouldn't know how you would contact him; I've only got a landline, except the RT. The same with Charlie who is due back tomorrow night. The other two should be at home just now." Pheby jotted down numbers and handed over the sheet of paper.

McInnis put the pocket book away, aware that he was being watched.

"It is a murder then, Inspector; not an accident?"

"Definitely a murder, sir."

"Oh!" Pheby breathed deeply, "I don't suppose you know who…"

"Not yet, Mr Pheby."

"I'll get that other list to you as soon as I can, Inspector."

"Thank you, sir." Bob McInnis nodded his thanks; he turned away and went down the steps, then took a few steps across the roadway, standing beside the harbour entrance with his back to the sluggish river Ellen below.

He looked from side to side in the powerful lighting, getting a perspective on the area; he knew how different it could look in daylight without the shadows and spaces. He glanced up and saw Hugh Pheby outlined, another shadow, in the window of the Harbour Master's office. McInnis would have liked to see the expression on the man's face.

He offered the man another nod before moving away, going back round the three enclosed sides of the commercial dock before passing the café and stepping onto the pavement at the side of the aquarium.

The incident van was parked in the public car park at the entrance to the harbour, surrounded by a flotilla of squad cars, like a huge liner coming in to berth. Bob mounted the two outer steps and pushed open the door.

It had sprung to life in his absence. The phone lines were now manned by a couple of constables; of the bank of computers at the back, only one screen was comprehensible to Bob, the one with a list of names and addresses. Of the three others, one had a diagram of wavy lines, one had flowers and a butterfly, and one showed a picture in red and black. He stared at this for a minute but it still didn't make any sense, no matter which way he turned his head to view it.

He shook said head, and turned away, homing in on Gareth. The young giant was sitting writing longhand notes in a corner, with a cooling coffee next to him on the table. Gareth would have stood up if Bob hadn't laid a hand on his shoulder. "Gareth, have you got the addresses of the boys that first reported the find?"

Gareth flicked through his day book and held it out.

"Thanks." Bob leaned over the table, copying them down. He handed the book back and started to turn away.

"They'll still be in bed, sir." Gareth pointed out the obvious, "They didn't get sent home till nearly two this morning."

"Ah, yes of course."

"I should try after breakfast, sir."

Bob nodded; he'd forgotten about breakfast. He spared a thought for Sandy, hoping that the man had eaten something. "Have you had something, Gareth?"

"Yeah, the café opened up early. They might be closed to the public but the coppers can make up the trade for them."

McInnis smiled somewhat wryly. "It's an ill wind that blows nobody any good, Gareth." He looked down at the serious face, "Make sure you get some sleep too; you can't function with a tired brain."

Gareth gave him back a cool look. He desperately wanted to say 'nor can you'. He'd conceived a fondness for McInnis the previous year, and the change in the man since he'd been widowed hurt the Celt in Gareth. Instead he said "Yes, sir." and turned back to his notes as McInnis left the van.

McInnis pondered; he couldn't do much for a while, still too early for interviews. He eyed the beckoning lights of the café. He supposed he'd better eat too. Not that the sight of that corpse had done much for his appetite, but starving himself wouldn't help either. He sighed and walked across the intervening space.

Having played with some toast and disposed of three mugs of coffee, McInnis now stood outside the café as the nasty little wind nipped around his exposed ears and he debated his next actions. A quick look at his watch showed twenty to eight. Twenty to eight meant Mary would be up; six children ranging from fourteen years to nine months, not counting his own child, meant she rose early.

He pulled out his mobile and moved into the shelter offered by the side of the van. "Hi, Mary."

Mary, answering with a child on her hip, smiled down the phone line. "Hi, little brother, how you doing?"

"I'm fine; I'm taking some sea air in Maryport."

"Oh! Who died there?"

"Don't know yet. How are you all coping?"

"We're packing steadily. Hector goes from Germany to Afghanistan in a couple of weeks. We'll just about have time to settle into the army digs over there before he goes."

"Are the brats looking forward to it?"

"Maria's not happy; she says we're tearing her away from all her friends. Typical teenager." Mary sighed. "She'll be fine once she gets there and discovers half her friends have been relocated too. Only we aren't supposed to tell her that."

She gave a soft gurgle of laughter. "You should see what she's done with her hair! Hector nearly had a fit when he saw the red streaks in it. She looks as though she's had an accident with the ketchup bottle."

"Ah! The joys of parenthood." Bob smiled down the phone. "How's my daughter doing?"

"She's listening in to this conversation with an eggy smile of satisfaction on her face." Bob heard Mary say "It's your daddy, cherub, isn't that nice," and a little gurgle in reply from his daughter.

"I haven't sorted much out, Mary, but her room's ready whenever you have to bring her."

Mary pulled a face at the phone. "I don't want to bring her at all, Bob. The children don't want her to go either. But I think she needs you, and I think you need her, so I'll be up on Monday. Mother Stover is supervising the brats and helping us pack up, so she says she'll baby-sit for me."

Bob allowed another tired smile to appear on his face for a minute. "I bet she'll love that!" His sister and her mother-in-law had an ongoing feud about the way the children were raised. Mary believed in casual compliance. Mother Stover expected instant obedience. However, they rubbed along tolerably well for all that.

"OK, love, give my baby a kiss from her dad and I'll see you Monday. Let me know when you expect to arrive. Take care." Bob flicked shut the mobile and sighed.

He didn't honestly know what he was going to do. There was the police crèche of course, but that was only eight to eight. His mother was willing, but it wasn't really fair to introduce a five-month baby into her independent life on a full-time basis; she'd turned sixty-three and a baby took energy. He shook his head; she would do what she could until he got sorted out. He just hoped he could sort it out fairly quickly.

He flicked open the phone again. Speed dialling, and waiting. "Sandy, have you eaten? Good. I haven't got to the teenagers yet, still abed apparently. Where are you?"

He listened to his partner, head on one side, as he watched a man turning a length of rope neatly around a bollard, before scanning a rather rusty boat moored some fifty yards away, and then heading towards him.

"Well, if none of the missing men match our profiles we'll have to wait for dentals and see if that helps." He nodded, "Well, get back to me on that, when they do answer. And, Sandy, have a couple of hours. It's going to be a long enough day and we can't do much more for a bit." McInnis moved in front of the path of the man from the boat. "Gotta go." He flicked the telephone shut.

"Good morning, sir." He shoved the mobile away in the inside pocket, pulling out his warrant card from the same place and held it up. "Didn't you hear that this is now a crime scene?"

The man pushed back a dirty cap with an equally dirty hand. "Yeah, heard that, but I had things to do on the boat. I ain't interfering with your crime scene." He smelt of fish and perspiration, with undertones of beer.

"Actually, sir, just by being here you're interfering. Can you tell me your name?"

"Can. Don't see why I should."

"Don't be difficult, sir! I've had a long day already and I can require you to account for your presence." Bob looked him up and down; the man was a brawny specimen, unshaven and a little truculent.

Apparently he was doing a little looking of his own. Bob was also unshaven and whatever the man read in Bob's eyes caused his attitude to undergo a slight sea change. "Name's Matt Phillips."

"Well, Mr Phillips, this is officially part of the crime scene of a murder. Now why are you here?"

"I was going to take the MARY LOO out on the next high tide. I have to work too. Fishing is difficult enough; I can't afford to miss a tide because some poor sap's fallen in the water. He should've stuck to the land. These posh buggers coming round in their swank yachts lording it over us. They want to play at sailor; they want to try some proper sailing first."

McInnis stood patiently while Matt Philips let off steam. When the man appeared to have come to a stop he started to speak himself. "I am sorry that you won't be able to take out your boat and carry on your trade, sir. However," he held up a hand to stop further comment, "this is now a murder investigation."

He watched the man sag slightly.

"Oh! Bloody hell!"

"Quite, sir. Perhaps you can account for your movements over the past week?"

Matt Phillips licked his lips, "When? Why me? I ain't done nothing."

"We will be asking everyone whose business is around these docks, their whereabouts, not just you, sir. Perhaps you could step inside the van and I'll have a constable take your statement."

Phillips nodded, but McInnis could see he wasn't a happy man. Gareth, emerging at this moment, his bulk effectively blocking the man's exit to the roadway, apparently set the seal on his day. He shrugged and slouched towards the van, going around the two policemen. Before he entered though he suddenly swerved and burst into a run.

Gareth might have been taken by surprise, but he wasn't slow. He gave effective chase and proved why the rugby team in his home town had been so sad to see him leave. The man landed on the unyielding concrete with the force of a newly felled oak, his chin making hard contact and his jaws clicking together with a noise reminiscent of a couple of bowling balls coming back into play.

McInnis was no slouch in the chase and grab stakes either. He was putting on the cuffs even before Gareth had managed to stand up. McInnis turned the supine head and examined the now bleeding chin of the unconscious man. "Now that was a stupid thing to do, Gareth. I only wanted his whereabouts and now I'm all suspicious of him." He smiled wryly.

Gareth grinned back. "Nothing like a little arrest to wake you up in a morning, sir. What are we arresting him for?" He lifted an eyebrow.

"I haven't a clue, Gareth, but I'm sure he's up to something. Perhaps you can find a nice specimen to stand guard over this –" he nudged the prone figure with a well shod foot"– while I go and speak to Mr Pheby. And while I do that perhaps you'd care to just keep a cautious eye on that hulk over there, just check he hasn't got any friends ready to drive away, or whatever boats do, will you?"

Gareth disappeared into the van and emerged with a local constable. "John here will watch over our sleeping beauty, sir."

"Good." Bob McInnis started to walk back towards the Harbour Master's office with Gareth, telling him of the recent encounter and why he wanted him to check over the boat. He carried on walking as the constable stopped at the MARY LOO and went down the metal ladder to the deck below him.

McInnis had covered half the distance when Pheby met him. "I saw things happening from the window, Inspector, though I couldn't figure out who you were with. What happened?"

McInnis ignored the question in favour of one of his own. "Perhaps you can tell me who owns that boat there, sir?" He pointed out the rusting boat sitting low in the water with Gareth just emerging from the cabin.

"Paul Saunders. He's moored in the Elizabeth dock most of his life. He doesn't take her out much these days. Sleeps on her sometimes."

"Hm." McInnis turned and began to walk back towards his prisoner who was making rather feeble movements to stand up. "And the gentleman currently decorating the pathway?"

Pheby squinted at the man McInnis indicated. "Brian Moore. He does odd jobs about the harbour; acts as crew occasionally when anyone is short of a man."

"You don't like him, sir?" He looked sideways at Pheby.

"He's too fond of the drink, and he throws his weight around a bit too much." Pheby grimaced. "Otherwise I don't know anything against him. When he's sober he's good crew."

They stopped as they came abreast of Gareth and the boat. "Anyone on board, Gareth?"

"No, sir."

McInnis gave a come-on sign to Gareth and the three men walked back along the quayside to where the man Pheby had called

Brian Moore was now upright and volubly protesting the handcuffs at his wrists to the local constabulary.

"Ah, Mr Moore, we'll get someone to look at your injuries in just a moment." Bob McInnis smiled somewhat grimly. "I don't suppose you'd like to tell me why you were on board that boat, or why you gave me a false name? So how about starting with why you tried to run just now?"

"I want a lawyer. This is police brutality."

Bob's mobile eyebrow winged up. "Well you can certainly have a lawyer if you want one but I assure you we haven't been in the least bit brutal." He paused. "Yet."

"You heard him, he threatened me." Moore looked at Pheby.

"I heard him say he hadn't been brutal, Brian. Now what the hell were you doing on old Saunder's boat?"

Bob said nothing as Pheby look squarely at the scruffy man.

"Weren't doing nothing. Just coiling the rope, didn't want anyone tripping on her."

"Brian, I could see you. You were on board the MARY LOO. I was coming to check you out when I saw the Inspector stop you."

Brian Moore shook his head. "I was just making things shipshape, nothing else."

McInnis sighed. "Take him inside and book him for trespassing for the time being, Constable. Get him some first aid and arrange for a solicitor if he still wants one." He turned his back and ignored the string of curses directed at the constabulary in general. He waited patiently until the noise was silenced by the decisive click of the door and then spoke to Pheby. "Now perhaps you can tell me where I might find Mr Paul Saunders?"

Pheby shook his head. "'I'll have to go back for the exact address, Inspector. He lives up on the hillside there, near to the old Roman fort."

"Thank you, sir. When you've got a minute then. We need him to see if he's had anything stolen, and we can't just go traipsing over his property without a warrant."

"Would you like me to phone from the office, ask him to come down?"

McInnis rubbed a hand over his face feeling the slight rasp, the late night and early morning was catching up. "Yeah, that might be best, I'll be away for a short time but he can always give his statement to one of the locals."

Pheby nodded and, turning on his heel, went back round the basin towards his office. McInnis stood watching for a minute. He was still looking across the water of the dock when Sandy spoke next to him. "What have you been up to now, lad? It isn't even nine o'clock and already you're arresting the natives of these parts. Solved the case have you?"

"I thought I told you to get a couple of hours, Sandy?" McInnis swung round and looked at the older man as he spoke.

"Yeah that's likely," Sandy's lips twitched, "I don't think, with you flinging men to the floor and beating them up!"

McInnis raised both eyebrows. "My, rumour flies round here faster than Concorde!"

Sandy grinned at him. "Actually I came back for my overnight case, and stuck my nose into the van to tell you I'd got us a couple of decent rooms. Between the curses of our 'guest' and the way young Gareth tells it, you single-handedly arrested a desperate criminal."

Bob shook his head, quickly bringing Sandy up to speed with the last hectic half hour. "I've no idea what he was up to, probably petty pilfering. I wish to God solving this murder might be that easy."

They moved off, going towards the squad car. "I'll take the car and drop off our bags then come back, Bob. Where are you going to be?"

"I'm going to find another local bobby and go and visit two young gentlemen and see what they've got to say to me about this body they found."

"Want me?"

"No. I meant it, Sandy, you look shattered, man. I'll see you at lunchtime."

"You need to sleep too, Bob."

McInnis shrugged. "I'm not tired. I'll grab some kip later." He looked at Sandy Bell, reading the protest on the man's face. "Leave it, man, I'm alright."

Bell sighed, but he had to admit he would function better with a couple of hours' sleep under his belt. "Alright, Bob, but be careful, you can't run on fumes for ever, lad."

They parted at the squad car, Sandy getting in and driving off; while Bob approached one of the other cars. Standing beside it was a constable so young he didn't look as though he owned a razor yet. Bob felt his chin again; he must get to his whiskers soon. "Are you here for any specific purpose, Constable, or can I get you to drive me to interview a couple of witnesses?" He showed his card as he spoke.

"Constable Pretty, sir. I'm waiting for Sergeant Meeks. He's in the incident van."

Bob nodded, not a flicker crossed his face. "Go and see if I can borrow you." He watched the young constable give a salute straight out of the manual and head towards the van, and savoured the enjoyment he would have when he told Sandy about Constable Pretty. The lad would be eaten alive by some of the criminals Bob knew, with a name and face like that.

He watched impassively as both Constable Pretty and Sergeant Meeks returned. "Perhaps you could drop me off, Inspector? Then you can have my constable to drive you where you want to go, but it's a small town you know."

Meeks' attitude was one of slight disgust that Bob should want chauffeuring around. McInnis, indifferent to the implied insult, shrugged. "Thanks, I need to see these two lads, and I don't know where they live."

"Ah, of course. Take him to see John Simpson and his brother, Pretty."

Constable Pretty saluted again and got behind the wheel. Bob climbed in the back with the sergeant and they set off; neither of them seemed inclined to conversation.

Pretty pulled up outside the station and Meeks got out. He stuck his head in the front window. "Take the Inspector where he wants, Pretty, and make yourself useful."

Pretty sat impassively in his seat. "Right, sir." He kept his eyes trained on the roadway.

McInnis was transferring to the front seat of the car; he held the door while the sergeant spoke to him. Meeks wrinkled his nose as he watched the inspector throw his wet coat on the back seat. "I'll see you later, sir. Pretty here is in training, so I'll trust you to keep him out of mischief."

McInnis nodded. He sat back in his seat after giving the address, and as they drove off said, "How long have you been on the streets, Constable?"

"Four weeks, sir."

"Like it so far?"

"Yes, sir, the Sergeant said I could observe, sir."

"And what have you observed so far, Constable?"

Oliver Pretty shot him a sideways glance at variance with the youthfulness of his face, assessing whether the inspector was making idle conversation or whether he wanted genuine opinions. The serious expression on the older man's face evidently gave him his answer. "About the case, or in general, sir?"

McInnis took his eyes from the road and observed the peach-fuzz face next to him. "Either, Constable."

The young man hesitated for a moment then said, "That Senior Constable you brought down with you, he breaks protocol, but only when it won't detract from your authority. That older Inspector, he lets you be in charge. You're not too proud to ask questions, and you don't like to hurt people's..." He paused, changing gears and preparing to turn left, he waited patiently at the corner, checking the street before moving off, then continued, "I was going to say feelings, sir, but I think I mean ego."

Bob McInnis said nothing for so long that Pretty began to wonder if his dream job had suddenly taken a nose dive.

"What on earth are you doing in the ranks, Pretty? You should have gone straight to university and come back in at detective rank." It was the tone of an indulgent uncle to his favourite nephew, and Pretty caught the hint of a smile.

"I wanted a taste of the streets, sir. They can teach you things a university degree can't."

"Ye...s and no, Pretty."

Constable Pretty pulled up outside a two storey semi-detached house. It had a well tended front lawn and borders, and an old model estate car parked at the side.

"This is where the Simpson boys live, sir." He hesitated. "Their dad can be a bit –" he lifted a hand and waggled it "– dictatorial. The boys tend to rebel a bit sometimes."

Bob hid a smile; this from a boy who couldn't have been more than three years older than them struck him as a bit comical. "Right, Pretty, in you come. You can do a bit more observing." Bob released his seatbelt and got out, waiting on the pavement as he spoke to the younger man.

For the first time he surprised a mild look of horror from the constable.

"Come in!"

"Yes, Constable, in." McInnis waited, his stance saying he would stay there until the young man got his body out of the car and on the pavement and it had better not take too long, while Constable Pretty undid his seat belt and climbed out of the car.

Pretty followed him up the path beside the neat border of staked dahlias, dripping, just at present, from the recent rain, and McInnis rang the bell and waited. The door opened to reveal a small girl of about nine or ten, her ponytails swinging as she stood turning her head from one man to the other, her eyes wide. She stared at them, and then past them to the police car, round eyed. A male voice in the background said, "Who is it, Lucy?"

"It's the police, Da." There was some curiosity but mostly familiarity. "But it's only Oliver."

A tall man in his mid-forties came to the door. "Hello, lad, have you come to see Jimmy? He's still in bed."

Bob decided he'd better assert some authority before things got totally away from him. "Good morning, sir, I'm Detective Inspector McInnis." He produced his card. "We have some follow-up enquiries to make of your young sons. Might I come in?"

James Simpson, after a very cursory look at the card, nodded, "Sorry, Inspector, we didn't intend to be rude. In you come." He turned and led the way down a corridor and into a small sitting room.

"Lucy." He turned to the young girl following them. "Go and knock on you brothers' door and tell them to come down, the police are here to see them." She turned to skip away. "And then young lady you finish tidying your room, or there won't be any Saturday swimming lesson for you." Lucy looked back over her shoulder, offering a pout, but continuing onwards.

James Simpson indicated a chair and sat on the sofa himself. Oliver Pretty went to stand next to the door and they waited in a comfortable silence for the appearance of the boys.

John and Christopher Simpson appeared within a very few minutes. It was obvious to Bob that they were not only tired but very chastened young men. They looked sideways, first at their father, and then at Oliver Pretty, who got a very brief smile from each. Then a look reminiscent of a badly straightened sheet settled on their faces, all creases and rucks, as they took in the strange man seated in their front room.

"Right boys, this gentleman is a detective, I want you to answer his questions truthfully."

James Simpson looked from face to face and sat back. Waiting.

"You are John and Christopher Simpson?"

The boys nodded in unison.

"Which is which?"

"I'm John, sir." John, Bob noted, had reached the stage where he needed to shave occasionally and where the acne was winning the fight over the facial hairs in a bid for territory.

"John. Tell me what you were doing out at the docks last night?"

"Chris and me were just messing about, one of the older lads gave us some bevvies and some alcopops, and we were daring each other to jump in the dock for a bet, like. We were a bit drunk." He slid a look across to his father. "Anyway, about eleven thirty we saw something in the water and we got a boat and went to look, and saw the head just floating there, and then we called Jimmy and he come and told us to wait while he looked." He stopped speaking as if someone had thrown the switch to 'OFF'.

McInnis shot a warning glance at Oliver Pretty as that young man stirred slightly. "And you agree with this statement, Chris?"

"Yes sir." It was whispered. Chris hadn't even got the benefit of acne to hide behind, his cheeks blossomed a bright red at being addressed.

"And who is Jimmy?"

"Jimmy is my oldest son, Inspector. He's a constable on the force here in Maryport."

"Ah, right." Bob McInnis nodded. "I'll have a word with him when he comes back on shift. It's been a long day so far. I'm sure we'll have his statement already. What did you do then, boys?"

"Told the Sergeant and came home when he said we could."

"Thank you for your time, boys." He looked across at James Simpson. "It was brave of them to come forward knowing they would get into trouble at home for doing so." He stood up, shook hands with the youngsters and, preceded by Oliver Pretty, left the house.

"In you get, Pretty; I'll drive us back to the docks." Bob sat in the driver's seat and waited patiently for the constable to buckle up. He swung the car round in the wide road and then said, "What did they say wrong, lad? They were obviously lying. It was all a bit too rehearsed."

Pretty opened his mouth and shut it again.

"Divided loyalties. If you intend to work your own backyard you must get your loyalties sorted out; this isn't the schoolyard anymore." McInnis spoke kindly but there was a hint of steel in his voice.

"You're right, sir," Pretty sighed, "on both counts. They were lying. That time of night they couldn't have seen that far through the water. The dock would have been nearly full, and it would have been too dark. They must have been in the water already."

McInnis glanced over, nodding, "Follow it through, lad," before returning his attention to the road.

Constable Pretty looked confused. "Sir?"

"If they couldn't have seen the head, then Constable Simpson…"

"Oh!" Pretty sounded as if he'd just discovered the corpse himself.

"Yes, not a nice position to be in, lad. Want me to come and speak to Sergeant Meeks?"

Constable Pretty frowned fiercely; it sat oddly on his youthful forehead, as if he'd been messing with his mother's make-up and drawn lines to prematurely age himself.

"No, sir."

McInnis said no more and they finished the journey in silence. McInnis was mulling over the new information, adding it to the knowledge he already had. He stopped neatly in the car park next to the docks. "What did you mean when you said I didn't like to hurt people's feelings, Pretty? Give me an honest answer."

Pretty looked across the space at Bob, assessing him in a way Bob had noted before. "You knew the Sarge was criticising you for wanting a car and driver, so you gave him an explanation. You needn't have, you're a senior detective. And..." He gave a shy smile. "You didn't laugh at my name even though you wanted to."

McInnis raised an eyebrow. "Go to uni', lad, the streets aren't for you." He climbed out of the car and strolled away. A mug of tea would go down very nicely while he got his head around the knowledge he was accumulating. He was beginning to find pieces of the jigsaw, but he hadn't found a corner yet or even a straight bit. He looked up at the sky where patches of blue were trying desperately to fight their way through the storm clouds. It might turn out a nice day after all.

He found a venerable gentleman waiting in the incident van. Mr Paul Saunders must be nudging ninety, he thought, and immediately felt guilty for asking the man to turn out and come down to the docks. However, like the storm clouds, the guilt was blown away by the rising wind of charm which greeted him.

"Detective Inspector. I'm so pleased I could come and help. I don't get a lot of excitement these days and to be involved in a murder, albeit in a peripheral manner, is quite a fascinating experience."

Bob found himself responding to the old world charm, relaxing for the first time since he'd come to the town. "I'm sorry to have brought you out in this weather, sir."

"Nonsense, Inspector, I don't melt. Now what's this about? Hugh said something about my boat being broken into, though how you can lock up a boat like mine, I'm blessed if I know."

"We caught a man by the name of Brian Moore leaving your boat earlier this morning. He failed to give us an account of his actions and subsequently tried to run off."

He stopped as Paul Saunders tutted, "Stupid man!"

"Well yes, sir, perhaps, up until then I didn't think too much about him being there." McInnis offered his fugitive smile, the one his wife had loved to see. "We need you to tell us if anything has gone missing."

"How delightful, I'm helping the police with their enquiries." Saunders stood up; his face might have declared him old but his body was of that peculiar sort, apparently made of wire and tanned leather that just kept going. "Shall we go and look? I haven't been down to the boat for about –" he gazed off into the corner of the van for a minute "– oh, I should think four weeks now."

3

Four hours later McInnis, reporting the conversation to Sandy over a hasty lunch, found himself smiling all over again. "He doesn't use the boat much, Sandy. Does a bit of gentle fishing in the summer, mainly rod and line work. He's employed Brian Moore now and again to crew for him." He paused, pointing a fork at his superior. "Mainly, I think, because he felt sorry for the man. He seemed quite capable of managing that boat on his own."

Sandy, carefully deboning fish and dipping chips in sauce before placing the loaded fork in his mouth, looked up. "So was anything missing?" He asked when he'd disposed of the mouthful.

"Mr Saunders thinks the tank was considerably fuller when he was last on board. He also thinks it hasn't been siphoned, so much as used. Says the charts weren't in the right order either. Got a bit technical for me. Moore isn't saying anything and Mr Saunders is considering if he should press charges for trespass." Bob laid down his knife and fork neatly at the side of the plate and took up the thick, white, pottery mug of tea, resting his elbows on the tabletop.

Sandy Bell frowned at the remains on McInnis' plate; the lad wasn't eating enough in his opinion. "And you say the boys were lying?"

"Had to be, Sandy." He shook his head. "If we could only just see the head of our corpse when we arrived, what chance had they of seeing it nearly two hours earlier?" He set down the mug and rubbed his face. "It comes down to familiarity, and I'm just not used

61

to the sea. I wasn't thinking tides, even when we were talking to Mark." He sighed deeply.

"No, and nor was he!" Sandy made a face of disgust at variance with the enjoyment he was receiving from his lunch. "I'll have to have a word with that young man." He picked up a slice of bread and butter and placed the few remaining chips on one side and carefully folded it, making a chip butty. He glanced up to find Bob watching him with a raised eyebrow. "You tell Sarah about this and you get to do all the paperwork and the legwork too."

Bob shook his head. "What me, rag on you to Sarah? I wouldn't dare! Anyway, I do all the paperwork already."

Sandy grinned and spoke a bit thickly round the butty. "What's next then?"

"Well I've spoken to these men, Low and Bassington. They come and go pretty much how they please apparently. They only have small rowing boats. They didn't see anything out of place they said, but one thing they did say was that Hugh Pheby keeps his own boat moored at that corner." He smiled grimly. "I think he's hiding something, Sandy, and I intend to find out what." He picked up the mug and finished off his tea.

Sandy did likewise before pushing back his seat and stretching out his legs. The café was full of the smell of damp clothing and hot vinegar. A rising tide of voices and the clink of cutlery washed back to the two detectives from uniformed men all eating hearty meals. The sun had finally come out and was hot through the glass as it bounced around the steamy room. "What do you want me to do?"

"I think I'd like you to tackle Constable Simpson, find out what game he's playing. It strikes me as natural, if somewhat stupid, to lie about something which has been exposed so quickly, Sandy." Bob McInnis kept his voice low. "I suppose he was trying to protect his brothers."

Sandy glanced around, but the little table they sat at was in a corner, and the local officers seemed to be giving them a wide berth. "I think his mistake is already common knowledge, Bob. I hope it doesn't create too many problems in our investigation."

Bob nodded his head. They needed the locals helping them to solve the murder, not protecting their own backs. "That's one reason I want you to tackle him, Sandy. I find I want to shake the young fool and that's not exactly a tactful response to the situation is it?" His mobile rang as he finished speaking and, with a muttered "'Scuse me," he pulled it out of his pocket and flicked it open.

"McInnis."

Sandy watched the frown gathering on the younger man's forehead. It looked like night clouds sweeping in off the sea, all dark and brooding over the sober landscape of McInnis' face.

"Stop apologising, Mary. If you have to come earlier, then you do. We'll think of something. Mary!" It was a slightly exasperated yelp. "Stop it, do you think I blame you for the vagaries of the British army! I'll see you tomorrow afternoon." His voice softened. "Take care of yourself, love." He flicked the phone shut and sat holding it, deep in thought.

Sandy watched him for a moment or two. He had no desire to get his head bitten off. "Look, lad," he touched Bob's hand, bringing the man's attention to himself. "Sarah and I, well we talked about this." He shook his head as the gathering thunderclouds further darkened on Bob's face. "We weren't gossiping about you, lad."

"No, I don't suppose you were, Sandy." He sighed and offered a glimmer of a smile.

"Look, Bob, Sarah, she's grieving as much as you." He held up a hand as the shuttered look started to appear. "I know you don't want to talk about Elizabeth, but Sarah, well, she got attached, it would help her, and you, if she looked after little Caitlin while

63

you're on this case. You can sort something out when you're back in Carlisle."

Bob shook his head. "It's not fair to either of you, Sandy. You really don't want teething and nappies disturbing your peaceful lives."

"Peaceful! With Claire forgetting the time difference and ringing us from Australia in the middle of the night, and my father ringing me up to go and change his batteries in his hearing aid at six in the morning!" Sandy grimaced. "Because, he says, the staff have enough to do in that home of his." Sandy shrugged. "Like I haven't. Your little girl isn't going to make much difference to my peace and quiet, Bob." Sandy sighed, "Truly, lad, it would help Sarah too."

McInnis frowned down at his hands. Yes, it did make sense, but he hated being beholden to anyone and this was his problem. He could accept his sister's help. She had been wonderful, breastfeeding Caitlin as well as her own small son, and then keeping her milk to feed the little girl alone.

Bob hadn't had much choice really; those first few weeks after the funeral were a bit blurred, even now. Mary had arrived with her youngest son and taken charge of his infant as if it was quite natural to add a seventh child into her already crowded life.

Hector, when Bob had finally surfaced enough to realise what Mary had taken on, had told him bluntly not to be a bloody fool. "Do you think you could have stopped her, man? I certainly couldn't, and wouldn't have if I could. My wife knows what she wants to do and gets on with it."

Sandy watched the small smile appear briefly on Bob's face, like a flash of lightning illuminating the sad features, and wondered what he was thinking.

McInnis came out of his abstraction, looking across at Sandy, noting the anxious look on the man's face. Hell, had it reached the stage were even his partner was afraid to speak his mind. He must be behaving like a right jerk.

"OK, Sandy, Sarah shall have the spoiling of Caitlin, for a few weeks until I get things sorted out. But," he raised an elegant finger, "you will accept the same amount as Mary and Hector did. Babies don't come cheap." He stemmed the protest before it got out of Sandy's mouth. "It's that, or the deal's off."

Sandy scowled, but Bob was shaking his head, "Take it, man, Sarah will need every penny."

Sandy was still frowning as Bob changed the subject. "Put it away for now, Sandy. We need to decide where to go next with this case. If you're happy to tackle Simpson, I'm going to harass Jonesy; he might be able to give us a preliminary time and cause, even if he won't have the tox reports back yet."

Sandy shook his head. "You're a braver man than I am, Bob. I wouldn't bother our Medical Examiner on a Saturday morning when he's only had the body a couple of hours. Yon man can be nasty tempered when he doesn't get his weekly round of golf."

Bob smiled grimly. "I want something to work with, Sandy, and so far nothing connects up at all."

Sandy shrugged. "I'll go and see this young man then." He pushed back his chair a bit further and stood up, scanning the room and catching the eye of Sergeant Meeks.

Bob watched him go out of the room with the local officer and then pulled out his notebook, looking over the information he had so far. As he'd said to Sandy, they had damn all to work with. He was just putting it away when a mug appeared at his elbow and Gareth blocked out the light with his bulk.

"A word with you, sir?"

"Have a seat, Gareth. What's up?" Bob accepted the offered drink and eyed Gareth ap Rhys with a little surprise; while he knew the man came from some obscure valley in North Wales he'd never heard quite so much accent before.

"I am sorry, sir, I have made the mistake."

Bob raised an eyebrow. "Sit down, man."

Gareth reluctantly sat down and took a deep breath. "I mentioned the fact that we couldn't see the corpse from the Harbour Master's window when I was talking to John, sir. The constable that helped us with the arrest of Brian Moore?" Gareth said, as Bob cocked his head on one side. "I shouldn't perhaps have said anything, but I was just thinking aloud like." Gareth looked thoroughly put out. "The next thing I know he's blabbing about it to some of the other men and, well…" He stopped.

"Out with it."

"Pheby's disappeared, sir."

Bob looked across the table at the constable, noting the misery admixed with anger on the man's face. "Stop beating yourself up man. If you can't trust the locals who can you trust? It might not have been you at all; I've been questioning the man too." He sipped tea and sat thinking while Gareth scowled into his own mug as if scrying for answers to the future.

"Fedrwn ni ddim trystio 'r saeson"

"I don't know what you said just then, man, but I hope I'm not included in the comment."

Gareth looked momentarily appalled. "Oh no, sir, I'm sorry, sir, I was thinking out loud."

"Well think more quietly, man, that's what you reckoned got you into this pickle in the first place." McInnis gave a significant look at the thinning crowd of officers in the café.

"Yes, sir." Gareth sat watching McInnis as they were left in an island of greasy plates and pushed back chairs.

"Right, Gareth, I want you to go visiting. I interviewed a gentleman by the name of Paul Saunders. He's worked in and around this port for most of his life. And he knows the people. Go and have a chat with him."

"What about, sir?"

McInnis looked the constable over. "I don't know, Gareth, I just have a feeling he might tell us things if we allow him to talk. Go and try out your powers of detection, man. Here's the address." McInnis pushed his book in front of Gareth and waited while the constable wrote it down in his daybook.

Gareth stowed the book and looked McInnis over. "With respect, sir. Are you trying to get me out of the way?"

"No, I think he might tell us something about Pheby and this dockyard." Bob mentally crossed his fingers; he didn't like lying, but the man was obviously seething and that didn't make for good working relationships, and it was only partly a lie.

McInnis stood up and so did Gareth. Bob reflected that it would be a brave man who would get in the way if the constable ever decided to take the law into his own hands. "Off you go and report back to me. And, Gareth, take your time, he's an old man but he hasn't lost any of his marbles and he's got lots to tell us, I'm sure of it."

McInnis turned away and went over to the counter to speak to the ladies behind it. He believed in good community relations and a simple 'thank you' could go a long way towards fostering them, aside from the fact that he had enjoyed his meal.

Once that little task was dealt with, he headed towards the incident van, pulling out his mobile on the way. "Hi, can I speak to Doctor Jones please? Yes, I know he's doing a post mortem, it's that

67

I want to speak to him about." McInnis sighed heavily and waited for the connection to go through.

"Jonesy, it's McInnis."

"I know it's you, Bob, what do you want? I thought you wanted this poor man dealt with quickly." The doctor stood outside the door of the autopsy room, leaning against the wall in his green scrubs.

"I do." McInnis leaned against the side of the incident van, watching the passing foot traffic. "I just wondered if you had a preliminary report for me."

"First you drag me away from my golf and then you demand the impossible."

"Jonesy, since when have you played golf in the pouring rain?"

"Isn't raining now."

Bob sighed again down the phone line.

"OK, OK, you should save that sigh for the dirty phone calls. This is only preliminary. He's dead. He's been dead about seven to nine days, I won't admit to a closer time frame than that, it's September and the Irish Sea we're dealing with here, and they can both delay decomposition. Toxicology isn't back yet so don't harass me about that, and that young man Forester has sent off some of the water and diatoms to the bugs man to see whether your corpse drowned in situ or somewhere else, or if he was dead before he hit the water."

Doctor Jones pushed a blue scrub cap back off his brow and frowned down at the corpse he could see through the autopsy room's porthole window. He'd opened the chest, laying the skin either side of the body like over-large lapels. He hadn't, as yet, used the rib cutters to get inside the cavity.

"I haven't got to lung and stomach contents yet, Bob, so don't ask the impossible of me. Drowning is notoriously difficult to determine, I've got to exclude as I go along." Dr Jones sighed. "We don't know what he was doing preceding death and we don't know his state of health before death; they both have to factor in.

"He was bound antemortem, and I believe put in the water conscious, or at least became conscious when he arrived in it. There are signs of struggle on the wrists. Not a nice way to go. Though I believe it was a recognised, and supposedly kinder, form of execution in the seventeenth century, *'cum fossa et furca'*, with drowning pit or gallows."

"Are you saying this was an execution, Jonesy?"

"I don't know, Bob, you're the detective. I'm just telling you what I've found so far. The man appears to have been deliberately drowned and probably aware of his imminent death, and he didn't go peacefully into this good night, he struggled. That's all I can tell you so far."

"No clue as to his identity?"

"Male, white, mid fifties, bit overweight, well tended hands, old appendix's scar, broken his left leg at some time in the past. I've done X-rays of the teeth but haven't got a match back yet. The fingertips have been stripped."

"What, deliberately?"

"No, no, washerwoman syndrome, Bob. I might try for a reversed fingerprint later, but give me time man. That's all the help I can give you. Now go away, I've got work." He hung the phone back on the wall bracket and with a quiet whoosh went back inside the chilly room.

McInnis was left looking at his phone and shivering in the chill from the wind outside. He put the phone away and went inside the van to see what progress had been made with the missing persons in the area.

Mark Forester, having travelled back from Carlisle, was dealing with a few missing things himself. He was squatting over a pile of junk on the quayside next to the steps. He had been accumulating a variety of articles from the floor of the marina basin. The biggest of these was a small rowing boat. This had taken considerable ingenuity to remove from the mud as it appeared to be buried in gravel. He wasn't even sure it was relevant, but it was next to the area where the corpse had been fastened, and it did appear to be newly sunk.

He had moved it against the wall under the Harbour Master's office. There didn't appear to be any holes anywhere, so it looked like the hull had been overturned and the whole thing submerged. There wasn't much in the way of sea life beyond the watermark on the bottom and the inside was still clean. He puzzled over it for a short time but couldn't see any reason for the sinking, and that was what kept drawing him back to it.

He had also recovered enough tin cans to set up an aluminium factory, and several occupied lobster pots. These had caused several raised eyebrows when they had been hauled unceremoniously to the surface. The lobsters had been somewhat surprised too. "I didn't think fishing inside the dock was legal."

"'Tisn't, Mark, at least I don't think so." The sergeant had found a man after his own heart in Mark, and between swopping stories about dives, they had found they had much in common. Now they both frowned down at the illegal catch as they stood amid the detritus of the harbour bed.

"Wonder if we can eat them or if they're evidence?"

"Well personally I wouldn't want any marine animal that had been near your corpse."

"Good point." Mark gave a tiny shudder of mingled disgust and horror. The two men eyed the crustaceans and their stare was returned with equal horror; the lobster didn't much fancy being eaten either.

"Should we let them out?"

Mark considered while the feelers waved piteously at him. "No. I think I'd better hang on to them, Jeff. Gruesome as the thought is, they might just contain evidence."

"So what do you want me to do with them?"

Mark scratched his head. "The aquarium, they can maybe store them for me?" He grinned. "Am I a genius or what?"

"I think the answer to that is better not answered, Mark." McInnis stood behind the two men, gazing with astonishment and some dismay at the accumulated piles of rubbish.

Jeff grinned impartially at both men, and then nodded towards the small dingy they were using to transport finds to the wharfside. "I think my lot have finally got whatever was holding him down; you're just in time, sir." He measured the draught of the small craft as it came towards the steps. "It's bloody heavy whatever it is!" All three peered down as a small, compact, and obviously heavy, stone was carefully removed from the boat and carried up the stairs. It was slung between two of the divers on a large section of canvas.

They arrived a bit red in the face and panting slightly, to gently set the stone down on the quayside at the feet of the senior officers, like a couple of red setters proudly bringing back the day's catch.

"Good God! It's a quern."

Mark and Jeff looked at Bob McInnis.

"A what, sir?"

"Top half of a millstone, Mark. Strictly speaking the hand stone or top half of a hand milling stone." McInnis stooped over the stone, looking at the rope still tied through the hole. He could smell the

71

weed and the seawater that had soaked into the rope, a compound of bilge water and brine.

Jeff and Mark exchanged another look; it said 'who knows about milling stones in this day and age?'

McInnis was still looking at the quern. "That, say about two stone weight: plus the man, I should say he was twelve or thirteen: altogether maybe fifteen stone dead weight. Someone with a lot of muscle put him in there, or are we looking for two someones?"

McInnis frowned down at the gritstone circle which was shaped like a doughnut; it had a slot at one side and the remains of a thickish rope fastened through the hole. "And where the hell did it come from? You can't pick these things up at the Co-op." He briefly thought of his wife, she'd taught him about millstones. He shut the thought down; he couldn't allow those thoughts on the job, they clouded his mind too much.

"You might get something off that rope where the knot has been tied, Mark." He turned to Jeff Lyell, his face hard and closed. "Is there much more down there?"

"Not much, sir. It's mainly feeling around in the silt now." Lyell eased his dry suit from around his neck and looked at the detective, wondering if the man was blaming him for not doing the job quicker. "We've nearly done all the hours we can for now; the last two have got twenty minutes more. It'll either have to wait for the other team or tomorrow. That's your decision, sir."

Bob McInnis stood rubbing his chin, unaware of the thoughts of the other man; his had strayed to the fact that he still hadn't managed to have a shave and that it was nearly three in the afternoon. He looked over the stretch of water, hearing the blue and white flag flapping on the end of another rubber dingy, and then seeing the sparkle where the late sun glanced off a rigid blue and white code flag, attached to a buoy that the divers had placed over the area where the body had been found.

"How far from the side is that?" He indicated the buoy.

Jeff scowled into the basin; the sluggish water slopped against the side making a small plop, plop sound as his men surfaced and placed things on board the boat before going under again. He ignored their activities, estimating the distance. "About four, maybe five feet, sir."

"It would take quite a bit of throwing to get a man," he glanced down at his feet, "and a quern, that far away from the quayside. Two could throw more easily than one, taking a head and foot swing."

"If you just rolled him, sir, and gave a good shove wouldn't he sail out that far?" Mark looked at McInnis.

"No, I don't think so, Mark." McInnis frowned at the area of concrete in a line with the wall.

"And how did he get here in the first place? A man walking along with one of those tucked under his arm might excite some comment."

"Could he have brought it earlier and left it ready, sir?"

"Wouldn't someone have noticed it? I don't know, Mark. What would be noticed lying around on the side of the dock?"

Mark scowled, glancing around at the various items propped up or neatly piled around the dockside. Netting, rope, crates, the odd stack of tyres. It was remarkably tidy. Nothing unusual met his eye, if you discounted the large pile that had been dredged up by the police during the course of the day. "I think it would have been noticed, sir. Pheby seems to keep fairly tight control of his area."

"Brought in a car maybe? It's easy enough to drive right round the basin." Bob McInnis looked across at the divers' long-wheelbased Land Rover and the small van of equipment parked behind it. They were parked well back from the edge of the quay, effectively blocking any access by other vehicles to the second dock.

"Nothing to stop them bringing a car right up alongside the edge between a couple of bollards. I wouldn't want to do it, on a dark night, but it could be done." McInnis was almost talking to himself as he wandered away from the steps and sighted on the area around the buoy. "Especially if you were familiar with the area."

He turned around to find the two younger men had followed him and now stood silently behind him as if playing a strange game of grandmother's footsteps. He addressed the sergeant, "I want the area around the gate dragged, and I may want you to look over the other marina before we've done. Is that alright with your team?"

Jeff nodded. "Tomorrow? I want to get my men warmed and rested for now, sir. They can't function properly and safely without that."

"That's fine. Mark here has got plenty to be going on with." He looked at the younger detective. "There are some marks on the quayside, I want you to examine and photograph them for me, Mark. I don't know if they are general wear and tear or relevant to the case." McInnis stepped back from the quayside and pointed out two rows of horizontal scratches.

"Damn! I didn't see them earlier, sir."

"No, I caught the glint of the mica just now; I think it must have been the angle of that fitful sun up there." Bob nodded up at the sky. "Neither of us saw them in the dark and rain this morning, but the diving team have blocked the entrance there and they've been using the steps. No one has parked there today that we know of."

Bob shrugged. "We don't know who has been parking here in the last few days, so I need to get them asking for witnesses, of cars as well as people."

Mark crouched down, looking closely at the scratches. "I'll see if I can get any traces from them but I doubt it, sir."

"Frankly so do I, Mark, but try anyway." Bob nodded at both men and walked briskly away again.

Jeff, following his figure until he turned the corner, raised an eyebrow. "Interesting bloke."

"Mm!" Mark for once wasn't being drawn, he was mad at himself for missing the marks and letting a mere detective spot something that a forensics man should have seen first. "Let's get these things sorted out and back to the lab, then maybe I can give him something to help solve this murder."

He wandered away to collect his camera and got busy with that and a pair of tweezers and then cotton buds and strange cans of spray. Jeff watched him for a moment or two before being recalled to his own responsibilities by a hail from the water.

Sandy and Bob were sitting in the quiet of Sandy's room at the bed and breakfast. There was a faint smell of aftershave and soap in the air from the shower Sandy had taken before their evening meal. They had a bottle of beer each, resting on the small table in the corner, and were seated on low armless chairs.

Sandy had donned slippers and removed his jacket to reveal heavy twill trousers held up by braces of a startling red and blue stripe.

Bob was trying not to look at them. He had shed his suit jacket but still had his tie neatly fastened around a freshly laundered shirt. He had managed to shave and sleep for a few hours after he'd left the quayside, but had woken around seven as the sun was going down to admire a spectacular sunset and eat dinner.

Having retired to Sandy's room they were now busy discussing tactics and exchanging information.

"So what you're saying, Bob, is we should be looking for two murderers."

"No, I'm saying maybe two. It might only be one person with a car and plenty of muscle." He frowned so fiercely at Sandy, that, that man, felt the need to defend himself.

"Look, the kids gave them me for Christmas; you have to be able to say truthfully that you've worn them, even if it's only just the once. It's sort of symbolic."

"Eh! I wasn't thinking about your braces, Sandy, though they are a bit..." He waved an elegant and expressive hand. "Why a millstone? Why not a heavy tyre or chain? Plenty of those around!"

Sandy shook his head slowly. "I don't know. It could just have been the nearest heavy object. What do you think we're dealing with here, some psychological nutcase?"

"I dunno, I'm just a bit worried by the method that's all."

"All! I'm bothered that there's a murder at all."

Bob grimaced. "Yeah, but this feels a bit... odd."

"All murders are a bit odd, lad." Sandy shifted in his seat, pouring beer into the tooth glass provided by the establishment. He watched the beer foam up as he spoke. "Definitely a man, think you?" He sniffed at the yeasty smell of the beer and felt his mouth begin to water.

"Not necessarily, Sandy. I've seen a few strong women in my time. But on balance, a man. It would take some effort to get that body in the water, man or woman."

"Jonesy still hasn't come back with any identification?"

"It's not like your precious CSI, Sandy. DNA takes time, and we haven't got a huge database to draw on either. I'm hoping the teeth might help, and we've got a few more reports of missing persons from around Cumberland. One or two might match."

"It's a pity we can't show the public a picture."

"I wouldn't want that picture to decorate anyone's living room, Sandy."

Sandy Bell felt as if a cold wind had touched him; no, he wouldn't want that either. "How about Mark, has he had a chance to find anything yet?"

"He'd got a huge pile of rubbish to sort through from what I saw on that dockside. I think it might take him a bit of time." Bob grimaced and then reached for the bottle of beer, unscrewing the cap and taking a healthy drink from the top of the neck of the bottle.

"We still haven't discovered the whereabouts of Pheby. No one saw him leave the harbour. I thought at first Gareth might have been mistaken. Thought the man might have just been away about his own business, but he seems to have scarpered." Bob set the bottle carefully down on the table again.

"He hasn't been seen at his digs, and his landlady says he came back mid afternoon and took some clothes away. She thought he was just doing a bit of washing or dry cleaning." He shook his head at Sandy. "I thought he was acting a bit strangely, but you know, Sandy, murder affects people; makes some of them twitchy. Everyone's got something murky to hide, or thinks they have, so I didn't have him watched."

"No more did I then."

Bob shook his head. "I should have spotted something off." He played with the beer bottle, rolling it around on its base and absently watching the surface level move around the inside. "Until we get an identity we don't know where to start looking for the murderer do we?" He raised tired brown eyes to Sandy's face.

"Do we look for a connection with the docks and the people who know the area? Is it someone who's visited, murderer or victim, and thought it would be a good dumping ground? Or maybe we're back to symbolism again. Jonesy said they used to execute people that way instead of hanging them," Bob spoke, as he frowned once more at his beer bottle.

"Can't see the odds on it myself, Bob. Whichever way you go you're still dead. I would have thought a good clean snap of the neck would be kinder than suffocation with water." Sandy grimaced. "But you're right, until we get a bit of identification it will certainly hold us back a bit, lad." Sandy took a sip of beer and licked the foam off his top lip. "All this symbolism stuff is a bit deep for me, lad. Murderers generally kill from motives of greed or fear, envy or rage, with the odd bit of ambition thrown in. You don't get many madmen killing really."

He put down the glass and looked across the quiet room at Bob, "I spoke to Meeks. I've rarely seen a man more put out, Bob. He looked as though he might commit a murder, and he certainly isn't a madman. He had James Simpson in the office so fast you could see the skid marks on the lino."

"What were the boys up to then?"

"Still don't know. Constable Simpson wouldn't say, even when Meeks suspended him. Meeks had their father bring the boys in and we all sat looking at each other. They wouldn't speak at all, even though their father tried bribery and threats." Sandy picked the glass up and sipped again, before using a stubby finger to trace the condensation on its side. "Tell you the truth, I don't think their big brother knows what they were doing; he's just trying to protect them. Whatever it was, I don't think they murdered that man."

"No, I don't think so either; I just hope it's not too illegal. What did Constable Simpson say? I take it he didn't sit in silence as well."

"He claims the boys came and told him they'd found a body under the water when they'd been diving in the harbour. It scared them both silly, but he claims they hadn't been drinking. He looked at his father at that point, Bob. I am thinking he was trying to give the old man some consolation or maybe save them some grief."

Sandy shifted in the seat. "Constable Simpson says he took their word about what they'd seen and the rest of the report about checking out the area and securing them was accurate."

"How about the fact that we could barely see the head when we arrived? Surely some of the other local coppers noticed it wasn't visible."

"They took Simpson's word that the boys had been on the water and looked down on the corpse through it." Sandy shrugged. "By the time most of the constabulary of the town got there it was an hour, an hour and a half later, and you probably could see it if you were over the top of it."

Bob raised an eyebrow. "Do we believe that?"

"Even if we don't, we do Bob. This is no time to be muddying the harbour waters with queries about the constabulary. I think they're just being loyal to their own. We'll find out what was going on more easily if we don't push at this stage."

Bob picked up the bottle, sipped, and thought about that. "Mark in on the general, local loyalty, conspiracy, Sandy?"

"Ye gods, no! The fool says he just wasn't thinking. He arrived, saw the head bobbing in the current and went from there. And I believe him, Bob." Sandy shook his head. "Hell! We were all half asleep when we arrived. You've never seen the boy so annoyed with himself. Between missing that bit and not spotting those marks on the quayside that you saw, he was too busy beating himself up for me to get a word in."

Sandy smiled somewhat grimly. "He'll learn. Give him a chance, Bob, I'm sure you can trust him."

Bob said nothing for a minute, setting the bottle down squarely on the lacy doily provided by the B and B to try and save their tabletops. It obviously hadn't worked in the past; there were enough white rings to symbolise the Olympic Games. "I hope to God you're right, Sandy."

Bob rubbed a hand over his hair. "I have to go and see about Caitlin tomorrow. I'll be as quick as I can but it's going to take most of the afternoon. How do you want to divide up the labour?"

"Let's wait for the morning, Bob; we might have a bit more info' to go on by then." He paused, looking across the small space. "I rang Sarah this evening before you got up. She can't wait to look after the little one." He smiled a bit crookedly. "She once told Elizabeth that she didn't know what the empty nest syndrome was." He shook his head, smiling even more wryly. "Myself I don't think her nest will ever be empty."

Bob sighed. "I miss Beth so much, Sandy, I'm sorry I'm being so difficult."

Sandy looked across, the pity he was careful never to show lurking at the back of his brown eyes. "Yes, lad, I know, we all miss her." He reached over and just touched the fist fiercely gripping the bottle. "It will get easier, Bob, but take your time, lad, I understand, and so does Sarah."

4

"There aren't many perks to this job, Bob, but getting to see a spectacular sunrise next to the seashore, has to be one of them."

"Yes, well, I thought we needed to get an overall look at the scene of the crime in natural light. Maybe see if a bird's eye view would help us see anything we might have missed before." McInnis shifted his feet and stared back at a black-backed gull which was gliding on the uplift next to him and giving them all greedy looks.

"That's known locally as 'The Three Kingdoms', sir." With a sweep of his hand in a fine calfskin glove, Mark Forester indicated the horizon over the sea at one side of them and sent the gull, flapping lazily, away. "Mainly because the Scottish, Irish and English all have a stake in the fishing rights."

The three men stood on the separating mound between the two basins and looked out over the view obtained from their lofty height. They could see the small town on their right just stirring to life, the orange-yellow sodium lights winking out down the hill as the sun fretfully advanced upwards, fighting its way through the thick liana-like spirals of smoke ascending heavenwards from early Sunday morning fires. The faint smell of coal smoke just reached the men as the wind veered and changed direction.

McInnis and Sandy both wore thick waxed Burberrys over their suits, despite the lack of rain. In addition Sandy had a muddy-brown scarf tucked into the top of his jacket. Mark however was sporting a soft leather bomber jacket and a white silk scarf. Sandy thought he looked like Snoopy fighting von Richthofen from the top of the kennel, but hid his smile. The boy had something to learn about fashion yet; thank God he didn't wear flying goggles too.

They looked downwards at the two docks. From this angle they could see the torpid activity of a few constables stationed to guard the site overnight. A large orange buoy was bouncing about on the water in the brisk wind, but the gates were still closed so the level hadn't changed since the day before, the sound of ropes and sheets hitting masts in a faintly musical clang. The sound drifted up from the few remaining yachts in the Marina as the wind nudged them about on the water.

The commercial dock was beginning to fill with water however; the tide had turned a full four hours since and the fishing boats were slowly hoisting themselves back up the walls on their mooring ropes. After the debacle the day before, Bob had spent a profitable hour studying tide tables in an effort to get his head round the scene he was now looking at.

"So tell me if I've got this wrong, Mark. Yesterday morning the tide was low at four 'o'clock. So if the murderer wanted to put the body into the water at high tide and at night, he'd have to have done it any time from Tuesday to Sunday of the week before last?"

Mark shook his head. "I'd need the tide tables, sir. But yeah, it runs in six to eight day cycles of low and high. So, high early this morning, would mean low about a week ago at the same time of day, roughly."

"So probably the best time to dump the body would be Wednesday or Thursday. Round about the eleventh?"

"No that won't work Bob. It was full moon last weekend. It would have been too bright the week before, he'd have been seen." Sandy shook his head. "I checked the calendar."

Mark was looking puzzled. "Why has he got to be thrown in at high tide, sir?"

"Because he wasn't gagged, Mark. So unless he was unconscious, and Dr Jones says he struggled so I don't think he was, then he had to go in over his head right away or he could have called out and attracted unwanted attention. The alternative is that he was unconscious, but the murderer still wouldn't want him reviving and yelling, so we still need deep water."

"Didn't the rope strangle him then?"

"Nope, probably drowning. Jonesy is being a bit coy about that."

Sandy grinned as the young forensics man scowled, and then turned his eyes onto Bob McInnis. "So you want a dark night and a high tide for the deed, Bob? Rather than a dark and stormy one?" His lips twitched as he saw McInnis register the reference to Bulwer-Lytton's novel.

"Yes I do, Sandy. It might be a secluded spot but it's still a lot nearer the town centre than I'd want if I was committing a murder."

"Personally I wouldn't want anywhere near a town centre if I was going to commit a premeditated murder. But there are always fools to keep us in our jobs, Bob."

Bob grunted an acknowledgement of the comment but his mind was obviously turning something over. "You know, Sandy, the more I think of it the more this seems like a crazy plan. Why not bury the body nearer to the original crime scene? Why drowning? Or if you can bring it as far as the sea, why not take it all the way out to sea? Mark, here, has just told us that that's a good fishing area. The fish were doing a good job of disposing of our corpse before we got to it."

"Thanks for that." Sandy gulped and looked a bit sick. He'd had freshly caught fish for his lunch the day before, he thought. "Maybe he hadn't got a boat or access to one."

"I don't think a murderer is going to flinch at stealing a boat, Sandy." McInnis turned and began to make his way down the slope of the mound, onto the commercial dockside. The other two followed him down.

Sandy shook his head and addressed the retreating back of his partner. "I've known murderers who filed honest tax returns and handed in valuables they found on the street, Bob."

Bob swung his head round and offered a brief smile. "Yeah! But there aren't that many saints around, Sandy."

He jumped the last foot and stood waiting for the other two to join him. "We need weather reports, Sandy. See if we can't narrow things down a bit. Until we know who it is, all we can run with are the facts we have got."

He turned to Mark. "There are several things I want you to do, Mark. First, the fishermen around here know the sea, so if they wanted to take a corpse out and dump it they could?" He paused, looking at the younger man.

"Well yes, sir, but I wouldn't fancy taking a small boat out on my own hereabouts. There's a tide race of seven to ten knots outside the harbour. And it might excite interest if you took a boat out and brought it back on the next tide. That wouldn't be good fishing practice. What's more it would be a risky business on your own doing a job like that."

"But two men...?" Bob let the question hang.

"Yeah." Mark puffed his cheeks out and sighed. "Two men could do it. I don't like to think any of my mates would have though."

"The other way is a single, knowledgeable man, who wouldn't risk it." The three men began to walk along the side of the wall. "Or someone with no knowledge who wouldn't risk it either." Bob paused. "Or someone who wanted the body found. Knowledgeable or otherwise."

"I need you to ask about, Mark." Bob kept strolling as Mark scowled across at the few fishing boats bobbing at their buoys in the dock.

Sandy looked at the pair of men in front, and then glanced in a seemingly casual manner around. He wanted to know who was interested in the doings of the police, and Mark especially. Even if Mark hadn't realised it, Sandy knew that in setting up the morning discussion in such a public place Bob was making sure the fishing fraternity were aware of Mark's position and authority as a police officer, not as the son of one of their mates.

Bob McInnis was continuing with his instructions. "I want you and the divers to finish dragging that bottom. I don't suppose you'll find much more in the marina. Then," he pointed, "I want them to check the hulls of a few of these boats. Something fishy, if you'll pardon the pun," he switched a grin on and off, "is going on, and I want to know what that Harbour Master was so scared about he felt he had to run."

He looked at Mark. "It could be awkward, Mark. You're going to be investigating men your father, or you, might know personally. You'd better speak up if you think there's going to be a conflict of interest."

Mark shook his head. "It isn't going to be a problem, sir."

"Well I hope not; we've got enough of a problem with the local lads covering for each other. Come and talk to us if you think it's all turning pear shaped on you, Mark."

Mark nodded. "Yes, sir." He looked at Sandy almost apologetically. "I've got the Lake District team coming over this morning. I thought things might go a bit quicker if we had more men to draw on. The water's pretty cold at this time of year, sir." He looked at Bob. "You said yesterday you might want more water searching; the divers can't stay down so long when the water's cold."

"That's fine, Mark, I said you were to organise the diving as you saw fit. I don't know enough about it. This is your area of expertise." Bob offered the younger man a smile of encouragement.

Mark nodded at both men. "I'll go and set things up with Jeff, see how he wants to spread the load." He walked away rapidly and the two detectives could see him scanning the docks and offering greetings to the few fishermen who had been allowed back on their boats to sort out their gear.

"He's a scamp, Bob. But he'll make a good Detective Inspector some day."

Bob nodded, but passed no further comment about Mark, remarking, apparently irrelevantly, "Have you met Constable Pretty yet, Sandy?"

"Constable who?"

"He's the young constable I shanghaied yesterday as a driver, Sandy. Constable Pretty. His brain bulges, and he thinks with it." Bob McInnis began to walk around the dockside in the wake of Mark Forester. "He's going to make a brilliant detective someday too. He cottoned on to the boys' lies and had the guts to tell Meeks about it, even though young John Simpson is his mate."

"I look forward to making his acquaintance then." Sandy's lips twitched. "Really? Pretty?"

"Yeah, and it gets worse, his first name is Oliver. I wonder how many have tumbled to the fact that he's a COP."

"Eh!" Sandy looked blank.

"Constable Oliver Pretty." Bob flashed a brief grin at his partner as he watched him mouthing the names, and then give a grunt of laughter.

"Oh! C.O.P. I get it."

"I told him to swap to detective rank as soon as he can. But I'm not sure being a DIP isn't worse."

Sandy gave a roar of laughter, "They'll call him dipstick. Ah! Well, I've surmounted the obstacle of being known as ding-dong. If he's good enough he'll overcome his name."

They finished the walk in silence, both thinking their own thoughts, until McInnis said, "I'm going to call in and see Jonesy before I come back, Sandy; he might have a bit more to give us." He halted at the door of the incident van. "I'll get things sorted out with Mary and Sarah and be back about tea-time."

"Take your time, Bob; you need to know the little one is settled for your own peace of mind. You won't be any good to us if you're fretting about her."

"OK, Sandy, I think I might steal Constable Pretty and a squad car and bring my own car back. I'll go and speak to Meeks."

Sandy gave him a speculative look. "Giving the lad a break, or picking those bulging brains, Bob?"

"Bit of both, Sandy, he isn't going to be flavour of the month with the local lads until all this dies down; they must know who told Meeks about the Simpson boys' statements."

"And you can get a bit more background on the locals while you're at it." Sandy smiled. "Go and organise yourself then Bob, and, Bob...?" He watched as the younger man stopped his forward movement. "Eat breakfast, lad."

"Yes, Dad." Bob pulled a face, changing direction and heading towards the café which was obviously doing sterling business among the local constabulary.

Constable Pretty was quite happy to act as chauffeur to Detective Inspector McInnis and said so in a quiet voice as Bob climbed into the car at half nine that fine Sunday morning.

"Having a bit of a rough time, son?"

"Nothing I can't handle, sir. I'm used to a bit of bullying." He gave a brief smile as he put the car into gear and pulled out of the parking area and over the bridge into the centre of the town.

McInnis nodded, but said no more as the young constable manoeuvred his way out of the town and into the Cumbrian countryside. When he was satisfied that Oliver Pretty knew how to handle the car on the narrow country roads he shifted in his seat and began asking questions. Quite what Pretty had expected to be asked about he wasn't sure, but to be questioned on the history of the town wasn't it.

"Well I know a bit of local history, sir. But how far back do you want me to go?"

"I want a feel for the area, Constable. Just start talking and I'll stop you if you go too deep."

"Er, right, sir." Pretty, paused, gathering his thoughts together. "Original name of the town was Alauna, sir, named by the Romans; they had a Spanish cohort here."

Bob raised a hand. "Maybe a bit more modern, lad. More the sailing history."

Pretty frowned, chewing his lip for a minute and scowling at the passing traffic as he thought. "It was Ellenfoot after the river Ellen, trade was chiefly fishing, herring mainly, and smugglers of course. But then the Senhouse family started to develop the town and the docks in the eighteenth century. It was named after a Senhouse wife and became Maryport."

McInnis raised an eyebrow. "Where did the smugglers come from?"

"Ireland, a lot of them, sir. There's a tunnel up near Bank End a bit south of the town. You can still see the entrance they used, but I think the other end is blocked now."

"The coastguard will never stamp it out entirely while the import taxes are the price they are and there's a quick, if risky, profit to be made. What else were the docks used for besides fishing or smuggling?" Bob glanced across as he asked the question.

"Export, sir, iron ore, coal, glass and Ismay had his origins here."

"Ismay?"

"White Star line, Titanic and Oceania, sir."

"They weren't launched from here?"

"Oh no, sir. Biggest ship launched here was about two thousand tons and that was launched broadsides into the river." Pretty changed down a gear.

"Now that I would have liked to see." McInnis tried to visualise such a big ship slipping sideways into the small, and muddy, river Ellen they had crossed on their way out of the harbour. "How on earth did they get it out to the shore?"

"Tugs. I'm a member of The Nomadic Society myself."

This comment appeared to come from left field and McInnis frowned and shook his head. "Eh! What have native tribesmen got to do with it?"

Pretty cast a smile whose mixture was compounded of shyness and slyness. "The NOMADIC was built in 1911 in Belfast in the next slipway to the TITANIC. She used to ferry the posh folks out to the big ocean going liners, including the TITANIC, sir. She's being restored over in Belfast. I hope to get over there to help do a bit of restoration work next year."

"Hmm!" McInnis hid his grin; nothing like a convert or a volunteer for shouting about a cause. He tried to drag the conversation forward a century. "So when did they stop making ships here?" Apparently he was unsuccessful.

"Before the First World War sir. Dockyards weren't big enough for the modern iron boats; the firms moved or died and the trade went to Whitehaven. The place really suffered during the Depression and the dockyards themselves closed in the early sixties, I think." Pretty slowed as they approached the outskirts of Aspatria and McInnis kept quiet as they went through the small town. When they were safely on the far side he took up the conversation again.

"They don't look as if they've ever been closed."

"They're still closed sir." Pretty looked puzzled.

"We've just fished a body out of one of your dockyards, lad, and it had plenty of boats in it."

"No, sir that's the harbour basin. Dockyards are where you make or repair ships, a harbour basin is where you load and sail from."

"Ah! So I shouldn't be calling them dockyards?"

"Well you can." Pretty glanced across, then returned his eyes to the ribbon of grey metal they were currently travelling on. "But strictly speaking they're only docks, not dockyards. The one where the body was found is the newer one and its name is the Senhouse Dock and the other, the commercial one, that's the Elizabeth Dock."

Bob McInnis sighed quietly, changing the subject slightly. "So aside from the few boats in the docks now, what keeps the community together?"

"Tourists, sir, and the Blues festival."

"No smugglers now?"

"Maybe, sir, but small scale and it's a case of 'watch the wall' for most of us as Kipling says."

"Even the police, Pretty?" He watched the dull red colour the young man's cheeks.

"I shouldn't think so, sir. Sergeant Meeks is a good officer and so is Detective Oakes. Maybe with one or two, but they really aren't a bad team, sir."

"Except when it hits family?"

"Maybe, sir." Pretty shrugged, "But I don't think that attitude's that prevalent among the force."

McInnis could see that Pretty wasn't going to be drawn any further on the subject. He sat back more comfortably to mull over the information and decide if it helped him.

Was the Harbour Master turning a blind eye to a bit of smuggling? Was that why he'd run? McInnis didn't think Pheby was the type to commit a murder in his own backyard and risk the body being found. The man knew too much about tides and docks to do something so stupid, surely. They'd have to investigate him, but McInnis didn't think he'd find a murderer lurking under that neat moustache, but he supposed he could be wrong.

His thoughts were derailed by the small train of information suddenly shunted his way from Constable Pretty.

"There was Fletcher Christian as well."

"Pardon?"

"Fletcher Christian, sir, he lived in these parts. You know, Marlon Brando and the *'Mutiny on the Bounty'*, sir."

McInnis, detoured onto a branch line, blinked a bit. "Marlon Brando?"

"Marlon Brando, sir, he played Fletcher Christian in *'Mutiny on the Bounty'*."

"So he did, Pretty. Though I am faintly surprised that someone of your age should know about him."

For the first time that day the serious face of his driver cracked into a huge grin. "My mum is a huge fan of Brando, sir. I think she's watched every one of his films." Once launched there was no stopping the boy, who was apparently also a huge fan of the screen idol. McInnis allowed the jetsam of film titles and fifties film stars to jostle around him while he thought about the reasons a Harbour Master might have to kill someone.

McInnis had enjoyed the company of the constable and said so when that young man stopped at the central police station in Carlisle. "Have a meal before you drive back, Pretty, and report to Sergeant Meeks when you arrive."

"Yes of course, sir, but don't you want me to take you back?"

"No, I'll be back later; I'll come in my own car. Off you go, and don't forget to have a meal." Which, Bob McInnis had to admit, was a bit ironical, since he himself couldn't have felt less like eating.

His car was parked round the back of the police station. He got in to find the half-drunk mug of coffee from Friday night still sitting in the little well next to the gear stick with, apparently, a miniature oil slick floating on the top of the black and murky liquid. McInnis leaned out and deposited the fluid on the car park concrete for the next rain to wash away, fastened his seat-belt and pulled out his mobile.

"Sandy, yeah I'm at the Station. I'm sending the lad back after he's eaten." He paused, idly tapping the wheel as he listened to his partner.

"Yes, I picked his brains. He's a bright young man; I'd love to second him to our neck of the woods." He swapped ears and fished out his notebook. "I've got the address here, are you going to try and see what they'll say without Dad present? It might work, Sandy."

He tucked away the book while he said, "OK, I should be back about six. Yeah, yeah, you behave yourself too; don't eat too much candyfloss." He was just flipping the mobile shut when he had a thought. "Sandy?" The mobile was silent. He pressed 'redial' and waited.

"Sandy, I've had a thought. Can you ask the Sergeant to take a small detail and check that Bank End isn't being used again for its old purposes? Send Gareth with them if possible. Smuggling, Sandy."

The phone muttered at him like a distant thunderstorm. "Yeah I think it's a reach too, but it won't do any harm to check. Bye, Sandy, see you later." He put the machine on the passenger seat and started the car, heading to Sarah's house and a meeting with his baby daughter.

He had seen his daughter only twice since the week she was born. Elizabeth, his wife, had been nearly eight and a half months pregnant and had joked on that fateful morning that if she got any bigger she'd never get behind the steering-wheel. She'd gone shopping; for baby clothes he remembered. The car had been shunted from behind at a road junction and the driver of the other car had sped away; witnesses differed about make, number plate and even the colour. The first he knew about it, the hospital was calling to tell him she was unconscious.

She'd suffered a massive haemorrhage from a whiplash injury, exacerbated by the raised blood pressure of pregnancy. They really only needed his permission to do an emergency caesarean and turn off the machines afterwards. He'd walked around in a daze for weeks. Mary and Hector had taken charge. It wasn't that he didn't love the child. But he'd hardly got used to being a husband and suddenly he was a single man again.

He drove over to Sarah's, feeling his stomach churn and his mouth dry. The last time he'd felt like this was when he was a rookie cop. It was the first time he'd given evidence in court, he'd been terrified he might make a mistake, and not entirely sure what he would do if he did.

He parked outside the three-bedroom semi that belonged to Sandy Bell and his wife and turned off the engine. He could feel the sweat sticking to his back as if he was developing a fever. "Oh! God, I hope I can cope with this." It was a whispered prayer. He released his vice-like grip on the wheel and climbed out, slamming the door and locking it. All the while feeling he was in some sort of bad dream, and his feet were moving in that slow, unreal way, only dreams have.

He squared his shoulders and pinned a smile to his face. A firing squad might have held more appeal. "Hi, Mary." His sister must have been watching out for him, she'd swung the door open before he got to it.

"Hello, little brother." She carefully examined him from under thickly lashed brown eyes as she reached out to take his hands and draw him into an embrace and the house. "Sarah has just popped out for five minutes. She'll be back soon. Come and say hello to your daughter."

Bob nodded, but he was beyond words now. Mary slipped an arm around his waist and led him inexorably forwards. His daughter was sitting, propped up in Sandy's TV chair, cushions surrounding her. She was trying to clutch a set of multi-coloured plastic keys, without much success. Big brown eyes lifted and took note of the entrance of the two adults and as she was distracted she neatly whacked herself in the face with them.

The wail didn't mean much, it was only a minor protest of frustration, but Bob found himself hoisting her up and holding her before he'd realised what he was doing. Suddenly he was hugging her tight against his shoulder, the soft, round, heavy head resting in the curve of his neck. He felt tears at the back of his eyes and turned away from Mary, feeling embarrassed.

Mary, however, was tactfully walking out the door saying, "I'll put the kettle on, love, while you get reacquainted."

Bob sat down, taking a firm grip on his emotions and his daughter, placing her on his lap. "Hello, Caitlin. Aren't you a lovely little thing then?" He looked at the rose-pink jumper and denim jeans her aunt had chosen to array her in. She was a dainty little thing, like her mother had been.

Caitlin was unimpressed by compliments, but quite fascinated, apparently, by his tie. She reached out a slightly sticky hand and tried to grab.

Bob smiled down at her, the smile for the first time in nearly six months reaching his eyes. "Oh I don't think so, darling." He gently restrained the waving hands and handed over the plastic keys. While his daughter tried to put them all into her mouth, a feat on a par with stuffing a melon through the eye of a needle, he examined his prize.

"I don't remember you having all this beautiful black hair." He smoothed the tufts down, balancing her carefully. As an uncle to Mary's six children, handling babies wasn't what he'd been afraid of. No, what he'd been terrified of, he thought, was the searing pain of grief he'd experienced whenever something brought the memory of his wife back. This moppet might bring Elizabeth's presence racing back, but it was a good feeling, not the heartbreaking one he'd been expecting.

He was gently bouncing the child when Mary returned with two mugs of steaming tea and a baby bottle on a tray.

"She's due for a feed. I've brought her enough formula for the next two weeks, but she eats a tiny bit of solids now too." She passed him the bottle and a large white muslin cloth and sat down in a chair opposite.

Bob, accepting simply because the bottle had been placed in his hand, now looked across. "Shock tactics, Mary?"

"Well, love, the sooner you start the better. It's not as if you haven't fed a baby before."

"No I suppose not, Mary." He expertly tipped his daughter on his arm and inserted the nipple, making sure she wasn't sucking air along with the milk. "How long have you had her on the bottle?"

"Only about a fortnight, since Hector got his papers. She's taken to it well. Sarah knows all her formula and food details, love. She'll make sure you don't go wrong." She smiled across at him as he nursed the child who had her eyes closed and a blissful expression on her face as she gently kneaded the chest of her father.

"I'm going to find it really hard parting from my niece, but I was right, you need each other." She nodded to herself and sat quietly drinking tea as he tended to Caitlin.

"I'm in the middle of a murder, Mary."

"You'll always be in the middle of some crime, Bob, it's your job. But your daughter needs to share your life." She brushed hair out of eyes as deep a brown as her brother's, "Don't fret, Bob, we'll all be here for you. You're not alone."

She grinned impishly. "Mum will be fighting Sarah to baby-sit, and Granddad Fielding will want a share too. It's not going to be a case of being alone, but trying to get time alone with the moppet, believe me. If I hadn't been breast-feeding I'd hardly have had a look in myself. She's a happy little thing."

Bob gently removed the nearly empty bottle from the slack mouth from which a tiny dribble of milk dripped, then looked up. "Yeah? I hope you're right, Mary." He set the bottle on the low coffee table, and used the cloth on the pink lips. "Because there's a hell of a difference between looking after your brats and handing them back, and having one twenty-four/seven." He grinned a bit wryly at her chuckle; propping his daughter up against his shoulder and, while he inhaled the baby smell of talc and sweet milk, patted the small back.

A phenomenal burp rewarded his efforts.

"She's good at that, no colic to keep you up half the night, though the teeth might."

Bob kept the small body resting on his shoulder; a snore like a small two-stroke engine buzzing next to his ear. He leaned forward and took a sip of tea, making a face at the tepid drink.

"Drink it fast or drink it cold, Bob, when you have infants about."

The siblings sat exchanging news while the baby slept contentedly between them. Not even the return of Sarah disturbed her slumbers, or being placed in a cot in the little room which belonged to Claire, Sandy's teenage daughter.

"I've set the monitor." Mary came down the stairs and placed the little cube on the kitchen table; they all listened to the snuffling sound for a moment or two and then Bob put it in the centre of the table and continued to place cutlery at Sarah's directions.

He had been trying to say how grateful he was but Sarah wouldn't let him.

"She's a darling, Bob, and I shall love having her. When you've got yourself more organised, we'll sort something out. I'm not trying to steal her from you. Not that I wouldn't like to." Sarah was matronly, tending to plump. But there were good strong muscles under the squishiness and a good firm character under the soft manner.

"I couldn't wish for better for her."

"Away with you, man!" Sarah blushed rosily as he came over and dropped a peck of a kiss onto her cheek. He smiled disarmingly at her, his slow and quiet smile, and Mary blinked back tears because she loved her baby brother and that smile had been missing for too long.

Mary had gone soon after lunch. She'd tiptoed up to the crib and kissed the little rosy cheek, and backed out of the room very quickly because she knew she would be in floods of tears soon. Caitlin was as dear to her as her own children.

Bob had hugged Mary hard and watched her go. "I bet she stops somewhere and has a good cry." He looked across at Sarah, who nodded her agreement.

"Yes, probably, we're funny creatures."

"I've got to go and see the Medical Examiner this afternoon before I head back."

"Why don't you take Caitlin with you, it's a fine afternoon." Sarah paused then said, "Unless you're going to that nasty morgue place. You're not to take Caitlin there."

"What do you take me for, Sarah?" Bob smiled across at her. "No, I'm going to Ryan Jones' own home office. I rang before I left Maryport, he said he would have a preliminary report for me."

The small wail interrupted them and sent Bob upstairs. His daughter, nappy changed and toy in hand, came down with an angelic smile on her face. Bob put her into an all-in-one suit with zips and poppers and received a big bag from Sarah. He looked slightly horrified.

"The minute you only take one nappy, she'll go through two and leave you without a spare. But if you've got a spare you probably won't need any at all." She shrugged philosophically. "Babies are like that."

Bob took both baby and bag and headed to his car, where he and Mary had earlier installed a baby seat in the back. "In you get sweet-pea. He fumbled the seat straps around her small person and emerged from the back seat with a triumphant grin. "I'll be back in about two hours, Sarah."

"Babies don't care about anyone's schedules but their own, lad, so you might like to make that an hour and a half."

"Oh! Right." Bob nodded, before climbing in to the front of the car and dumping the changing bag on the passenger seat. He checked his watch then headed across the city to the accompaniment of gurgles and mutterings from the back seat. "Heavens! It's worse than having a criminal in the back, Caitlin, you do go on." He looked in the rear view mirror at his daughter industriously chewing her fist. And smiled again.

Ryan Jones greeted Bob at the door and led him indoors. He had company. Doctor Jennifer Lowther was seated in one of two big leather chairs that flanked the fireplace in the study of the old Victorian house. The fire was small, but a very comforting sight nevertheless. As Bob entered the room she was just about to sip from a mug. The mug stopped halfway and her mouth formed an 'o' shape along with her big green eyes.

Bob looked around trying to find what had surprised her. Behind him Ryan Jones was saying, "We've got some delightful company, Bob. I believe you met Jenny yesterday?"

Jenny stood up, setting the mug on a side table and coming forward. "Do let me hold her Inspector, she's adorable." She reached out to take Caitlin from her snug position in Bob's arms and he began to see what Mary had meant. He smiled a bit wryly and handed over his daughter.

Ryan Jones watched the transaction with a strange expression on his face, but didn't say anything about it, merely enquiring if Bob wanted a coffee.

"Yes, that would be nice, Jonesy." He went and sat in the other leather chair, watching curiously as Jenny Lowther sat next to Ryan Jones' quiet wife on the old damask-covered sofa and the pair began to talk to the baby.

The Medical Examiner, returning with a small paper file and a blue pottery mug, handed over the mug and put the file down on the coffee table near the sofa. "We have an identity, Bob."

Bob nodded over the mug's rim. "Will it help?"

"Oh, I think so."

Jenny looked up, "He's Doctor Neil Sandman. He asked me to take over his practice for three weeks while he took a much needed holiday. He was supposed to be spending a couple of weeks in North Wales."

"Oh, I'm very sorry, Doctor."

"It's OK, I didn't know him well, Inspector. We'd only met a couple of times, he seemed like a very pleasant man, and his patients all speak well of him. I can't imagine who might want to murder the poor chap." She looked down at the child who was pulling at the long braid of light brown mousy hair resting over one of her shoulders and gently disengaged the fist, saying, "I bet you do that to your mum too." And missed the wince of the Jones'. However no one offered to correct her.

"How did you find out?" McInnis looked across at Ryan Jones, "Teeth?"

"Yes, teeth, but before that I'd discovered one of the very new pacemakers. They're tiny these days. Hadn't got to it when you called yesterday, but I ran the serial number and there were all the details. I rang the surgery just to double check; Jenny checked his itinerary and the poor man hadn't turned up at his bed and breakfast."

"You'd think they'd have rung to find out why he hadn't come."

"'T'isn't their business to run after the clients."

"No, I suppose not." Bob sighed. "Still we can make a start now."

"Why would he be at Maryport docks, Inspector? If he was catching the train to Wales he'd go into Carlisle."

McInnis looked at the serious face as Jenny Lowther rested his daughter against her shoulder and began, instinctively, to pat the pink-clad back as she asked the question. Caitlin, oblivious to others' needs, stopped the grizzle she had been starting, and wriggled against the feminine body, her legs trying to find purchase against the softness.

"I don't know, Doctor. We need to track down his car as well." He found he was quite jealous of Jenny's ability to quieten his daughter on so short an acquaintance. He set down his empty mug and said, "Perhaps I'd better have her."

Caitlin sat happily on her father's lap as if she'd been doing it since birth. The grizzle disappeared like magic, and she started to suck a fist, leaning contentedly back against him and examining her late seat with big eyes which were beginning to droop.

The hand holding the child firmly had a broad gold band on the third finger and Jenny Lowther, noting it, watched the interaction and suppressed the twinge of envy. So that's why he'd ignored her. Her lips twitched upwards; it was good to know she wasn't losing her allure, she thought. Why were the nice ones always married? Then answered her own question. Because they were nice.

McInnis was continuing to discuss some of the details with Ryan Jones. She tuned back in as he was saying, "It was definitely a handstone. I was thinking about your comments, Jonesy, about drowning being a form of execution. I wondered, do you think it was symbolic?"

Doctor Jones shook his head. "God knows, Bob. I don't. The man was a good doctor by all accounts. I met him once at some conference or other. He tried to keep abreast of modern trends; he worked himself into the ground for his patients according to the receptionist at the surgery. I can't think why anyone would want to kill a doctor, for heaven's sake."

"Well, we'll move over there tomorrow and start talking to people. I think the dock might have been the primary crime scene, but it wasn't the place where the murder was plotted." He deftly turned his daughter around and rubbed her back, rocking her gently. "I'd better get back. Sarah warned me about the next feed." He hoisted his small companion and scooped up the file in passing.

Doctor Jones smiled. "I'll see you when you get back to Carlisle, Bob. You know to ring me if you have any questions. The full report will be ready Wednesday or Thursday."

McInnis nodded farewell at the quiet Mrs Jones and the attractive young doctor and turned away. Ryan Jones walked with him out to the car and stood watching him stow Caitlin safely in her seat. "Has your sister brought the baby for a visit?"

"Nope." Bob stood up and shut the rear door. "Caitlin's going to live with me now."

"Oh!" whatever the good doctor thought of that he refrained from speaking for a minute or two. Eventually he said, "That's good, Bob, very good."

McInnis smiled. "Well we'll certainly hope so, Jonesy." He stopped with his hand on the driver's door. "By the way what does, now wait while I get it right, *'vedrum thim trustio season'* mean."

Ryan Jones winced. "Was that Gareth who said that to you?"

Bob nodded, a smile sneaking onto his mouth before he knew about it.

"I hope he wasn't addressing you; you could do him for insubordination." At Bob's shake he went on, "You've rather mangled what I believe is the language of God, but I think what he might have been saying was 'you can't trust Englishmen' or possibly the English. Does that make sense?"

"Indeed it does, and I can only be grateful that no one else understood him either." McInnis raised an eyebrow as Jones laughed.

"I'll see you around, Jonesy." He climbed in and drove away, leaving the Medical Examiner to go back to his wife and guest.

5

Telling Sandy about his day Bob McInnis found that smile creeping up again. His daughter had crept into his heart and settled down there, bottom in the air and thumb in her mouth. She was thawing out parts of him that he'd frozen, and Sandy could see the old wicked sense of humour lurking at the back of his eyes.

"So how was my lovely wife?" Sandy leaned back in the low chair he'd used the night before. He could just see the harbour and the sunset from the window of the bed and breakfast, and he watched the glorious swirl of orange and red as he spoke to Bob McInnis.

"Oh! I've fallen in love with her all over again, Sandy. I gave her a kiss, just like you would." He watched the flush suffusing Sandy's face as his partner transferred his gaze from outside to in. The red on Sandy's face could have been a reflection of the sunset, but Bob wasn't entirely convinced of that. He waited until the man was ready to burst with indignation, then said, "When you're in company that is."

Sandy deflated and laughed.

"She says, and I quote, 'tell Sandy he isn't to have more than one lot of chips a day!' So have you exceeded today's quota?"

"Mind your own business." Sandy picked up his mug of tea and drank deeply before continuing. "The little one settled OK?"

"Oh yeah, your Sarah was enjoying herself when I left, telling Caitlin about her bath-time. My daughter seemed to understand

104

every word." His lips twitched. "Now let's talk murder." He pulled the file out of a battered briefcase he'd brought into the bedroom and laid it on the bed, leaning over to start pulling papers out.

"This is Jonesys' preliminary. Doctor Sandman was fifty-six, had a heart condition which had been partially fixed by a pacemaker. That's how we got his identity so fast." Bob smiled grimly. "I wonder if our murderer knew about it?

"He was a little deaf, not badly apparently, and he definitely died in the dock. His lungs had sea water and various plankton and diatoms, whatever those might be, found in the water of these parts, and also in his bone marrow. Jonesy says that's not conclusive of drowning but a damn good indication." Bob looked up at Sandy and smiled wryly.

"He had been tied before he was pushed in, and that included the stone around his feet which must have prevented him from swimming upwards." McInnis took a sip of his own tea, wetting his throat and then setting the mug carefully back down; he raised his eyes again over the paper and looked at Sandy, who was listening intently. "Nasty, Sandy.

"The tox report shows he'd no alcohol in his blood, but the water can dilute all sorts of things, so the tox is a bit skewed. There was no bruising except that found from the swelling of the ropes in the water and some..." Bob paused, reading the notes to himself, "...some passive congestion and lividity of the face and head. Jonesy seems to be implying he wasn't roughed up, Sandy; my guess is he was taken totally by surprise." McInnis laid the flimsy sheets down and picked up the mug again.

"Are you thinking it was someone who knew him then, Bob?"

"It was someone he allowed to get close enough to tie him up without too much protest, Sandy."

105

"You'd protest if even I came at you with a rope and started to tie you up, lad. Do you think he was into bondage?"

Bob looked startled for a minute. "My God, Sandy, sometimes the way your mind works!" He shook his head. "I was just speculating. I certainly hadn't got as far as S and M tendencies. From what I've learnt so far he was a respectable married man."

"Even respectable doctors can be into sadomasochism, Bob."

"Well yeah." McInnis felt his cheeks growing a bit warm. "But I really don't think so, Sandy."

"So speculate, lad! Why else would a respectable doctor allow himself to be tied up?"

"Robbery gone wrong, but you'd need one person to threaten and another to do the tying up."

"I suppose drugs might be worth stealing."

"How about threatening his wife for a pin number for his card?"

"Still difficult, Bob. How are you gonna threaten and tie up without putting down the weapon or whatever, and if it involved threats to another, they could identify just as easily. What does the wife have to say?"

"Apparently she's gone into shock; she thought her husband was in Wales."

"Sarah would expect to hear from me every other day at least." Sandy cocked his head on one side. "Why didn't she go with him?"

"We can maybe question her tomorrow, Sandy; it might have been her, she's close enough to him for him to allow it. Wives get fed up of husbands for all sorts of reasons."

"And you talk about my mind!" Sandy sniffed indignantly. "Why else would you allow yourself to be tied up?"

Bob scratched his head, then shook it as if trying to shake free ideas. "Kids playing Red Indians with granddad, but I don't know if he's got any, and they'd hardly follow through and drop him in the sea. To pacify a nutter who was threatening to top himself. Dunno." Bob McInnis shook his head again, frowning. "I really don't know, Sandy."

Sandy shrugged. "I'll think about it and see if I can come up with any better suggestion that meets with your approval." He grinned. "What else did you learn while I was hard at work and you were kissing my wife?" His lips twitched.

Bob countered with a question of his own. "Did you check up on the smugglers' cave?"

"Yeah, nothing. The end is blocked off, looked like there'd been a cave-in at some point. It would take a stick or two of dynamite to get through that rock."

"So you've been playing down the beach while I've been hard at work then?"

"Bloody cheek!" Sandy grinned and finished his tea. "I take it that little gem of information came from Constable Pretty."

"Yeah he's a bright lad, with a few strange addictions. He's really into Marlon Brando." Bob looked puzzled.

"Nothing wrong with Brando."

"Before my time, granddad." Bob grinned. "How did they get on in the commercial basin? Find anything?"

"Not a lot, you'd better talk to Mark in the morning. He got a bit too technical for me. He was enjoying himself, got rigged out and went down in a suit. He told me it was a dry suit but it looked wet to me, so I'm all confused!" Sandy smiled across the room and Bob shook his head at him. Sandy liked to pretend he didn't understand, but Bob knew he was a shrewd officer and the ignorance was largely a pose.

"Any witnesses, Sandy?"

"Nope, not so far. We've asked around on a best guess of the murder happening a week last Friday. It was teeming down most of that night, pretty dark despite the moon. One –" Sandy ticked it off on a finger "– no one was wandering about in the rain to see anything. Two, the murderer had plenty of cover for the deed, and three –" he touched a third finger, "– there was a harvest supper at the other end of town. Anyone who was out was up that end; it was a community do."

"Fishermen?"

"High tide wasn't until half five on Saturday morning. The poor man could have been thrown in any time between half eleven the night before, though that's not likely, low water was at half eleven, and high at half five next morning. I reckon about two thirty, enough water in the basin to drown him and no one around getting their boats ready for the day."

"Damn, we're getting good at this tide thing, Sandy." Bob McInnis smiled across the room.

"Aren't we just." The smile Sandy exchanged disappeared from his face like a fade-out on the small screen, leaving it serious and a bit blank. "But it means we haven't any witnesses, Bob."

McInnis sighed. "How about the handstone? Anything on that?"

"Ah! Now there we are making a bit of progress. It actually came from the Roman museum up the hill. They hadn't missed it, but then they open by appointment this late in the season. The curator's a pleasant chap. Knowledgeable too." Sandy shoved a hand through his hair. "Let me get the notes, Bob."

"Why the museum, Sandy?"

"Ah! That was Mark; he suggested they might know where such things might be found, something about not buying querns at the Co-op." Sandy looked quizzically at Bob, who only smiled a bit lop-sidedly. "Made him think, did you, Bob?"

"Who me, Sandy?" McInnis watched as Sandy leaned over and pulled his daybook and a pair of wire-rimmed glasses out of the rumpled jacket he'd abandoned, like an old skin, on the end of the bed. Sandy carefully fixed the glasses around his ears, flicked through and began to read to himself, his lips moving silently as he refreshed his memory.

"OK, it was the top or handstone part, of a gritstone quern, of the early fifth century according to the senior SIC boys. Probably used by the Romans to grind maize but also had traces of silver in it. It might have belonged to a Christian, there's a cross cut into the side and an inscription to some Roman god." Sandy looked up, and over, his glasses at Bob McInnis. "Apparently they tried to cover all the bases when it came to ergot and fungal rust."

"Stop showing off, Sandy; you've got no more idea what ergot and fungal rust are than I have."

Sandy grinned. "Aw! Let a man have a bit of fun." He went back to his notes. "Ergot's got another name, St Antony's fire." He watched the light switch on, in Bob's eyes. "Yes, I thought that might ring a few bells, Bob. Remember that case of poisoning young teenagers when you first partnered me? We thought it was LSD or mercury at first, hallucinations and nausea antemortem."

Bob nodded. "I remember. Half a private school taking sick isn't something you forget too easily, Sandy. A couple of those kids lost limbs when the gangrene set in, and all because the rye bread was infected."

"Hm! yes, poor wee things, it was a nasty case." Sandy shook his head, "Anyway to get back to our quern. As far as the curator could tie it down, it must have gone missing about a month ago. I've borrowed the visitors' book." He stretched an arm and pulled a nicely bound book from under his coat. "I don't suppose our murderer would be stupid enough to sign his name, but you can never tell."

Bob eyed the thick book and, taking it off Sandy, turned to the start of September. He found at least fifty names covering the pages, all praising the displays. "We'll set the local lads to tracking these down, Sandy. As you say, nobody could be that stupid surely, but it's something we need to check."

Sandy hesitated a moment.

"What, Sandy? Spit it out."

"I was just wondering how you recognised a quern so quickly, Bob. Mark said you knew what it was straight away."

The glow dimmed in Bob's eyes. "You remember Beth and I went for our honeymoon to Norfolk?" Sandy nodded, wishing he'd kept his mouth shut. "She belonged to the Society for the Protection of Ancient Buildings, SPAB, they have a Mills Section, and we had a lovely time exploring one of the working ones; it's all to do with renewable energy. Querns were just added interest from that." He sighed, looking across the room at his partner, his eyes so miserable Sandy could have kicked himself.

Bob caught the same look of misery now settling behind the lenses of Sandy's glasses. "Don't fret man, there are bound to be reminders, one of them is probably being bathed at this very minute by your wife. We'll get through this. I don't regret my marriage, only its brevity."

The moment was interrupted by a knock on the door of Sandy's room. As Sandy opened the door Gareth stood, like a replaceable door, in the gap. "In you come, lad." Sandy waved a hospitable hand.

Gareth nodded and moved cautiously; the walls seemed to shrink inwards exponentially as he advanced. Bob shuffled along on to the spare bed and made room.

Sandy indicated a seat. "No need to be formal here." Bob, looking at the comfortable carpet slippers and the striped braces once more on display, reflected that it would be difficult to be formal in the sight of that attire.

Gareth sat and the bed dipped, despite being a good solid interior-sprung mattress. "You said to come and pass my report on to Inspector McInnis this evening, sir."

"That's fine, Gareth." Sandy soothed and smoothed, then sat back, removing his glasses and waiting patiently for the constable to relax as well.

Gareth looked a bit uncomfortable trying to maintain his balance on the bed, but he pulled out his daybook and prepared to deliver information.

"You asked me to go and see Mr Paul Saunders, sir."

Bob nodded.

"You'd gone to bed, sir, when I got back yesterday afternoon and I was trying to mend a few fences in the evening."

"Since you don't trust the English, that was a wise move, Gareth. Always get to know your enemy." Bob ignored the faint gasp of horror from his constable and smiled a bit slyly. "So what did that delightful gentleman have to say to you?"

Gareth, a bit red in the face, looked from Bob to Sandy and back, but since they appeared to be waiting for his report he took a deep breath and started. "I didn't quite know what you wanted me to ask him about, sir. But once you got him started there didn't seem any stopping him anyway."

He allowed a faint and unprofessional smile to cross his face. "He's ninety-one, sir." Gareth seemed a bit stunned by the man's age. "Lived in the town all his life, except for the War. He remembers the dockyards declining, and the Depression era. He can remember when there was a battery up where the old Roman fort is and a battalion of men, the blackout, and the renewal of the docks themselves in the sixties. He was really fascinating to listen to, sir."

Gareth settled back a bit on the bed, warming to his subject and beginning to relax. "Just imagine, he and his wife had the first television in the town. They got it for the Coronation and the entire street watched. He said those that couldn't get in the front parlour stood at the window, and others stood behind them on stools all looking in at the screen. He says they still stick together as a community, even now."

Bob shot a glance at the slight cough from Sandy but held his peace; the boy had stars in his eyes. Evidently Gareth had found a friend for life.

"He said when he retired he joined the wetlands conservation. He used to go and help count natterjack toads, up on the Solway." Gareth grinned at them both. "He's going to take me to see and hear them one night, sir." He grinned impartially at both inspectors; he looked like a small boy told he could go fishing with his dad, which, Bob thought, was about the level of the treat.

Gareth was continuing. "He told me all about the jubilation in the council when Maryport harbour was declared an SSSI for the small blue butterfly. Apparently the farmers, mostly, are quite happy to live in an area of outstanding natural beauty, though it upset some of the fishermen. You can't fish for peeler crab around here now, they're protected."

Gareth wound down after a while. He'd obviously had a great time but as he now said, "I don't see how it helps us solve the murder, sir."

"It gives us a flavour of the neighbourhood, Gareth. What I'm getting is a picture of a tightly knit community that has weathered a number of storms, both physical and economic, and is still here. The young ones haven't left entirely, the older ones keep an eye on them, the sense of pride in the town is still there." Bob nodded at him and looked across at Sandy. "I don't think we'll find our murderer here; I think this is just where the crime was committed."

"Yeah, I'd go along with that, Bob." Sandy smiled a bit grimly. "We still need to discover what the Harbour Master was up to, and those boys, but whatever it was I don't think it was murder. When I saw them today they still refused to talk."

"Did Mr Saunders have anything to offer about the murder?"

"No, sir, he said the same as you; he couldn't think of anyone living here that would do such a thing."

"Thanks, Gareth, you've done a great job."

"I really enjoyed it, sir, but as I said before, it doesn't help us much except in a negative way."

"Elimination is half the job when you're hunting a murderer. Didn't Sherlock Holmes say, 'eliminate and whatever is left must be the answer'?" Sandy smiled at his two bemused subordinates. "You two really should study Conan Doyle; I've told you before."

Bob and Gareth exchanged a look that, eliminating all else, Sandy described as pity for the old man, and Gareth got up to go.

"We'll be going to Greystone in the morning, Gareth; we have an identity for our corpse, a Doctor Sandman from that town. I'll brief the DS here and then leave the bulk of the grunt work to them. You'll be coming with us. Good work."

"Right, sir." Gareth hesitated just a bit too long to be ignored.

Bob raised an eyebrow and waited.

"The Welsh sir? I really didn't mean you, but who...?"

"Ryan Jones was kind enough to translate, though I'm not at all sure I agree that Welsh is God's tongue." Bob smiled, a slightly wicked glint in his eye. The giant before him looked more than a bit put out, and Bob thought Ryan Jones might be hearing some more of his mother tongue, if not any that God would say, in the very near future.

"Ah! Right, sir." Gareth got himself out of the room in good order and Sandy shut the door behind him, and let loose the chuckle he'd been suppressing. "I thought when you asked me to take our young friend there with me this afternoon, that you were looking for a couple of impartial witnesses to whatever we might find. But it seems I was wrong. What goes on, Bob?"

"I forgot you weren't there, Sandy. Gareth blamed himself for the Harbour Master doing a runner; he thought it was because he spoke in front of the town force and they'd blabbed. He damned all Englishmen, in fluent Welsh." Bob gave a slight chuckle.

"I don't think it was anyone babbling myself, I think it had something to do with that bloke I arrested yesterday. But that problem can wait; we have a murder to solve."

"Tomorrow, lad. I'm ready for my bed. Go away, and leave me in peace; I want to take my teeth out and unscrew my wooden leg." Sandy grinned at him from a set of teeth that the National Health would have been sued for making. It was a good smile that a crooked top incisor added to, but it patently wasn't patent.

"I can take a hint, Dad." Bob picked up his own jacket which, unlike Sandy's, had been hung neatly on the back of a chair, and left the room with it slung over his shoulder.

The next morning found Sandy deeply entrenched in discussions with Detective Sergeant Oakes and Senior Sergeant Jason Meeks. Bob McInnis gave them all a nod as he entered the incident room but headed towards the far end where Mark was listening to something a young officer was saying.

At least Bob assumed he was a police officer; the man was dressed in an old pair of jeans and a polo-neck jumper thick enough to have deprived several sheep of their winter coats. Bob came up quietly behind them and listened to the end of the tale, while he caught the scent of Mark's aftershave mingled with coffee, and an aroma like damp dog. His nostrils twitched.

"Well we've lifted over thirty of the little buggers and their picket fences but the divers keep putting more down. The rumour is that they've gone deeper than the fifty metre level, so we can't shift them."

One of the other divers grinned. "You've just got conspiracy theories on your brain, Carter."

"Who me? Nah, I reckon maybe Blair and Bush were secretly trying to relocate the terrorist detainees from Guantánamo to England, in exchange for terrorist gnomes in Wast Water."

"You are a strange man, Carter." A buxom young woman in a WPC uniform spoke. "And stop trying to scare me, my ex is in America and I want to keep it that way."

"You were married to a gnome?" Carter asked in return. "That explains a lot!" Then Carter caught sight of McInnis. He snapped to attention and Mark swung round going faintly pink.

"Sorry, sir, didn't see you. These are the divers from the Lake District, sir."

"That's alright, Mark. I was interested. I remember hearing that scientists had discovered the map of the genome about five years ago. Maybe you could use that to find the picket fences and bring the evil doers to justice."

He waited for the groan to disperse and the divers to relax. "What were you talking about?"

The first man spoke up. "Constable Carter Hickford, sir. There's been several deaths in Wast Water, sir. Divers staying down too long to look at a gnome garden that was placed underwater. We took it away for public safety, but there are rumours of another garden." He smiled a bit lop-sidedly.

"Unfortunately we can't dive below fifty feet, health and safety, so we can't check up or do anything else about it." He offered the information with a shrug of broad shoulders. "We can't play nanny all the time, but if it's going to endanger my men to rescue some silly sod, I object." He paused. "Respectfully, sir."

"Oh I don't blame you at all, Hickford. Are you in charge?"

"Nominally, sir, I'm taking turns with Sergeant Lyell from the Ayrshire division. He'll be along shortly."

"Well perhaps you can tell me what was discovered yesterday in both docks." Mark Forester started to move away but Bob stopped him. "I'm leaving you in charge here for another day, Mark, so hang around so that I can tell you what I want doing."

"Now, Constable." McInnis moved to one of the seats and sat down, pulling his notebook from his pocket and waiting patiently for Hickford to organise his thoughts.

"Marina dock, sir, that would be the Senhouse, we've recovered everything of note down there and DS Forester, here, has sent it off to the lab to be processed. There weren't any obvious weapons like guns under the silt. There was a decent boat that the other team pulled up; it had no palpable reason to be scuppered." He shrugged with an obviously habitual gesture.

"The markings on it identify it as belonging to the Harbour Master, sir." Mark Forester added the information and then waited for Hickford to continue.

"The other dock, the Elizabeth, not many boats there. Mark here," Hickford nodded at Mark standing patiently beside him, "said you wanted a general scout about and a look at some of the keels. The MARY LOO has a sling under her."

Bob raised an eyebrow. "Which indicates what, Constable?"

Hickford showed faint surprise but answered readily enough. "Means she is, or has been, used recently, to maybe bring something in without showing it on deck."

"You mean like drug smuggling?" Bob McInnis sounded faintly incredulous.

"No...o. It was too big a net for that; I'm not sure what, but maybe an illegal catch, sir."

"Nice work, Constable. Anything else?"

"Not really, sir. Most of it was just the usual crap you find in a dock. If anything it was cleaner than some I've dived in."

"Fine, carry on and report to Mark if you find anything else." It was polite dismissal. Hickford nodded but didn't shift from his relaxed stance. "I'd like permission to take a couple of the lads to look at some Roman pilings when we've finished, sir."

McInnis shifted his eyes to Mark, hoping the young man could enlighten him.

"I was telling Carter about the Roman harbour; it was built just along the coast, north of here and nearer the fort, before this modern one, sir. There are some oak pilings from it, they're petrified and you can see where some of the original Roman troops have carved their initials into them. They were always a special thing for new divers to have a look at."

Bob nodded. "Whatever, Mark. When you get through the work here, I see no reason why you can't dive in your off time. Just take care in those currents out there."

117

The two men turned away and Bob stuffed his notebook into his inside pocket and stood up; he watched as the group of divers trooped outside followed by Mark Forester. That young man still looked as though he ought to be on the cover of vogue rather than in forensic whites investigating crime, but, Bob thought, that would be a waste of a good brain.

He walked over to where it seemed Sandy had nearly finished his round up of information. Agreement seemed to have been reached as to the division of labour.

"Right, Inspector Bell, I'll get the lads busy on the door to door again, in view of our new info', and I'll set a couple of WPCs to phoning the people in that visitors' book and asking them tactfully if they've murdered anyone recently." Sergeant Meeks smiled like a bulldog sighting a juicy bone. He stood up and, as he walked away, DS Oakes slid sideways to allow Bob McInnis to sit down.

"What can you tell us about Greystone, Sergeant?"

"Little market town about three, four, miles from here as the crow flies, bit further by road, population is shrinking, the youngsters are moving into the cities. Typical rural pattern, no work and house prices the next generation can't afford, so they go looking for work and don't come back." Sandy listened to the croaky voice; it was obvious Oakes's cold wasn't much better.

"Much crime there?"

"We have a bobby drive through during the day and an unmanned police station. The teenagers get a bit noisy, there's some underage drinking and a bit of vandalism but nothing desperate." Oakes sighed. "But then that's what I'd have said about Maryport."

"I think you still can say that." Bob looked across the small table. "It's a very pleasant place and the people we've met have been both helpful and polite."

Oakes scowled. "Helpful, when half my force is colluding to pervert the course of justice?" It was obvious to his two listeners that Oakes was seriously upset.

"I hardly think one green constable trying to protect his younger brothers counts as colluding, Oakes." Sandy looked him firmly in the eye. "Give the boy a chance, he'll probably tell you everything when he's had a bit longer to think about it."

"I always said the policy of making them train away from home was the best one."

Sandy nodded; he turned the conversation back to the town of Greystone. "What's the population size?"

"Couple of thousand. Mainly older people with a sprinkling of middle aged. They closed the local school and the post office, there's a bus three times a day into Maryport and what kids there are, are bused in to school here. Those that aren't brought by their parents." Oakes sniffed and pulled out his handkerchief. Bob noticed it was a blue checked one today.

He spoke to the snuffling man in front of him. "How did they rate the services of the Doctor?"

"Dr Sandman was semi-retired: he'd been ill, heart I think." Oakes paused to put the hanky away and sat back in his seat to allow a PC to provide him with a mug of coffee. She looked at the other two detectives, who shook their heads.

"Anyway, he cut his list right down, said he could cope with the people of the village, but didn't want a huge practice anymore." Oakes sipped coffee. "Everyone benefited. He had a job and they had a doctor on tap without having to come into town to see one, and with no worry about transport. It doesn't often work like that."

"No, I don't suppose it does." Bob pushed his hand through his hair. "I suppose they'll have to travel now, which is a pity all round and something the murderer probably didn't even think about."

"Is there somewhere we can stay there while we investigate, or had we better hang onto our rooms here?"

"Small pub, but it only has a couple of rooms if I remember rightly. We had a missing teen to investigate a few weeks ago. I stayed out there a couple of nights. It's small though; probably better if you stay here."

Bob nodded, and Sandy said, "I'll see to that, Bob."

"Anything else you want to know, Inspector?"

Sandy frowned down at the table. "Not for now." He looked up. "We'll be in touch, Sergeant, and Sergeant, stop beating yourself up; you've got a good steady bunch of men."

Oakes finished his coffee and set the mug down. "Yes, sir." But he didn't sound convinced and they watched him go over and start issuing orders in that hoarse voice to a couple of PCs.

"He isn't going to forgive himself easily, Bob, and some of the blame does lie with him. He was cruising to retirement and not keeping a sharp eye on the troops. But they aren't that bad a bunch for all that."

McInnis nodded his head, he agreed, but the murder was the thing uppermost in his mind. "Let's get a move on, Sandy. I'll take my car and meet you at Sandman's surgery."

6

The small rural town, village would perhaps be more accurate, Bob thought, of Greystone, nestled in a valley just off the main Carlisle to Maryport road. It had an ageless quality about it, the houses of grey slate, so that Bob found himself looking at them afresh. This area he knew from his A-level Geography studies at school, should be gritstone moorland, not this grey mix of sandstone and slates.

The town seemed to consist of a main street with a few side streets going off. A pub at one end and a chapel at the other, with a huge old Anglican church dominating the middle of the town centre, like a misplaced skyscraper. The church spire was out of all proportion to the small cottages nestling under its shade, like cygnets under a swan.

He parked on the main street, sighing as he did so. He felt tired today and wished, briefly, that he'd chosen a different career where people weren't killed and he didn't have to deal with the aftermath. He looked around, spotting the sign for the surgery just up the street and, locking his car door, began to walk along the pavement. The chilly wind nipped at his face but he found it was waking him up a bit too; he sniffed the fresh smells lingering on the rain-drenched air.

There was a baker's somewhere; he could smell the sweetness of cooking sponge cake. The soft tinkle of a bell drew his head momentarily towards a crowded butcher's shop. Then his eyes sought and found the doctor's surgery standing in isolation on the other side of the road

Jenny Lowther was sitting in her office with the door open when he arrived. He saw her stand up, even as he came through the open glass door of the reception area. The small nondescript dog was at her heels. "Inspector, after they rang through from Maryport I cancelled all the appointments this morning, so that you can do what you have to, here in the surgery."

She flicked back the long, silky plait and stood watching him. Her eyes, a shade of moss green, observed his face carefully. "I hope I did right."

"Yes, thank you, Doctor." McInnis, after the briefest of looks at the woman in the pretty blue wool dress, was taking in the fittings and fixtures of the surgery.

"It's a very small surgery, but then he only had a very small list. He didn't do anything very major here."

"I'm going to have to look at some of the patients' notes, Doctor; is that going to be a problem?"

"Not from me. What else will you need to see?"

"I shall have to interview his wife." McInnis was unaware of the slight grimace that drifted across his face for a moment. "His receptionist, he did have one, and a practice nurse?"

"Oh, Yes. Hayley Noble and Alison Lythe are both available. I'll get them." Jenny turned away, but he stopped her with a quiet word.

"I'll get to them; first I want to look around the surgery."

His arrival had been observed from behind several net curtains in the village. Speculation was rife. Of course both the receptionist and nurse had talked. Those that had had appointments cancelled had also talked.

At number ten High Street old Mrs Hall had been due to have her leg dressed, and she was quite indignant that it had been put off until the next day. She had hobbled down the street to the butcher to buy a pound of sausage and enjoy a bit of complaining in company.

Mr Bailey at number thirty-seven was equally annoyed; he wanted his prescription renewing. The fact that he'd left it until the last tablet before ringing the surgery was, he considered, nobody else's business. However Lyn Gregory from one of the side-roads wouldn't hear a word against the doctor, even though her twins were both down with croup again.

"It's not the poor Doctor's fault he got murdered."

"I never said it was, but why that young woman can't see us and sort my leg out, is what I don't understand."

"Well all she had to do was sign the prescription and I could get on with things."

"Doctor Sandman always insisted on seeing you for renewals, Jack Bailey, and well you know it."

"He came out for the twins twice during the night, this summer; I don't know why anyone would want to kill him." Lyn gently rocked the twins in their double buggy. "I don't know what I'm going to do now, if I have to take them into Maryport every time."

The butcher, a thin bespectacled man who had been trying to get payment for the sausages for five minutes, managed to get a word in at this point. "There's going to be a lot struggling now that he's gone. I shouldn't think we'll get another doctor here." Before anyone else could speak he quickly pushed the package over the counter. "That'll be one pound seventy please."

Other families were speculating about the fate of the doctor and the town. Trevor Paton talked to his mother while he helped her to get dressed. Not that he expected an answer; his mother had Alzheimer's. He still talked to her though, telling her snippets of gossip. And being his mother's carer meant he hardly ever saw anyone else to talk to.

"It will mean we have to go into Maryport, Mother, in the wheelchair. You like travelling in the van and going up in the chair lift on the back don't you?" He spooned cereal into her mouth. "We'll go for your last checkup on Friday, make sure that nasty cough has gone, and see what they have to say."

His mother continued humming tunelessly as he tried to get her breakfast into her.

The Johnsons had lived in the town all their married lives and last year they'd celebrated their diamond anniversary. They discussed the events of the weekend, while Angus helped Violet into the specially adapted shower and handed her the facecloth. "There you are, dear, it's got soap on."

"I wonder how we'll manage for appointments now, Angus. Can you give me the loofah thing, darling? I want to reach my toes." Angus obediently handed her the long pole with the sponge adaptation that the nurse had come up with so that Violet could reach her feet without bending over.

"We'll manage, Vi. I'm sure one of the girls will come over and give us a lift into town."

"Yes but I hate to ask them, Angus; they've got enough to do." She sponged vigorously for a minute. "He was such a lovely chap, Angus." Angus watched a bit helplessly as the tears came into his wife's eyes.

Philip Twentyman wasn't being quite so complimentary. He lived alone; his wife had died of cancer several months before. Now he leaned over the fence, smoking a noisome pipe, and between puffs expressed himself to his neighbour, a buxom young woman who was pegging out washing, and who kept an unobtrusive eye on him. "Well I think it's just deserts, Anne; if he'd seen to my Mavis earlier she might be alive now."

The young woman shook her head but didn't actually contradict him. It was a favourite theme with Philip Twentyman, when he wasn't complaining about the government and the youths of the town. She knew that his wife had left it too late to go to see the doctor. Mavis had been having bowel problems for months, but 'hadn't liked to bother anyone'. She had been as uncomplaining as he was vociferous.

Unfortunately the police were going to be bothering them and several other worthy citizens before the day was through.

Bob McInnis stood at the small surgery door now, looking around at the desk and chairs where the late Doctor Sandman had dispensed advice and medicine in equal parts. He could smell the slight aroma of antiseptic hand wash and something Bob always associated with new Elastoplast.

He looked at the corner where a small plastic table and chair with a box of books and toys sat rather forlornly. His roaming glance next took in the big round glass jar half filled with sand and topped up with small cacti. It was set on a high shelf out of reach of small children. There was a black couch hidden discreetly behind a set of partially drawn pale green curtains. His eye came back to the desk.

Jenny Lowther spoke behind him. "I haven't altered things in here; it's a nice set up."

He nodded. He didn't think this was the primary crime scene, but if it was, it was too late. Along with antiseptic and Elastoplast he could smell polish, and the desk had the patina acquired from years of elbow grease on good wood. "You've got a cleaner for the surgery?"

"Yes, she comes in every day at six. Patsy Collins."

"We'll need a word."

"I'll give you the address, Inspector."

He nodded again, filing the name away for future reference.

"Why are you here, Doctor Lowther? I would have thought you'd want a more modern practice." McInnis walked forward into the room and sat down at the desk. He began to pull open drawers, noting the scripts and forms tidily arranged in them. He looked up when she didn't answer immediately.

"Several reasons, Inspector."

McInnis cocked an eye waiting, his hands stilled on the desk.

"I'd almost reached burnout in the practice I was in. We have a list of nearly fifteen thousand between the three of us, but it swells to impossible proportions in the visitor season." She leaned against the door jamb, watching him.

"I've just recovered from a bad bout of pneumonia, and while I'm happy to start work again, my partners felt it might be better if I had a gentle run in."

McInnis looked her over, seeing the tiredness on her face and moving aside. "I've taken your seat, Doctor. Do sit down."

"No, it's fine. I'm not ill now, Inspector."

"Nevertheless." McInnis gestured to the chair. Jenny came in and sat down, and McInnis moved over, shutting the door and coming back to take the patient's chair opposite her. The little dog flopped at her feet as if he'd been chasing rabbits all day and McInnis, seeing it, smiled. "What's he called?"

"Jack." The dog raised an ear and opened one eye when he heard his name, but didn't move any other muscles. "You wouldn't believe it to look at him, but he's a rescue dog for the Lake District team. He comes alive on the fells." Jenny poked the animal gently with a blue court shoe and was rewarded with a deep sigh.

Bob smiled down at the animal and then looked at its mistress, "You said several reasons, Doctor."

126

"I'm wondering if I'm in the right trade, Inspector. I know I said I was happy to start work, but seeing people suffering day after day, not just the volume of them, but the emotional impact too. Sometimes I'm not sure how much longer I can cope with it." She smiled at the serious face watching her. "And then something good happens and I know why I do it."

McInnis found he could get right alongside her feelings; he'd been feeling the same only that morning. "Yeah, it can be tough, but then it can be rewarding too."

He paused a minute, getting his questions lined up. "Tell me what you know about the doctor?"

"I only met him twice, once at the interview and once when I came to take over. I don't know anything about him really."

"OK, what have you learnt about him since you took over? You must have learnt something. You're working with his patients and his people."

Jenny Lowther nibbled a lip, gently tugging at a small piece of dry skin while she thought. "Most of his patients love him. He was conscientious, caring, even loving. He was firm. He kept excellent notes, not just about what was wrong but what he'd suggested and prescribed and why." She looked at McInnis. "He did callouts, which he shouldn't have done. His heart condition was worse than he let on to his wife. He was a bit old school. He felt that medicine was a vocation, not just a job."

McInnis watched as the woman in front of him frowned in concentration.

"He told me he couldn't and wouldn't play God, so if any of the girls wanted abortions they would have to go to Maryport. I wasn't to authorise it."

McInnis raised an eyebrow. "Did anyone, er, want an abortion?"

"No. No one has come asking, I've seen a couple of unmarried teens for routine pregnancy checks. They seem happy to be having babies." She shook her head, her plait swishing gently against the soft blue material.

"His people?"

"You mean Hayley and Alison?"

He nodded.

"Hayley has been his practice nurse for fourteen years; she lives in the town and was brought up here. She's competent, reliable, and keeps up with the latest nursing trends. It suits her to work here; she's married to a local man who works in Maryport." She shook her head. "She gets a good salary and when the surgery closes she'll lose a good job."

"How about Alison?"

"Bit flighty. I was surprised she was still in the town; I would have expected her to be looking for work in Carlisle. She does her job, acts as secretary too, I wouldn't say well. She doesn't talk about the patients outside the surgery, but she does pass comments to Hayley sometimes which I didn't think were entirely appropriate."

"Any reason either of them would have cause to dislike the good Doctor, enough to kill him?"

"What you mean like sexual harassment or getting fired?" Jenny looked startled at the thought.

"Well, anything like that, yes."

"You have got to be kidding me!" She sat upright in the chair, her eyes narrowing as she took in the man in front of her afresh. "He was a nice gent, he loved his wife, and he paid his employees well. They're all going to be out of a job and out of pocket now. I've never heard a whiff of gossip about him and the girls. How can you ask such things?"

McInnis shrugged. "I have to ask, it's my job, I don't always like it. But sometimes something good happens and I know why I do it." He batted her words back at her with a faint smile.

A soft knock at the door heralded the entry of Sandy Bell. He poked his head round like a snail checking the outside world, and then allowed the rest of his body to enter the doorway. "Hi, Bob, Doctor Lowther. Have you made much of a start, Bob?"

McInnis shook his head. "Just general enquiries so far."

Jenny Lowther stood up. "Would you like a cuppa while you exchange information?"

Sandy offered a smile and a nod and came the rest of the way into the room and stood at the side of the desk, making the room itself feel like a broom cupboard. Jenny smiled impartially at both and left, and Sandy dropped into her seat.

"First impressions, Bob?"

"Nice little set up, respectable life, nothing obvious to suggest he'd be a murder candidate. I haven't talked to anyone but Doctor Lowther yet."

Sandy waited. "And?"

Bob scratched an ear. "Well I don't think she topped him to take over the surgery."

"No, I didn't." Jenny watched the faint colour wash Bob's cheeks. "But thanks for dismissing it." She wrinkled a pretty nose and came through the door with a couple of mugs, milk and sugar, on a tray. Her eyes, Bob thought, were mocking him a bit but it wasn't malicious.

Jack the dog, who had raised a lazy head at his mistress's voice, now sniffed at Sandy's shoes, then dropped back into an apparent coma.

Sandy nudged the inert body with his toe to get a quiet huff, but no other sign of life. "Energetic wee beastie, ain't he?" He smiled across the room. "We're sorry to put you out, lass."

"That's alright, Inspector; Dr Sandman is even more put out. My American colleagues would say he was 'metabolically challenged'!" She raised finely shaped eyebrows and smiled a bit sadly at the detectives. "I'll get out of your way. The Doctor lived next door, and I've been lodging with his wife while he was away. You can come and find me if I can be any further help. Jack, walk!"

The dog sprang to life at the command and shot out of the room, his whole body quivering in anticipation. He seemed suddenly to be made of coiled springs as he waited expectantly at the front door.

The two detectives watched as he followed tightly at Jenny Lowther's heels as she quietly left the surgery. She flipped the closed sign on the door before she shut it behind her.

"So bring me up to speed, lad, and then we'll see how we're going to divide the labour here. I haven't told them to bring the incident van yet; I thought we'd go a bit softly to start, but seeing the size of this place that seems a bit redundant." He smiled a bit wryly. "Before I get to the first interview, they'll know how many sugars I put in my tea." He suited the action to the word.

Bob acknowledged the truth of the statement as he watched a small child pressing her nose to the glass door and being pulled away by a red-faced damsel. "Yeah you're right, Sandy. Better whistle it up and then we'll have a place to rest your weary body in private. They've all but finished with it over there; the rest of the work can be done from the station."

He paused, sipped some of the tea, and then began to tell Sandy what he'd learnt so far about the doctor's set-up. "We'll have to interview of course, but I don't think the receptionist or nurse are

130

likely suspects. Maybe cast a closer eye over the receptionist. I'll take her if you want to handle the wife?"

Sandy shook his head. "I think I'd like us to work in tandem actually, Bob. Cover our butts till the van gets here. I've got a feeling in my water."

Bob looked at him curiously but shrugged. "Just as you like, Sandy." He'd come across Sandy's 'feelings' before, and learnt to trust them.

"The nurse first I'm thinking."

Bob stood up and went out into the bright, if somewhat chilly street. The doctor's house was obvious as soon as he turned his head, a bungalow standing to the side of the surgery building, with a gravel path and Jenny Lowther's car parked in front of it.

Bob strode across the intervening ground, the gravel crunching under his feet like a spilt packet of cornflakes, and rang the bell. Apparently he was expected. A thin, almost anorexic, young woman, with a nasal twang and enough metal on her fingers to form an effective knuckleduster, answered the door. "Yes?"

"I'm Inspector McInnis. I'd like a word with Hayley Noble, over at the surgery."

The young woman looked him over with a great deal of curiosity while she shouted for Hayley. "I'm Alison. You'd be from Carlisle then?" She pulled her skinny rib jumper down over a flat chest, and licked her well coated lips.

"That's correct." Bob stood his ground, his nostrils flaring slightly at the smell of burnt toast wafting down the corridor to him from the nether regions of the house, admixed with some heady aroma from the damsel in front of him.

A plump young woman of about his own age appeared. "Hi, I'm Hayley, how can I help?"

"Police, Ms Noble, we need to have a word with you." He swung his head. "And you Miss. I'll ask Ms Noble here to fetch you when we're ready."

Hayley nodded, "I'll just get my bag. Won't be a mo'." She swung away and he was treated to the somewhat criminal vision of too much bottom in too little jean. Hayley disappeared into a side room and emerged again pulling on a thick, oatmeal coloured, cardigan, which did nothing to diminish her size. "Right you are."

Bob stood back and she headed for the surgery, allowing him to follow. He shook his head; she really shouldn't wear jeans, he thought. He caught up with her in time to open the door for her and indicate the surgery. He closed it and then followed her through. Sandy had been busy. He'd brought another chair from the reception and arranged the chairs so that one of them could write at the desk.

"This is Inspector Bell, and I'm Inspector McInnis. Would you like to sit down?"

Hayley plopped down on the seat near the desk and looked them both over. "This is a terrible thing to have happened."

"Yes, it is Ms Noble, but we're hoping you might shed some light on the Doctor's murder."

Hayley Noble looked at Sandy in a considering way. "Well frankly I don't think I can. When Jenny told us about it last night, I thought and thought, but he was a lovely man was Doctor Sandman. I wouldn't have said he had any enemies at all, only he must have mustn't he?" She paused for breath. "You don't think it could be a case of mistaken identity do you?"

Sandy shook his head. "No we don't think that."

"Well I think it's a great shame and I don't know how the village will cope. It really isn't in anyone's interests here to get rid of the poor man. He was always available; they're going to have to go to Maryport now you know, and what with the lack of buses and everything, well it just doesn't make any sense." She paused for breath and Sandy quickly got a question in.

"Can you tell us which of his patients the Doctor saw regularly, and help us to eliminate those he hasn't seen for the last six months, Ms Noble?"

"Course I can, and why don't you call me Hayley? I'll go and get the files." She began to stand up but Sandy shook his head.

"No, just a minute, Hayley. Let's finish asking you questions first and then you might show Inspector McInnis where they're kept and give us the list."

She subsided and Sandy, seeing her mouth begin to open, quickly put another question. "When did Doctor Sandman make his arrangements to go on holiday?"

"Let me think –" without pausing Hayley carried on speaking "– it would be August, I think, we had the rep through from Numark and then the man about instruments, the Doctor used to like him visiting." She smiled at them both impartially. "Then it would be the rep from the dressing firm. Yes it was the middle of August, because Sid always takes his holiday in August and he was telling the Doctor about how he'd spent the week at Llandudno, and Doctor was so distracted he bought three boxes of silver nitrate dressings instead of two from him, and they're so expensive and we only use them for old Mrs Hall." She stopped, looking from face to face. "August."

Sandy took in the slightly stunned expression on Bob's face and covered his grin with a hand and a fake cough until he'd got his mouth under control.

"Now, having decided in August, who would know about it in the town?"

"Well everyone, I mean it wasn't a secret; he told us, and he'd tell his patients so that they could visit him before he went. Some of them are a bit set in their ways; don't like to deal with a locum. He liked to make sure his patients were happy, didn't like to leave their care to other people if he could help it. He told us, Alison and me, as soon as he'd got the bookings through, because he said he'd got a locum, but he didn't want her run off her feet. Poor thing has been really poorly you know, got trapped in a mine or something and got pneumonia." She wound down again.

Sandy felt as though he was trapped in a Gilbert and Sullivan operetta. The words hammering out at him.

"Thank you that's, er, very clear." Bob inclined his head, standing up. "We may need to ask you a few more questions later. If you could show me where the files are kept and indicate the ones most recently used, and then perhaps you'd be good enough to ask Miss Lythe to come over." He went to the door and opened it, waiting silently for her to gather her handbag and precede him from the room.

He came back five minutes later. "I don't know what she's like as a nurse, Sandy, but she'd drive me crazy as a person. I sincerely hope we haven't got to re-interview. She'd never get around to murdering anyone; she's too busy talking them to death."

"Aye, lad. She might be a great nurse but she can talk the hind legs off a donkey."

Bob grinned across the short space. "I hope the next one's a bit quieter."

"Och, lad, you get a lot from yon noisy ones; they tell you all sorts of things you hadn't thought to ask." He stopped as a knock at the door, followed by the strong aroma of heady perfume, heralded the arrival of Alison Lythe.

"Oh! There are two of you."

Bob came forward and offered her a seat while Sandy's lips twitched. "I'm Inspector Bell, Miss."

Alison Lythe lowered her bony frame into the chair recently occupied by Hayley Noble; there seemed a lot more chair suddenly. Not only was she about half the size, she apparently hadn't anything much to say either. She waited for their questions.

"Now, Miss, perhaps you could tell us of anyone you think might want Doctor Sandman dead."

"I can't think of anyone."

Sandy exchanged a glance with Bob McInnis. "Come, come, surely the man wasn't a plaster saint, Miss, he must have offended people occasionally?"

"If he did I'm not aware of it."

"Didn't he ever pass remarks about people when he was handing you their notes to write up?"

"The Doctor did most of his own notes; I only wrote referral letters, things like that."

"How about arguments? You might have heard the odd harsh word when you where sitting out there in reception."

For the first time she looked uncomfortable. "'Tisn't for me to say."

"Oh but it is, Miss Lythe. The Doctor has been brutally murdered, and we need to find his killer. It's important that you answer us truthfully. This isn't gossip."

Alison Lythe looked at Bob; it was the sort of look a vulture gives when it sights a fresh meal. "I wouldn't like you to think I gossip, Inspector." She turned away from Sandy, her action cutting him out of the intimate conversation she seemed to want. McInnis stiffened.

"This is a murder investigation, Miss; we don't deal in gossip, only facts. If you have overheard something then tell us about it."

She lowered her voice and moved forward in her chair, narrowing the distance between them. "You might like to ask some questions of Mr Twentyman, and Mr Bailey; they had words with him a time or two."

McInnis sat well back in his chair, looking past her at Sandy. "Inspector Bell will look out their notes in a minute."

Sandy, picking up the expertly tossed ball, addressed her sternly, forcing her to face him. "What reasons have you for naming them, Miss? Would you give us some specific reasons?"

Alison Lythe pouted, turning around again. "Oh I couldn't do that. It's just they shouted a bit when they visited and Mrs Twentyman died a few months ago in mysterious circumstances."

"Is there anyone else that argued with the Doctor, Miss Lythe?"

"Well I wondered why his wife married him. I mean he wasn't a young man any more, and you'd think if he wanted someone young he'd want someone who understood his job. Wouldn't you?"

"Perhaps, Miss." Sandy looked her over. "I think that will be all for now. We'll contact you if we need to ask you anything else." Sandy stood up and opened the door pointedly for her.

She looked from one man to the other and got reluctantly to her feet. "Oh I do hope I can help you, Inspector McInnis."

She left the room, ignoring Sandy who left the communicating door open while he watched her walk away. He looked across at his partner and gave an exaggerated shiver. "Call me strange if you like but I wouldn't like to have to talk to her alone if I wasn't feeling well, Bob."

"No, me neither! We'll have to investigate these men, Sandy, and the wife. She didn't actually answer the question did she? Just went and implicated the wife. I've yet to see Mrs Sandman but I should think Alison Lythe would be jealous of any red-blooded

136

woman with flesh on her bones and wouldn't have minded doing the wife a mischief. Do you think she had designs on the good Doctor?"

"Undoubtedly! I think she's got designs on anything with a pair of trousers and a good bank balance, so watch yourself, Bob. I was right to make sure we worked in tandem, only I thought it was going to be the wife we had to be wary of." He raised a comical eyebrow and pretended to mop his brow.

The two men went through the reception area around the back of the small curved desk and towards a dark door with a Yale lock. This door was unlocked however. Sandy pushed it open to reveal a pokey cupboard, the walls lined with files. Bob, following, gathered up a book from the desk and he and Sandy stood at the door looking in.

"The nurse showed me the list of patients, Sandy. If we just backtrack through the book we can figure out who's been to visit frequently, and if there has been any problems with their treatment."

Sandy eyed the files, stacked like soldiers on parade. "I think that's going to be a job for the local lads. They can let us know about frequent users, expensive treatments, maybe delayed treatments, and any queries about cause of death, Bob. I think for the moment we'll go and talk to the wife."

They continued to gaze at the serried ranks of paper. "Who else might have cause, Bob?"

"Patients, relatives of patients, either one of those dissatisfied with the treatment or professional conduct, other professionals." Bob shook his head ticking off options on his fingers. "Jealous lovers and/or wife." He smiled a bit wryly. "We need to check his financials, and these reps the nurse mentioned." He frowned. "I'll think of some more in a bit I'm sure, Sandy." He shrugged. "Do you want me to get the van through?"

"Yeah, might as well. I asked Gareth to do a bit more checking up on Pheby. If we can catch Gareth, he could come through with the van. I pinched the car." Sandy grinned.

They closed the door, hearing it snick shut behind them. "I hope they've got spare keys." Bob replaced the appointment book on the desk.

They left the surgery, shutting that door as well. "The house is over here, Sandy." Bob spoke on the phone as they walked over, asking that the incident van be sent over.

The door bell was answered promptly when Bob rang it. The vision in front of him made him blink a bit. The woman was stunning. Mid twenties he thought, her long red-gold curls held off her face by a couple of barrettes. She had blue eyes, currently red-rimmed and with dark shadows under them. And she was in an advanced state of pregnancy.

Her voice was husky when she spoke. "Are you the police?"

Bob nodded and Sandy spoke, pulling out a warrant card, "I'm Detective Inspector Bell, and this is my partner, DI McInnis."

"Come in please. I'm Maureen Sandman." She backed away from the door, and swivelled herself around in the narrow passage. "Do you mind coming into the kitchen. It's a bit warmer in there."

The men exchanged a glance, and followed her down the passageway to a door at the end.

She went through and Bob heard the less than dulcet tones of Miss Lythe. "Who is it, Maureen? I said I'd go."

The detectives, when they entered, noted she didn't look as if she was going to go anywhere.

"I'm sorry to turf you ladies out into the cold, but could we have a word with Mrs Sandman alone?"

Jenny Lowther swung round with a kettle in her hand. "I'll just finish making Maureen a cuppa and then I'll be out from under your feet." She looked pointedly at Alison and Hayley who got up and came towards the men.

Both stood aside to allow them to pass. "Would you mind terribly if Jenny stayed, Inspector? I'm afraid I keep passing out."

Jenny smiled at the slight paling of the male cheeks. "I'll just be down the corridor, love; they can come and get me, if they have to. I don't want to admit you, Maureen, so sit down and stay down will you." Jenny spoke firmly, and Maureen produced a twitch of the lips which couldn't really be called a smile, but defied any other description.

Maureen Sandman sat down near an Aga cooker in the corner of the room. It was a cosy room, modern enough to be labour saving without being so high tech as to feel like an operating theatre. Bob went to a small kitchen table and sat down, and Sandy, after waiting for Jenny Lowther to give Maureen a mug of tea, held the door and closed it after her before sitting down himself.

Both men eyed the young woman with some surprise. "I'm sorry for your loss, Mrs Sandman."

"Yeah, me too." It was said quietly but the depth of misery could have filled the Grand Canyon. "You'd better call me Maureen."

"How long have you been married, Maureen?" Bell smiled gently at her.

"Four years, Inspector Bell. I met my husband in a cave." The fleeting smile just touched her lips and then was gone again. "We knew it would raise eyebrows, but I loved Neil very much and he loved me."

"Yet you didn't go away on holiday with him?"

"Like this!" She indicated her stomach which Bob could see moving slightly under her smock as the baby stirred. "Neil wanted to explore the Great Orme; I wouldn't have got in the entranceway. He needed the break, and if he'd stayed here people would have called or rung. 'Just for a little advice, Doctor.'" She smiled sadly again. "He tried to take a holiday at home earlier in the year. It was impossible."

"Didn't you worry when you didn't hear from him?" Sandy enquired.

"Oh! But I did."

Bob looked puzzled. "When did you last hear?"

"Friday. I must admit I was getting a little anxious yesterday. Then Jenny came and told me he had died."

The two men exchanged puzzled looks. Bob frowned. "Just how did he communicate, Maureen?'

"Text messages." She stirred in her chair. "What's wrong, Inspector?"

"Might we see your mobile, Maureen?"

She gave Bob a puzzled look. "Of course, I was expecting you to want it. It's on the table there."

Bob looked at the small pile of clutter. Amidst the morning mail, a pot of Michaelmas daisies in a red jug, a bowl of fruit, and a piece of oddly shaped stone, a small silver mobile lay. It had a blue flashing light at the side, signifying an incoming message.

"You seemed to have someone wanting you now actually." Bob rose and, gathering the phone, took it across the room to her.

She looked at it a bit sadly. "It's probably someone else with condolences, Inspector. They've been ringing all morning, ever since the news broke on the radio and gave Neil's name. I finally put it on mute."

She pressed the button and then gave a small gasp, the skin of her cheeks blanching white. McInnis took it from the hand which had gone limp and said, "Sandy?"

Sandy however was already out the door and calling for Doctor Lowther.

Jenny Lowther came rapidly out of a side-room and down the corridor towards him. She didn't spare a glance at the two men but went directly towards the new widow.

"OK, love," Maureen was already coming around. Jenny held her wrist, monitoring her pulse.

Sandy, looking for him quite alarmed, said, "I think you'd better stay, Doctor."

Bob, satisfied that nothing drastic was going to happen, looked at the mobile.

"*Having a good time, my darling, Poppy, Wales is beautiful if wet today. I'll send you a postcard, miss you, love Neil.*"

"Sandy." He took the couple of steps across the room to show his partner the text message.

"Can we carry on this interview, Doctor? Or would it be better if we left it for a while."

"I'm OK, Inspector. I'm sorry about this; my blood pressure is a bit high. Neil was keeping an eye on me." She pulled herself upright in the chair. "Are you sure there hasn't been some terrible mistake?"

Sandy shook his head, looking like a basset hound denied a bone. "No I'm sorry, we're very sure. It was your husband."

"Jenny said it was better if I didn't see him. I thought maybe he'd been washed along the coast and got a bit –" she bit a lip and her voice hitched "– a bit bashed in the sea."

"No, sweetheart." Jenny glanced at the men still standing looking anxiously at Maureen Sandman. "I didn't like to tell you yesterday. Neil's been dead for maybe a week now." She watched a little anxiously but Maureen didn't faint again. Maybe her body could only take so many blows at a time.

"A week? But, but, he's been texting me, every day."

Bob stepped back and began to go through the calls and texts received over the past week. The messages were brief, but loving. They didn't say a lot. There was a text every day from Neil Sandman. He nodded at Sandy, but the person who spoke was Jenny Lowther.

"God, that's cruel!"

Bob nodded. "Yes, but we might be able to track it. We need to get this to the forensics boys, Maureen. I'm sorry."

Sandy held out his hand. "I'll deal with it, Bob. I've got the squad car." He left the kitchen quietly and Bob sat back down again, wondering whether he should carry on with the questioning just now.

He watched her smooth the side of her bump, gently massaging in a way he remembered Elizabeth had done near the end of her pregnancy. "When's the baby due, Maureen?"

"I've got six weeks to go, Inspector. Have you any children?"

"He's got a gorgeous baby girl called Caitlin. Haven't you, Inspector?"

Bob nodded.

"I couldn't wait to have this one; Neil and I were so looking forward to the birth. It's a very special moment between a husband and wife isn't it?" The slow tears began to drip down her cheeks.

Bob had no idea what to say. The woman before him couldn't physically have murdered her husband, and unless she was one hell of an actress, she had loved her husband a lot. He sought inspiration from the surroundings, fastening on two seemingly unconnected things. "Did you get the haematite from the cave you met your husband in?"

For the first time he saw a break in the grief that hung about her like a thick blanket. "It's a coprolite actually." Maureen Sandman sniffed back tears.

"Is it? I haven't seen one of those to handle." McInnis picked it up a bit gingerly, turning it over in his hand. It felt reassuringly cool and stone-like.

Jenny, willing to distract her patient a bit, smiled. "I did the same, Inspector. The idea of dinosaur do-dos on the table is a bit, er, yeuk! But fossilisation takes away a lot of the 'yeuk!' Doesn't it?"

McInnis nodded again.

"There aren't many policemen who know their haematite from their coprolite, Inspector," Jenny quizzed him.

"No, nor many doctors, Doctor."

"Neil knew. He loved geology. He's got a big cabinet in the front room. I'm a geologist myself, Inspector." Maureen Sandman seemed to be getting a grip on her emotions, McInnis noted. "I came here because it's a spur of anomalous rock; there's a vein of limestone, and lots of shale. The shale and sandstone have been exploited, but there has been relatively little work done with the limestone." She seemed to be trying to distract herself.

"I thought most of the limestone was much further over, near Haltwhistle and Hexham. At least that's where the lead mines are." Bob was happy to assist her distraction.

Jenny Lowther raised an eyebrow. "You do know your geology don't you?"

"Only A-level stuff, Doctor, and only as a hobby." But his sharp eyes were watching Maureen. "I'm going to come back later; perhaps you'd better go to bed for a bit, Maureen. You don't look well."

7

Bob had stood up quietly and left the two women alone, closing the door to the kitchen after him and leaving the house without speaking to the others in the sitting room.

He came out onto the main street and scanned the town centre. It hardly warranted the name town, he thought. There was a little more activity in the three or four shops he could see. There were a few mothers with toddlers, a sprinkling of old men turned out of the house while their wives turned out the front rooms. One or two of the men had greyhounds at their heels, the dogs' long thin bodies seeming almost emaciated to McInnis.

The church clock startled him by chiming eleven and he found himself gazing up at the tall steeple, at the circling crows calling as they were disturbed from their perches. The air smelled of woodsmoke, imminent rain and the drifting aroma of pipe tobacco. It didn't seem the kind of place to have murder committed in it, but he knew better than most that murder could happen anywhere.

He walked across to his car and unlocked it, climbing in and sitting behind the wheel. Who was sending texts to the widow? Who was so isolated they hadn't heard about the murder on the radio or TV? Who hadn't seen a paper and continued to keep up the pretence that Doctor Sandman was alive, and why? He pulled out his notebook and started to put questions down.

He had been sitting for ten minutes, thinking, when a tap at the window disturbed his reverie. He leaned over and opened the

145

passenger door. "I thought you were taking the mobile to forensics in Carlisle?"

"Was, met the incident van coming in as I was leaving the town. I've given it and the squad car to Gareth to take on, and I hitched a lift back with the van." With a sweep of his hand Sandy indicated the heavy vehicle pulled up behind him and nearly blocking the narrow high street. "We need to find a place to park it; any ideas?"

Bob McInnis shrugged. "Could maybe park it on the surgery forecourt. It'll damn near fill it, but they aren't exactly going to be overflowing with patients today."

Sandy nodded and went back to speak to the driver. McInnis got out, waiting for Sandy to return. He was idly watching the passing traffic when a familiar face drove by.

"Hi! Sandy!" Bob was scribbling in the notebook he still held in his hand, as he yelled.

"What's up?" Sandy came rushing over.

McInnis pointed out the car which had accelerated rapidly past the van, going up onto the pavement and endangering passing foot traffic in its efforts to get away. It was headed rapidly out of town.

"That was Pheby. Blast! He looked right at me, Sandy. We've got his number plate now and a description of the car." Bob stared off at the dwindling car exhaust. "I could maybe buy him, just not thinking about the murder, and going somewhere for the weekend. But that man had the guiltiest expression I've seen for a long time."

Sandy shook his head in frustration. "I'll get on to traffic; get a watch set for the man. Nothing else we can do. It's not as if we can pin this crime on him. At least I don't think so; I haven't turned up anything to connect him yet and he'd know by now who was dead, so he'd hardly be sending the grieving widow texts. Unless he's more devious than I give him credit for. What do you think he was doing here, Bob?"

"God knows, Sandy. You deal with traffic; I'm going to see if I can pry any information out of the locals." He strode away on the words.

Sandy watched him go; now there was a man who was seriously pissed off, he thought, but better that way than the general indifference that Bob had worn like another skin for the past few months.

McInnis stepped into the nearest shop, a small newsagent cum dairy. He was confronted by a young woman in a colourful sari, he did a double take.

"Can I help?"

He was somewhat relieved to hear a Birmingham accent. "Do you know many of the local families?"

"Not really, love, we've only been here ten years." She offered a whimsical and rather charming smile. "We're still strangers."

"Ah! I don't suppose you know the name Pheby?"

"Oh! Sure I know them; they live down Church Street. Well, Mrs Pheby does, her husband died about five years ago. Her son comes in sometimes, nice man."

"Can you give me an address?" He watched her eyes narrow cautiously. "I'm a police officer."

"You'll be about the poor Doctor then. I heard as how he'd been found in the docks where Hugh Pheby works."

"That's right." Bob accepted her self-explanation and pulled out both warrant card and notebook, waiting expectantly.

"Here you go." She swung a thick book round in front of him. It appeared to be the order book for newspapers and magazines. He

147

jotted down the address and stood reading the varied reading material of the population. Women's magazines and genealogy maybe, embroidery and woodwork, OK, even a magazine he assumed dealt with diving, given their proximity to the coast.

He raised an eyebrow at the more lurid magazines on order however. Someone evidently had, or wanted a bit more, spice in their sex life. Ah, here was the doctor; he and some other man took a caving magazine and there was a magazine on geology. That would be for the doctor's wife he assumed. The nurse evidently had some sort of medical thing ordered. An interesting way of finding out the tastes of the community, he thought. "Thanks, you've been very helpful."

He was just heading out of the shop when his progress was halted by the sight of a large white toy monkey. It had long thin arms and legs, and the most ludicrous smile on its face. The last time he'd seen a smile like that had been on his daughter's face yesterday, when she'd finished filling her nappy. He turned around, pulling out his card case. "I'd like to buy the monkey."

The young woman came out from behind the counter, taking the toy down from the stand, offering him a lovely smile. "Is it a present? Would you like it wrapped?"

"Yes please."

"If it's for a little one, be careful she doesn't choke on the hair."

Bob thought of his sister. "I don't think that will be a problem."

He paid for the toy and took the package. As thank-you gifts went, it certainly did, and the sooner the better. Before Mary had gone to Germany. It wasn't his Caitlin but it might remind her of the child.

He walked out carrying the bag as Sandy came towards him. "Any luck?"

"Yeah."

"What you got there?"

"Present for Mary." He opened the car door and threw the carrier on the back seat. "I've also got an address for Hugh Pheby; his mother lives in the town. I should think he came here Saturday, and then when he heard who was murdered on the radio this morning, decided he'd better get out."

Sandy's lips twitched. "I didn't think anyone had been murdered in radio circles today, though there's one or two I'd like to see seriously impaired on Radio One."

"You know what I mean, Sandy!" Bob slammed the door shut and looked across at the huge van crowding out the small parking space in front of the surgery. "Do we need to go and talk to the local coppers?"

"Nah, I've set one of them on, trawling through that list. Four more doing door to door, checking to see when the Doc was seen last and where, and another couple looking for his car. It's not at the railway stations; I've had calls back from Carlisle and Workington."

"Been a busy bee haven't you."

"We aim to please."

"And you've carried me long enough, Sandy. But thanks anyway."

Sandy shot him a quick look. "You've just been a bit off your stride, lad. We all have times like that. But it's nice to have you back."

Bob started heading in the general direction of the church.

"Are we just out for a stroll or have you got somewhere in mind?"

"Sorry, Sandy, I thought we'd pay a call on Mr Hugh Pheby's mother."

"Sounds like a good plan." Sandy began to stroll beside him. "Did you get any further with the widow?"

"I would say there was brains as well as beauty there, Sandy. We've got to check the money, but I don't expect it to go anywhere. Unless there's a first Mrs Sandman somewhere in the wings arguing about who gets what."

Sandy glanced up as they passed the church, measuring the steeple. "Hell of a church that."

"Yeah it could probably accommodate the whole parish now." McInnis also glanced at the building and the graveyard surrounding it. "It will have one more resident soon, Sandy, and it's a damn shame."

"Let's give her justice then, lad."

Bob grunted quietly, "Ah, I thought Church Street would be easy to find."

They walked slowly up the street, reading off the numbers until they came to the right one. "I think, Sandy, you'd better handle this one. You're always better with the older ones," his lips twitched, "got more in common with them I suppose."

Sandy gave a smothered laugh as Bob rang the bell, and then straightened up as an older woman opened the door. "Can I help you gentlemen?"

"Mrs Pheby?"

"Yes."

"Police, madam."

"Proof, gentlemen."

Both detectives dug into pockets and came out with identity cards which were scrutinised carefully.

"How might I help you?" She didn't offer to invite them in.

"We understand your son was staying with you over the weekend?"

"What of it?"

"We need to speak to him."

"Well he isn't here now; he's gone back to work. Good morning." The door was closed firmly in their faces.

Sandy looked at Bob. "Oh! Yeah! I handled that really well."

Bob shrugged. "He was here, he isn't here now, she answered our questions."

They turned away, Sandy hunching his shoulders as they left the gate. "She's watching me from behind those curtains I can feel it, Bob. I bet she's on the phone to Pheby right this minute telling him we've been."

"Nothing we can do about that, Sandy." He began to walk back the way they'd come. "Let's see how they're getting on with the patients, relatives, scorned lovers and disgruntled colleagues."

The incident van was quiet in contrast to the surgery and reception, which swarmed with men carrying files in and out of the small cubby hole of a store-room.

"Remember, it's a need-to-know basis, men. Only those names found repeatedly in the past six months." Sergeant Meeks was keeping a sharp eye on proceedings. He came over to greet the two detectives. "We're not checking them yet, sir. Just stacking them in the surgery."

They nodded and went through to be greeted by half a rainforest of paper stacked on the floor next to the desk.

"Oh! My! I'll make a start shall I, Sandy?"

Both men settled down to read. They'd been busy for over four hours by the time Jenny Lowther came to find them. "Inspectors." She greeted them both politely, observing the slight state of undress both had reached. Sandy's tie was in the usual half-mast position. His hair, alternatively, looked as though he'd been out in a particularly fierce gale. He had ink on his chin and a slightly wild glint in his eye.

Bob still looked relatively neat. His jacket was off, but placed carefully around the back of a chair. His rather conservative dark blue tie was still neatly tied, and his hair still apparently unscathed by his labours. Both looked up at her entry and McInnis stood.

"I'm sorry to bother you. I've just got to get one or two things out of the drawers. There are a couple of patients who can't wait until tomorrow."

McInnis stepped away from the desk. "I don't understand half these terms, but Dr Sandman kept meticulous notes didn't he?"

"Yes." She scooped a strange instrument from the third drawer; it looked to Bob's untrained eye like a duck's bill without the duck attached. She also took a handful of lollipop sticks without lollipops from a jar and stood back, holding them carefully. "Can I help at all?"

"Probably, in fact almost certainly, Doctor, but not just yet." McInnis eyed the oblong, metal box she was gathering from a shelf. "Is it an emergency?"

"I think it's probably a case of tonsillitis, the child is prone to attacks, but I'd rather treat it than have the poor mite throwing fits from too high a temperature." She started to leave then swung back. "You can talk to Maureen when you want; she's much more stable now."

"I think I'd rather interview when you're available nevertheless, Doctor. Perhaps you can answer one question though."

"I can try."

"Is she the first Mrs Sandman?"

"Yes, it was love at first sight for both of them and first love at that. Why?"

"Former spouses can be good murder suspects."

"Oh! Oh, dear." Jenny looked slightly appalled. "I shall make sure only to have one husband then." She smiled a bit cheekily at them both and left the room. She made her way through the few police left in the reception area; they seemed to have commandeered the desk and chairs, and a small array of used mugs sat on the counter. She hoped fervently that someone would wash them up.

Going out into the late autumn sunshine she sighed. He'd stood up, she thought, and there weren't many that did that. She got into her car and drove to the far end of the town, sternly rebuking herself for lusting after another woman's husband.

Jenny Lowther had been the first in a series of interruptions. Mark came in ten minutes later, bringing the smell of the sea with him and some interesting news.

"Afternoon, sir. We've got another body."

"What? Where?" Sandy Bell swung round from the desk, frowning fiercely over his glasses at the forensics man. "Why didn't you tell us?"

"I'm telling you now, sir, Detective Sergeant Oakes has viewed the body, but since we scooped it out of the side of a cave, underwater, I didn't think you'd want to travel back to look at a stretch of sea." Mark looked at them apologetically.

"That's fine, Mark. You can show us the location when we come over tonight." Bob McInnis sat back. "Just fill us in on the details you have got, and we'll go from there. Do you think it's connected to our Doctor?"

"Hard to tell, it was in a pretty manky condition, sir."

"What kind of word is 'manky', Mark?"

Mark just stopped the shrug as he caught sight of Sandy's face. "I don't quite know how else to describe it, sir. It had been in the water for a bit and it was badly battered, probably by the currents and rocks. I've sent it off to Doctor Jones for autopsy."

"Ah, your final three, would it be in then?"

"Don't know, sir." Mark looked at the serious face of McInnis. He admired a man who not only listened, but remembered. "Given the place we found it, it could have been trapped under there for a couple of weeks. It was in a sort of opening off the pilings, and it's pretty chilly in the open water now."

McInnis recalled Jonesy's comments about September and the Irish Sea. "So give us what you have got then, man."

"You remember I was going to take a couple of the divers to see the pilings, sir? Well we'd been over both basins and still had a bit of diving time left so I took Jeff and Carter down for a quick look. The pilings really are something special, you can see the bark and the carvings, and..." His voice became suspended and he rather thought he might be, if he didn't get a grip on his enthusiasm. "You really don't want to know about that?" He glanced from Sandy's scowl to Bob's frown.

"Sorry, sir. Anyway the pilings are near a series of shallow entrances. I've not explored them, but I always thought they were part of the Roman harbour fortifications; maybe dry docks or something like that. This body was just washing about near the entrance to one of them."

154

"How did you get it out?"

"Jeff and Carter moved it, sir. It wasn't fastened down or anything."

"Age?"

"Undetermined as yet, though I would say youngish. What clothes remained are youthful, I think. And definitely male." Mark swallowed. "He was in rather a revolting condition, sir. Jeff and Carter couldn't do much more than bring up the body; and we nearly ended up with several pieces, it was only the clothes that kept the limbs in situ; and they were more than a bit rotten. We were nearly out of time too.

"They're going to take the teams out there tomorrow and explore the area. But it will be even slower work than the harbour; it's not a good time to be out in open water, heading towards October."

"OK, Mark, we'll have to take it as it comes." Sandy was still looking annoyed, so his next words came as something of a surprise. "You did right not to drag us back over there. Now, what does your gut say about this body? Connected to this or a separate case? Accident or murder?"

Mark paused, thinking about it. It was the first time Sandy Bell had asked him such a direct question, and it implied a degree of respect he didn't think the older man had for his abilities. "Too soon to give a cause and therefore to determine whether it's connected." He spoke slowly and a little cautiously, expecting to be corrected.

Sandy continued to look at him. "And your gut?"

"My gut says it's too much of a coincidence, sir; two bodies in the water in my town, which I know to be a backwater, is a bit more than I can swallow. I don't see what possible connection they can have all the same."

"We'll go with your gut nevertheless. We'll treat it as connected, and not bring in a separate team to deal with it. Well done, lad." Sandy nodded at him. "You'd better go off the clock for a while. Jeff Lyell was telling me about the diving yesterday. You must be tired, lad."

"Oh! But!..."

"I need you to dive with the team, Mark, if possible. I assume you've passed your fitness since you were diving today?" He waited for the nod. "I can't afford to miss any clues because you're too tired to spot them." Sandy smiled. "Off you go and get some rest."

Mark Forester was tired, but he was also a bit stunned. He wasn't used to the senior man being so pleasant. He nodded, and then received his third shock of the day.

"Hello, Inspector, Jenny said you'd like another word with me." Maureen Sandman came into the room, leading with her bump and a smile. It was true the smile barely stretched her mouth and certainly didn't reach her eyes but it was a brave effort for all that, and all the men recognised it as such.

McInnis and Sandy stood up immediately, and Bob held out his chair. "Sit down, Maureen; I'm sure you shouldn't be standing."

She cast him the slightly exasperated look women have been giving men ever since creation. "I'm having a baby, not ill, Inspector. I bet you drive your wife nuts." There was a certain teasing element which made the reception of the comment all the more puzzling.

"I'm a widower, Maureen." It was said quietly and denied the need for pity.

"Oh, God! I'm sorry, Inspector."

Mark, with a tact he hadn't known he possessed, led her forward to the chair at the desk, pulling it out for her and seeing her settled. "You might only be pregnant but that's one hell of a bulge you've got there, Mrs Sandman. How long have you got to go?" Mark looked at the pretty face turned up to him and prayed she'd take up his conversational gambit.

"About six weeks. Are you another inspector?"

"I'm only a Detective Sergeant, my name's Mark Forester, but I'm headed for those giddy heights, yes."

Sandy sat back down and took off his glasses. "It's good of you to come over here, Maureen. It is true we have a few more questions, but only if you feel up to it."

"That's alright, Inspector, I want you to find out who did this to Neil." She glanced across at the silent McInnis leaning against the examination couch, who offered her a faint smile.

"The first question I want to ask is how your husband went on holiday, car, train, what?"

"He was going to take the car to the station and then catch the train. I offered to take him but I'm a bit big behind the wheel now!" Maureen looked down at her bump and Sandy caught the faint sigh from Bob McInnis.

He turned and faced her more fully, drawing her full attention towards himself and partially excluding his partner, to give Bob a minute to regroup. "We need to know if your husband was having any problems with any of his patients." He indicated the mass of files. "We can go through these, but they only tell us who is ill and who might have had contact with him."

"Neil didn't really talk about his patients to me, Inspector. He was a very ethical man; it wouldn't have been right to tell me."

"Surely he passed the odd comment, between husband and wife?" McInnis asked the question quietly. "Something like, 'I had old so-and-so in, grumbling,' without going into specifics."

Maureen Sandman frowned in thought. "There's Mr Twentyman, I know he grumbles, but he grumbles about everything, Inspector. Neil didn't say anything to me, but I've heard them down at the shops. He said Neil was guilty of negligence when his wife died. He wasn't." She said it fiercely. "Neil was the most conscientious Doctor I know and I know the comments hurt him, but Mr Twentyman had to blame someone."

She brushed wisps of red hair off her face. "Some of the youngsters complained that he wouldn't dish out the morning-after pill without talking to them. He didn't hold with abortion under any circumstances. I heard some of the mums-to-be talking down at the clinic." She looked at Sandy. "They stopped talking when they noticed me. Not that they were nasty or anything."

She moved restlessly on the hard chair. "I really can't think of anyone who would hate him enough to kill him."

She absently rubbed her bump while she thought. "There's Paddy's husband," She shook her head. "I think he's still in jail though."

"Who's Paddy?"

"She was one of Neil's patients. Neil testified against her husband, for wife battering. She wouldn't leave him, kept saying it was her fault, but then he hit the child and she came to Neil. She's in a safe house."

"Give us the name and we'll check." Sandy nodded across at McInnis.

"Paddy McCulloch. No, wait, that wasn't her proper name… it was Paula, her husband was Morris I think."

"Any idea where he was tried?"

"Neil went to Carlisle to give evidence, so I suppose there."

McInnis stepped outside and pulled the door to, while he phoned through to Carlisle. He'd get them to check records and find out if the man was still inside.

"OK. Now we have to ask." Sandy coughed. "Was your marriage alright?" He kept his face as blank as a sheet of unused paper.

"It was a marriage, Inspector, we had our rough moments. If you mean were either of us thinking of leaving? No. Did we row? Sometimes. We were intelligent people who didn't always agree."

Sandy absently rubbed a finger under his nose. "Did the age difference create problems?"

Maureen put her head on one side. "Let me think. Well, we had different tastes in music, and of course I wanted to party all night and visit night-clubs twice at the weekends." She patted her bump and watched the little patch of red grow on Sandy's cheeks. "Of course we had problems, Inspector, but nothing that we couldn't handle." She softened her tone. "I'm sorry, I love Neil and I know you have to ask, but I'm going to miss him and I didn't want my marriage to end."

Sandy nodded. "I think that's all for now. Thank you, Maureen."

Mark, who had been standing silently by, now helped her to rise. "I'll see you home, Mrs Sandman." He looked across at Sandy. "I'll meet you back at the B and B sir and show you where..." he stopped, deciding that mention of 'manky' bodies in front of the new widow wasn't such a good idea.

"Fine, Mark, off you go."

McInnis came back into the room as Mark escorted Maureen out. He gave her a polite nod and the two senior men watched as the new widow left and then McInnis shut the door after them. Turning round he looked across the room, cocking his head on one side.

"Impressions, Sandy?"

"I think the same as you do. It was a good marriage. She didn't want to get out of it, she was happy despite the differences in age and morals."

Bob looked at him, raising an eyebrow.

"I think she didn't quite approve of his rigid moral stance, Bob. She thought that he was sitting in judgement slightly, on those girls who asked for the morning-after pill."

McInnis sniffed. "I'm not sure I approve of abortion myself, Sandy. It depends on the circumstances. Maybe after a rape, or if there are too many kids already, but…" He shook his head. "Maybe I'm too good a Catholic." His lips twitched. "Nevertheless, I agree with you, she loved him and she didn't want him dead."

"This is the second time we've had the name Twentyman given to us, Bob."

"Yeah, we're going to have to talk to the man. I've found Twentyman's wife's files in the mortuary stack. If I've understood it correctly, and there's no guarantee of that –" he shook his head as he poked the file "– that poor woman didn't come to see our Doctor until it was far too late to do anything but stop the pain. She died within seven weeks of first visiting."

"I've been scanning the teenagers. There aren't that many. Oakes was right, most of them have moved on. It's a shame, Bob; this is a nice quiet rural village."

"No work and no future, Sandy."

"Yeah." He looked at his watch. "It's about time we were getting back to Maryport; I want an update from the teams on this new body. I think our suspect can wait. According to my file," Sandy pushed another file with a stubby finger, "Philip Twentyman is in his seventies; I don't think he'll be doing a runner overnight."

Mark, having escorted Maureen Sandman back to her kitchen, was making her a cup of tea. He was also thinking about who could have committed the crime. He agreed with Sandy and Bob, this young woman hadn't.

"There you go, Mrs Sandman." He handed her a pottery mug and sat down near her on one of the chairs at the table.

"I think you'd better call me Maureen. You really don't look old enough to be so formal."

Feeling slightly indignant Mark looked across the room. "I'm twenty-eight."

"Same age as me then." She hesitated a minute. "I am sorry about the Inspector; Jenny said he'd got a baby daughter so I thought..."

Mark moved uncomfortably on his seat. "Yeah, well..." He scratched among his curls, his face mirroring his embarrassment while he fixed his eyes on the maternity pinafore in a slightly fascinated way. "She died in a car accident." He glanced away guiltily. As a single child he hadn't had much to do with pregnant women, but his eyes were drawn back to the slight movements, however hard he tried to avoid them.

Maureen, aware of his gaze smiled. "It's OK I don't mind you looking. In fact," she held out a hand, "come and feel."

"Oh no," he looked horrified, "I couldn't do that." For a man who spent half his life handling the revolting remains left by others and analysing them, the expression was ludicrous and the feeling worse.

"I don't mind." She continued to hold out a hand.

Mark looked at her face.

"Neil used to love feeling the little one bump about. He said it was different when it was your own child." The voice, in stark contrast to the face, was full of tears.

Mark took the proffered hand, stretching forward in his seat as she rested his hand above a small bulge which gave a tiny kick. He would have jerked away but she held his hand firmly against her. "What do you think, geologist or footballer?"

Mark smiled. "Ballet dancer!" He patted the little limb and sat back.

They were all sitting around tables in the dockside café; its furniture had been rearranged to form three parts of a square. Sandy Bell was standing in front of them, next to a whiteboard on which he began making notes.

Only one of the ladies who normally presided behind the tea urns was present, and, swathed in a pinny, she was vigorously rinsing dishes in the sink before putting them in the dishwasher. The air held the waning smell of the delicious lamb hotpot and roast chicken many of them had enjoyed for their evening meal. Now they drank tea, relaxed, and waited for her to leave.

Sandy opened the proceedings as she closed the door, nodding at Oakes and the two senior divers. "We've decided to treat the two victims as connected at the moment. We aren't sure if our second body is actually a murder victim, or a swimmer or fisherman who has been in difficulties. However, DS Oakes hasn't as yet found any missing persons in Maryport who might fit that category. Tomorrow I'd like you to widen the search to Cumberland." He paused and used a penlight to point to names.

"As far as the murder of the Greystone Doctor is concerned, we have eliminated Doctor Sandman's wife. She isn't physically capable of killing her husband, her finances are comfortable and she will be reasonably well off, but there certainly isn't enough in the kitty to pay for a hit."

"These three ladies –" Sandy moved the light down "– are the nurse, Hayley Noble: the receptionist, Alison Lythe: and the cleaner, Patsy Collins. I believe we can dismiss the nurse and cleaner. There is no earthly reason why they would want their employer dead. Both are going to be out of a job and seemed genuinely upset at his death. The cleaner has been questioned about the state of the surgery and states it was 'just as usual, nothing out of place since the Doctor left for his holidays'."

Sandy kept the pointer on Alison Lythe. "This young woman might repay further investigation. She was plainly jealous of the wife and obviously felt herself slighted. Women can act irrationally in those circumstances." McInnis heard the slight Scottish inflection and gave Sandy a curious look; his partner had picked up something he hadn't, evidently.

Sandy moved on to the second list of names. "We've got reason to believe this gentleman and several others on this patient list might have held grudges or disagreed with the Doctor's treatment for themselves or their relatives. These interviews will be conducted over the next few days.

"DS Oakes, would you like to fill the team in on the body found today?"

Oakes stood and moved over beside Sandy who stepped back and leaned against the side of a table where he could watch faces.

"As some of you know, the divers were taking a little well deserved paddle this afternoon." He smiled thinly. "Which will teach them not to take busman's holidays! They were examining the old Roman harbour and discovered a body trapped on the sea floor. We haven't yet determined anything about the poor chap except that he is a male, and he is dead." He cleared his throat, taking a sip of water from a glass in his hand.

"The autopsy will take place tomorrow, hopefully. I've asked the diving teams to clear things with their branches so that they can continue diving for a further few days here in Maryport unless they are needed urgently elsewhere. We need to establish where this body has appeared from." He paused, looking at McInnis and Bell. "I know for a fact that there have been a few dives lately in that area. Certainly some in August and the first week of September. I can't help feeling they would have noticed a dead body among the ruins."

Oakes waited for the slight chuckle to subside. "Until the site is explored there isn't much more we can tell you about that. However," he paused, sipping again, "I have made contact with Andrew Hamilton; he runs a charter boat out of the harbour and he rang from Ireland to say he was on his way back. He heard the news on the radio and he thinks he might have seen something a week last Friday. He spent the night on board his yacht in the marina basin that night."

He cleared his throat. "Fred." He nodded at a tall thin man who stood up.

"I'm with traffic, sir. Further to your message about Mr Pheby, we've had an all points bulletin out for his car, but no one has spotted him yet. We'll keep looking."

"Are we any wiser as to why the man is evading us?" Sandy put the question to the group as a whole but only got shakes of the head.

Mark coughed and stood up. "You know we found the boat next to the body, sir?" He waited for the nod. "We found markings to show it was Pheby's, and it was recognised by some of the fishermen. Well, we can't find a scratch on it. No obvious reason to scupper it. Cocks are all in place, oars were damaged but still in the rowlocks, which is odd, and the painter is still attached. In fact it's a mystery why the thing was down there."

"I'm ignorant, lad. Why shouldn't the oars be in the rowlocks, and what's an artist got to do with our mystery?" Sandy grinned at Mark.

"You would ship the oars when you moored it, sir," He caught the gleam of mischief on the older man's face. "You would take them out of the rowlocks and put them in the boat, otherwise they would be in danger of floating away or catching on things. And a painter is a rope to tie the boat to the side, sir." His lips twitched; closer acquaintance with Sandy Bell was letting him see another side to the senior detective. He didn't think Sandy was really that ignorant. He did however think the man was making everyone think a bit more about this new information.

"Any idea when it was last seen?"

"Can't get a definite on that, maybe a fortnight ago, maybe longer. Those we asked seemed to assume he'd taken her out of the water for the winter, sir."

"OK, keep at it, we might get lucky. Any further ideas concerning Thomas Moore?"

"He's been fishing for peeler crabs, sir." Gareth stood up and spoke up. "I remembered Mr Saunders saying they were protected, Moore said he was 'borrowing the boat'." Gareth put the phrase in 'brackets' with his fingers. "To do a little unlicensed fishing and selling the crabs at a good profit down Liverpool way. He decided he'd better tell us when the second body turned up; I think he was genuinely frightened that we might slap a murder charge on him."

He paused, frowning fiercely. "We're charging under the Wildlife and Countryside Act for fishing unlawfully in an area of outstanding natural beauty." Gareth watched the nod of acknowledgement from Sandy Bell, and sat back down again.

McInnis looked at the group from his seat. "Have we any idea yet what the young Simpson lads were up to and if it's germane to this case, or just mischief on their part?"

Oakes looked across the room to where McInnis was sitting slightly apart from the rest, taking notes. "They aren't, as yet, talking to us. For the moment we're leaving them to think about things. I personally don't believe they have had any hand in this murder, sir."

"No, Sergeant, nor do I, but I need to establish just what they have been up to so that we can eliminate them." He offered a pleasant smile to the local constabulary present.

"Just so, sir."

Sandy took the floor again. "Right, ladies and gentlemen, tomorrow those of us with the short straw will carry on with the interviews. The divers will dive. Mark, as you know, I'd like you to be with the teams, see if you can pinpoint what needs dredging up, and have a look at these caves you think you've found. And gentlemen," Sandy paused, "I don't want any other bodies on my plate, so take care in these waters.

"Those of you who have been over at Greystone today I want some more door-to-door interviews. The good Doctor must have been seen. I want a timeline of his final day in the town, and I want his car found.

"Dismiss." He watched as the men trooped out, and then looked across at Bob.

"Do you want to do the interview with Hamilton tomorrow, Bob, work in tandem with Oakes and see what this skipper has to say? You can pull all the information together for me this end. Then maybe re-interview the Simpson boys. You're right, they're a thread we need to snip off."

"Yes that's fine, Sandy," he sighed. "You don't have to keep me away from Mrs Sandman though, I'm not as fragile as all that." He watched the faint wash of colour.

"Am I as obvious as all that, Bob?"

"Only to me." Bob gave him a light punch on the shoulder and they turned and left the room together.

8

What was obvious to McInnis next morning was that Oakes was still annoyed with his team. He nagged them for information and growled at them when they hadn't got it. Bob watched the man, and the local constables, sympathetically, for five minutes and then spoke quietly to him. "Walk around to the marina with me, Sergeant."

Oakes nodded and with a final flurry of orders left the incident van after McInnis' tall figure.

"What did you want to look at, sir?"

"Nothing in particular, just refreshing my mind." They strolled along, enjoying the late autumn sunshine. The few fishermen about were mainly working on their boats, sorting gear. McInnis gazed down into the commercial basin. He thought the tide was coming in, but couldn't be sure. It was certainly low. He looked down on the decks, noted nets and lobster pots, smelt tar and seaweed, heard soft voices and the occasional laugh. It was a gentle, ageless scene.

"You get a different perspective when you look from this angle don't you, Sergeant?"

"I suppose so, Inspector; I don't really think about it, I've worked here most of my life and the docks have been part of it."

"And it's your turf, Sergeant. Do you resent our intrusion?"

"No, sir." Oakes flushed. "I couldn't have handled this lot, and I know it."

"Do you think I'm here today to keep an eye on you?" It was said quietly and gently.

Oakes's face rivalled a tomato for redness; his nose, still sore from his cold, was a beacon in the centre. "Er." He paused just too long.

"I'm not. Inspector Bell was stating facts yesterday. He certainly doesn't think you need watching. He trusts you, Oakes. Now, might I suggest you allow a bit of that trust to seep through to your men?" McInnis shook his head. "Men don't work well with resentment at the back of their minds."

He stopped at the corner, under the Harbour Master's office, and looked out across to the causeway. "Let it go, Sarge! A young Constable with mixed loyalties doesn't make the whole force rotten. They're working damn hard and so are you. But work at the right thing, man. The murder."

He brought his gaze back to the silent man next to him. "Show me this other entrance to the marina Pheby was talking about. He said it was at the end of this marina somewhere."

Oakes said nothing, but he began to stroll along the other side of the long mound. They'd reached the end together and McInnis was looking at a set of stone steps leading upwards before Oakes spoke again. "You're right, sir, I was letting it get to me. I was feeling guilty, and with cause." He glanced across at the silent inspector. "I've let Sergeant Meeks shoulder much of the day-to-day work just lately. I'm taking early retirement at the end of the year, but that's no reason to take my hands off the reins just yet."

"No, Sergeant, but don't ruin their mouths for the next rider." McInnis flashed a brief smile, like a ray of sun through clouds, and then turned to the path again. "I don't think our murderer came this way, not carrying a heavy body, inert or not."

He looked around; the sea wall was a solid line against the encroaching sea, a muffled hiss and splash in the background indicating the presence of the tamed beast that was the sea trying to get into the boating sanctuary.

The back of the marina had several storage huts but otherwise presented a further barrier to sand and sea. "There isn't another way in is there?"

"No. It's either down the steps, on the road, or by boat through the marina gates."

"Damn!"

"Sorry, sir." Oakes looked justifiably surprised as McInnis swung around and looked the length of the basin towards the gates which were now open to sea traffic.

"We assumed the body was thrown in from the dockside. What if someone brought it in, in a boat, and dropped it in the harbour from the seaward side? Mark said no fisherman worth his salt would take a body outside the harbour, too much risk with your tide race. But what if he came down the river Ellen and along the harbour entrance way?"

"I'll get some men to check the empty dockyards and slipways, sir. See if there are any signs of recent use around."

"Perspective, Sergeant, and territory. I'm not even sure I knew there were slipways along there." McInnis exchanged a smile. "Let's get back. I'll see if I can bring a different perspective to bear on the Simpson lads shall I?"

"It might be as well, sir." Oakes nodded. They discussed tactics as they walked back; then Oakes went to reorganise his men slightly, setting them to check the new sites while McInnis took his car and headed for the Simpson household.

The boys should be at school. McInnis wanted a quiet word with their parents first if possible. The house was quiet, the dahlias lifted their heads to the weak sunshine and the lawn had obviously been freshly mown. He walked confidently up the path and rang the bell.

"Good morning. Mrs Simpson?" He raised an eyebrow at the sturdy woman who answered.

"Yes, can I help?"

"I'm with the police," he said, fishing out his warrant card. "I'm going to have to talk to your lads again, but I wondered if I might have a word with you first."

"Me?"

"Well, you and your husband."

"James is at work." She held open the door. "You'd better come in, Inspector. I'll give him a ring; he works in a garage down in the town. He might be able to nip home for a bit."

McInnis was shown into the same sitting room as before. He took the offered seat and relaxed back into it; it was proving to be a strenuous case.

"I'll just go and phone. Would you like a drink, Inspector?"

McInnis shook his head. "No I'm fine, thank you." He watched her leave, her movements quick as she whisked a tin of polish and a duster from the sideboard on her way out. He smiled to himself; he'd seen his mother perform the same conjuring trick a few times when unexpected visitors came, inconveniently, to call.

He sat pondering the case in the quiet of the room, the tick of a carriage clock the only sound. He closed his eyes for a minute, thinking, and became aware of the polish and the sweet smell of cut grass. Maybe he should go and see Jonesy again tomorrow, see if

171

he'd managed to do an autopsy on the new body. Then frowned as he realised he was making an excuse to go to Carlisle.

He analysed his motive, turning it around. Yes, he did need to see Doctor Jones, but even more he needed to see his daughter. He wanted to reassure himself that she was OK. Not that he didn't trust Sarah Bell. He did. But his daughter had been taken from the only mum she'd ever known and he wanted her to know the parent she had got left loved her deeply.

Just then the mother of the Simpson boys returned. She brought with her a tray of coffee and some biscuits. McInnis, rising in a slightly startled manner at her entrance, held the door for her.

"I know you said you didn't want anything, Inspector, but James will, when he comes, and I need a sit down. So help yourself if you've changed your mind." She set the tray down and McInnis waited while she sat and then seated himself again.

McInnis smiled across the small coffee table as he heard the slight sigh, like a summer zephyr, issuing from his hostess' mouth. "I've got the beginning of term meetings with Lucy's new teachers this afternoon, so I'm trying to fit everything in this morning."

"And I've come along disrupting you even further. I'm sorry, Mrs Simpson."

"That's alright, Inspector." She gave a slightly wicked smile. "We women are good at multi-tasking; I'll catch up." She cocked her head and McInnis caught the slight snick of the front door. "That'll be James." She poured a mug of coffee and liberally sugared it, setting it down as her husband entered the room.

James Simpson entered and leant over his wife offering, without any embarrassment, a kiss to her upturned mouth, then sitting next to her. "How might we help you, Inspector?" His large hands, McInnis saw, were grimed with oil, and the faint smell of that and diesel clung about him like a strange miasma. He sipped coffee and looked enquiringly across the intervening space, his whole body radiating a forced calm: like a dog held tightly on a leash.

McInnis took stock of the two people in front of him before speaking. They complemented each other. James Simpson was stern, his wife relaxed; he was defensive, she was open. Did this mean he knew something she didn't or was it just their natures?

"I'm doing my best to eliminate your boys from my investigation; their continuing silence isn't helping much." McInnis smiled slightly. "I don't, for one minute, think they had anything to do with the murder. But I do believe they have been up to something illegal."

Simpson opened his mouth and McInnis saw his wife gently rest a hand on his arm and give it a squeeze. "Let the man finish, love."

McInnis nodded at her by way of thanks. "It's not easy being a parent, you love them and want to shield them, and teach them right from wrong, and when they get it wrong you fear for them. But..." he sighed, "your boys are muddying my waters and I need to eliminate them. No charges will be pressed." McInnis looked sternly at them.

"They came forward as good citizens should. Whatever they have been up to will be forgotten." He offered a faint smile. "Providing it isn't something against someone else, rather than the law. Even then, we'll try to get whoever it is to accept payment for damages and abject apologies."

Simpson was frowning deeply. The clock was ticking off the seconds of thought and the phone ringing broke the silence jarringly. Mrs Simpson excused herself and left the room, leaving the door open. They heard her speak softly and then the receiver being replaced with a soft ting.

As if this had been the cue, James Simpson started to speak. "They'd been fishing. I promised them a rowboat this summer, but work hasn't been so good, and we just couldn't afford it. They'd been boasting last term; they wanted to go out with their mates and claimed they'd got a boat. Apparently they've been borrowing the Harbour Master's boat without his permission, to do a bit of fishing." His wife stood at the doorway and looked across at him.

He paused, sipping coffee. Mrs Simpson came in and sat next to him and he set down the mug and took her small hand in his. "I should have told you, love."

"I already knew, darling. Lucy knew, and she can't keep a secret to save herself." She gave a wry smile. "I thought it better not to say too much." She swung round and looked at McInnis. "They're good lads, Inspector, and we try to give them things, but money's tight at times with four of them. What they were doing was wrong but I'm sure Hugh Pheby knew about it and turned a blind eye. He's always seemed a reliable man when it came to that harbour of his."

"So they were fishing on the night the body was found?"

"No…o, Inspector." James Simpson seemed relaxed now, "Chris, Christopher, says they'd put a couple of lobster pots down in the harbour entrance. They used to fasten them to the harbour wall. They thought Pheby was wise to them. At least they couldn't find his boat." He sighed again. "They hadn't been drinking at least. But when they found the body they freaked out a bit and rang my eldest son, who was on duty. The rest you know."

McInnis stirred in his chair. "Alright, I still need to talk to them, but basically they've been setting lobster pots in a protected area and pinching a boat on a regular basis." He thought of Thomas Moore and his crimes. Could they let the boys off and still prosecute the man? Maybe, the boys were just doing it for fun; he was doing it for profit. And what about Pheby? How much did he suspect, and know, of what was going on in his harbour? Was that why he was doing a vanishing act?

McInnis stood up. "Thank you both for being so honest with me. I'll deal with this as quietly as possible. Can you arrange for the boys to be kept off school tomorrow morning so that I might have a word with them?"

James Simpson nodded but said, "What about my eldest son, Inspector? James has always dreamed of being a policeman." The elder James Simpson looked across the room as he too stood up.

"I can't promise anything there I'm afraid, but I think you'll find that the governing body will understand his motives, if nothing else," He offered a tired, somewhat wry smile. "We're good at motives after all."

Sandy Bell was being motivated too; he was motivated to take cover in the incident room to escape the cheerful chirruping of the nurse. Not that the woman meant any harm, he thought, but her scattershot pattern of speech left him feeling slightly breathless himself.

He and Gareth were wading their way through snowdrifts of paper. It piled and heaped and cascaded off every available surface; hopefully somewhere in it all there was the shape of a man who had committed a murder.

They had more or less eliminated the fishermen from Maryport; either they were alibied or there was just no motive they could discover. Which brought them to the people of Greystone. Sandy Bell had rarely encountered a more law-abiding, if slightly boring, group of people.

"So what have we got, Gareth?"

"Well, Chief, this lot." He thumped a sheaf of papers down, flattening them onto the surface of the desk with a large hand. "They have never been in trouble with the law, not a parking ticket between them, they haven't seen the Doctor in the last year and they have come forward willingly to offer statements." He moved his hand to a second pile. "This lot are a little less clean. You've got your odd speeding and parking, a few minor D and D's at the Christmas season. But that's about it for them." He picked the pile up and laid it on top of the first pile at right angles.

Sandy scratched his chin, nodding at the third pile. "And that lot?"

"I've got half a dozen, what you might term, hostile witnesses, Chief." Gareth flicked the pile with a finger. "We've got three teenagers. One with an ASBO."

"For?"

"Mainly affray, but graffiti, fighting, history of bullying, right little tough." Gareth sniffed. "The two others, they would be your typical teenager looking for something to do and finding mischief for their idle hands. The other three, well I don't think they need concern us, they used to live here but one has joined the army and is currently in the army detention centre, one is serving time at Her Majesty's pleasure in Lincoln and one is, well, actually no one knows where he is, Chief. Name of Eric Potts. Dropped off the radar apparently, last sighting… Carlisle about six weeks ago."

"Let's have a look at it." Sandy flipped through the notes. "This will be the young man Sergeant Oakes said they'd been looking for, his notes are very thorough." Sandy Bell glanced up. "The parents reported him missing after seventy-two hours, but since he's been running away since he was thirteen and they haven't been able to control him for most of his teenage years they aren't that worried about him returning."

"If you read a bit further, Chief, you'll find he hit the mother and tried for the father. Who, it seems, gave as good as he got."

"Nice family. Anything on the father?"

"Nope. I've got his interview here somewhere." Gareth shuffled several piles onto the floor and handed Sandy three pages clipped onto a brown file. "That's the interview about the Doctor. The rest is his dealings with the police, concerning his son."

"Give me a summary, Gareth?"

"As I said they lost control of him. When he occasionally went 'walkabout' they reported him missing, but, as I read it, weren't too thrilled when the police brought him back. This last time they reported him missing, but told the coppers he wasn't welcome in their house anymore."

Sandy Bell sighed. "Well if he's been gone six weeks I doubt he had anything to do with our murder two weeks ago, but we'd better tell the Carlisle station to keep a look out for him just in case. What else we got?"

"Patients. We've eliminated most of them. You said you wanted to visit Philip Twentyman. So the locals have left him for you. Oh! And that guy McCulloch."

"Who?" Sandy frowned.

"Guy with spousal abuse."

"Oh yeah! Doctor Sandman was the witness for the prosecution, what about him?"

"Still in clink. Got another eighteen months to go according to the county court and I checked, he's still in, not earned any smarty points at all for good behaviour."

Sandy scrubbed his hands over his hair, then straightened his tie. "Come on then, lad, you can help terrorise a seventy-something

177

with a grudge." They stood up and, nodding at a couple of constables still doing a frantic tap-dance over the computer keyboards, they left the stuffy van for the bright light of an autumn day.

"Look, lad, a strange orb in the sky." Sandy nodded at the sun sending fingers of light through the clouds to hit pavements wet from the overnight rain. Gareth gave a faint chuckle. "Which way to this Mr Twentyman. Do we need the car?"

"No, sir. It's just along the road."

Gareth had abandoned his waterproof, after one of the locals had asked him where the fair was and if he always carried the big top for them. Even so he was a big man, especially when he'd got his flak jacket on, the equipment slung around across his front like a bandolier. They strolled up the street with the measured policeman's walk immortalised by *Dixon of Dock Green* and *The Bill*. Sandy, glancing at their shadows, grinned. "Have you stopped growing yet, lad?"

Gareth cast a puzzled frown at his superior. "Of course I have, sir. I'm only six two though. My *tad*, he's six six."

"Never mind, Gareth, you make up for it in breadth." The town was busier this morning, Sandy Bell thought. Bad news travelled and the natives wanted a look at the bad news. "That's it lad, you intimidate them."

Bell's face had the look of a wolf sighting prey as his gaze encountered a couple of old ladies obviously discussing events over the garden fence. One uttered a faint squeak and dived into the local butchers. "They sound just like cackle cheats, sir."

"They sound like what?" Sandy lifted an eyebrow and gazed at the young giant. He watched the faint flush.

"Er! Chickens, sir."

"Hm!" Sandy filed the comment away to share with Bob McInnis.

"Here you are, sir, number forty-two."

The door appeared to be built on substantial lines for a standard semi-detached. Sandy almost expected it to squeak and to be answered by Igor the butler with a limp and a lisp, so the slightly wizened man, wearing glasses strong enough to replace the Hubble telescope, and in his own personal cloud of tobacco smoke, was rather a disappointment.

"Well what do you want? If you've come to sell me something I haven't got any money, the government only give me a pittance and then they take it all back in taxes."

Sandy, a bit taken aback, closed his mouth which he'd opened preparatory to announcing himself, and looked at Gareth. Gareth was plainly a police officer. His insignia gleamed, his flat cap sat on the head of an unmistakably stern-faced minion of the law.

"Well speak up! Don't stand there blocking the light; I can't afford to heat up the whole of Cumberland."

Sandy stated the obvious. "We're with the police, sir. I'm Inspector Bell, sir."

"Well about time too! I reported those pesky boys for upturning my dustbins three days ago."

"Er, we haven't come about the dustbins, sir."

"Well why not? I've just told you I pay my taxes; I'm entitled to some service. You'd think after the time I spent in the army making this land safe for you youngsters, you could at least keep me safe in my own home."

Sandy, still floundering slightly, was saved by a young woman who appeared behind Mr Twentyman. "Mr Twentyman, they'll have come about the poor Doctor."

Philip Twentyman peered at them over his glasses, and under eyebrows like the eaves of a thatched roof, and then looked over his shoulder at the woman. "Well, that shouldn't stop them dealing with my dustbins."

"Can we come in, sir?" Sandy moved forward. "While we are here about the murder of your Doctor, I'm sure my Constable will be able to enquire about the trouble with your dustbins."

He threw Gareth to the wolves without a qualm and as Mr Twentyman turned away he shook a finger at his neighbour and said, "See. If you deal with them firmly you get results, Anne Winchester." Gareth and Sandy crossed the threshold.

"Now, sir," began Sandy. By dint of some nimble footwork, Sandy had advanced beyond the sacred portals to the inner keep. This house really was Philip Twentyman's castle. Any minute Sandy expected to hear the drawbridge being pulled up. "We understand you weren't too happy with the care you received for your wife from Doctor Sandman."

"Of course I wasn't. The man was incompetent." The pipe wagged up and down in the corner of his mouth as he spoke, a pointer underlining his words.

"What form did his incompetence take, sir?"

"I've paid all my life for the National Health. I expected the man to spot the trouble and get my wife the treatment she needed; and instead he gave her an aspirin and told her it was too late."

"Did he not offer you any explanation, sir?"

"Muttered some mumbo-jumbo about her leaving it too late. In this age of scientific wonders, I wonder he dare say such a thing. I think he just didn't want to treat her because she was too old. It's all the same you know." He shook a finger, stained the colour of a caramel toffee under Sandy's nose. "They don't want to be burdened with old people clogging up the system. I've heard about it on that there *Panorama* programme, bed blocking or something they call it, as if it was our fault."

"Do you think your wife was refused the correct treatment then, sir?"

"Of course she was, isn't that what I'm saying?" Sandy had never seen a fool at the court of the king, but he now understood the meaning of the word capering, as the elderly man in front of him jigged about in a fury. "There's poor Mrs Paton; he wouldn't admit her to hospital either, incompetent that's what the man was. You should be looking for his murderer among those he's deprived of treatment, I say."

The young woman Anne, standing just behind him shook her head slightly at the two police officers. Sandy gave her a quick, small nod.

"And can you suggest anyone who might have wanted their revenge for that, sir?"

"Why should I? That's your job." He shook the finger again, this time at Gareth's chest. "And don't you be forgetting to see about my dustbins, young man."

Gareth, a silent and awed spectator, now incited more vituperative comment, though all he said was, "Yes, sir. I'll look into it."

"And that's another thing, you foreigners coming here and taking over our men's jobs, why can't you find work in your own country? I suppose that's why there isn't enough money to treat us old folk. Too many of you lot taking up the beds in the hospitals."

With Gareth thus rendered speechless, it was left to Sandy Bell to extricate them before Philip Twentyman consigned them to the dungeons. They sidled away towards the door with a stream of words washing over them as they made their retreat.

"Phew!"

"Yeah, Gareth, 'Phew!' Indeed." Sandy pretended to mop his brow. He walked through the gate and stood breathing deeply on the pavement. "I knew I should have left him to Bob."

He remained standing outside the gate until Gareth, a monument of patience said, "Sir?"

"She tipped me the wink, Gareth."

"Who, Chief?"

"Anne, whatever her name was. I think she might have something to add."

He leaned against the gatepost and watched the passing foot traffic and a few minutes later his patience was rewarded. Anne came out onto the road.

"I live next door. I keep an eye on him."

"Well I admit I think he could do with a keeper." Sandy smiled a bit wryly and got a grin in exchange.

"Would you like to come in for a minute?" She led the way up the garden path and put her key in the Yale lock.

When they were all inside, and she'd walked through to the kitchen with the police following like dogs hoping for a few crumbs, she smiled nicely at them and nodded at chairs. "Do you want to sit down?"

"No thanks, Miss. What was it you wanted to tell us?"

She swung around and, picking up the kettle, began to fill it from the tap, speaking over the noise. "His wife, you should know poor Doctor Sandman did his very best for her. There was no way he could have got her better. She didn't go and see him; she was a quiet woman." She put the kettle on the stove and Sandy heard the click, click of the pilot light, before she turned around and faced him, leaning against the sink to talk.

"I'm not surprised. I'm only surprised she got a word in at all."

"Yeah. Well Philip, Mr Twentyman, he's harmless enough; he just likes a good grumble. I don't mind really. But he shouldn't say that about the Doc; he did all he could for poor Mavis."

"What was that about Mrs Paton?"

"She lives over the back fence. Her son cares for her. She's got Alzheimer's. She was sick the other week, a nasty chest infection. The Doc gave her antibiotics and had the nurse in every day to help look after her. It was better for her than going into hospital; they had her in for one night and apparently the X-ray unit was a shambles after they'd finished with her." Anne grinned again. "She gets a bit aggressive when she doesn't recognise anyone."

"Right." Sandy nodded thanks for the information. "Do you know of anyone who might hold a grudge?"

"No, the Doc was a good sort. He turned out at night and, what's more, he had time to talk if you went to the surgery. Didn't rush you for the next patient. It's a shame, it really is."

"Well thank you for your help, Miss Winchester."

Sandy and Gareth strolled back towards the van in the incipient downpour. "I think we can take him off our list too, Gareth. I had high hopes of our Mr Twentyman." He sighed so lugubriously that Gareth gave a chuckle.

"Really, Chief?"

"No not really, Gareth, but I hate these murders where the murderer can be any one of a dozen and you have to wade through piles of paperwork in case you miss your man. Are you sure you want to be a detective, lad? It's mostly paperwork you know."

Gareth, who was aware that Bob McInnis normally did the bulk of the paperwork, said nothing. He still wanted to be a detective because he'd seen the satisfaction the team he was currently working with had from the job. He wanted that satisfaction for himself, instead of having to hand over his clues to someone else.

Mark was searching for clues too. The area he was searching in had all the charm and delight of the inside of a wellington boot: dark, sweaty and smelling of rubber. He hadn't done any diving inside caves before and found he didn't really care for the experience, at least not when it came to caves where you had to push your tank in front of you to get through the space.

Jeff and he had gone down on the first dive of the day; the 'dry docks' had proved to be caves. At first they'd thought they were shallow erosions, but the third such cave had gone back, and back some more, until they found a narrow passageway at the top.

Jeff was in the lead, Mark second, and a young female Constable, Robyn, third. All Mark could see was the light from his headlamp, reflected off his tank, and occasional glimpses of Jeff's flippers. He tucked his elbows in a bit more and wriggled forward, concentrating on his breathing. Jeff had gone through once and assured them, via the intercom, that there was a larger opening at the other end. Mark hoped to hell the man wasn't kidding.

He emerged like a cork from a bottle; with a whoosh of energy he shot forward into a deeper cave. Jeff was grinning through his face mask; he made the sign for OK and pointed upwards as Robyn appeared. They put their tanks snugly back into position and began swimming, paying out line as they went. Nobody wanted to get lost underground and underwater.

Mark couldn't see much. The water was much clearer here, it was true, but the Stygian blackness outside their own overlapping circles of light was total. He signalled back 'OK' and they all swam upwards.

As he went higher he became aware of lightness in the water. It was like surfacing from a deep sleep and becoming aware of the sunlight touching your eyelids, a reanimation of consciousness after being immersed in a dream world.

They bobbed up in a cave, treading water at the surface of a large underwater pool. It was huge and the limestone seams high above them reflected back their lights, as if a huge zebra was moving across the cave roof. They swept the surface with powerful flashlights, searching for further exits. Jeff pointed again towards the side; a blacker area indicated another cave just at the surface of the water. They began swimming towards it.

Jeff swam cautiously to the entrance, shining his light up the silvery pathway. The passage was narrow, but led out of the water and would allow them to half stand if they followed it upwards. He checked their supply of gas, calculating how long it had taken them to get to their present position and how much exploration time they had left before they needed to get back.

He pointed upwards, then indicating his tank showed thirty minutes before turning round. Thumbs up from the others and he half swam, half crawled, upwards into the passageway. He thought he knew what he was entering.

Mark was frankly staggered at the size of the next cavern. They had been half crawling, half walking for several minutes when they emerged into it. Far above them a tiny hole of daylight could be seen in the almost cathedral-like dome. He pushed his face mask up and unclipped the mouth piece.

"Wow!"

"Wow indeed." Jeff had also freed his mouth. "This is some place Mark."

"What the hell is it?"

"Mine workings I think; that should be an exit to the surface up there."

Robyn nodded. "I've heard about something like this further south, in Derbyshire. Castleton, that was the place Jeff. Remember, that pot-holer, found the Titan's main shaft back in ninety-nine?"

"I don't think that was a mine, I think it was natural limestone erosion."

"Whatever." Robyn looked around. "No, you're right, Jeff, that bit over there looks man-made." She flip-flopped her way cautiously across the rough surface with Jeff following, heading for an area which sloped gently upwards.

Mark was still standing gazing in something like awe at the vast size of the place. "God, this place is fantastic."

The two others looked back at him. "It sure is, but we haven't got radio communication this deep so we can't stand touristing too much Mark."

They moved around the cavern looking at the exits, several of which went off for a few dozen feet and came to dead ends. Eventually they found one that continued upwards. Mark moved slowly behind them. They had been climbing steadily for about five minutes when Jeff smacked his lips and looked across at Robyn. "You got acid?"

She nodded, "I was just thinking that myself."

They glanced back at Mark panting slightly behind them, "Mark, put your mask on."

Mark looked both a bit puzzled, and dazed. "Eh?"

Jeff walked back and pulled the face mask down onto his face, turning the mixture to the small reserve oxygen tank they all carried.

He took several gulps off his own tank then spoke to Mark. "Listen carefully, Mark. We're going back now, this place is heavy in CO_2, I can taste it." He breathed again while he watched Mark's breathing ease. "Let's get out of here!" the voice came tinnily through the intercom but it was clear to Mark.

They made their way rapidly back through the tunnel and down onto the shore of the underground pool. Jeff spoke through the intercom of his suit, keeping a constant check on Mark's condition, but the forensics man appeared to be fine. They stood on the internal shoreline while he did a final check of their status.

"The least sign of something wrong, Mark, let me know. Slow and steady, lad, but let's get back to the boat."

The journey back was uneventful; they knew where they were going and took careful checks of each other as they retreated. Being helped onto the RIB Jeff looked back and checked his companions again as he pulled off his helmet. All three sat quietly for a minute before they spoke.

"Damn! That was close."

"I'm not even sure I know what 'that' was."

Jeff smiled a bit grimly. "The cave was full of carbon dioxide, Mark; I could taste it."

"Yeah, I've tasted it once before. It's like acid in the back of your throat. You were behind us, Mark, I think you probably got a bigger dose."

"I didn't notice anything wrong," said Mark.

"No, that's the problem, can't see it, smell it, feel it. It just kills you." Jeff smiled grimly.

They travelled back to shore and the unit's truck. Jeff said very little, but he kept glancing at Mark. They were changed and in warm clothing and sitting in the rest area before he spoke. He called across to one of the other men. "Boyd, got a fag for a desperate man?"

The policeman addressed nodded in some surprise and brought over a packet of cigarettes. "Thought you quit, Jeff."

"I did, but I've decided it just might have saved my life."

The cigarette was offered and Jeff had indulged in a couple of long drags, and a good cough, before he offered an explanation to Mark. "I want you to get a check-up before you go back in the water, Mark. In fact you're not on my team until you do."

He took a more gentle assault on the cigarette. "The cave was full of CO_2. I smoke, and so does Robyn; we're used to poor air quality so it didn't get to us quite so quickly. You, my lad," he pointed a finger and cigarette, "are too clean-living, you were panting. I bet you've got a thumping headache." He raised an eyebrow in question.

"Bit of one." In truth Mark could feel the pain behind his eyes like a red-hot needle.

"See a doctor. And I don't want you near the water until you've got the all clear." He went on to debrief the rest of the team. "Tomorrow we go back in. I think that body might have come down from the cave; I want to know how it got in there. We take extra O_2 and we keep alert. We need to find a local who knows the geology round here, a farmer, walker, miner, someone. See if we can't find the land entrance to that cave."

"I think I might know a geologist." Mark offered the comment. He didn't like being excluded from his own domain, but he wasn't so egotistical that he couldn't see the sense in the diving leader's comments. He'd sat quietly, wondering what he'd say to Inspector Bell. He felt he'd let the team down; now he saw a way to redeem himself.

9

Part of the diving team was gathered at the Greystone doctor's surgery. Morning clinic had finished and the evening bout hadn't started. The room wasn't crowded, at least not compared with students filling a telephone box for the *Guinness Book of Records*; trouble was this wasn't a telephone box, and those in it weren't students.

Both Sandy and Bob were sitting in chairs; they wore equally anxious expressions normally seen on expectant fathers. Mark was behind the green curtains surrounding the examination couch. He hadn't objected to them being in the room, it wouldn't have made a lot of difference if he had. Jeff leaned against the door alongside Robyn, their dark police uniforms adding to the sombre feel of the room. Sandy noted casually that they were holding hands and filed the information away for future reference.

Jenny emerged first, leading with a sympathetic smile in her eyes. "No damage done, the exposure was minimal from his account, and he's a healthy young man."

She watched the two older men sag slightly in their chairs. Bob had arrived on the doctor's doorstep twenty minutes ago with such a serious expression, she wasn't sure if she was to be arrested or to attend a multiple pile-up. He'd more or less plucked her outside and hustled her across to the surgery at such speed she wasn't sure if she'd walked or he'd carried her.

The others had been waiting at the glass doors, looking between them anxious, bewildered, or just plain scared, according to their inclination. What Bob McInnis felt she had no idea, but his actions shouted concern, so she'd responded.

Sandy had briefly filled her in with the events of the last few hours for the diving team. Now she spoke to him as the senior person present. And the one with the biggest frown on his face.

"I'll give him something for the headache, Inspector Bell." She nodded at Jeff as she addressed him, "But he can go back in the water whenever he wants."

Mark came through the curtain, fastening his white shirt. "I told you I was alright, sir. It was only Jeff being ultra careful. Not that I blame you." He looked at the senior constable. "You can't take foolish risks when you're diving."

Jenny went over to the small sink and washed her hands, turning as she used the paper towel and threw it in the swing bin near the door. "Well, gentlemen, I'm for a cup of tea. Why don't you come over to the house and Mark can pick Maureen's brains."

They filed out and stood outside the glass door while Jenny locked it, then Jeff stopped Sandy as the others kept walking. "He did things by the book, sir, I'm not criticising him. But I blame myself; I should have tumbled to the risk as soon as I saw all that still water and limestone. It's a perfect set-up for choke damp," he saw the puzzlement, "stythe…. like firedamp only with CO_2 instead of methane, sir."

"We can aye be wise after the event, Lyell, I'm just as culpable, I didn't ask if he'd done any cave diving. Just took it that if you could dive in water it was all the same thing."

Jeff nodded, "Well, we can stand here blaming ourselves or we can learn from it, sir. Do you want me to take him back down? I can keep him off the team; he's not officially a member."

Sandy thought about it. "No. That implies a lack of trust in the pair of you. If you want, and he wants, take him down again. We'll see what our geologist has to say." They began to stroll after the others.

The kitchen was full of big men and Maureen Sandman, looking much better, her maternity dress today a pretty shade of lilac, was officiating over the teapot and kettle.

She wasn't quite sure why Jenny had brought them all back, but assumed it was something to do with her husband's murder.

Jenny was fishing mugs out of the dishwasher and lining them up on the work surface. The men and Robyn sat down around the small table, their elbows almost touching in the confined area. Mark introduced them, waiting while everyone was served with their poison of choice before nodding at Jeff to open the questioning.

Jenny came and sat down next to Maureen, and Jack, her dog, stirred enough to wander over and sit down with a thump at her feet, looking hopefully at the assembled company. He was about to be disappointed, no biscuits fell his way.

"Mrs Sandman, Mark here tells me you're a geologist?"

"Call me Maureen and, yes, that's right." An expression of bewilderment sidled across her face; whatever she'd been expecting it wasn't to be questioned about geology.

"The diving team," he looked at Jeff then waved a hand at himself, Mark and Robyn, "well we've got ourselves a limestone cavern, off the foreshore. It comes inland a fair way, and we're trying to find a safer way into it. Have you got any maps of the underground areas? Caves, and old mine workings, and such?"

Maureen started to rise but Jenny stopped her. "Tell me, and I'll fetch them." Maureen directed her to the cabinet in the sitting room and looked at the police. "Is this to do with Neil's death?"

"We think it is, Maureen. Mark found another body yesterday and we think the two deaths might be connected."

191

Maureen looked across at the young forensics man. "I thought, that is Jenny said, it was found in the sea?"

"Yes it was, but we were investigating the site and it led upwards away from the sea and inland towards a series of caverns. You were telling me there was a geological anomaly hereabouts. I think we've just been in the middle of it."

"Oh how wonderful!" For a moment Maureen's eyes sparkled with interest. "Neil would love to..." She stopped and the men looked at each other in embarrassment.

"I'm sorry, Maureen, we can ask elsewhere. It was thoughtless of me." Mark looked like a whipped puppy. He started to stand, but Maureen reached out a hand, looking squarely at him.

"No, it's OK. I'm being foolish. Neil would want me to help." She looked up as Jenny returned with a sheaf of papers and small booklets.

"These what you want, love?"

"Yes." Maureen shifted her bulk so that she could spread a map out on the tabletop. The men obligingly placed their mugs on the corners to keep it down, and shuffled sideways to give her room. Sandy reached into an inside pocket and put his glasses on, and they all leaned forward, looking at the paper in front of them as if it contained the secrets of the Rosetta Stone.

"Now, this is North-West Cumberland. You can see that it's colour coded for the different rocks. If we start with Scafell Pike across to Shap it's volcanic."

"Ye gods, Bob, I didn't know we had volcanoes here!" Sandy looked in a horrified way at Bob, as if he'd just discovered that his favourite ginger nut biscuits were actually deadly poison.

192

"We haven't, Sandy. We had." Bob exchanged a quick amused smile with Jenny, who was desperately trying to change a gurgle of laughter into an unconvincing cough.

Maureen looked at Jenny in a puzzled manner, but continued, "The next block, Egremount up to Cockermouth and across to Blencathra, they're known as Skiddaw rocks, unique to that area. Then you've got a narrow band of limestone circling it, above that gritstone, and above that sandstone. But," she laid a gentle fingertip on the area next to Maryport, "if you look at the map, the gritstone and sandstone meet just about where we are in Greystone, and between them there's this little outcrop of limestone. That's your anomaly."

"OK, I've got that." Jeff was frowning at the map. "Now was it mined, for lead?"

"Very good, Sergeant. Lead it was. A small independent mine. Didn't last long, it was played out within twenty years, back in the 1890s. That's what brought me here four years ago; I'd been studying some old journals and read about it, and wanted to see for myself."

"So you know where the entrance is?" Jeff beamed at her and then his face fell as he watched the curls swaying with her negative shake of the head.

"'Fraid not, Sergeant,"

"Oh!" Jeff looked at the others.

"Didn't you spot any metallophytes?" Bob said looking first at Maureen, and then at Jenny, hoping for inspiration. "What would they be around lead?"

Jenny shook her head. "I dunno."

Maureen smiled. "You are an interesting man, Inspector, and you're right, I looked. I found some pansies and sandwort, on the bouse and shoad ore, but I couldn't find the entrance to the mine."

Bob nodded in understanding.

Sandy, who'd been turning his head in the manner of a man watching a quick-fire game of ping-pong, now held up a hand. "Will someone tell an old man what the h… what you're all talking about? And you," he pointed a finger at his partner, "shut up! You've used more words I don't know in five minutes than I want to think about."

Bob smiled, and Sandy noted that the twinkle went all the way to his eyes. "Sorry, Sandy." He didn't sound sorry though.

"You." Sandy pointed at Jeff. "Why should it be mined? And keep it simple; me and the lad here have got headaches."

Mark grinned in his turn, but held his peace.

Jeff Lyell looked apologetically at the two inspectors. "Where you get limestone, you sometimes get lead, sir. That's how a lot of the old miners spotted the source material. There was a lot of limestone in that cavern and it looked as if it had been worked."

"Shafts and machinery?"

"Not quite. Back in the nineteenth century there wasn't that much heavy machinery; dynamite but not much else to cut down the heavy work. What's more, lead shafts are vertical. That's what tipped me to it, sir. Those shafts we were climbing went up at a shallow angle, say about 1:250, from the main chamber and you could see the rotten timber in some places where the miners had been standing, but essentially we were headed up an offshoot from a vertical shaft."

He looked at Maureen. "We went through a flooded cavern, a shaft, a partially flooded one, another shaft, and then we were in the clear, and into another shaft more vertical than the first two."

"Hang on a minute, I thought mines had levels."

"Depends what you're mining, sir. Coal, that goes along a seam, horizontal. Lead that goes beside a seam of limestone, vertical." He watched as Sandy frowned down at the table absorbing the information.

"Alright, lad I understand that. Now, why assume that yon corpse had come from the shaft?"

"DS Oakes said divers had been down to look at the Roman harbour this autumn, and hadn't seen the body. It had been in the water for a bit, sir." He glanced across at Maureen and gave her an apologetic look. "But they hadn't seen it. It had to have come from somewhere. Either out at sea and washed up, or inland and washed down."

Sandy shook his head, not in denial, but more to stem the flow of information for a minute. Everyone waited in respectful silence as he gazed into space and absently stirred his tea.

Eventually Bob started to speak. He didn't get beyond, "Sandy?"

"Haud thee whist." It was said testily.

Bob obediently shut up again. He'd been Sandy's partner for getting on for four years now and had learnt that that tone didn't mean annoyance, just deep thought. He looked at the others around the table, finally coming to rest on the quiet face of Jennifer Lowther. She'd left her hair loose today and it hung in a long golden-brown waterfall, framing her face and curling up at the ends around her shoulders. He cocked his head, admiring the look of her. She, it seemed, was more concerned with monitoring the doctor's wife.

Bob wondered how long Jennifer would stay. Would she keep the surgery going? He wasn't sure how it worked but he had a feeling you had to buy yourself into a practice, and with no one to share, that could be a pricey business.

He made a mental note to see who might be interested in a snug little practice in the country, or even who would benefit from a practice closing down. He shook his head quietly, what kind of word was practice? Didn't they know how to do it right? His musings were interrupted by Sandy.

"So what it amounts to is this, you –" he pointed at Jeff "– think the second body might have come from the caves. Which you now tell me are probably mines. And because of the body's position and the estimated length of time it's been in the water, you think the crime scene is inside those mines."

He swung round, his face gentling as he looked at Maureen. "And you, tell me that you think there is a mine somewhere around here, but you don't know the entrance. I suppose you've asked around the locals, lass?"

Maureen nodded.

"Aye I thought you would have." He looked at Jeff. "We've got to find that crime scene, and while I understand you going through the entrance you have got, I want another entrance. I'll lay a pound to a penny the crime wasn't an underwater one. You never mentioned diving equipment on yon corpse did you, Mark?"

Mark shook his head. "No, it was dressed in ordinary clothes, sir."

Sandy pushed back his chair. "I'm going to get some men; I want this area searched for that mine." He swung around again, looking at Maureen. "Have you still got the journals?"

"Yes, Inspector."

"Good. Bob, get 'em and take 'em to some of your research friends. I want someone to try and see if we can't find something through the paperwork. Two pronged is maybe quicker."

McInnis nodded; Sandy had evidently got some plan on his mind. He knew Bob had avoided the circle of researchers that Beth had introduced him to during their short marriage. To be asked to visit them, Sandy must want something more than just another entrance to the cave.

Sandy, issuing orders to Jeff while he put his glasses away and straightened a tie which would be back at half mast in the space of an hour, left the room and the mugs behind. Mark and Bob were left with the two civilians, who were sitting at the table with slightly stunned expressions on their faces.

Bob smiled nicely at them both. "He's hard to hold when he gets the bit between his teeth." He looked at Mark. "Take it easy for the rest of the day, Mark." He held up a hand. "Yeah I know. The Doctor here gave you the all clear, but I don't want to have to go and talk to your father, I hate that job." They exchanged a look. "If I might have those journals?"

"I'll get them for you, Inspector." Jenny stood up and came around the table, ignoring the other two, to follow McInnis out of the room.

He followed the jeans. Now that, he thought, deserved to be showcased in jeans, unlike the last bottom he'd followed. Beth would laugh at his description. He sobered; there wasn't a Beth to share the joke with anymore.

Jenny, turning around from a shelf of books and magazines, was stunned by the misery she surprised in his eyes. "Inspector? Is something wrong?" She reached out a hand, only to snatch it back when she caught his icy look.

"No, Doctor I'm fine. Are those the journals?"

197

He didn't look fine to Jenny Lowther; he looked like a man in pain. But she could hardly ask outright if he didn't want to tell.

McInnis reached out a hand and took them from her.

"I don't actually know which journals you need. But these are the ones Maureen talked about earlier in the week. I was going to have a shufti; it pays to know where you might need to go, to rescue a body."

"Shufti, from the Egyptian 'to look', Beth used to..." Bob stopped speaking, turning around and going swiftly back out of the room towards the kitchen.

Jenny stood looking after him, blank astonishment on her face, clutching some more, slightly dusty, journals to her size thirty-six bust. What on earth had she said now? He really was a strange man. Handsome, but strange.

Left alone, Maureen scrutinised the young forensics man's face. "What did he mean you've got the all clear? Are you ill?" She scanned a face which might look embarrassed, but otherwise was healthy.

"It's nothing to worry about. I had a little accident while we were down in the caves."

Maureen leaned back, looking him over more carefully. "Did you fall?"

"Nah, just a bit too much CO_2."

She checked his face. "Nasty! It can sneak up on you. Jenny gave you the all clear?" She laid a hand on his arm.

"Oh, yeah! Don't worry."

"What did Inspector McInnis mean when he said he didn't want to talk to your dad?"

Mark rubbed a hand over his hair, making the curls flatten and spring back up with its passing. He looked like a small boy who'd been caught with his hand in the cookie jar. "It was scary for a bit there, that's all."

"Well, take care." She smiled at him and Mark, with the enlightenment of a thunderbolt, realised he'd just done the unforgivable: he'd fallen in love with another man's wife. He pushed back his chair, avoiding her eyes as he looked at the mugs on the table.

"Do you want another drink?" He was amazed at the calmness of his voice as he stood up.

"No thanks, I'll only have to go to the loo, again." Maureen, unaware of her companion's thoughts, gave a small chuckle. "I think this baby must be practising pirouettes on my bladder now."

McInnis entered the room as Mark took the first few mugs to the sink.

"Inspector, did you find the right journal?"

"Er! No."

Mark must have caught something in his tone, for he swung around from the sink and looked at Bob curiously.

"Er! Doctor Lowther wasn't sure which one I needed to look in."

"I'll come and have a look for you." Maureen struggled to her feet as Mark moved closer to her. He laid a hand under her arm and helped her up.

His actions distracted Bob enough to bring him part way out of his misery; Jenny, coming through the door with several more magazines in her hands, finished the job. He took a firm grip on his emotions, shoving them behind the door marked 'private' in his brain. Pretty soon, he thought, he'd be afraid to open it, in case everything tumbled out onto his head, like Charlie Brown's toy-closet.

Jenny laid her burden down on the table. "I wasn't sure which one, Mo', so I brought them all."

Maureen subsided onto her seat again with a slight wince, rubbing softly at a limb which was poking out.

McInnis watched her and offered sympathetically, "I really am sorry to trouble you, Maureen."

"No it's alright, Inspector. Let's have a look at these journals." She began to sort them into two piles on the table while the other three watched. "Those are the ones for the Permian/Triassic periods, that's not it." She pushed them to one side, "Now, it's one of these." She started flicking through the contents pages.

Bob and Jenny pulled up chairs and sat down again, each taking a section of the small pile and began reading the contents pages themselves. Mark shrugged; he remained standing next to Maureen's chair watching the search.

He hadn't a clue what to look for, and he had other things on his mind. He looked down on the red curls near him, absorbing the faint smell of honeysuckle he would forever associate with the young woman near him. What the hell was he going to do about this situation? It was ridiculous; he didn't even believe in love at first sight.

He was lost in thought when he became aware of being addressed, and not for the first time, he gathered.

"Mark, stop wool-gathering man! Maureen asked you a question."

Mark, finding he was the cynosure of all eyes, blushed furiously. His fair skin had been the bane of his existence in his teenage years and he thought he'd overcome the habit. Evidently not!

"I'm sorry, I was thinking about something else, sir."

"That was obvious. She must be some looker, man, to bring that expression to your face."

Mark directed a different expression towards McInnis, one that any sergeant in the army would have had no problem in classifying as dumb insolence. "Sorry, sir." The blandness rivalled wallpaper drying for interest.

Maureen, who'd been looking from one man to the other, now said, "Mark, can you describe the shafts you went through before you got to the final one? How wide they were and the angles? I've had an idea, I don't know if it will help but…"

"Yeah, sure." He paused, thinking about the route before telling her, "Finally we came out in this huge cavern, there was a tiny hole to the surface way up in the roof, and the shaft we took was at a gradual angle. But there were several shafts; most of them were dead ends though."

Maureen had been sitting with her finger inserted in the pages of a journal; now she opened it and swung it round so that he could see it. "How deep would you say your cavern was? Do you think it could have been one of these 'bell pits'? It says here that they are usually about thirty to forty feet deep." She tapped the page.

Mark glanced at her face and then picked up the journal and began to read. McInnis and Jenny Lowther watched as he frowned over the description. Eventually he laid the paper back down. "Yeah, that's actually a fairly good description. But it says the miners would sink a new shaft. Ours went onwards both ways."

"OK, but what I was thinking, I was looking for the kind of disturbance you would get over on Alston Moor. The Nenthead mines had hydraulics and reverberatory furnaces. Lots of stuff is still visible. But if it was a bell pit mine there wouldn't be that much outside now. What's more I was probably looking in the wrong place."

She turned to another journal. "This was the original article that I found, Inspector, but maybe you should take this one too. See what your friends can make of it."

"Thank you, Maureen, you've been very helpful." McInnis stood up with a slight scrape of his chair. Mark handed over the first article and Bob picked up the second. "I'll get these back to you as soon as possible."

"I don't think you need worry, Inspector, I'm not likely to be hunting for mines, or fossils, or anything else, for a little while, given my size." She offered him a gentle smile and smoothed her dress over the bump at her front.

"Er, No!"

"I'll see you out, Inspector." Jenny stood too, and with her dog at her heels walked towards the door. "I'll just give Jack an airing, Maureen, before evening surgery. Won't be long." She nodded at McInnis who was holding the door for her.

Mark suddenly became galvanised into action. "I'll come with you, sir. I can tell Jeff what we think we might have discovered." He seemed to Bob to be desperate to go.

He shot out of the door behind his superior with barely a backward glance at his hostess. Maureen heaved herself up as the front door swung to with a gentle thud. They were a funny lot the police, always jumping about and rushing off. She began to stack the remaining journals into a pile.

Sandy was organising with gusto. Men who had been gently ticking along found themselves caught up in the maelstrom of his energy. He took all but three women police officers off the paperwork, and the rest were astonished to find themselves cast out into the cool September afternoon, some to start disturbing townsfolk, others set to climbing up the nearest hillside with instructions to look for pansies, among other things.

McInnis caught up with him in the incident van. He went and sat down at the corner table and started to organise his notes while he waited for Sandy to finish giving instructions.

"We aren't going to find it tonight, Sandy. It'll be dark before they've even started on the foothills of the young mountain out there."

"I'm not daft, Bob; I've only got a handful searching for the mine itself."

"Did you really tell them to look for pansies?" Bob couldn't have stopped the smile if he'd tried. "I wasn't sure Gareth had got it right; he looked as scandalised as a Nonconformist told to go to the pub."

Sandy grinned in his turn. "Yeah, well, I was half serious, Bob. But actually I've got them canvassing the village to see if there are any old folk whose parents or grandparents might be able to give us a lead."

"I don't think you'll find anyone about here that old." Bob raised an eyebrow.

"Och, you know what I mean, lad. We need to find the entrance this end and if what that lassie says is right, maybe we can connect our two bodies."

"What are you thinking, Sandy? That the Doctor was killed for showing too much interest in the whereabouts of the cave, and the same person killed both? Why not leave the body there then?"

"Dunno, Bob. Maybe someone wanted information from the man?" He sighed heavily. "We haven't found a really good motive yet that could be acted on. Every time I think we might have found someone either they haven't really got a motive or they haven't got the means, or dammit, they're alibied." Sandy sat down with a soft thump opposite, rubbing his hand over his hair and yanking his tie down.

"We're missing something, Bob."

"What have we got, Sandy?"

"We've got a dead doctor who was abducted by means unknown, for reasons unknown, nearly two weeks ago, and dropped into Maryport harbour, with a millstone around his feet." Sandy scowled.

"And we've got a body found in the sea less than half a mile away, which has probably, but not necessarily, come from some caves that have their origin in the same area as the good Doctor. Only this body is anything between two months to two weeks older and many years younger. On the face of it, Sandy, they have nothing in common." Bob looked across the table, his serious face frowning at his partner's frustration. "But your gut and mine, and even, God help us, Mark's, say they are connected. We just can't see the connection."

Sandy nodded somewhat grimly then pointed a stubby finger "That the journal?"

"Yes." Bob McInnis pushed it and the second one forward, filling Sandy in on the conversation about bell pits.

"These damn murders are full of things I don't understand Bob. What with the diving and now mines, I'm more than just at sea, I'm buried inland too." He grimaced, the lines of his face wavering like a heat haze on hot tarmac.

"Are we any further forward with Doctor Sandman's timeline?"

"We know he got up early to visit a pair of twins with colic at two in the morning of the day he was due to start his holiday. I've spoken to the young mum and he did call. She was quite upset about him dying, as much for herself as the Doc I think.

"We know he planned to visit Mrs Paton on the same morning with a recommendation, according to his notes, that her son should have more help caring for her. Those are documented on the computer." Sandy shook his head in frustration.

"One of the constables went round and checked. Mr Paton, her son, says the Doctor never came. They're on the phone, but the son, who's the sole carer, says he just thought the Doctor had been too busy, so he hadn't worried or called, since it wasn't urgent. It was just a final check-up. His mum has had a nasty chest infection."

"So some time after visiting the babies and before going home for breakfast and bidding his wife goodbye, the man, and his car, disappeared. We haven't found his car, Sandy. We've had a few more reports since your initial one and they've been thorough. Maryport now has several wrecks it didn't know about, but no doctor's car so far. They'll keep looking though."

"Have we any idea what might have taken him to Maryport, Bob?"

"I was at the small cottage hospital when Jeff turned up with Mark and Robyn this afternoon. They generally get the local GPs to check on their own patients there. They were a bit surprised actually; he was very good about visiting his patients and hadn't called on one. Then someone remembered he was due to go on holiday so no one worried too much.

"He was a local, but no, Sandy, that weekend he didn't turn up and he wasn't missed. He must have been dead already. He was going to Carlisle to catch the 8:15 train, and planned to leave his car in the long-stay car park there. It's not there, you checked with traffic yourself."

"And the car hasn't been found this end either. Damn!" Sandy rubbed his hands over his face, smoothing away the wrinkles for a minute. "Someone must have seen him after he left home. It's not as if this place is crowded with streets; if I have to knock on every damn door myself, Bob, I'm going to find someone who saw him leave."

They sat quietly thinking. The two female constables at the other end of the van got up and left their computers, going off duty. The detectives continued to sit; the only sound in the van was the increasing rain on the roof which was rapidly turning into a persistent drumming sound. Bob McInnis glanced upwards and opened his mouth to pass a comment, then closed it again as Maureen Sandman came into the van.

Both men stood up as she stood just inside the door, shaking the water off her wildly curling hair and pulling her wet dress away from her legs. Sandy pulled a chair forward. "Lassie, you should have asked one of the constables to fetch us, instead of coming out in this." He in turn looked at the roof.

She took off and shook her cardigan. "It's alright, Inspector, I don't melt." She moved to take the seat. "Though it is coming down much heavier now. I've only walked a few yards."

Bob offered a clean handkerchief, and with a quick smile she mopped her face, and then laid it over the arm of the chair to dry. They waited for her to finish fussing with it. She glanced from man to man. "I had an idea, I don't know if it's any help but…"

"Yes, lass?"

"Well, Neil gets the caving magazine, I'd forgotten. Only Jenny brought some through to the kitchen with the other journals. I know Mr Paton got it too, because Neil said they compared notes and talked about articles sometimes. Maybe Mr Paton might be able to help you. Only you'll have to go and talk to him; he's looked after his mum for three years now so he hasn't been able to get out and do any caving. Especially since his wife left."

The detectives looked at each other.

"I understand your husband was due to pay Mrs Paton a visit, the day he was to go on holiday."

Maureen shrugged. "I'm sure he mentioned something about it at teatime on Thursday; she'd been ill and he had some results. He didn't always tell me where he was going, Inspector. He was very particular about patient confidentiality, but I remember that, because he said he would take his bags in the boot and go straight to the station from there and wouldn't come back. He had an early train and he hated feeling rushed."

"Didn't you wonder at him not coming back to bed?"

"Not really, I've not had an easy pregnancy and I've been tired. If he had a call-out he often went into the spare room when he got back so that he wouldn't disturb me. I just assumed he'd let me sleep, and I've had the texts so I wasn't worried."

"Didn't you wonder that he didn't kiss you goodbye?" Sandy smiled to take the sting out of the question.

"He wasn't a very demonstrative man, Inspector. So no, not really."

She chewed a lip, thinking. "What does Trevor Paton say?"

McInnis looked at Sandy then at the young woman. "Mr Paton says he didn't turn up."

"Oh!" She paled slightly.

Mark, making a precipitate entrance at this moment, felt his stomach plunge like a horse on the brink of a precipice. He'd come to find Sandy, to tell him of his conversation with Jeff. He stopped, holding the door open in a nerveless hand while he took in the scene and the presence of Maureen Sandman.

"Shut the door, Mark. You're wringing wet, lad." Sandy eyed the forensics man with some surprise, as the normally brashly confident young man hesitated in the doorway.

"Er, it's OK, sir. I can come back."

"No it's fine, Mark, I'm just going." Maureen stood up, pushing curls back off her face and pulling the pink, fluffy cardigan back around her shoulders. She looked past him to the outside. "The rain's easing off anyway."

Mark swung his leather jacket off and around her shoulders as she drew next to him. "I'll walk you back, Maureen." He offered a faint smile to Sandy and Bob. "Won't be a minute, sir."

The door clicked behind the couple and the two remaining exchanged a glance of puzzlement. "What was that about?"

"Boy's finally learning some manners."

"I'm not so sure, Sandy." Bob raised an eyebrow and the corner of his mouth, making a comical face across the table top.

"You don't think! He couldn't! It isn't seemly; the lass hasn't been widowed a week."

Bob McInnis shrugged. "Just a thought. He was behaving a bit oddly earlier." He shrugged again, dismissing Mark's possible romantic interests in favour of murder. "Will you go and see this Mr Paton then?"

"I think we'll both head over there; it's between home and there that the trail has gone cold. And if yon lassie is right he might know where the mine entrance is, though I don't hold out much hope."

"Me neither; if he had found it you'd think he'd have told the Doctor and his wife about it."

208

Mark returned, wearing his leather jacket and a very serious expression. "I just came back to tell you Jeff's plans for tomorrow, sir, and then I was heading back to Maryport. I think the pain relief is making me a bit stupid to tell the truth."

"So, don't hover, man. Tell us." Bob pushed out the chair previously occupied by Maureen with his foot. Sandy was still pondering the thought of Mark smitten. He looked the young man over as if finding a clue in his murder investigation that didn't belong there. As Mark sat down, puzzlement and astonishment crossed Sandy's face in rapid succession, like a kid chasing a ball through busy traffic.

Mark filled them in: Jeff was going to dive again the next day, but he was taking the whole of his team, and leaving the Lake District team topsides, ready to dive if necessary. "He says I can go down with him, sir. But if you don't mind I'd like to head back over to Carlisle and into my lab. There's work waiting and I might find something, working on what we have, rather than looking for more."

"No, Mark, that's fine." Bob paused. "So long as it isn't a case of not wanting to get back on the horse, man." There was a hint of concern in Bob's voice.

Mark was shaking his head almost before Bob had finished speaking. "No, it isn't that, sir. I'll go back down to prove it to you if you want."

"You don't have to prove anything to me, Mark. Just so long as you're happy about it."

Mark nodded. "I'm going to my parents' home, sir. I'll head over to the lab in Carlisle first thing in the morning, unless you contact me." He stood up and left the van.

"Nah, you're wrong, Bob; he can't wait to get to his lab."

Bob, dragging his mind from assassinations to amorousness, cast his partner a look calculated to kill. "Of course he can't; he knows it isn't 'seemly' too." He sighed, "Come on, Sandy, let's go and talk to Trevor Paton."

The house was within walking distance of the incident van. They strolled past the churchyard and noted the sexton busy digging a hole over near the far wall. An idea prompted by the sight led Bob to remark, "When's Jonesy releasing the body? Any idea?"

"Not sure, sooner the better now, then perhaps Maureen Sandman can move on."

Bob shook his head. "How's she going to move on with his child inside her?"

"We all have to, lad, regardless." He spoke quietly as he cast a look from under his brows, but Bob didn't appear to have heard him. He was looking from the rough map he had to the road sign.

"This is it, Sandy, corner of the high street and Church Lane."

The door to the small bungalow was at the side, while the end faced the main road. It had a thin plastic roof, shielding the door from the elements. Its supports seemed to be provided by a garage forming an extension to the house itself and metal rods outside the door. While McInnis waited for the door to be answered, he turned his head, looking for the source of a faint and persistent squeak, like a very tired mouse on a treadmill.

The noise seemed to be coming from a tumble-dryer in the garage; it was squashed against the wall beside a trail bike. A large car, for want of a better word, stood just inside the garage, with a disabled sticker on the front windscreen. Sandy nudged Bob to get his attention. As Bob pondered if it was actually a converted van the door was opened.

Trevor Paton answered the door with a metal spoon drooping in his hand and an expression of defeat on his face. "Can I help you?"

He looked at their faces in turn and then he looked back down the corridor as a loud clattering noise came from the kitchen. "Come in, I've got to..." He disappeared down the corridor and the two detectives stepped over the threshold and closed the door as they heard him say, "Mother, don't touch that, please." In tones one would use to a toddler.

Sandy took the lead as they followed the source of the voice. Trevor Paton was gently guiding his mother towards a seat. McInnis took in the laundry basket at one side of the stove with an upended pan sitting in it. The laundry would have to be done again. Unless, that was, they liked tomato-stained clothes.

Trevor got his mother sitting and gave her a bunch of keys. She began to turn them over and over in her hands. He straightened up, running a hand over his greying hair and glancing at the washing. "Would you mind keeping an eye on her for a minute while I put that lot back in the machine?"

He grabbed the basket and went out through a side door. Sandy looked at Bob, and then they both looked with a degree of pity at the elderly woman playing with the keys and humming to herself. She ignored them.

"My God, Sandy." Bob wrinkled his nose; the place smelt, a compound of cooking and unwashed dishes and a faint undertone of urine.

"Yeah! And he seems to have some sort of a disability himself. His right hand, did you notice?"

"Yeah, tough."

They kept a cautious eye on her and found themselves seats, gingerly sitting on the hard kitchen chairs as they waited for Trevor Paton's return.

"Sorry about that." He came back into the room, a very thin and white faced man, drying his hands on a towel, his eyes automatically checking the state of the elderly woman. "What can I do for you? "

"I'm DI Bell and this is DI McInnis. We have the Constable's report of course, but we just wanted to ask a few more questions. Partly about Dr Sandman."

"Yes. Well, Dr Sandman said he'd call and check with me, before he went away, but it was just to make sure she was over her infection, after the hospital sent her home."

"And he didn't come to see you. Weren't you worried?"

"Not really, it was just a catch-up after all. I thought maybe he'd had an emergency to attend or something." He turned away. "Do you mind if I carry on while she's quiet? I have to get dinner and she can be a bit restless."

"No, sir, that's fine."

"I don't see many people; I never leave her on her own. It's a twenty-four/seven job Inspector Bell, and I didn't even know about the Doctor's death until the Constable told me." He sighed. "She wrecked the TV."

Bob raised an eyebrow at Sandy as Trevor turned away and started to get equipment out of the cupboard.

Trevor looked across at his mother, checking her, and then filled and put a pan of water on the back of the stove. "I'll need to do some more shopping. Thank God for home deliveries! It's a good job that hadn't started to heat up." He got a jar which, from its colour, had more tomato in it.

"Spaghetti. It doesn't take much chewing, and it's quick. I haven't much appetite these days." He set the pasta boiling and turned back to them.

"You said 'partly', what else did you want to know?"

"Mrs Sandman told us you used to go caving, sir. We wondered if you'd found any caves around here?"

He frowned at them, before turning away and slicing some bread. He went over to his mother, offering her the slice before turning back. "She was probably hungry, that's why she spilt the sauce. Why would you want to know about caves, Inspector? The Constable said Dr Sandman had been found in Maryport."

"He was, sir. But we have a second body now, and we believe it came from a cave near here."

"If you've got the body surely you know where the cave is."

Sandy scratched his ear as he looked at the puzzled frown on the man's face. "Not exactly. The body was found in the sea, but near a cave entrance underwater."

"But you just said you wanted to find the cave." Paton frowned at them and then turned away to check on his food.

"I'm sorry, sir, we're talking at cross purposes here. We've found a second body in the sea near a cave entrance, but we need to know where the same caves come out on land. Our police divers reported seeing the sun at the top of one cave so it must come out somewhere inland."

"Ah! Now I understand. But why come and ask me? I've hardly left the house in the past three years. My mother keeps me busy. So busy that my wife has divorced me and taken the children with her." He spoke with his back to them, but even so they could hear the bitterness underlying the quiet words. "I really don't think I can help you, Inspector."

Sandy pulled the offending ear again. "We were told you still get the caving magazine, sir."

"A man must dream, Inspector, or go mad. But I understand why you're here now. Unfortunately, I can't help you." Paton looked

213

at his mother as she sucked on the crust of bread. They read pity and frustration on his face before he looked up. "I must feed my mother; is there anything else I can help you with?"

"No, sir, we'll see ourselves out."

Paton nodded, turning and beginning to put the pasta and sauce into a plastic dish.

"Shoot me before I get to that, will you, Bob. I'd hate to lose all my marbles and be a burden like that woman is to her son." They headed rapidly back to the area commandeered by the police for their vehicles, to the detriment of the flow of traffic.

McInnis grunted his agreement. But there was something he'd heard or seen in that house, that struck him as odd, and he couldn't quite put his finger on it. He said as much to Sandy.

"I dunno, Bob, the man is too damn busy with his mother to be committing murders. He never gets time off for good behaviour seemingly. Twenty-four/seven he said and I, for one, could believe it." They halted at the squad car where Gareth was sitting waiting, his shift over several hours before.

"I don't think he murdered the Doctor; as you say he'd never have the time. But he said something, Sandy..." McInnis got in the back of the car and leaned back smothering a yawn.

Sandy looked at him and shook his head. "Gareth, take us back to the B and B; my partner can't keep up the pace."

10

The pace was slower the next morning. Sandy headed back to Greystone, he hoped that he'd find a contingent of extra men there to do a bit of searching for him, though even he had to admit it was terrible weather for it. He'd asked for a helicopter to do a few 'fly-overs' but the weather was worsening by the minute.

As he and Gareth drove along the winding road to their destination the windscreen wipers began to go into overdrive. One of them appeared not only to be leaving a repetitive streak but to have a repetitive squeak too. "This will put paid to my helicopter, Gareth."

Gareth, his eyes glued to the murky windshield, grunted in a very un-respectful way. "I don't much fancy crawling about the scenery either, sir."

"No, you and most of the rest of my force. I'll just have to hope we've got a bit of a break in the town itself."

Gareth grunted again. He knew what that meant, hours pouring over interviews or walking from house to house, where as like as not they didn't even offer you a cuppa.

Sandy glanced from the young man to the weather and relapsed into silence. Not that he blamed Gareth for a mood as grey as the clouds currently tipping their load on the car roof. The whole thing was slowing down, including the squad car; he watched Gareth change down to fourth as the wipers went into frenetic mode.

They needed something to work with other than patients with grudges. "Did we get anything back yet from Mrs Sandman's phone, Gareth?"

"Not yet sir; forensics said they would try and track the texts supposedly coming from her husband, but the number calling her was out of area."

"You'd think his wife would have wondered at that."

"Why sir, he was supposed to be out of area and she expected texts from him. No reason to suspect that it wasn't her husband calling from his phone."

"Whoever it was that was texting must have got her private number from somewhere."

"We asked about that, sir. Several of the townswomen who are pregnant had it; she'd got a list of friends and family on there, plus the butcher, baker and candlestick maker." Gareth sighed, slowing the car further and going down to third gear.

"Eh!"

Gareth risked a hasty glance sideways. "I only meant she used it to phone tradespeople in Maryport, chief. She must be lost without it if she hasn't got a list of those names."

"OK." Sandy sighed with relief as they rounded the last bend that brought them within sight of the thirty sign for Greystone. "I'll see what the knock on doors produced last night, Gareth. And you, my lad, can assist me."

Bob McInnis wasn't looking for assistance, but he'd got it anyway. He and DS Oakes were in an unappealing little room off the main office of Maryport police station. A small narrow window let in dubious light; a naked bulb didn't add much to the aura, besides being one of the new eco-lights which looked so ugly to McInnis.

216

McInnis settled on his seat and shivered slightly. The room had three sides to the weather and it felt damp and chilly. Oakes was laying the groundwork for the interview with Andrew Hamilton.

"So you say you run a charter, Mr Hamilton?"

"Yes, I've got a nice little six-berth yacht. I take private parties out, sometimes across to the Irish Coast, and sometimes down towards Liverpool."

"Do you manage the boat by yourself, Mr Hamilton?"

"No, my son acts as crew most of the time; we came in on the morning tide." He looked up as a constable came in with a tray of pottery mugs and set them down on the wooden table.

"Thanks, Constable." McInnis looked up at the fresh young face of Officer Pretty; so did Oakes.

"On the door, Constable."

Pretty went over and stood at parade rest next to the door. He watched as Oakes handed over a mug to Hamilton.

"It's very good of you to come in, sir."

"I must admit I'm glad of this coffee, Sergeant. I've only had about four hours' sleep. It was a lousy crossing too."

"Yes, sir, I can imagine." McInnis had seen the waves outside the harbour entrance that morning as he'd looked out of the bedroom window of his temporary abode in the B and B. The waves had made him feel distinctly queasy, and he wasn't even on them. He didn't think he'd make a very good sailor.

"Can you tell us what you think you might have seen, before you set out on this latest trip, sir?"

Andrew Hamilton set the mug down and rested his hands around it while he looked at the two officers who waited patiently for him to gather his thoughts. He gazed off into the right hand corner of the room for a moment or two looking at a damp patch on the ceiling which had started spreading some time ago and now appeared to be making a takeover bid for the wall too. He brought his thoughts and eyes back into focus, looking at the officers seated before him. He nodded at McInnis as that man pulled an A4 pad towards him and held his pen ready.

"I generally sleep over, the night before I sail. I like to make sure everything is on board, supplies of food and fuel, bait and such like. But my son, who's also Andrew, but we call him Drew, he likes his own bed. He got married this summer, so that's understandable. My wife says she gets a decent sleep when I'm away, claims she doesn't have to listen to me snoring." He offered a grin.

"Anyway, I'd gone to bed about midnight Thursday, high tide was at five, and Drew was supposed to be coming on board at four thirty with the couple of men who'd hired us. We were hoping for some sea bass."

He picked up his mug and took a sip. "About four or thereabouts, something disturbed me – I thought it was my son in the car, I'd hardly been to sleep a couple of hours, so I was feeling a bit groggy, not to mention grumpy." His lips twitched wryly. "I got up vowing vengeance on my son for disturbing me, but when I got out on deck I couldn't see much at all. It was thick cloud and pi..." he paused, watching as Bob finished writing and held his pen, looking at Andrew inquiringly. "Well anyway it was raining hard. Visibility was seriously restricted."

"What did you do then, sir?"

"I scouted around the boat, called Drew's name but he hadn't come on board. I felt a bit uneasy though; there's been a bit of diesel siphoning going on down at the harbour and I'd got a full tank. So I went down and got dressed again and came up on deck with a torch intending to check and see if anyone was about."

Andrew finished off the mug, and sat back looking out of the tiny window which gave the appearance of travelling through a car wash, as the water sluiced down. He returned his gaze to the two policemen, "It was raining as hard as it is now and I wasn't inclined to mess about too much. I checked the ropes and the buoy and just as I was going back down to the cabin I heard a splash and maybe a voice but I just thought it was someone else throwing over a tyre as a fender, to prevent bumps; it was pretty choppy on the water. I didn't think any more about it until I heard about Dr Sandman being found in the harbour."

"That's very clear, sir." McInnis laid down his pen. "If I could just have a few more details?" He began asking questions, filling out the story; the names of the passengers, when they'd booked. When the son had arrived. If he had seen anything odd as he'd brought them around to the boat?

At the end of two hours the police felt they had got all the information they were going to get form Andrew Hamilton who, despite the rain, felt as though he'd been wrung dry.

Constable Pretty escorted him out of the building and returned to the small, almost cell-like, room. McInnis nodded to him. "Give me your impressions, Pretty."

Constable Pretty, a spasm of something terrifying crossing his face, gulped and drew himself to attention. "Yes, sir." Then he relapsed into silence. Neither senior man thought he'd gone dumb; they waited for him to speak.

"He told the truth, sir, about the fishing and hiring but he was lying when he said he didn't check out the splash. Sir." Pretty stopped abruptly.

"How do you come to that conclusion, Pretty?"

"He looked out the window, sir."

219

Oakes raised an eyebrow, looking out the window himself. "It's pissing it down, Pretty. Why shouldn't he look out the window?"

"No, sir, when he started he looked right, gathering his thoughts and recalling events. When he started to lie, he looked out the window, it's on the left sir. He was creating, making things up."

"So why do you think he started to 'create', Pretty?" Bob asked the question almost gently.

"He shouldn't have been annoyed at being woken. He said his son was coming on board at four thirty. He should have been stirring at four anyway. Perhaps he was already awake stealing a bit of diesel himself, sir. Running charters costs a bomb, and diesel has gone through the roof this summer. Maybe he saw someone else doing something they shouldn't have been doing but didn't want to betray them."

"Do you think he saw the Doctor being dumped?"

"No, sir. He came forward, and maybe he needn't have, but he might have figured that Mr Pheby would have given you his name, so he was covering himself. I think he heard something. But then I think he got on with his own business because he saw it was a dark night, sir." Pretty relapsed into silence standing in front of the two detectives, his blues spotless and his face serene.

Oakes allowed a grin to appear on his face. "Those, young man, were the conclusions we had come to. You and I are going to check out his story a bit more and see if we can find out just what the man is hiding from us.

"Dismiss." McInnis ordered, and they waited while Pretty left the room.

Oakes and McInnis stood up. McInnis handed over the file. "I think it probably gives us confirmation of the time the Doctor was put in the water, don't you, Oakes?"

Oakes nodded.

"I'm going across to Greystone later today. Is there anything else we need to know before I go over there?"

"Not at present, Inspector."

"Before I go I'm going to see the Simpson boys. I've spoken to their parents and you have my written report."

Oakes nodded. He had indeed had the written report of the parents' interview. He had been awed by the copperplate handwriting and overawed by the recommendations for the whole family.

McInnis had suggested that Constable Simpson be given a severe reprimand and sent to a different area for the remainder of his training, but that no other punishment should be given. McInnis suggested that his record should not be marked either. Considering the chaos it had initially caused the Carlisle men, Oakes thought that was more than generous.

As to the parents, while they had attempted to pervert the course of justice by withholding evidence, McInnis again recommended that no action be taken. Given that sort of generosity, Oakes felt he could trust the man to interview the teenagers. It had taken him some time to acknowledge that he was not just defensive about his own role, but also the impressions he had wanted to give of his town, and his people.

"I'd like to take Constable Pretty with me?" There was half a question. Again Oakes was conscious of Bob's generosity. He wasn't sure he, in the same position, would have bothered to ask.

"I'll tell him to meet you outside with a squad car when you're ready, sir."

"No, don't bother with a squad car. I'll take my own."

"Right, sir."

221

"Half an hour, I have a couple of phone calls to make."

"Sir."

The rainwater ran noisily in the gutters and down the drainpipes as McInnis and Pretty pulled up in front of the house. McInnis was driving; Pretty had been surprised when he was told to get in the passenger seat, but not as surprised as he was when he saw their destination.

He sat absolutely still for a minute as they drew up, looking straight ahead up the road to the Roman fort that could just be seen at the top. Bob McInnis gave him a casual glance before getting out of the car. The expression on Pretty's face could have been caused by indigestion, but McInnis thought it was more probably an indigestible thought.

As they reached the front door he said, "Observe, Constable."

James Simpson let them in, casting a look at the car neatly parked on the roadway. "Inspector? The boys are in the front room."

"You have the right to be there, Mr Simpson, the boys are minors, but I would like to talk to them alone." He waited, standing on the doormat while Simpson thought.

"No, Inspector. You do what you think right. Give me your coats." He turned, hanging up the raincoats and leading the way into the same quiet room. The boys sat together on the settee, looking as if they expected to be hauled away in chains any minute. "Answer the Inspector honestly, John, and you, Chris." He left, closing the door quietly behind him.

Oliver Pretty stood just inside the door, his eyes sympathetic. Bob McInnis sat down opposite the boys on an easy chair, allowing the coffee table to act as a barricade between them. He pulled his notepad and pen out of his pocket and held them both in his right hand while he unbuttoned his jacket and sat back slightly.

John eyed him for a minute in the silence. "We're sorry, sir. It wasn't Chris' fault; I borrowed the boat, he just did what I told him." Chris, going a painful dull red, shook his head but didn't speak.

"And you, Chris, are you sorry?"

"Yes, sir." As whispers went, it certainly did, it slithered off into the ether, hardly registering on the decibel scale.

"You realise that you have caused the police a great deal of trouble by not telling us the truth. You involved your older brother in the lies, and that could have caused him to lose his job."

"Yes, sir." John was now a floury white, in contrast to his younger sibling.

"As to the theft of the boat –" McInnis stressed theft, and watched them both wince "– you will apologise to Mr Pheby and make any reparation he thinks fit."

Two heads nodded in unison.

"Regarding the setting of the lobster pots," he looked at them both severely, "I wish you to visit Mr Paul Saunders. I believe he lives near here. He's an elderly gentleman, so mind your manners. You will oblige me by following his orders."

"Yes, sir."

"Officer Pretty here will report back to me if you misbehave again. That will put him in a very difficult position." He glanced across the room at Oliver Pretty, who maintained a straight face with some difficulty.

McInnis sat forward and for the first time opened his notebook. "Now I have one or two questions to ask you."

He waited for the nod. "When did Mr Pheby's boat go missing?"

He could see the cogs turning; the boys looked at each other. "It was the weekend before last, sir."

"No it wasn't." Chris shook his head and turned to his brother, holding a low voiced conversation. "It was Friday, 'cos I wanted to go to Ben's and you said no, let's go out, and then we couldn't."

"No, that was Thursday."

"No, Thursday we had football, it couldn't have been then."

McInnis couldn't for the life of him stop his lip twitching; he hoped there wasn't going to be a long argument.

"Oh, yeah!" John thought a bit more; McInnis watched as he ticked off days on his fingers, and then poked his brother with the longest digit. "It was Saturday. I was right."

He looked triumphantly at McInnis. "We went out Wednesday night to put the traps out, down near Bank End. It's not a very good place, but it was a bit rough on the sea. We should have gone back for them Thursday, only we had a special footy practice and we couldn't get out later. Friday, Dad made us clean our rooms, and his car." He scowled. "He won't give us pocket money if we haven't earned it."

"Quite right too. Earned money is always sweeter." Bob thought he'd better get them back on track. "So you went to try and rescue your pots, and any lobsters, on Saturday and the boat was missing?"

"I've got a Saturday job, so it was Saturday evening and the light had nearly gone, and so had Mr Pheby's boat. We thought he'd laid it up for the winter, sir." John frowned. "We haven't been able to rescue those lobster pots either, and they cost a lot!"

"Not to mention the poor lobsters caught in them." Bob watched the red riding high again in each boy's cheeks. "I'll get one

224

of the police divers to get them for you and release your captives, if they're still alive. He paused, looking the boys over.

"So you put pots elsewhere?"

"Yeah, in the harbour. You're not supposed to, but we didn't think there would be any harm. Anyway Mum and Dad were at the harvest supper with Lucy. We didn't want to go to that, with all those old people."

McInnis couldn't prevent the grin this time; it had stolen onto his face before he had time to repress it. The horror of attending the harvest supper, when you were a teenager, was something he knew from first hand.

"Now, the night you spotted the body, how did you manage to see it?"

"We've got snorkel gear, sir. I tried to pull up the pot in the harbour and it was stuck fast. We'd got it tied to a bollard on the corner of the dock. I said 'let's get the gear and go down,' 'cos we didn't want to lose our pot. So we nipped home and got the stuff and went back out again. Mum an' Dad were watching TV; we'd never have been allowed out so late if they'd known what we were up to."

McInnis sobered his face. "Alright, so you got your gear and went back, then what?"

"We dived and saw the body." John was going white again, and McInnis thought Chris was a nice shade of green. He looked how McInnis had felt that morning, thinking about going out on those rolling waves.

"And then?"

"We didn't know what to do, so I rang Jamie on my mobile and he came in the squad car and let us get changed before he rang the station, sir. I am sorry we got him into trouble, sir. It wasn't his fault. What will happen to him?" John looked sick too now, as though he'd finally realised that his big brother was in big trouble.

"You leave your brother to me. But remember that all actions have consequences; everyone has to take responsibility for their own actions. Especially when they affect others. Make sure you think in future." He put his notepad away in his inside pocket. The boys sat looking at him, both silent again.

Bob McInnis sat back watching them for a minute. "Now I suggest you get back to school. What excuse did you give your mates?"

John looked horrified. "Didn't tell them anything, sir."

"Well when they ask, and they will, I suggest you tell them you're helping the police. That will boost your street cred; you should always try to keep deceit within shouting distance of the truth because the truth is important, boys, no matter how painful."

"Yes, sir." It was a muted chorus.

McInnis stood up, holding out his hand, as the boys also stood up. He shook each of their hands in turn. "You've been helpful boys. Now don't forget to see Mr Saunders." He pulled a card out of his pocket with the address printed on it.

"No, sir. I mean yes, sir," John nodded vigorously as he watched the tall detective leave the room followed by Oliver Pretty.

Pretty maintained a discreet silence while McInnis said his goodbyes to the parents. "The boys are to visit a Mr Paul Saunders as part of their punishment, Mr Simpson."

Simpson nodded his head. "I know him, lives just up the hill. And James?"

"Constable Simpson will probably be asked to transfer to a different division for a time."

"Thank you, Inspector."

McInnis raised an eyebrow. "For what? You've got a decent set of kids, and we all make mistakes."

He offered both parents a smile and turned and left.

They were in the car and travelling back to the police station before Pretty asked the inevitable question.

"Why did you take me, sir?"

"You tell me, Pretty."

"Because actions have consequences, Inspector?"

McInnis took his eyes off the road and then nodded, before going back to the traffic.

"Good actions and bad actions, especially when it affects others?"

The nod again.

Pretty watched the slightly stern profile for a minute in silence, before asking, "What is Mr Saunders going to do?'

"Mr Saunders belongs to the Wildlife and Wetlands Trust; hopefully he can teach those two a little about conservation. He also owns a boat and needs some crew now that Brian Moore is under arrest." McInnis flashed a grin which was reflected in Oliver Pretty's eyes.

While McInnis might have been satisfied with his morning's work, the same couldn't be said for his partner. Sandy Bell was being frustrated by the weather at every turn. The helicopter couldn't go up; the divers couldn't go down, and the men couldn't go out and search.

He'd satisfied his zeal for action by setting up a whiteboard and arranging a timeline for the doctor's actions for the twenty-four hours prior to his holiday. He looked at it as he sat slumped in his chair eating a ham sandwich. He had the most miserable expression Bob had seen since Sandy had been told by his wife that they were going on holiday, and she'd already packed.

Bob's arrival didn't appear to relieve the gloom. "What's the matter, Sandy, forget the mustard?"

"Hi, Bob." Sandy transferred the hangdog look to his partner.

Bob came and sat down at the small table opposite the white wall. He put a pile of magazines on the table amidst the crumbs, and pushed a white paper bag across with an elegant hand. "Get it while it's hot."

Sandy looked at Bob's face and then at the bag. He started to reach out and then stopped. "What's the catch?"

"No catch, but if you don't want a hot apple pie…" He reached out again, only to have his hand slapped and for Sandy to gather the bag and sniff as he opened it.

The hand that went in and abstracted the pastry was faster than an addict finding some speed. His eyes gleamed almost as brightly as the sugar-dusted, glossy pastry. Sandy spoke a bit thickly through hot apple. "It's appreciated, but I'm sure I'm going to pay for it somehow."

Bob shook his head. "I went into the little paper shop up the road. I had a hunch, and I wanted to check it out. I saw those pies in the warmer, and thought of my boss." His lips twitched.

"So what was your hunch?"

"It didn't pan out, Sandy."

"Tell me anyway, and then we can be miserable together."

"You remember I went in to try to find out if Pheby had an address in the town?"

"Yeah."

"When I was looking over the magazine orders, I spotted the two men Sandman and Paton; they both took the caving magazine."

"So? We knew that, Bob." Sandy took another bite and set the pie down to fan at his open mouth for a moment. He swallowed hastily and took a sip of what Bob presumed was tea. "Hot!"

"Yeah! I'd never have guessed." Bob grinned. "Anyway, I just wanted to see if there was anyone else who took it.

"And?"

Bob shrugged. "Nah. It was just a thought. The young woman in there was grumbling about that lad Eric Potts though; he hadn't picked up his order for the last six weeks, so I brought them along. I wondered if that guy Paton might like them. Thought he might enjoy them."

He lifted the first one to show Sandy the title: 'MOTOR CROSS'. "He'd got a bike in that garage stuck at the side. She gave me them at cost, said she'd already cancelled any more, said Potts would have to come and re-order if he wanted them."

"Yeah. Nice thought." Sandy pulled out his handkerchief and wiped his mouth and fingers. "Now, what's the catch?"

McInnis contrived to look innocent as a choirboy; he succeeded, if you accepted that they invariably had frogs or spiders to put down the choirgirls' necks.

"I was wondering if I could head over to Carlisle tomorrow. I could get the prelim report from Ryan Jones on our second body."

"And maybe call and see Caitlin?"

"Well, if I was over there already."

"You don't need to wheedle for that, Bob." Sandy grinned. "Sarah told me last night that she's getting broody just caring for Caitlin. She says the baby's a little darling."

They exchanged a smile of understanding. Then McInnis stirred and got himself a mug of the liquid they laughingly called coffee, and sat back down to bring Sandy up to date on the progress over in Maryport.

"Andrew Hamilton was lying; we'll find out what he was really up to. Oakes will interview the son and see what he has to say. It'll take time but we'll find out what the man was doing. I said Oliver Pretty was bulging with brains, Sandy. He was spot on with his observations; not one rookie in a thousand would have seen the flaws in Hamilton's statement."

"How about my divers? Mark rang through to say the weather was too bad for any diving today."

"I stuck my nose in the lorry before I came over; both teams were talking jargon and cleaning equipment. Jeff Lyell says he'll get them in the water as soon as he can. He actually said he was glad of a day's respite for them."

"What did you want to see them for?"

"I heard of some prisoners who might need releasing." Bob grinned around his mug, telling Sandy about the Simpson boys and their lobster pots. "I wanted to ask Jeff if he could do me a favour and go over there and let the poor things out if need be."

They continued to discuss interviews for a bit longer, until they were interrupted by one of the senior constables coming in. Since a small window of dry weather appeared to be starting, he wanted to know if the inspector wanted a search beginning.

"How long is this window going to last?" Personally Sandy thought the window was probably the size and description of the pantry window back home, small, dirty, and mostly useless for shedding light, but he didn't say so.

"The helicopter crew said they were going up now and expected maybe three hours, sir, before they were grounded again."

"Right, get the troops up and away then, man. Don't stand there talking to me." Sandy swung back to Bob. "We might not know where it is but we've managed to eliminate some areas where it isn't anyway."

Bob watched as men poured into the room, grabbed yellow jackets, and swung rucksacks onto shoulders before heading out again. He looked at Sandy. "I think I'll join them, Sandy. I've put in a good few hours walking the fells this summer, and an extra pair of eyes might help." Neither of them remarked on why he'd been walking the fells of the Lake District.

"OK, lad, but you take care out there. No solo walking today."

Bob McInnis gathered up one of the visi-vests and slung it over the top of his waxed jacket; he picked up one of the flasks that one of the women PCs was preparing for the searchers. "I'll get my boots and waterproofs from the car." He strolled out of the van as Sandy shook his head. He wouldn't want to roam the fells at the back end of September when more sleety rain was promised, but Bob seemed to need the consolation and isolation to get him through.

When Bob McInnis returned from his car, kitted out with boots and his own rucksack, the teams were being divided into fours and given map references of their search areas. He was surprised to see Jenny Lowther similarly kitted out, with Jack at her heels.

She smiled at Bob from the depths of a hooded jacket, little curls of mousey hair poking out around the mock fur edging. "Jack and I are getting cabin fever; we thought we'd join the search."

Gareth swung over to them, his bulk huge by virtue of the rucksack and the big fluorescent-yellow waterproof. "Sir, there are three of us left so I'm to come with you and the Doctor." He cast a look of puzzlement at the team leader, as that man stood packing away maps that had been spread on the bonnet of a Land Rover. "He said we'd still be a four-man team." He looked down at Jack, who was wearing a bright orange dog jacket and sitting panting at Jenny's feet. "I suppose he meant the little dog, sir."

Bob's lips twitched and he glanced across at Jenny Lowther to surprise a distinct twinkle in her eye as well. But all he said was, "Yes, you're probably right, Gareth. Doctor Lowther, this is Gareth ap Rhys; he's one of our senior constables."

Gareth showed them the map and they walked over to one of the police Land Rovers, throwing their gear on the back seat. Gareth looked at McInnis. "Shall I drive, sir?"

"No, thanks." Bob opened the passenger door and lifted the little dog into the passenger footwell before standing back to allow Jenny to climb aboard. He slammed the door and walked round to the driving side. "Don't stand dreaming, Gareth. Get in the back, and for this little jaunt I think you'd better call me Bob." He lifted an eyebrow.

"Yes, sir." Gareth climbed in the back and, with a faint smile, McInnis swung himself behind the wheel and started the engine.

"It's about ten minutes out of the town and then you'll have to navigate for me, Doc."

Jenny glanced back over her shoulder at the solid bulk of Gareth behind them. "If he can call you Bob, I think I'd better be Jenny to everyone."

Bob McInnis smiled faintly in his turn, but passed no comments, just shifted in his seat and changed up a gear. The next comment again came from Jenny Lowther. "There's a farm track

232

about five hundred yards further, on the right. Take that." She watched as Bob flicked the indicator. "It peters out into a field according to the map, and then it's uphill and on foot all the way."

They turned and jolted along the uneven surface, grass doing an excellent job of cleaning the underside of the vehicle as it brushed up from the centre of the trackway.

The way led first between fenced fields, and then out, as predicted, onto a field bestrewn with erratic rocks and a few unhappy sheep. McInnis nodded at them as he pulled up and applied the handbrake. "They always look miserable," he nodded at the sheep, "but in this weather I don't blame them." He jumped down, his wet weather gear rustling, and slammed the door as the others joined him in the open. He checked his watch with the other two.

"According to the weatherman we've got two and a half, maybe three, hours. It's two fifteen now. We turn back regardless at four. Agreed?"

The others shrugged into their rucksacks and nodded agreement. Jenny leant down and released the catch on Jack's harness. "Off you go, Jack, seek."

The terrier-cross headed up the hill, first racing and then sniffing while he waited for the others to catch up.

The pace was steady; all three were experienced walkers who knew that rushing an uphill climb just left you short of breath. Bob McInnis, after a few minutes of watching the others, looked across at Gareth. "Did you do much walking in Wales?"

"Mainly in Snowdonia, sir. Mountains are mountains, but the colours are different here. It's a bit more grey in Snowdonia except when the sun shines." He continued to stride up the hill as if he was patrolling along a flat street.

"You said you were in the mountain rescue didn't you, Jenny?"

"Actually I'm a 'body' more than a rescuer these days. Jack needs constant training. We're members of SARDA, the Search And Rescue Dog Association. He's had a glorious holiday for the last two months, because I haven't been able to take him out on the mountains." She also strode along confidently. She watched her dog affectionately as he covered twice the distance in half the time, sniffing and snuffling in every small pile of rocks he found.

"Yeah, I was told you'd been ill, something to do with being trapped in a mine?"

"That would be Hayley I suppose. I certainly wasn't trapped in a mine; I was on a search and rescue and we'd been in the mountains for over twenty-four hours. Despite wet weather gear I got a soaking, it's been a bad summer overall, up here in the North. Apparently I had the germs already but getting half frozen and exhausted allowed them enough of a toe-hold to give me pneumonia." She could feel Bob reassessing her face. "Hey, I'm fine. Trust me, I'm a doctor."

"If you cease to be fine, let me know; we can as easily go back as go on." Bob looked at her seriously, to get a twinkling smile in return.

The three of them climbed steadily upwards. At about seven hundred feet they stopped on an outcrop and Bob pulled out his binoculars. He stood scanning the area. The other two waited patiently. Gareth looked off to the West. "You can just get glimpses of the sea from here, sir. I didn't think we were that close."

"It's deceptive, Gareth; I would say that was a good three to four miles away. Let's have a look on the map; we're off the beaten track here but according to the GPS finder…" They huddled around the plastic-covered square of paper, comparing it to the small instrument. "We're here, and that's the main road to Maryport down there. That stretch of coast must be above the old Roman Fort."

234

Bob traced an elegant finger along the route they'd taken. "If we head off in that direction," he looked up the rocky stretch in front of them, "we should be able to see a bit more." He dropped the map back into the front of his rucksack. "Everyone OK?"

"Yeah, fine."

Gareth nodded, turning to look across the hillside. "I know the signs of slate mining but I'm not sure of the signs of lead mining. I'm just looking for scars on the landscape, sir."

"That's all any of us can do, Gareth. It's over a hundred years since this mine was worked, apparently. We can look for limestone outcrops, and deposits in the streams. That was the way the old miners used to find the stuff. It was called shoad ore." He grinned disarmingly at them. "I looked it up after Maureen spoke about it."

"Think of the kudos you could have garnered if you'd not told us that." Jenny turned towards the uphill climb.

"And think of the egg on my face when you found out I didn't know any more than that. I'm an instant expert on all sorts, I am." McInnis grinned at the chuckle from Gareth.

For the most part they climbed in silence, as Sandy would have put it, 'saving their breath for cooling their porridge'. The next ridge was on the fifteen hundred contour line and had required a steep scramble upwards. They stood at the top looking around. Jenny had rosy cheeks and her hood had long since come down; her face was nicely framed by wildly curling hair, and her green eyes sparkled with enjoyment.

Jack came and sat at her feet, panting and with his tongue dangling, as she stood looking round the area. "Not much limestone visible and no streams to quench your thirst, Jack." The little animal shuffled nearer and lifted his chin for her to scratch.

Bob McInnis was checking his watch; he'd unzipped his jacket and now stood with slightly damp hair from the settling dew and exertion. "I don't know how much further we should go; you're right, this doesn't look like limestone country but..." he stamped a foot. "Hear that? Hollow, just like in the Peak District. There's caves under here somewhere." He pulled out the map again.

"I think we might head along the ridge, and we could try and get down that track there and cut back to the Land Rover. What do you think?"

Gareth looked at the map. "There's a stream bed marked a bit further along from that, sir."

"Let's see how long it takes us to get there, Gareth, agreed?"

"Agreed."

They set off again; Jack had ceased to race quite so much and seemed to be content to stay a few yards in front of them. McInnis, watching him, remarked that he must be part goat.

"He was a sorry looking specimen when I got him from the RSPCA. He'd been dumped by the side of the roadway and was too frightened to move. He was just a scrap of bone and hair, and not much more than a pup. I've had him nearly four years now. He's a great little animal, really bright and eager to find bodies."

"Ah! Yes, you said you were a body. I've heard about them. Have you, Gareth?"

"Yes, sir, we get them in the Snowdonia Mountain Rescue Team too. People who train their dogs to find bodies, by being hidden bodies themselves. Takes a lot of dedication that does, Miss." He watched the dog snuffling about among the dying heather and bilberry bushes. "Has he found many?"

"About four so far. People are foolish, they go into the mountains without proper equipment, and think if they have a mobile with GPS locator on it, they don't need a map too. Then they get lost or have a fall and it's 'Oh, dear! Why can't we get reception up here?' Dangerous foolishness!"

"Would you believe I've seen people climbing Snowdon in trainers and with no coats? Just because it's a sunny day and the train takes them most of the way, it doesn't mean it can't turn nasty very quickly up there." Gareth shook his head. "Mind they're mainly southerners and *saeson* too."

Bob turned his head away and grinned. He always found it interesting when Gareth forgot himself and talked freely. That quick turn of the head was to prove a decisive turn in this case, though Bob didn't think so at the time. Jack was running back and forward to an outcrop where a new stream, brought about by the recent rain, was tumbling in a splashy and spectacular manner over the ground.

"Has Jack found something?"

11

The helicopter crew had found something too. They didn't find it necessary to run in circles, but from their elevated height they could certainly see at least three sets of police searchers in the small area, including McInnis and his small team up in front of them and further west.

The navigator and the 'eyes' pointed downwards, then began radioing their position back to the base. Sandy, standing in the incident room listening to them, smiled grimly.

"They've got a car they think, sir."

"Yeah! I heard. Who's nearest?"

The woman PC manning, or in this case womanning, the bank of equipment, was already calling up team leaders to get their positions.

"We've got a team nearby, sir; they'll take about ten minutes to get to it. They're a little off the pathway."

"Right, tell the helicopter to mark the position. Any other team, who can get there in the next twenty to thirty minutes, can go; otherwise I want them to carry on searching for this mine entrance."

"Very good, sir." She started to relay messages to the teams.

She stopped rather abruptly and Sandy wondered at her silence. "Sir, Detective Inspector McInnis is on the line, sir. He says they have another body. A child's body, sir."

"Oh, God!" Sandy reached out a hand. "Give me the headphones, lass."

Bob came through with hardly any static. "Sandy?"

"Yeah."

"We've got a child's body. Or a skeleton at least. The Doc thinks it must be several years old; it's jammed in a culvert. The little dog found it actually. Any chance we can get the helicopter to lift the remains out? I can see it circling from here."

Sandy could hear the drone over the headset himself. "I'll get them contacted, Bob. Can the Doctor give cause of death?"

"Impossible to say at this stage, Sandy. Possibly blunt force trauma to the head. But that could be damage from being tossed down the mountain. This stream is spectacular."

"OK Bob, keep your line open until I can get a team and the chopper to you." He looked down, but the PC was already using a different line to call in the nearest group.

Sandy walked impatiently up and down the inside of the incident van. An aura of excitement emanated from him, like that usually seen outside shops at the start of the New Year Sales; at last they seemed to be making some headway. He was rather in the way of the senior constable checking off men as the groups returned, but that man could hardly tell a senior detective to get out of the way.

The helicopter had managed to land about ten minutes' walk away from the site and Sandy had the radios, hands free so that he could hear what was going on. Nothing much was. He could hear them talking amongst themselves, and occasionally Bob's voice issuing a string of orders but without a picture of the area it was just so much static. Eventually he interrupted. "Bob, talk to me, lad."

"What, Sandy! I'm a bit busy here."

"Yeah! So I can hear, lad. Tell me what's going on, brief as you like, but tell me."

Sandy could hear some muttering and then Bob McInnis came over loud and clear. "There's a new stream caused by the rains and we believe it's washed this body down from higher up the hillside. I've got three teams working their way up the stream to see if they can track the original dump site. They're also making sure that anything lost by the body on the journey down is found."

"OK I've got that. Do you want more men up there?"

"No, Sandy. It's nearly five now. By the time the men get here the light will be all but gone. I'm going to call them back soon, even if we haven't found anything else. I want everyone off the hill before night sets in. We know where we're looking; I'll have men up here at first light scouring the area. The chopper crew are going to take the body back to Carlisle. They're nearly out of gas and flying time, so they must go anyway."

"And the car?"

"There are a couple of teams at the site giving it a once over; I don't know if it's the Doctor's yet. They haven't got back to me."

"That's fine, Bob. I'll debrief and stand down the men this end. Take care, lad."

The two detectives, each at his separate place, dealt with this new body and its investigation and disposal. Bob, true to his word, had everyone off the mountain and back in the town before the light had gone for the day. Gareth went to check in and report their return as Bob escorted Jenny Lowther back to the doctor's house, a hand tucked under her elbow.

"Thank you for your help, Jenny. I'm not sure we would have spotted that body without little Jack doing what he's been trained to do. I just wish it hadn't been a child." He looked down at her face. "You look tired; are you OK?"

240

"I'm just tired as you say, but I can relax now, but you, you've got to find out whose it is now, haven't you?"

Bob nodded soberly. "We'll have to go through the records and find the names of missing children who fit the size and time frame."

"I can't give you a time frame, I'm afraid. It could have been exposed on the hills or buried and deteriorated that way. I'm just not an expert on that. I can tell you that it still had a couple of milk teeth so maybe under ten. And there are signs of old breaks on the arm bones. They've been set and healed, but badly. I wouldn't say there'd been much medical intervention there." She stopped as she reached the door of the house; her green eyes had lost all their earlier twinkle. "I hate child abusers!"

"Yeah! So do I." McInnis frowned down at her.

"You'll keep me in the loop, Bob?"

"If you want, but I don't think this has anything to do with our present case. We'll probably hand it over to a different detective; we've got enough on our plate already." He offered a faint smile. "I'm going to see Ryan Jones tomorrow. I'll ask him to send you a copy of the PM."

"Thanks, will you have time to see your wife, and that baby of yours, while you're over there?"

Bob could feel himself withdrawing from her, his face going stiff and cold as if he was still isolated on the mountain. He did his best to block the reaction. "I'm a widower, Jenny; I thought Maureen would have told you. I'll make sure you get the reports, and thanks again." He turned away abruptly and Jenny was left standing on the doorstep wishing she'd found the damn mine, then perhaps she could have hidden in it, or any other dark hole for that matter. She watched him walk away; she'd not just put her foot in it, she'd damn near got the shoe leather the other side of her appendix.

Sandy watched as Bob came into the incident van. He wondered what was going on in his partner's head at that moment. Bob looked defeated. His shoulders slumped as he reached the privacy of the police van. Sandy poured a cup of coffee and came over with it. "Have a seat, lad, was it bad?"

"Not really, Sandy. Just a skull and a few bones." Bob sat down heavily behind the table and rested his head back against the side of the van, closing his eyes for a few seconds. "The team has found most of the rest of the bones that were missing; they just backtracked up the stream and found them dotted here and there as if the water had washed them apart. It was a young child according to the Doc. Maybe under ten, possible signs of earlier abuse. We'll know more when Jonesy's had a gander at it. It was just a pathetic pile of bones, and rather sad."

Sandy looked around. The van was nearly empty now, the last of the team had gone and only a couple of PCs were busy talking to the senior constable over near the computers. Sandy lowered his voice. "So what else is troubling you, Bob?"

"I'm not sure I can talk about it here, Sandy." He offered a faint tired smile. "Don't fret, man, I'll sort myself out. I won't wreck the investigation."

"Stuff the investigation." Sandy spoke quietly but vehemently as he sat down opposite. "I thought you were finally getting it together again, Bob."

"I am! It's just, I seem to run up against reminders at every turn, and I don't know whether to be sad or happy about that."

Sandy shook his head. "Drink your tea, lad, and go and see your daughter. Gareth would like to have a trip back to Carlisle; he can meet up with that young lass he's secretly courting."

"Don't be daft, Sandy. I need to give you the report."

"Daft I might be, Bob, but we can't do anything until the morning, whether you give me your report now or then." Sandy cocked his head, looking at Bob McInnis.

McInnis shook his head. "I've got to go over tomorrow, and I'll see Caitlin then. Let's get back to Maryport and I can fill you in on everything, over there. I'll be better for a meal and a sit down."

Sandy started to shake his head then caught the look. He offered a faint laugh. "OK, I'll stop fussing; you're right of course. You need to sort out the teams for tomorrow, providing the weather is kind to us."

"Even if it isn't, Sandy, we have to go back up there and gather the evidence. It's a pity Mark is away in Carlisle."

"Mark can get himself back over here; I want my team doing the forensics."

Bob McInnis raised an eyebrow but said nothing, burying his faint smile in the mug of hot coffee. He wondered if Mark realised he'd been elevated to Sandy's team, or just what that meant!

He set the mug down. "Come on, Sandy, let's get back and then I'll tell you about my afternoon."

Sandy's bedroom at the B and B was warm, dry and cosy. The curtains had been drawn against the returning rain, and the central heating was pumping out several watts above tropical, the steamy atmosphere aided by Sandy's recent shower. They had eaten, barely exchanging a word, too hungry and tired to say more than was necessary. Now, however, they were drinking tea, in Sandy's case very sweet tea, and, revived slightly, they prepared to fill in the gaps in each other's information.

Sandy opened the batting. "So, Bob, tell me what reminded you today."

It wasn't the question Bob had been expecting. Sandy was usually more careful about seeming to pry into his partner's life and emotions.

"I must have looked rather bad for you to be this blunt, Sandy."

"You were." Sandy sniffed, running a finger under his nose. "I probably wouldn't be this blunt, but this case is getting me down and, truth to tell, I'm missing Sarah, so God knows how you're feeling." He looked seriously at Bob. "Was it the fact that it was a bairn that you found up there?"

"That didn't help." Bob sighed. "But no, it's having to tell folks I'm a widower. I see the look of pity or disbelief on their faces. I can cope with the grief, Sandy, but the pity gets to me."

"And who was pitying you this time?"

Bob looked embarrassed. "I'm not even sure she was, now I come to think of it. I'm so used to it, I see pity where none is offered. It was Doctor Lowther."

"Ah!" Sandy shook his head, "Concern maybe, Bob, but not pity, not from that lassie." He picked up his mug and drank deeply while he thought. "I don't know what to advise, Bob. Except to grow a thicker skin, lad. People do care and you can't stop them."

Bob nodded, "I know, and thanks." He too drank tea, and the silence settled. When Sandy set his mug down on the scarred dresser, McInnis took it as the signal to start with the day's report.

He pulled out the map he'd been using and started to tell Sandy about the walk. "We'd got a fair way up the hill, looking about, none of us really knowing what to look for. Jack was scouting about as dogs do. About here." Bob pointed on the map and then waited while Sandy found his glasses and wrapped the arms around his ears. "About here, there's a new stream, I think it was flowing down a track made by some lunatic riding one of those light trail bikes.

244

I've seen that kind of track before, further down the country; they tear up the landscape and ruin the footpaths for everyone else."

"OK, so your skeleton came down with the fresh rainwater?"

"Well, not the whole skeleton, Sandy. What Jack found was a little skull minus the bottom jaw, and several ribs and a few other bones. All jammed up against a huge stone erratic."

"You and your erratics!" Sandy shook his head smiling. "What the hell are they anyway?"

"Roughly, they're boulders dropped from the bottom of an ice sheet as it retreats, Sandy. You find them all over the Lake District."

"Well why can't you call 'em boulders then?"

Bob shrugged. "I suppose because not every boulder has got there by being dropped by ice." He watched Sandy's face of annoyance, with a mixture of amusement and affection.

Sandy sighed deeply. "Never mind your erratics, tell me about your body."

"OK." McInnis rubbed a hand over his hair, gathering his thoughts which had been momentarily scattered as badly as the erratics. "We found the skull, and when the teams arrived, I set them to walking the ground uphill. They recovered most of the poor thing's skeleton. I need them to carry on searching tomorrow, make sure we've got it all and anything else that might have been hidden with it. We really need to find the place it's come from."

He brushed the hair back again. "I don't know if this is a dump site. Or if the child had run away and got lost on the hillside. It's a bit early for labelling it murder, Sandy. If it wasn't for the signs of abuse Jenny Lowther spotted, I'd go with lost."

"Yeah you're right. Now this car that the helicopter spotted and the second team found. Could it be Doctor Sandman's?"

Bob scratched his head. "It was behind us over the ridge and into the next valley here, Sandy." He pointed on the map. "See, this is Greystone and there are these paths climbing towards the ridge. We went up this one and the team who found it were behind us and nearer to the town. The ridge runs parallel to the town headed out to the west and the sea. But this part where the car is, well, it curves away up north.

"The car was up this dirt track. The original team say it's largely overgrown. They wouldn't have gone along it if the chopper hadn't directed them that way; they were searching the lower slopes.

"No plates on the car, they'd been removed, but right colour and make. Nothing in it on first inspection. I need to arrange for it to be brought back down, get the wagon from Carlisle to transport it to where we can do some sort of proper forensics on it."

"How did the chopper manage to see it?"

Bob's lips quirked upwards. "Sunshine reflected off the back window. The track fades out into a large rocky area with almost a wall of rock at the top, forming part of the ridge we were walking. The car was tucked into the neatest little crack in the rock; any other angle and they wouldn't have spotted it. In fact ten more minutes and the angle of the sun would have been too low to catch the back screen. Fools for luck we are, Sandy."

"If it is the Doc's car what the hell is it doing half-way up a mountain, Bob?"

"I dunno. I suppose the murderer might have dumped it up there, but whoever it was would have to get back down again."

"Lends more credence to your theory of a two-man job, Bob. If one drove it, and the other followed, and both came down in another car."

"Ye...s, I need to get the tyre treads checked out. I'm not sure which to set Mark on first, Sandy, body or car."

"The child's been dead a wee while, lad, it'll keep a day or so. Let's concentrate on the car shall we? We can send a couple of teams to walk the area and get anything else brought down by the rain. But let's deal with one thing at a time."

"You're right, as usual, Sandy." Bob sat back, sipping at the cold tea and pulling a face. He set the mug back down with a click. "If you get things organised this end, I'll nip across to Carlisle tomorrow morning and see Jonesy and fetch Mark back with me."

"That sounds like a plan, Bob, but take an hour to see your daughter as well; you both need it. Oh, and, Bob."

"Yes?"

"Get Sarah to send me a couple of clean shirts, there's a good lad. I didn't expect to be over here this long."

Driving back to Carlisle on Thursday morning, Bob's spirits lifted. The sun was out despite the fact that it seemed to have rained half the night. He'd woken up several times from vivid dreams in which Elizabeth was walking away from him and talking to him over her shoulder. He couldn't hear her and kept running to catch up, but she always seemed to be just out of range. Nevertheless he remembered her smile as she'd spoken. It warmed the cold part of him.

He glanced back in the rear-view mirror at the large teddy bear on the back seat. It was a wonderful shade of rose pink. He'd bought it the day before, along with the biking journals, and been assured it was safe for his daughter to play with; it seemed to be gently smiling at him. He smiled back.

Doctor Ryan Jones was in the small cubby-hole he called an office, just down the corridor from the autopsy room. He was morosely stirring something cloudy in a plastic glass, with the end of his biro, when McInnis came in.

The biro lifted out of the glass for a minute, dripping slightly on several files before indicating the seat opposite. Bob sat down quietly, eyeing the mixture.

Ryan Jones gave a final stir and tapped the glass, before dropping the biro and downing the contents in two large gulps. He set the empty container down and pulled a face worthy of the gurning championships. "Yeuk! Indigestion. I knew I shouldn't have succumbed to the temptations of the lobster."

McInnis reflecting on the various lobsters he'd seen over the past week, vowed, yet again, never to touch such crustacean again. Not even on a Friday. He waited respectfully for the coroner's antacid to kick in.

"Right then, Bob, I suppose you've come about your second body?"

"Second and third, Jonesy."

"You keep piling them up like this and I'll have to share my bonus with you, Bob."

"Thanks, but I'd rather do without the bonus and have fewer bodies."

Doctor Jones grunted and shifted in his seat. "Right," he said, scrabbling on the desk and coming up with a file. "Male, name, Eric Potts, age n –"

"What?" Bob shot upright in his seat.

"Mean something to you does it? I only got the info first thing this morning myself." Doctor Jones looked at him over the top of his reading glasses. "His prints were in the system and you really don't want to know how I collected them, but it involves soft-rinse."

"How long's he been dead, Jonesy?" Bob ignored the comments about soft-rinse; he did actually know, and he didn't want to think about the removal of fingers and re-plumping of flesh.

"All in good time, Bob." Jones transferred his gaze back to the paperwork. "Our Mr Potts is, or rather was, nineteen. He's been dead between two and three weeks. I had the entomologist take a look see at some of the bugs that had been feasting on the gentleman, and he was above water for about seven days before he became immersed in Davey Jones' locker. Some of the larvae had drowned, apparently at that stage in their cycle, so he tells me." He frowned. "It's not a branch of the science I care for." He gave a slight shudder. "Creeps me out a bit. I'm going for cremation myself."

Bob said nothing verbally but the expression on his face must have said a lot.

"Yes, well Mr Potts had sustained several blows to the face, one of which cracked the occipital bone. Also a number of blows to the ribcage. Unfortunately the tissue was too degraded to get a boot print, Bob. There were defensive marks on the hands and arms; I'd say your boy had been in one hell of a scrap. One of the blows to the ribs punctured a lung and nicked the liver and those together are what killed him. He bled internally."

"A fist fight or blunt force trauma?"

"A fist is blunt force, Bob, but I know what you mean. Probably fists, difficult to be totally accurate but I didn't find anything to make me think a weapon was employed; the other guy would have had a few bruises too."

"So Potts didn't drown?"

"No, there was fluid in the lungs, but that was probably his own as he went into shock. He died from injuries sustained in the fight. Then at some stage was put into the water somehow."

"What, you think someone went back and threw him in?" McInnis raised an eyebrow in astonishment.

249

"I didn't say that." The coroner shook his head. "I said he went into the water. It's your job to figure out how he ended up where he did. He died and then went for a swim in the briny, somehow.

"Now as to your third body, what I've got of it, and this is just a prelim, understand; the poor soul would be about eight or nine I'd estimate by teeth and epiphysial growth. There are greenstick fractures of both arms that have healed without treatment."

"Spiral or straight?"

Jones felt his lips twitch. "Getting good aren't you? I told you I'd have to share the bonus. Straight breaks. The arms weren't twisted to cause the injuries; child might have fallen or received a sharp blow. There was also some growth over the right shoulder socket, I'd say it had been dislocated at some time and reset."

"Cause of death?"

"Difficult to say for sure, Bob. I've only got the skeleton and not all of that. I've detailed the missing parts in the preliminary report here, give you an idea what else you should be looking for. Most of the phalanges and metatarsals are missing, but then those little bones are hard to spot. Haven't got all the backbones either. No soft tissue or organs to work with. The skull does show staining inside, it might be caused by a blow to the head, there's a hairline fracture, but these bones have been exposed for a good few years. It could just be wear and tear, Bob."

"How many years, Jonesy?" He held up a hand. "I know you can't be accurate, but maybe a ballpark figure to give me a clue where to start looking."

"Hundred, hundred and twenty?"

"How much?" Bob looked as if he'd been hit in the face by a wet fish.

The side of Doctor Jones' mouth lifted. "I'm getting a forensic anthropologist to have a look but I don't think you're going to find the relatives of that little person easily, Bob."

McInnis rubbed both hands over his face, and then the left one over his hair, sitting back and looking at the coroner who was smiling somewhat crookedly at him.

"Sorry I can't be more helpful, Bob. I've thin-sectioned a bit of the femur; if I can count the osteons I might be able to give you a more accurate age of the child and I've taken a scraping of marrow from one of the long bones and from the inside of a tooth, but it might be too old and dry to get you any results. So don't hold your breath on that one. I'd need to have something to compare it with anyway."

Bob sat with an abstracted look on his face and Doctor Jones waited for the brown study to end with good-humoured patience. He wasn't doing anything; he was waiting for some results himself.

McInnis eventually stirred. "Thanks, Jonesy. I'm not quite sure what to do about the poor thing, but it can't have any bearing on the current case."

"Body will be released next week, when I've finished the forensics."

"Let me know, I'll have it laid in the angels garden at the cemetery." Jonesy nodded. That was typical of Bob McInnis; he never made a fuss about his religion, but he cared enough to see that an unknown child should have a Christian burial.

McInnis stood up. "You'll send the report through to the Carlisle desk?"

Doctor Jones nodded, "You can take this one with you, Bob." He handed over Eric Potts' file.

"I'll inform his parents. They'll probably be relieved, and not know how to say so." McInnis shrugged.

"Nice lad was he?"

"Oh! Yeah, the police reports say he gave 'em hell."

"Probably one of our misunderstood youth then." Jonesy stood up and walked Bob to the door. "I'll let you know about the other child, Bob."

McInnis went outside, getting into his car and putting the report into his briefcase before driving to the second appointment of the day. He wasn't looking forward to meeting the young lady he'd rung on Tuesday afternoon, charming though she was.

"Nancy?" The brunette who answered the door was long-legged and as ugly as the back of a bus, but she had a charming smile and a heart of gold. She leaned forward now and kissed both Bob's cheeks in a friendly manner, enveloping him in the smell of *Charlie* and a hint of must.

"In you come, Bob. I've got some info for you but I'm not sure it's all that helpful."

"Anything is helpful at this stage, Nancy."

"Tough case, eh!"

"Yeah you know that quote, something about not having a beginning and not being able to see the end. Well that's this case. The problem's as murky as the water we've pulled our two bodies from. We don't know how they got there and we can't see an end in sight." Bob was aware that he was talking to keep Nancy from asking questions but he couldn't seem to stop himself.

Nancy led the way into the sitting room and sat down beside a coffee table overflowing with papers; the source of the musty smell became obvious as she brushed against the books and papers. "Relax, Bob." She smiled up at him as he stood irresolute on the carpet before her. "I'll ask once how you're coping and expect a short answer, or none at all, then you can be easy."

Bob McInnis had met her at his wedding; she'd been blunt and friendly then, too. "Sorry, Nancy."

"So, how are you coping?"

"Sometimes good, sometimes terribly."

"Give it time. Now this research." She moved briskly forward, both in her seat and her conversation. "A nicely intriguing puzzle to get my teeth into."

Bob sat down opposite and tried to smile across the table at her; it was an effort she rewarded by not fussing him further.

"I've found references to your mine, in several places."

"I'm amazed you've found any references. You haven't exactly had long."

"God bless *Google* and all who sail in her. Plus I have a few friends around who'd do a favour for Beth, and through her, you."

She ignored his slight wince and carried on. "I think I might even be able to pinpoint the entrance for you, but I'll get to that in a minute. It was a bit of a fly-by-night operation in the 1870s to '90s. They were mainly dealing with lead, but were probably looking for silver."

"Silver?"

"Yeah, you often get the two in the same seam. It's called argentiferous galena. The earliest mention I've found is about the Romans mining for silver in this whole area. They used a lot of slave labour and the conditions were appalling. But since the native Britons were already mining for it, I don't suppose they thought the conditions were that bad."

She paused, finally finding the paper she'd been looking for among the pile on the table between them. "Ah, here we go." She picked up a pair of glasses hanging against her non-existent chest and placed them firmly on her nose, then waved the paper at him before she started reading. "This is by a guy called Thomas Sopwith. He was an agent for the Allenhead mines and he installed some pumps there. It was an ingenious method of getting fresh air into the mine by having water running down a pipe in a continuous stream and dragging the fresh air with it, called a water blast. The water got to a pool at the bottom and the air was forced into the chambers and levels." She checked to see her audience hadn't glazed over from boredom, looking at him over the upper rims of the glasses.

Bob's alert face reassured her. "Now his use of these water blasts was documented and your little mine owner wrote to Sopwith, telling him how they'd managed to implement it in their mine. There's a nice description here." She laid the paper down.

"Also." She picked up another paper. "They got done for breaking the Mines Act of 1842, – no women or children under thirteen." She waved the paper. "This is a copy of the *Parliamentary Papers* of 1842 and this –" she picked up yet another sheet "– is Chadwick's report on conditions among the poor, which has your mine in it, and was how they were caught out, and eventually fined, for breaking the law."

She laid the papers together. "I've found a name. 'The West End Mine'. There's a map too, got that from one of the geology societies. But it's not very accurate; still, it might narrow your search down a bit more." She laid more papers on the increasing pile. "I'm afraid that's all I've been able to track down so far, Bob."

Bob sat back smiling. "You've done a fantastic job, Nancy. I can't tell you how much will be helpful. But at this stage I'll take anything I can get, and this is more than just anything."

Nancy sat back, pulling off her glasses and beaming at him. "Good. We aim to please. Now, will you stay for a coffee? It's –" she looked at the carriage clock on the mantelpiece "– eleven. Have you got time?"

Bob shook his head. "I want to see Caitlin before I get back to Maryport."

"Fair enough, but you will come and see me again, Bob, and bring Caitlin?" She watched his face, reading the refusal he wanted to give. "I miss Beth too, and it would give me pleasure to see her baby. How else are you going to pay me for all this research?" She swept a hand over the piles of paper in front of her.

She watched the embarrassment on his face. "Just so. I'll expect a visit now you've been to see me again."

12

While McInnis was visiting old friends, Sandy was visiting old crime scenes. He didn't like moving out of his comfort zone, but since his partner had gone off to Carlisle he had no option but to put his boots on and drive up the hillside, which was as far as he was concerned very uncomfortable.

It hadn't proved as bad as he'd expected. The Land Rover had driven a good way up the trackway, imperilling the lives of several sheep it was true, and ruining the homes of a whole family of rabbits, but it had climbed the hill, followed in close formation by forensics in another Land Rover and a lorry for the abandoned car.

They parked on the rocky outcrop, pulling into the lee as much as possible. He and Gareth, who'd done the driving, climbed out into the teeth of a gale. Sandy, rapidly zipping up his jacket, shuddered, and raised his voice to the men disembarking from the vehicle which was getting up close and personal behind them.

"We'll keep back until forensics have done their job." He looked at Gareth also busily fastening poppers on his heavy fluorescent coat. "Not that they'll get much; this wind is the *coup de grace* to any tracks, I should think."

He stepped to the side and allowed two of the Maryport men to come forward with big, metal cases. "You know what I want lads. Tracks if possible, anything that might have been dropped or abandoned: sweetie papers, fag ends, chewing gum. Do your best."

The two men nodded. It wasn't exactly their first day on the job, but Sandy wasn't an officer to argue with when he got the bit between his teeth.

He stood back now, watching them work. "What do you think, Gareth?"

"Like you said yesterday, sir. Right make and colour, and hidden away. Chances are it's the Doctor's. How it got up here is anyone's guess."

"How would you get back to civilisation if you'd left it up here, Gareth?"

"On Shank's pony," Gareth looked about, "it's a steep climb and on foot it would take an hour, maybe two, if you weren't fit, to walk back down."

"How else?" Sandy was also looking about and had spotted some interesting tracks next to the car door.

"Get a mate to follow you?" Gareth shook his head. "I'm not shining am I, chief?"

"You're not doing badly, but look more closely at the area around the boot of the car."

"Ah!" It was a long drawn-out sigh. "Gottya, chief."

They stood, shoulders hunched against the spiteful wind which kept spitting icy particles at them, and watched forensics do its worst.

One of the men was placing little numbered triangles on the ground like a *maître d'* setting a table, badly, for a huge dinner party. The other followed behind like a Japanese tourist unwilling to miss a thing for his holiday scrapbook.

"They've got some sort of tracks anyway." Sandy sounded satisfied. The man came over after twenty very energetic minutes.

"Sir." He sketched a salute. "If we could bring the wagon forward we'll pull it out of the hollow and load it. Then we'll finish up on the ground up here."

Sandy nodded agreement, waving forward the police wagon which had followed them up the tracks. Gareth, watching them, muttered and then moved rapidly over to the Land Rover, climbing in and backing it onto an area of even rougher ground to let the lorry through.

The men in the lorry were experts, which was just as well. It wasn't going to be easy to manoeuvre the four-wheel high top and get it on the ramp. Sandy watched them with admiration as they swung around in the very rocky and confined space.

The car was checked over and then, clad in a white coverall and wearing less than fashionable blue vinyl gloves and plastic overshoes, one of the men drove it up the ramp and onto the low loader.

"Neat piece of work, Gareth." Sandy turned back from watching operations and looked at the space where the car had been. "Well, I'll go to the foot of our stairs."

"Pardon, chief?" Gareth looked where his boss was looking. There, tucked into the hillside, was a portcullis-shaped metal grill over a dark hole.

"Good God! We've found the entrance and we weren't even looking." Sandy was grinning all over his face. "You wait 'til I tell Bob about this." He motioned the forensics men forward. "Come on! Don't stand gawking in the wind, lads, do your job and then maybe I can do mine."

The men, who'd been exchanging a few words with their colleagues on the low loader, cast slightly guilty looks at each other and came over. "Right, sir, shouldn't take too long now. If you want to move over to that bit, where we've processed the scene, it'll be out of the draft a bit for you, sir." The senior man pointed to a corner near the mine entrance.

Gareth, nothing loth, moved forward with his boss, and they stood in the lee of the stones. The difference was felt immediately, the wind dropped away, and the smell of damp, slightly mouldy earth was wafted up to them from the entrance. "Do you think they were implying anything by that, Gareth?"

Gareth, who was a cautious man at the best of times, returned a very deadpan, "Couldn't say, sir."

Sandy grinned wickedly. "Very diplomatic, my lad. You'll go far."

"Sir?" The senior forensics constable hailed him.

Sandy moved swiftly over, his faithful shadow following.

"I've got boot prints, sir, and the imprint of a bike." Even as he was speaking he was squeezing a white plastic bag of 'Shake 'n' Cast' and setting a frame around one of the prints. "Sam, get the tyre prints, I'll do this."

"Two go in and one comes out. Interesting, Gareth." Sandy rubbed his chin and stared at the marks on the ground. "Make sure you get lots of photos, lads. I don't want to have to come back up here again!" He stepped gingerly around the prints and looked at the gate. "When you've done that, see about printing this." He nodded at the rusting metal. "Not that I've got much hope of anything, given the state of it. But that might give us something.

"Fetch the torch from the car, lad." He waited patiently for Gareth to return.

"Here you go, Chief."

"Can I get a bit nearer?"

"Yes, sir."

Sandy stood close to the gate, taking care not to touch its decomposing metalwork, and held the beam of the powerful light directed into the cave-like interior. He moved the beam inch by inch along the sides, sweeping along the roof and floor and shivering slightly as the cold air reached him from the interior. "Whoever they were, they went in; this padlock looks new. Forensics should get a print off that, if they've been careless." He smiled with satisfaction. "I don't suppose we've got anything to undo it?"

"Sorry, sir. We came for a car; I could maybe try to jimmy it open or I've got a set of bolt cutters."

"Nah, don't worry, we aren't dressed for roaming about in caves. Especially me." He stepped to the side away from the overhang, and then walked away from the entrance until he was looking at the cliff face from a distance. Gareth stood next to him, looking upwards but not seeing anything but rock and sky.

Sandy came to a decision. "I'm going back down. I've had an idea. Gareth, you can stay up here and guard this 'ere hole. I'll send Bob and Mark up as soon as they get back from Carlisle." He looked at his watch. "They should be here between two and three; it's nearly a quarter to twelve now."

Gareth nodded. He went over to the Land Rover with Sandy and collected his rucksack from the back seat. Sandy climbed into the driving seat and buckled up. "Got your over-trousers in there, lad?"

"Yes, Chief. And a flask and butties."

"Good. I'll send Bob up as soon as I can." He reversed and started down the track, travelling slowly and cautiously. Gareth stood and watched him for a minute then moved back towards the men still busy with their printing and photography.

"What was that all about?" Sam looked at the looming bulk of the Carlisle man as he asked the question.

"Dunno. I'm to make sure nobody steals the hole until he gets back." His lips twitched wryly. He went into the cover of the overhang, watching the men work methodically.

Bob might be a good Catholic but he could be a good Methodist too, and he was being methodical. His young daughter was asleep when he'd arrived at Sandy's house. Sarah exchanged the bag of dirty washing he offered her for a cup of steaming coffee and a kiss on his cheek. Bob had blinked a bit at the kiss, but then he'd just smiled at her.

He sat down in her sunny kitchen to pull together the information he'd been given that morning, and to see how it affected the information he already had.

He was reading over the material from Nancy and sipping coffee when Sarah came back into the room. She sat across from him at the kitchen table and pushed a slice of fruitcake towards him. Bob laid aside his notes and accepted the plate with a murmur of thanks.

"I had an idea when Sandy rang last night, Bob, but you might not like it," Sarah said nervously.

Bob raised an eyebrow.

"I don't want to seem pushy, Bob." Sarah, unusually for her, hesitated. She loved Bob like another son, but he always seemed to keep just a small part of himself hidden.

"There's a house for sale up the road, five doors down." Sarah blushed a bit. "I don't know whether you could afford it," she held up a hand, "I'm not being nosy. But I wondered if you'd think about moving. Your little flat hasn't got a garden or much room, and Elizabeth was telling me you were thinking of moving even before..." Sarah tailed off.

Bob shifted on the hard wooden chair and looked at the cake in his hand, then he laid it carefully down and picked up the mug. "Yes we were, Sarah. Beth wanted a garden for the baby to play in." He kept his eyes steady on her blue ones, his hands gripping the mug.

"If Sandy and you were called out, I could nip down and baby-sit, or even bring Caitlin up here until you got back."

Bob cocked his head on one side. "I'll have to think about it, Sarah. Not you caring for her, you're an angel for taking us both on. But I need to check on prices and finances. It does sound like a plan though." He offered her his slow and quiet smile, and Sarah blinked back tears because she loved him like her own children and that smile had been missing for too long.

She buried her nose in her own mug while she got herself under control. When she was sure she could talk without giving anything away she nodded at the paperwork. "Are you any nearer a solution to who killed the poor man?"

"I think we're getting somewhere, Sarah. In any case we'll be back in Carlisle by the weekend, I should say. Whether we've caught our man or not."

"Can you tell me about it? Sandy hasn't said much on the phone. And the newspapers don't seem to have anything new." Her nose wrinkled as she questioned him.

"Yes, well that's a deliberate ploy on our part, to fool everyone into thinking we know more than we do." He grinned around the mug, "What do you want to know then?"

"Last night Sandy said you'd found a third body? A child?"

Bob's face lost its brightness and Sarah was sorry she'd said anything.

"Yes, we were searching for a mine entrance and Jack the dog, has Sandy told you about Jack? He's a terrier and he normally works

262

with the mountain rescue, only his mistress has been ill, so he's having a holiday. Well Jack went sniffing about among the rocks and found a little skeleton."

"Oh the puir wee bairn. It wouldn't be your murderer that did that. Not a skeleton."

"No. Sandy doesn't even know yet, but the skeleton was over a hundred years old."

"Perhaps he was working in the mine."

"Eh!" Bob looked puzzled. "No we didn't find it in the mine. We haven't found..." His voice trailed away. He frowned in thought and then got up and dropped a kiss on the nut-brown curls. "Sarah, you're a genius."

"I am!" Sarah looked up at the tall handsome man smiling down at her. "Of course I am."

They smiled at each other and the spell was broken by a little whimper from the baby monitor. "Away and fetch the child. You can give her her bottle while I heat up some soup for you."

Bob climbed the stairs and poked his head around the door. The grizzles ceased, turned off like a tap at the sight of a face. "Hello, sweet pea, are you ready for your lunch then?"

Caitlin, it seemed, was ready for a nappy change first. She lay gurgling up at the mobile that had appeared as magically as the changing table in the small neat room. Her arms waved about as she tried to catch piglet swinging above her head. Bob snapped fasteners shut and hoisted her up into his arms. "There, all clean again. I see you've got some new toys young lady. You could get spoilt here couldn't you? Now hang on while your dad washes his hands and you shall have your lunch." He settled her against his shoulder and went into the bathroom.

Bob carried her downstairs, enjoying the unique smell of a baby, talc, milk, and soap, and something that was just Caitlin. He sniffed at her and then felt foolish, but he did think she smelt like her mum. That faint musky-sweet odour he'd always delighted in.

Sarah was trotting about the kitchen as he went in. "Here sit down, here's her bottle." She set the bottle on the table in a plastic jug of warm water.

Bob settled himself, and the child on his lap, and gave her the teat to suck. "You've been spending money, Sarah."

"Aye well, you left plenty for me, and you'll need the things yourself when you take her home." Sarah was guiltily aware she was making excuses; she caught sight of the pink bear. "Anyway, you bought her that creature." She grinned across the saucepan she was busy stirring.

"So I did, Sarah." He looked down at the child blissfully absorbing her lunch.

"She's a wee darling, Bob." Sarah too directed a loving look at the child.

"It's just as well you love her, Sarah; you're going to be helping me for a while yet." Bob looked up and lifted an eyebrow.

"Good." She came forward, setting bread and soup in front of him. "Give me the child and eat your lunch. You'll be needing to get back, if I know Sandy." She scooped Caitlin up and sat down next to him, watching while he ate the food.

They exchanged a few comments about Caitlin, but Bob didn't go back to the case. He finished his lunch and sat nursing Caitlin as she played with a round ring Sarah had brought out of the freezer locker of the fridge.

"She'll have a tooth by next week, Bob." Sarah was cleaning the table and putting bottles in a steriliser. "They grow fast at this age, every week something different."

"Yes. I can see changes already." He smoothed down the soft black hair. "I don't know how I'd have managed this week without you, Sarah."

"Your mother would have stepped in, but it's better this way. She's been round three times this week already."

Bob's face reflected his worry. "She's not been awkward?"

"Away with you, lad, we get on just fine. She couldn't cope and so she admits, but she missed the child while Caitlin was with her aunty, and she's making up for lost time."

"So am I, Sarah." He smiled down at the baby who was busy dribbling all over the ring and his hand. He sighed. "I'd better go and get Mark and get back over there. Sandy will have solved the case while my back is turned, and will be crowing about it."

"Not him, he hates having to write up the reports!" Sarah grinned at him, wiping her hands on a towel and coming to relieve him of his happy burden. "I'll take care of her for you. Quicker you go, the quicker you get back, lad."

She walked him to the door with Caitlin on her broad hip and waved him away with a smile.

Mark and McInnis were making good time back to Greystone. Mark, it was true, was very quiet, but McInnis, being a quiet man, was grateful for that. He was busy thinking and so was Mark. He had shot off to Carlisle in the hopes of putting distance between himself and a certain young woman, only to be hooked back into her orbit almost straight away. They had reached Aspatria before Mark spoke. "Sir?"

"Yes." Bob took his eyes off the road and glanced across to his passenger.

"How do you know when you're in love?" Mark realised it wasn't a very tactful thing to say the moment he'd opened his mouth. He went a dull red and shook his head. "Doesn't matter."

Bob McInnis shook his head in his turn. "An impossible question to answer, Mark. 'You just know', hardly seems adequate." He lapsed into silence and Mark was just breathing a quiet, if heartfelt, sigh of relief when Bob spoke again. "It's wanting to be with someone, not just the sex." He flashed a grin across. "Not even the sex, Mark, but the company, sharing jokes and everyday things." He thought of how he'd wanted to tell Beth about the tight jeans of Jenny. "It's sharing, and caring."

Both men sat silently until the town of Greystone was a blip in the distance. "You'll have to give her lots of space, Mark, and if it's love, you'll manage that. Just be there for her, man. She's going to know all about it after the child arrives, and she needs someone to share the special moments with. I know all about that."

Bob looked rather sadly across the space, at the horrified look on the silent man in the passenger seat. "Don't worry, you haven't been that obvious, Mark. Just…" he pulled up and parked, setting the handbrake and turning slightly in the seat, "just take things slowly." He offered a smile of companionship. "Now put it away. We have a murder to solve." He stepped out of the car and they made their way across to the incident room.

Sandy was waiting for them in the incident van. As he remarked when they came through the door, it was beginning to feel more like home than home, they'd been living in it so much. "Grab a mug of something hot, Bob, Mark. I want you up the hill."

He lifted a file. "I've just had a report through from Sergeant Oakes; he was carrying on the search for the Doctor's car which

266

we'd already found. Fortunately I hadn't got back to him." He grinned at them as they sat down opposite.

"You," he pointed at Bob, "apparently said something to make him think he should start looking through old dockyards."

"But..." Bob frowned.

"Tell me in a minute. He hasn't found the car; I'm almost certain we have. Still need confirmation from the chassis number. But Oakes, he's discovered what Pheby has been up to, caught him moving his equipment."

Bob sipped tea and grinned. "I told Sarah, you'd solve the case while I was away."

"I dunno about solving the case, Bob, but at least we've got one thread snipped off. Pheby isn't a murderer, at least I don't think so; he's dealing in boulders, and not the erratic kind."

"Boulders!" It was a puzzled chorus.

"Boulders, stones, gravel. This blasted case seems to be strewn with rockery. But Pheby, he's been doing a bit of quiet dredging down the river Ellen, at the side of the old dockyards. Then selling it off."

The younger men exchanged glances; the glance clearly said 'poor old man's finally flipped'.

"Er! There's nothing wrong with selling boulders is there, Sandy? You bought some in the summer yourself, to do the rockery for Sarah."

Sandy scratched his head in an absent manner. "N...o nothing wrong, provided you go to a reputable dealer. But this stuff, it's coming out of an area of outstanding natural beauty. It's illegal to take anything from the seashore for commercial purposes in this area, and Hugh Pheby was using a little backhoe. I don't think he was doing up his patio!"

"It's not exactly 'seashore'."

"It," Sandy swung his glasses over his nose, then read from the notes, "'affects the tides and amount of silt in the water, thereby influencing the natural habitat of the marine life,' even though it's just up the river." He pulled off the glasses and grinned at them again, like a small boy enjoying the push and shove of the playground. He knew it was going to end in tears for someone, and he knew it wasn't going to be him.

Mark, a silent listener, nodded. "I've seen the damage you can do with just a little breakwater; it can shift a whole sand dune in a season. The channels change and the animals have to adapt to new areas or die."

"Yeah, well, we got him. Oakes is even now holding him for questioning. The gentleman isn't talking about his activities, but he will." Sandy shook his head. "He knows better, Bob. I'm headed over there as soon as I've given you the relevant info'; I want a word with Mr Pheby. Muddying my investigation and wasting man hours." He scowled suddenly, his expression not boding well for the absent Pheby.

"Fair's fair, Sandy, if he'd hung in there we wouldn't have known about his activities, it's true. But we'd still have been searching there for the car. Actually I'd suggested to Oakes that we might find some clue as to how the Doctor got into the dock. I wondered if it could have been by boat down the river Ellen to the sea."

"Aye, maybe that's something we need to keep on with. Now if you two have finished lollygagging about, I want you up the hill. I need a mine processing." He grinned again as he watched his bombshell explode over their heads. It was a satisfactory reaction; he hadn't missed the pitying looks of a few moments ago.

"Yeah! I got the mine."

"Well I've got a name for it: 'The West End Mine'. What's more I think I might have a worker for it."

McInnis was small-minded enough to enjoy topping Sandy Bell's announcement.

"My God, he must be ancient."

"Nope, I think it could be our child." McInnis raised an eyebrow.

"That's some researcher you've got there, Bob."

Mark, who was now totally lost, coughed gently.

Both men looked at him; Sandy nodded. "Fill him in on your way up to the mine, Bob. This is what I've got so far." He began to tell both men about the removal of the car and the revealing of the metal gate. "I left it virgin for you to process Mark. That was a brand new padlock on that gate; you might get prints. Whoever went into the mine left boot prints in the soil inside. Have you got the right kind of gear to go rambling around in a mine? I've got some caving helmets but that's all."

"I can go in the entrance but I wouldn't want to go too far in without a bit more than that, sir." He paused. "I might be able to find some extra gear. I think I might be able to lay hands on a Draeger or an O_2 sensor alarm, fairly quickly."

"Whatever they are!" Sandy shook his head. "I don't blame you Mark. Go get them if it won't take too long, otherwise process just inside and I'm getting a caving team over tomorrow."

Mark stood up and, offering each man a smile in turn, went out of the van.

"How about you Bob, happy to go up there and try your powers of deduction?"

"I've got my walking gear in the boot. Wet weather gear, good boots, ropes, but I'm not keen on venturing too far in, Sandy, not when I don't know where I'm going. We'll process what we can and then wait for the team."

"That's fine, lad. Now give me the rest of your news."

"It's like I said, Sandy. Jonesy thinks the skeleton is from a small child, possibly under ten years of age. He also thinks it's somewhere between a hundred and a 120 years old. Difficult to estimate that kind of thing and we haven't found the entire skeleton for him." He paused, holding Sandy's eyes a minute. "I'd like to detail a couple of men to find the rest of the skeleton if you don't mind." He held up a hand. "I know it's even less urgent now, Sandy. But I'd like to do it anyway."

"OK, Bob. I'll arrange it."

"Your Sarah gave me the other idea, Sandy. She misunderstood me and thought we'd found the skeleton in the mine, but I wondered if maybe it had come from there." He rubbed a hand over his cheek. "I've contacted Jonesy; he's going to check for evidence of lead phosphate in the bones. It's not conclusive; he tells me you can find that in modern kids exposed to petrol lead, and in older people who had lead-painted soldiers as children. But it might be there and we might be able to make two and two, four. We can but try."

Sandy pondered the information. "I don't see how it helps the case, but I do see your need to do it, Bob, so yeah! Go for it. Now let's get you kitted out and up that hill. I'm going to take the squad car to Maryport. You may have that Land Rover with pleasure. It's like riding a bucking bronco coming down, so take care, and bring Gareth with you. Poor lad must be frozen by now."

Gareth was, if not frozen, at least standing in the equivalent of the refrigerator aisle. The forensics men had gone about half an hour ago, offering him commiserations for a lousy job. He didn't really mind though; he felt as though he'd learnt a lot from watching his two favourite detectives at work. This gave him an opportunity to think about what he'd seen over the last week. He would so like to spot the murderer before they did.

He examined the gate again and wondered what it was Inspector Bell had noticed that had galvanised him into action. He could see the car tracks, the bike tracks, the footprints; he could even see a couple of smudged fingerprints now that forensics had covered the padlock in grey dust. He shook his head; the Inspector had seen all those – well, not the fingerprints, but the rest. What had sent him galloping off back to town leaving him, Gareth, on this windy hillside?

He clicked on the torch and peered into the cave-like interior of the mine's entrance. The Inspector had been looking into the cave when he'd had his idea, hadn't he? Gareth quartered the area with the light. It didn't help. It was still just a dark and rather dank space. He sighed, turning and setting his back against the cold stone, relaxing and waiting for McInnis and Mark Forester to arrive.

Sandy, meanwhile, had arrived at Maryport. He was shown into the same small unappealing room as Bob had been in the day before; it was still chilly and now had a flourishing damp patch under the window as well as on the ceiling.

After the preliminaries of name and address Sandy settled on the hard seat and looked sternly at Hugh Pheby. The bright blue eyes looked back at him without expression.

"What were you thinking about, Mr Pheby? There are more than a few people who look up to you. You're young for this position and as far as we can tell, you maintained a good clean harbour and oversaw the safety of folks well. Why do this?"

Pheby shrugged but didn't answer.

"Come on, lad, we've caught you red-handed. You aren't trying to deny what you've been up to surely?"

Oakes looked up from the notes he was taking in addition to the tape recording that was being made. "Answer the man," he almost barked, and Sandy winced slightly, he was used to the quiet tones of McInnis. Still it might be turned to good account, good cop, bad cop.

"Now, Detective Sergeant Oakes is angry with you. You've mucked up his nice clean town and spoiled his record for peace keeping; you should be grateful it's me talking to you. He'd like to arrest you for this murder and tidy up his bailiwick all in one go." He watched the blue eyes; the pupils dilated slightly, as Pheby looked from one man to the other.

"I didn't murder the Doctor."

It was a start, thought Sandy. "Then why run? If you'd stayed put we probably wouldn't have cottoned on to your operation."

"It was my boat."

Sandy sat waiting. When it became obvious that Pheby wasn't going to add to the statement he rubbed a hand under his itchy nose and said, "What about your boat?"

"My boat, it went missing the weekend you said he died. I thought maybe it had been used to dump him."

"Well, and if it had, so what?"

"You'd start looking at me and find things out."

"We did that anyway. When did your boat go missing?"

"Saturday. It was there on the Friday evening when I went home and not there on the Saturday morning when I came back on

272

duty. At first I thought the boys had borrowed it, but they always bring it back."

"So you knew about the Simpson boys?"

For the first time a faint smile appeared on Pheby's face. "Course I did. Poor buggers just borrowed it to do a bit of fishing. They weren't doing any harm." He looked scathingly at Oakes. "I kept them from worse mischief in your precious town."

Oakes opened his mouth, but Sandy nudged him under the table with a well shod foot and spoke first. "Did you know they were fishing for lobsters and crabs?"

"Crafty little buggers! That's illegal."

Sandy hid the smile, at the indignation in the man's voice.

"No more illegal than selling stones from the area. In fact it could be argued that what you did was worse; you knew it was illegal. They apparently didn't, and you were one of the people who should have told them it was wrong."

Pheby reddened and replied in an argumentative manner, "It's all very well making this an SSSI but people have got to live here and survive. You can't live on pretty butterflies and flowers. You have to have work of some sort. There isn't the fishing or the charters to bring in the wages now."

"And who might these impoverished people be?" Oakes asked the question and got a sullen look. It was all that either policeman was going to get from him for the next twenty-four hours, except for a request for a lawyer and bail.

He got the lawyer but was refused the bail. They'd had enough trouble catching him the first time. Habeas corpus came in handy sometimes.

Oakes and Sandy sat in the sergeant's office after Pheby had been taken away to await his lawyer. Both had mugs of strong tea

273

and both had strong feelings. Sandy Bell was hiding his better than Oakes.

"I'm sorry, Inspector, he shut up and it was my clumsy handling that caused it."

Sandy shrugged. "It happens, don't fash yersen, man." He drank deeply of the mug. "It might even be better this way. There's nothing like a night in the clink for loosening a relatively innocent man's bowels and tongue. We'll see how he feels about talking tomorrow."

Oakes also drank, then remarked, "I've got some good news might cheer you up."

"Yeah?"

"We finally found a name that rang bells in the museum visitors' book. Eric Potts. Now if only we can lay hands on the little scoundrel we can ask him a question or two. I somehow don't see him as being there to improve his mind."

"I can tell you where he is." Bell's mouth twisted wryly, like he'd just got hot tea on a sensitive molar. "But he won't talk to you."

"I'm not always as clumsy, Inspector."

"Still won't talk, he's dead."

Oakes's face was a picture, possibly Picasso or another of the more modern artists. It certainly wasn't as pretty as a Monet. "Bloody hell!"

"Just so. Let me fill you in on the saga of Eric Potts so far, Sergeant."

13

The saga of the finding of the skeleton the previous day, and Bob's research so far, kept both him and Mark occupied while they jiggled and jolted their way up the trackway towards the distant heights.

"So what's your idea, sir? If we've found the mine entrance already, why would you connect the child's skeleton with the mine?"

"Call it a hunch, Mark. Sandy gets fey moments, I have hunches. It's what makes a copper more than just someone who likes doing puzzles!" He smiled a bit grimly. "The criminals hate coppers who have hunches."

"It must be based on something?" Mark was genuinely puzzled.

Bob sighed. "It's all pretty amorphous really; there's the fact that where we were walking had that hollow sound you get in the peaks. Especially in limestone country. As if you were walking over a honeycomb of rocks, which I suppose in the Peak District you are."

He changed down yet another gear as they steadily climbed upwards. "I'd been reading about the early miners; there were all sorts of terms I didn't understand, but I got the general idea. The skeleton was coming down a stream. After a storm a miner would go out and look for the raw ore on the mountainside that had been brought down by the rains. Then he'd follow the stream upwards until he spotted the seam."

"Yeah I've heard of that, Maureen called it 'hushing' I think. She was telling me there were over a hundred different minerals in Cumberland. The old miners used to make mineral boxes of all the different ones they found. She's got a wonderful one in the front room that belonged to her husband." He fell silent and Bob glanced at him, but the young face was giving nothing away.

"What else?" McInnis ignored the silence, continuing his itemisation of clues he'd garnered so far. "The skeleton was dated from the time of the mine, according to Jonesy. It had straight greenstick fractures, and a dislocated shoulder.

"Now I've seen that kind of damage before; I saw a small child's shoulder dislocated when the mother pulled it out of the way of a speeding car. They pop out easily in youngsters. There were some graphic pictures in my research, of kiddies pulling huge wagons of coal and slate. I just wondered if that was how the dislocation occurred." He smiled lop-sidedly. "Not many speeding cars back then."

He looked across at Mark as they crested the hill and pulled onto the large open area in front of the mine entrance. "All pretty flimsy stuff really."

"But worth checking out. I can see that." Mark swung out the door and dropped to the ground. "Hi, Gareth, are you frozen?"

Gareth walked over to meet them. "Not too bad, sir. The team from Maryport went away about three quarters of an hour ago. I've been pondering the case and watching rabbits."

McInnis came round from the driver's side. "And which was more interesting Gareth? Here, I thought you might appreciate this." He handed the constable a metal flask, which, when opened revealed hot coffee. "Sandy said you'd got a flask, but it isn't exactly warm up here."

Gareth grinned his thanks. "Actually the rabbits were a bit boring, but I did have an idea about the phone, sir." He poured himself a capful and handed the flask to Mark.

"And?"

"Well, you know we were wondering how the person had got Mrs Sandman's mobile number? What if the murderer was using it all along? It wasn't in the Doctor's possession when he was recovered." He looked up expectantly, a bright child expecting praise from his teacher. The smile dimmed. "And you've already got there haven't you, sir?"

"Well, yes. But you did get there, Gareth. It might have been an unknown number, but only someone who was close to the Doctor and his wife, or had the phone, would know she was called 'Poppy', by him. We've checked out all those who were close enough to know, and that didn't amount to many, half a dozen at most, so it had to be someone using the Doctor's phone itself." He paused, "And someone who wasn't in touch with current events either."

Bob patted him on the shoulder. "Give yourself a chance, man. I've been at this a bit longer than you. If we find the phone we've probably found the murderer. We've got the number tapped, so we can trace it, if 'whoever' is stupid enough to use it again. But I don't think we're looking at someone that stupid." He nodded at the cooling drink. "Drink up and tell me how the team got on this morning; we don't want to be duplicating."

Bob stood back observing the area, while Gareth drank the coffee and Mark queried him about the activities of the Maryport men. He wandered away from the other two and clambered up the steep side of the ridge.

The others watched his activities with some astonishment. He stood on the ridge, the wind whipping at his coat and tossing his neat hair into disorder. He turned slowly in a circle until he could see back to the area he'd been on the day before. "Gareth, come up here a minute." He waited patiently until both men had climbed up to him.

"That's where we were yesterday isn't it, over there?" He swung an arm up and pointed across country, his back to the sea.

Gareth squinted into the wind, carefully checking out the scenery. "Yes, sir, that would be the top of the hill where the little child came down."

"Yes, that's what I thought." He turned to Mark. "I think you might have swum under this hill, Mark." He offered a smile. "I think your light in the sky at the top of that cave might be somewhere over there. What do you think?"

Mark nodded, taking in the scenery himself and trying to orientate himself. "Could well be."

"Yes, I think I'll just phone through to Sandy before we start; we could maybe get the lads to check it out while they're looking for the child's remains."

The men went back down and Bob called Sandy up.

"Aye, lad, I thought it might be the case, but I hadn't been on the hill, so I wasn't sure. I saw it when I was up there this morning. I've already asked the team to go a bit higher and check it out. I meant to tell you but I forgot."

"That's great, Sandy." Bob grinned at the two men listening in to his side of the conversation. "I'll put these two out of their misery and talk to you later." He stowed the phone and filled Gareth and Mark in as the three men strolled across to the mine entrance.

Gareth, scowled. "That's what he saw; I thought it was something inside the cave."

Bob chuckled at the expression on his face. "At least you knew he'd seen something. He didn't tell me!"

Gareth, at last seeing the funny side, grinned. They turned to the business at hand, Mark remarking, "I've brought bolt cutters."

"The Maryport men printed the lock, sir, said they couldn't get anything off the chain though."

"Yeah, I can see." Mark still put protective gloves on to cut through the metal chain attached to the padlock, like the proverbial knife through butter. "I'll go first and use the Draeger."

"What's one of those, sir?"

"CO_2 detector, borrowed it from Doctor Sandman's house. If it goes off we retreat in a swift and orderly manner. Got that?"

"Yes, you're the boss here Mark." Bob sniffed.

They pulled the gate open and, strapping cave helmets on their heads, advanced cautiously. Mark pointed at the boot prints. "Go round the edges, while I take a few photos."

"Give me the camera, Mark, while you do what you have to do."

"Close, wide and comparison, sir."

Bob resisted the temptation to state the obvious as he took the camera and started to line up the prints.

Gareth, bringing up the rear, held the powerful police torch high to give them maximum spread of light. They advanced into the entrance millimetre by millimetre. Snails overtook them while they dallied over each tiny detail and made certain it wasn't a clue before they went further in.

McInnis found the spoil heap first. However, since it wasn't his first day on the job either, he called, and then waited patiently for Mark to come over, merely documenting with the camera.

Mark arrived and looked at the finely ground dust and the stone it was scattered over. "Why this stone, sir?"

"Because that –" Bob pointed down "– is the bottom of my quern, Mark."

Gareth gazed in some awe at the round stone as he held the light steady. "How do you know? It just looks like the other stones lying around."

"No it doesn't, Gareth. That's gritstone. Inside this cave you've got limestone, that's the whitish stuff; there's sandstone, the red stuff; there's mica, it's glinting at you whenever you flick your light over it; bit of quartz and fluorspar, and a lead seam, the dull stuff. But no other gritstone in sight." His voice left an echo as they all looked about and thought about his words.

He held his own light steady. "The powder on the stone, that's lead ore; mind you don't breathe it in. I can't figure out why anyone would want to grind lead ore though." He turned his head away, carefully exhaling and breathing in, holding his breath as he bent closer to the fine powder.

"I'll get a sample and then bag the stone. Fetch me a big bag will you, Gareth?"

Gareth moved cautiously back to the entrance and Mark's big case of forensic material. "That Draeger still working, Mark?"

"Yeah, we're fine; Maureen told me what to look for." He glanced back to the entrance; they had advanced a good fifty feet now. The circle of light that represented the world outside was covered with a curtain of rain and dullness.

McInnis flashed his light around, ignoring the implications of Mark's statement about Maureen, for police business. "There are two tunnels leading off this entrance, Mark. I think I'd rather have a bigger team before we explore them. But I would say this was how our Mr Potts got into the mine system; what do you think?"

"Someone, in fact two someones, have been in the habit of visiting this mine on a regular basis for several months I should say." Mark nodded at the collecting bags he'd been accumulating. "I need to analyse a bit more, but I've got summer grass seeds in some of the prints. There are bramble seeds in one of them, that season's only just started, my mum always picks blackberries at this time of year; she was talking about making jelly only last weekend." He grinned at Bob.

"We need to match prints to Potts' shoes; if he's been here we can eliminate his prints and see what we've got left." He paused as Gareth returned. "Take care, but see if either set of tracks goes into those tunnels, Gareth." He watched as the constable stepped cautiously towards the blacker areas from whence a light breeze could be felt and an even lighter smell of damp and stone and mouldiness. "He'll make a good detective." He smiled at McInnis.

"Yes, we think so too."

Gareth called them after a careful look around. "There's a fresh lot going in and they don't come out, sir. This one." He indicated the left-hand tunnel, his voice echoing slightly from the opening.

"How'd you know they're fresh, Gareth?"

They moved towards him, making sure they didn't stand on any of the prints. This necessitated clambering over the rocks close to the sides of the cavern as the way towards the entrance funnelled. Both men used their hands to support themselves. McInnis gave a muffled yelp at one stage and shook his hand. "Caught it on a sharp bit."

They arrived next to Gareth who held his beam steady on the evidence. "See, sir, it's been made by a wet boot and it has bits of broken heather in it. I was looking at that pink heather for over an hour, the rabbit burrow is in the middle of it. It's from just outside here, and it's got fewer flowers than the stuff outside, not as many as you get when it's in full bloom. That's appeared in the last couple of weeks, I'm sure of it."

Mark waited for the photos before gently tweezing the heather from the imprint and looking at it carefully. "I think you're very probably right there. Heather degrades slowly, that's why the Scots picked bits and kept it in their bonnets. We'll get it, and a cast of that boot print, back to the lab and have a good look at them."

Bob pointed further into the tunnel. "I'm not sure, but would you say there'd been a fight around here, Mark?" He pointed at the scuffed earth with his torch.

Mark went forward slowly and knelt to examine the area. "Yeah, I think you're right, Bob." He cast a guilty look at Gareth, then at McInnis, who shrugged.

"I don't think Gareth will break discipline if you call me by my first name here, Mark." He cautiously advanced. "Fight?"

At the nod he smiled grimly. "We might just have discovered where Eric Potts met his end."

"No that can't be right, Bob, one set of footprints go onwards." He gently touched and measured the depth with his fingers. "They aren't deeper, so it isn't one man carrying another either. We still haven't quite solved the mystery have we?"

McInnis shook his head. "No, but I think it's time we made a move out of this place. It's nearly six o'clock. Doesn't time go fast when you're having fun?" He flashed the light over the area. "Let's go. I'll get a team up here tomorrow and some decent lighting. We might be able to find out a bit more then."

He fished in his pocket as the others preceded him out into the evening light, wadding a clean handkerchief into his palm. It stung like an adder bite.

The trip down the hill had been conducted in almost total silence. All the men were tired. It had been a long day with a lot of emotions sloshing about. Gareth had put the new police issue padlock on a freshly assembled chain and added a further barrier in the shape of several yards of yellow police-issue tape. Then he'd climbed in the back with a thoughtful expression on his face.

Mark was also thinking hard. They had found an old abandoned mine, with obviously new footprints in it. The lead couldn't be the draw; anyone mining that would need a bit more than a grindstone to extract enough to make it commercially viable. Unless they were going to make a bit of lead shot, or a toy soldier.

"Should we be searching for owners of shotguns, Bob?" The question and informality popped out before Mark had thought about it. "I mean…"

He trailed away as McInnis cocked his head on one side and thought about it. Mark thought his goose was cooked as the senior man didn't speak for a few minutes, and the silence in the Land Rover was only broken by the shushing of the grass against the sides of the car doors.

"You'd need a shot tower. Where's the nearest one? It might be difficult to use it anyway, without drawing attention to yourself." He glanced across. "Unless they had moulds, but they're not exactly ten a penny either. It's an idea, Mark, but if there was access to a shotgun why beat someone up? Or drown them for that matter. Still it's your idea, run with it, man."

Mark nodded and went back to his thoughts. Bob McInnis' thoughts were running in a different direction. There was something about the quern, he'd been told or read. He shook his head in frustration at not being able to bring it back to mind; it was something Sandy had said, he was almost sure. But what?

When they arrived back at the incident van, most of the day staff had quit. In fact on first entering it had a distinct *Marie Celeste* feel to it, with papers set out, abandoned mugs, and computers with various strange screen savers on. Bob had been standing still until he realised he was being spoken to; his fascinated gaze had been fixed on a series of pipes which kept building and dissolving on one of the screens.

"Sir, do you want me any more tonight?"

"Eh! I'm sorry, Mark, I was dreaming."

"Do you need me anymore? If not I'll get this lot back to Carlisle and make a start."

"No off you go, but stop and eat first, Mark. We've been on the go since midday."

Mark nodded, "OK, I'll return this Draeger and grab something, then I'll be on my way."

"Fine, Mark." Bob's attention was back on the pipes. "I'll come over with you; I want a quick word with the Doc, myself."

The two men turned and walked out again. "Mark, do you think that the pools you were swimming through could have been water blast reservoirs?" He looked enquiringly at Mark as he explained about the air-conditioning system that had been invented for the lead mines near Allenhead.

"Maybe. It might give us something else to look for up the hill."

"Yes, that's what I thought."

Gareth, staring after them as he lifted his gear from the back of the Land Rover, stood scratching his head for a minute, looking at the bulky rucksack and the retreating backs of the detectives. He wasn't quite sure how he was to get back to his digs in Maryport. He shrugged. He'd find someone to hitch a lift with if necessary.

McInnis wasn't thinking about Gareth and his transport problems; he was puzzling over the transport that had been carefully removed to Carlisle, among other things. If you had the ability to open a padlock, why didn't you hide the car inside the mine? He thought there had been enough room to get the car in; there was certainly enough headroom for the first twenty foot; they had been standing upright until then.

They parted at the surgery, Mark towards the house and McInnis going through the glass door and into the well lit reception area. Jenny Lowther popped her head out as he pushed the door shut. "Did you want me, Inspector? I haven't got any more customers."

McInnis rubbed his hand over his hair. "I think I need your skills, Doctor." He lifted his left hand which had a vicious and dirty graze on the palm. "I caught it crawling about in the mine entrance. It's a bit 'manky' as Mark might say."

Jenny looked at the hand and nodded silently to the surgery door. She waited for him to enter and then followed, closing the door after him. Bob stood by the side of the desk waiting for her.

"Come over to the sink and I'll give it a rinse then maybe we can see what the damage is."

Bob found the small sink promoted a closeness with a woman which he hadn't allowed in nearly six months. He moved uneasily as she ran the tap water over his palm, breathing in the mixed aromas of something herby and antiseptic vying with something lightly floral.

"Hmm! Not as bad as it looks, but nasty all the same."

She left him standing as she went to gather up a sterile cloth and came back to pat it dry. "Let's have you sitting down, Inspector, then maybe I can see if it needs a stitch." Jenny sat opposite the silent man and, turning his hand face up, laid it on the desk. "How's your tetanus? Up to date?" He grunted as she gently probed the wound, removing several pieces of grit. She glanced up at the policeman's face; it was a bit pale. "Nearly done."

She gave a final sweep with swab-wrapped forceps, and sat back. "Steri-strips I think. How did you manage to drive back without arguments?" She went over and got dressing equipment out of a cupboard, coming to sit back down as McInnis pulled the bloodstained hanky out of his jacket pocket and smiled faintly at her.

"How do you know we didn't argue? To tell the truth I think they were too busy to notice, actually."

"You didn't answer. Tetanus?"

"I probably need one."

"I'll dress this and then you can roll up your sleeve."

Jenny finished the light dressing and busied herself drawing up the dose as he shrugged out of his top jacket, and rolled up his shirt sleeve. He turned his head away, addressing a line of books above the desk, he said, "And now you know my Achilles heel, Jenny, I hate needles."

Jenny gave a faint chuckle. "Well I'm glad to know you've got one; mine is dentists. There you go, all done." She patted the arm and watched as he pulled down the cuff. "I wanted to see you again, Bob. I'm sorry I upset you yesterday."

Bob watched the faint pinkening of her cheeks with some surprise as she bent and fastened the small button for him.

He gave a faint shrug. "You weren't to know. Sandy tells me I must either learn to accept people care, or grow a thicker skin." He gave another small shrug.

"I should go for the thicker skin for now." Jenny smiled at him, a slightly gamin grin that proved she overcame her *bête noire* enough to visit the dentist regularly, deliberately misunderstanding him to give him space, and save his face a bit. "Your daughter is going to require several injections before she gets to school age." She helped him on with his jacket as he stood up. "Keep that hand dry for a day or two, and if you start to throw up come and see me. You might just have lead poisoning."

Bob looked at her, an arrested look on his face; he'd just had a thought that might lead to an arrest anyway. "Give me the symptoms."

"I was joking, Bob. That much exposure shouldn't cause any damage."

Bob shook his head. "Yeah, I understand that, but give me the symptoms."

Jenny looked at him curiously, sensing his urgency. "I don't know all of them off the top of my head; it's not something that walks into the surgery on a daily basis. Let me think a minute."

He waited in respectful silence.

"OK, little children can be retarded, but that's long-term exposure. We do sometimes see hobbyists or people working in the paint industry with symptoms. Nausea, loss of appetite and collateral weight loss. Kidney failure, there's a reaction in the red blood cells but I'd have to look that one up. Anaemia, insomnia." She shook her head. "I'm sorry I'm failing 'lead poisoning 101' aren't I?"

"Don't worry about it, Jenny. It was just a thought."

She smiled at him. "Come and have a coffee and tell me about it." They turned to walk out in companionable silence. Jack, who had been resting under the desk, emerged to give a shake and a small yip. "It's time he stretched his legs."

McInnis waited patiently while she locked up the surgery and Jack went and cocked his leg against a bush. Then they headed for the lit windows of the comfortable home that the former Doctor Sandman had occupied. "How long will you stay here now, Jenny?"

"I've extended my leave for two more weeks after this, but I'm contracted to the Penrith surgery for over another year, seventeen months actually, so I'll have to go back. I'm sorry to leave the village without care though."

"Could you not take over the surgery?"

"Got a few thousand to spare?" She raised an ironical eyebrow. "No, Maureen will have to sell the practice, and it's not that big, which is one of the problems, but it's more than I can afford. Not many doctors want to take on a little isolated village, and even less will do the callouts Doctor Sandman did."

Bob held the door open for her as he followed and went to shut it as Jack shot in on her heels. They both heard the quiet murmur of voices as they walked down the passageway. Mark was sitting at the table talking to Maureen who was in her favourite chair by the Aga.

"Hi, Mo', how you doing?"

"I'm fine, Jenny. Mark here has been telling me about the mine opening." She caught the faint frown McInnis threw across, "Don't worry, Inspector, not the police business, though you let me in on a bit of it the other day." She smiled quietly at him. "Just about the entrance itself."

Mark nodded as Bob smiled faintly at him.

"I was asking if there were any signs of tracks up there. It might help you date the mine if steam engines had been used to haul the wagons."

McInnis sat down as Jenny moved towards the sink and filled the kettle. "Actually we have a name for the mine now, 'The West End' it was called. 1870s to '90s. So there could have been wagon tracks, but we didn't see any signs of them."

"Did you know that British Rail got its standard gauge from the Romans?" Jenny swung around from switching on the kettle and grinned at them.

"Pardon?"

Jenny leaned back against the work surface, looking at them. "It's one of those silly facts I learnt when I first started caving. Roman carts were built with wheels four foot eight inches apart; they wore ruts in the roads, and ruts in the Roman mines. Then the steam engines took over in some of those same mines and used the standard gauge left by the Romans."

Bob rubbed an ear. "It's a nice irrelevant fact. But I don't think this mine was a Roman one. He paused, thinking. "Mark, did we measure the entrance?"

"Yeah. Five two."

"I can't figure out why the car wasn't stowed inside. Nicely hidden from prying eyes. At five two, the entrance was wide enough."

"Don't think it had the height even if it had the width, sir. Maybe whoever left it didn't have a padlock key?"

Bob shook his head. "It just doesn't seem right." He looked at the fascinated faces of the two women. "I apologise, ladies. And to you too, Mark; now I'm talking police business."

Jenny nodded at him. "Coffee, Bob?"

"Yes, and no more shop talk."

The men kept the conversation light, while they drank coffee and ate a piece of Maureen's chocolate cake.

"This is wonderful." Mark smiled around the slice he was polishing off. "But shouldn't you be resting?"

"I don't know about that, I've got this urge to wash floors and turn out drawers. And since I've done that already, I thought I'd bake."

"Oh! Yes, I remember Beth doing that, she said it..." Bob stopped speaking, looking at Jenny with pain writhing over his face.

"Finish the thought, Bob." Jenny spoke softly to him, laying a hand on his, as the other two held their breath.

He looked at her, and then took a deep breath. "She said it was the nesting instinct and she made me laugh because she claimed she'd empty the bank, buying nesting material."

There was an infinitesimal pause before Maureen spoke. "I said something similar to Neil. He couldn't believe how much stuff we needed for one small baby. He said we'd need to borrow Trevor's van to load everything for a day trip."

"Say that again." Bob looked at Maureen, the grief crowded out by ideas, like rugby fans trying to get in before the kick off.

"How much stuff…"

"No, not that." Bob shook his head in frustration,

Maureen looked at the urgency on his face; it was the face of a man seeing his train leave the station, without him.

"We needed heaps of stuff for a day trip?"

"N…o that wasn't it." He stood up. "Thank you for the coffee, I've got to go." Maureen exchanged a look with Jenny. It said 'Help. What did I do now? Find out!'

Jenny walked behind him as Bob headed to the door. Becoming aware of her, Bob stopped and opened it for her. They went through silently.

Jenny led the way to the front door, then turned, blocking his exit. "I'm sorry, Bob, we've upset you again."

290

"No." He smiled, a quirk of the lips. "No, I've been hiding the good bits because I was afraid of the bad bits."

Jenny raised an elegant eyebrow.

Bob tried again. "I wouldn't let myself remember anything at all, but Beth and I, we had lots of good times. I needed to remember them. So thank you, Jenny. But, it wasn't that, I had an idea about the case; I need to go and think about it some more."

He offered his gentle smile, and Jenny fell just a bit more in love with the troubled man in front of her. She wisely kept her thoughts to herself. "I'll let you go then, but if I can help, I'm here."

He nodded and opened the door. "You look after Maureen's health; I'll get her some justice."

14

McInnis had driven back to Maryport a thoughtful man. He'd found Sandy morosely sprinkling ginger biscuit crumbs amid a sea of hand written notes.

Bob greeted him saying, "Hi, Sandy. You look like I feel. What you doing, casting your biscuit crumbs on the waters in the hope that they'll come back buttered?"

"The answer's here, Bob. I know it is." Sandy set the half-chewed biscuit down and looked across the room as his partner sank wearily onto the end of the bed, the only available space, as both chairs were heaped with files.

Bob's response echoed Sandy's frustration. "Yes, I feel the same way. We've got all the clues. We just haven't managed to put them together in the right way." Bob rubbed a hand over his hair and yelped softly as a few pulled on the sticking plaster.

"What you done?"

"Just a graze, the Doc's checked it out." He sighed. "Let's start at the beginning, see if we can't get something."

"OK, but I need a mug of tea if I'm going to do that."

"So do I." Bob nodded at the kettle. "I'll put that on, while you sort this lot out." He indicated the paper drifts.

Once they'd settled, Bob now on a chair and minus his jacket, they began to organise things on a sheet of paper on the floor between them, a couple of red markers lying ready to hand.

"OK, on Sunday the fourteenth of September…" Sandy started reeling of the time-line.

"No, let's go back a bit further, Sandy. Doc Sandman has arranged to go on holiday. He plans to be away two weeks and three weekends. His wife doesn't get too upset about him leaving without kissing her goodbye because, a. he's not demonstrative, b. she's nearly thirty-four weeks pregnant and he doesn't like disturbing her sleep when he does callout and c, she's had texts on her mobile, she believes came from him, since he left."

"The Saturday morning his holiday is due to start…" Sandy took the red marker, "the thirteenth; he had a call out at two in the morning. Mrs…." He looked at Bob for inspiration.

"Gregory."

"Yeah, Gregory. Her twins have got croup. He goes to see them. We know he left her at about three. Give or take a minute. Then we lose track of him. Anything else for this time Bob?"

"Yes, Andrew Hamilton. Up to no good, we've yet to determine what, but he admits to being awake at four that morning, possibly hearing a vehicle and hearing something go splash in the harbour. Oakes hasn't found any more out has he, Sandy?"

"He was interviewing the wife and son today, but he hasn't got back to me." Sandy rubbed his chin.

Bob checked his notes. "Because of tide and times we're fairly certain that the splash was Doctor Sandman going into the harbour anyway."

Sandy nodded and followed through the thought. "And that a vehicle was involved. But whether it was his or some other person's, like the murderer's for instance, we don't know." He wrote 'vehicle heard' on the sheet and sat back. "What next?"

"Next would be the Simpson boys coming to 'borrow' Pheby's boat later that day, which he admits had disappeared by then. The boys couldn't find the boat either. Now we know that that boat was underwater, still with its oars shipped and line..." he grinned at Sandy, "beg pardon, painter, flapping about. Question is, was the boat used in the murder to bring the Doc round to the drop site and dump him overboard? If so what was the vehicle Hamilton heard? Was the boat sunk to hide any trace of the murderer?"

"Well they're good questions, Bob, and hopefully Mark might get us some answers." He paused, exchanging pen for mug, and drinking before looking over the rim at McInnis. "The next event would be the following Friday. The Simpson boys having thrown a set of lobster pots over the side of the harbour wall during the week are desperate to retrieve them. How did they hope to do that Bob?"

"I think they had their eye on a dinghy but couldn't get to it." He raised an eyebrow. "What I want to know, Sandy, is why the body wasn't spotted during the preceding week? You'd think that at low tide someone would have noticed it floating about. If I understood Mark correctly, with his threes, from say Wednesday onwards, it should have been visible at low tide." He scrabbled among the papers. "Look, this is the tide table."

Sandy accepted the paper thrust at him and peered at the small print. He handed it back. "Explain, lad."

Bob took the paper, running his finger down the line of figures. "Low tide from Wednesday onwards happened at roughly one thirty in the afternoon and then got gradually later. According to this chart it was even lower, most of the time, than the night the boys found him."

"Now that's a damn good question, Bob. And one I hadn't spotted."

· "OK, let's file that for the minute and keep on with the timeline."

"Midnight the following Friday, the boys discover the body while trying to get their pots, and call their big brother." Sandy nodded as Bob wrote it down. "He delays a bit to keep them from trouble, which didn't work." He pointed a ginger nut at Bob and then dunked it. "After that," he bit into biscuit, "we appear on the scene." He munched, "Where does that get us?"

"We ain't finished yet. Eric Potts disappears six weeks ago but has only been dead about two. He might have been found among the Roman harbour ruins, but we think he's come from a cave complex over near Greystone. Yes?"

"Yes. So?"

"So the chances are, he either saw or heard something, maybe he was up at the mine, minding his own business, grinding lead ore for his own purposes. We believe he nicked the quern." He grinned. "And we said nobody would be stupid enough to sign the book if they were stealing it!" He grinned again, then continued. "The killer comes up to dump the car, and Potts sees him acting suspiciously and they get into it, and the murderer kills Potts too."

"No that won't work, Bob, the quern was around Doc Sandman's feet."

"He could still have surprised our murderer with the car."

"True." They sat in thoughtful silence.

"What if they were in cahoots?" Sandy set his empty mug down. "Eric Potts wasn't known to run with a pack but he might have had a partner."

"To do what, Sandy? The only activity we could see happening up in that mine entrance was with the quern. And it looked as if they were using it to grind lead ore. Though Mark did think they might be making lead shot." He shook his head. "You use a quern to grind corn and wheat and barley, not ore." His mouth twitched up at Sandy's comical look.

295

"No, hang on!" Sandy, suddenly emulating gazelles, made a leap for his jacket, sending a pile of papers sliding onto the floor. Bob raised an eyebrow, but continued to sit as the older man pulled his report book from his jacket and flipped it open, muttering to himself like a lunatic.

"Here." He in turn thrust something at Bob. "I need my specs. What does it say?"

Bob, confronted by the spidery handwriting, wrinkled his nose and began to read out loud. "Early fifth century, Roman quern, used to grind," He stopped, a grin sliding over his face and surprising them both. "Used to grind maize, this one had traces of maize and silver ore. Of course, Nancy said the Romans mined for argentiferous galena around here. That's silver to you and me, Sandy."

"So they could have been trying to make a quick buck, Bob."

"Yes, and it could be thieves falling out when one uses the quern to weigh someone down in the harbour. Yes, I can see that." Bob nodded. "But who would have a connection with Eric Potts? He didn't strike me as the brightest candle in the box. Who told him to go looking for silver in the mine? And did the same somebody also tell him to steal the quern for extraction purposes?"

Sandy scowled in frustration. "It has to be someone who knew both Potts and the Doctor, and had a connection to both and the opportunity to sneak out at night and kill the Doctor. Someone who has the opportunity to mine for silver without exciting comment." Sandy sat back, his momentary excitement dimming.

Bob handed back the book and absently smoothed the dressing on his palm. He stared at the dressing for so long that Sandy was beginning to worry. Bob began to speak slowly, still looking at the dressing. "When Jenny dressed this, she joked that I should report signs of lead poisoning to her. I wondered at the time if we might spot the person who had been in the mine by seeing signs of lead poisoning in them, Sandy. Trouble is I can't think of anyone who fits the bill."

"Tell me, I'll have a think."

Bob scratched his chin then repeated the symptoms he'd gleaned from Jenny Lowther. "Can you think of anyone, Sandy? Someone with those symptoms, motive for murder and no alibi."

Sandy shrugged. "Not off hand, lad." He shrugged again. "Let's have another cuppa, while I think."

Bob shook his head. "No more for me."

Sandy got up and put the teabag into the mug, whistling tunelessly through his teeth. When he had the fresh mug he looked across at his frowning partner.

"We still haven't found a motive."

"No, I know, Sandy. That's been worrying me all along. The Doctor was a conscientious man, who delivered his care to the best of his ability."

"He had his detractors, Bob. He was against abortion, probably euthanasia, and certainly believed in calling a spade a spade and not a garden implement. For the most part his patients appreciated the time he was prepared to give them."

"He didn't attend one patient."

"Who was that then?"

"Mrs Paton. But it's a bit difficult to visit her in hospital when you're at the bottom of the harbour."

"No, you've got that wrong. He was supposed to see her for a check-up before he left for his holiday. Trevor Paton said the Doctor was going to look her over before he went away."

.

Bob McInnis shook his head. "She was in hospital, that night; the staff on duty said they were surprised the Doctor hadn't been in to see her before discharge, but then they remembered he was going on holiday and didn't worry about it. He'd seen her a couple of days before."

The two detectives looked at each other and then both said, "I'll get my notes."

Before either could act there was a knock at the door and the smiling face of Detective Sergeant Oakes appeared around it, like a harvest moon around a cloud.

"Sorry to interrupt, Inspector Bell, but I've got some good news for you." He took a further two steps into the room, and then his gaze took in the papers and files scattered like so much lumpy confetti on the carpet.

"That's alright, Sergeant, we could do with some good news."

"Well, sir, we finished the interview with Hamilton, his son and his wife and..." a look of unholy joy found itself in unaccustomed surroundings as the Detective Sergeant smiled at them, "his girlfriend."

Oakes came over as McInnis lifted a pile of files from the chair to the floor and went to sit on the end of the bed. "I find myself strangely interested. Do tell us more, Oakes."

Happily, Oakes waded through paperwork and sat down. "It seems Andrew Hamilton has been having an affair for eighteen months now. His wife knew about it but kept mum."

"Why, a God's name? I wouldn't want to stay with a man," Bell grinned, "OK, a woman, who was betraying me with another."

"Me neither." McInnis nodded.

Oakes shrugged. "Finances, a comfortable home and, from what she said, wife status without married woman obligations." He watched the other two as their eyebrows quirked in astonishment.

"Anyway we got them all in for interview; the son didn't know anything except what his father told him about the splash and vehicle. But the wife was a different kettle of fish. We started out gentle like, asking about when he went to the boat and his regular habits while there. That's when she dropped the bombshell. 'Why didn't we ask the floozy he kept for sailing nights?' You could have knocked me down with a feather.

"Guess who his floozy is?"

McInnis exchanged a glance of puzzlement with Sandy. "Haven't a clue, but judging by your expression we know the name."

"Yep, Alison Lythe. Sandman's receptionist."

"Good grief. So that's what she was hiding! She must have had a hell of a shock when we came enquiring about the Doctor, especially when she realised she must have been on the scene at the time."

"You're not joking, Bob. I thought she was jealous of the new wife. She'd worked for him for nearly ten years, and I thought she was looking for a cushy billet, but she was probably scared of the Doctor condemning her morals."

"Could well be, Sandy."

"That's more or less what she said to us." Oakes grinned again. "Very upstanding man the Doctor. He wouldn't have liked her having an affair with a married man. Believed in morals and duty, did the Doctor." He sat back a little in his chair.

"So she admitted being there?"

"Oh, yeah!. Couldn't wait to tell us everything she knew once we cornered her. She alibis Alex Hamilton, if he needed one. It's not surprising he was a bit put out when he thought his son had come to the docks early. Son didn't know anything about Alison and was vociferous in his defence of his mother. Obviously Hamilton didn't want the son to find the girlfriend on deck." A sly grin turned his lips up. "It gets even better though." Oakes was leaning forward in his chair again by this time, his face as full of excitement as a kid on Christmas morning.

"Come next week for the next thrilling instalment," said Sandy, nodding across the room. "Don't keep us in suspense, man."

"Hamilton rolled over on Pheby. They had a deal going. Pheby used his rowing boat to fetch the stones, and Hamilton sold them in Ireland for a good profit, which they shared between them.

"Good news, sir?" He settled back in his seat again.

"I never did like him for the murder. But yes, great news, Sarge, it clears up several mysteries and snips off a hank of threads."

"So what did I interrupt, Inspector? Can I help?"

Sandy looked at McInnis and then at Oakes. He prodded the paper on the floor with his toe. "We're trying to get motive and opportunity; we were just about to discover which of us had been lied to by a certain man. Trouble is he's disabled, I can't see a motive, there's no connection I can think of with Eric Potts, and his opportunities are severely limited."

"And who might that be, sir?"

"Trevor Paton," Bob spoke.

"Yeah." Sandy sighed as he watched astonishment make a quick dash across Oakes' face. "Bob, what did the hospital say?"

McInnis found the file of notes. "They said that, Mrs Paton had come for a final X-ray before being declared cured of a chest infection. Your hospital isn't exactly big, but it was nearly empty. Mrs Paton threw a wobbly in the department and they ended up sedating her and keeping her for the night." He wrinkled his patrician nose. "The staff thought they were doing Trevor Paton a favour. They were giving him a night off. Told me he was worn out with the care of his mum and even a night's break, which was all they could legitimately offer, might help."

Sandy nodded. "Now in my interview with Paton, himself, he implied she was at home, and the Doctor was coming to give her a check-up before going off on holiday." He paused. "Someone else told me she'd wrecked the X-ray unit. Who the hell was it?" He stared blankly into space while the other two waited in respectful silence.

"Anne somebody or other. Lives next to that old guy who told Gareth to go back to his own country."

Oakes frowned. "But I thought Constable Rhys was a Welshman?"

"He is. Silenced the poor lad completely. What's more I don't think he's sorted out the dustbins yet. Twentyman. That was the name."

While Bell shuffled forward in his seat and began flipping over folders like a high wind through leaves. Oakes and McInnis had identical looks of confusion.

"Sandy, are the dustbins relevant?"

Sandy looked up, two files clutched in his hand and a look of triumph on his face. He frowned. "No, of course not." He waved away the interjection. "Now how did Paton know that the Doctor was out and about at three in the morning?" He scowled at the two men as if they were responsible for the puzzle.

Oakes rubbed his fingers up and down his neck, stretching the skin upwards. "Who was he visiting again?"

"Mother of twins. Lyn Gregory, croup." Bob supplied the answer.

Oakes smiled happily again. "That one's easy; she lives down Church Lane. I remember interviewing her about Potts when he went missing. Potts' parents live next door to her. Doctor Sandman would have to pass Paton's door to get to hers."

"Still doesn't explain how Paton knew he was about at that time of day." Sandy shook his head.

"Except," Bob said the word slowly, "that he said he didn't sleep much. He could have been looking out of the window, seen the Doctor go down the lane and waylaid him on the way back."

The three men looked at each other, trying the idea out for size. "All right, so you've got him in position, Bob. He was going there anyway and didn't apparently know that the old lady was in hospital for the night. If Paton waited for him, and intercepted him – hang on, no that won't work, how did Paton stop the car?"

"Why should he have taken the car, Sandy? We walked there; it was less than five minutes from the surgery. If the Doctor was on foot, Paton could have just popped out and invited him in for a minute."

Oakes was watching the fast rally of words, turning his head from one man to the other.

"So we give him, opportunity, no alibi, but what the hell was the motive and how do you connect him to Potts?" Sandy asked sitting back, absently scratching his head. "It's a bit thin; maybe we just misunderstood the guy."

Silence reigned again, in fact it poured into the room, bringing gloom with it. "I need to sleep on it, Sandy."

"Yeah, me too."

Oakes, taking this as his cue, exited stage left wishing them both a pleasant good night. For a minute or two there he'd actually been contemplating abandoning early retirement. He knew he couldn't take the stress though; he'd already got two stomach ulcers.

Bob and Sandy parted for the night almost straight afterwards. Bob headed for the comfort of his bedroom and had reached the stage where he had taken off his shoes, jacket and tie, when the phone by the bedside rang. He sat down, his mind divided between the case and the problems he was having washing and keeping a dressing dry.

"Hello?" He spoke almost absently.

Jenny's voice in his ear was a surprise. "I wasn't sure whether to bother you or not, Inspector."

"What did I do to become 'Inspector' again?" He settled firmly on the side of the bed, aware suddenly of the fact that his feet were cold and the radiator in front of him, and under the window, hot. He stretched out his toes, so that they just touched the base of the heating.

"Nothing, I'm just never very sure what to call you."

"Oh!" He frowned at the phone.

"Look, Inspector Bob..." She heard his chuckle.

"Makes me sound like that children's character, *Bob the Builder*, my nephew is so fond of."

"Bob, listen will you?" She sounded just as exasperated as Beth used to, he thought, then realised the sharp pang of grief wasn't there. His mind wandered away up this dusty by-road to examine the phenomenon, only to be brought up short by her "….is the most common sign of peripheral neuropathy in lead poisoning."

He snapped back into the present abruptly. "I'm sorry, Jenny, say that again; I've got a lot on my mind at the moment."

He heard the patient sigh down the line. "I said, I've looked up lead poisoning for you, and as well as all the other things I mentioned earlier, the most common side affect is something called wristdrop. It happens when the peripheral nervous system becomes affected. It takes weeks of exposure to develop though, but it stays affected because lead takes so long to be expelled from the body."

Bob was no longer lounging on the bed. He was sitting upright, remembering Trevor Paton handling a spoon which drooped in his hand as he opened the door to Sandy and himself. They had both thought he was disabled in some way, but maybe not. Or maybe not in the way they had imagined.

Jenny, waiting on the end of the line and listening to the gathering silence, said, "Bob. Isn't it any help?" She could hear the smile in his voice as he answered her.

"I think it might just be the final thing needed to convict someone. You've been a great help, Jenny."

"No problem. Take care of that hand. Wear one of your forensic gloves to keep it dry."

She put the phone down and Bob's lips twitched, "I would have got there." He spoke to the air as he crossed the room and fished in his briefcase for a pair of blue latex gloves, easing one over his hand and the dressing before going to take a shower.

The next morning both men had finished their plan over the toast and marmalade. "We can pull him in for questioning, Bob, but who's going to look after the old lady? I'm almost certain he's our man. That bit about the wrist that the Doc told you last night, is the clincher for my money."

"We still haven't got a motive, Sandy."

"Perhaps he'll give us one. Come on, lad, eat up. You'll be cooking for yourself tomorrow."

Bob picked up his cup obediently, but grinned before he drank it. "Oh, no I won't, I'm staying with you and Sarah this weekend, while I get Caitlin's room sorted out at home."

Sandy gave him a surprised look, like someone who'd expected a monsoon and felt the heat of a summer day instead. "Will you indeed! And there was me looking forward to some peace and quiet, with only my father and daughter disturbing my rest at three in the morning." He too picked up his cup. "Drink up. We've got a murderer to arrest."

They made their way to the police station to gather a constable or two. If Paton had managed to throw the doctor into the harbour he was stronger than he looked and they wanted no arguments about his coming in for questioning.

Oakes greeted them and, almost before they were through the main doors, said, "I was talking to the hospital this morning, asking about this infection that Mrs Paton was supposed to have." He nodded as a couple of constables saluted on their way out on patrol. "Paton has an appointment this afternoon at two. His mother has another X-ray due; apparently they found something on her lung at the last check. Maybe cancer." He led the way into his office and the Carlisle men sat down opposite his desk.

Sergeant Oakes seated himself. "If we hang on a bit the hospital could perhaps look after his mother while we interview him. What do you think, sir?"

Sandy and Bob exchanged a look. McInnis spoke, "I think it sounds like a good plan. Do you want to be present at the interview, Oakes? It's your town and you've done as much of the work as we have."

Oakes recognised it for the compliment it was, and flushed under their fascinated gaze. He nodded his thanks. They were drinking coffee as they waited when he put another piece of the puzzle in place. "By the way, I've got a couple who moored their boat right next to the harbour entrance for a couple of days, the Wednesday and Thursday, they sailed Friday on the five o'clock tide; they've been up to Scotland for a few days, second honeymoon and incommunicado." He watched as Sandy nodded approval. "They told me Pheby said it was an empty berth."

"And Pheby could have told us, if he hadn't been hiding his own activities." Bob almost growled the comment.

Pretty entered as they drank yet more coffee and finalised plans for the afternoon's interviews. He offered a salute and handed a thickish file to Oakes, standing back respectfully.

"Ah! Constable Pretty," Bob nodded, "have you met DI Bell?"

Bell looked at the slim youth, smiling kindly. "I hear you've been a great help to us, Constable. We appreciate your input."

Oliver's face reflected his astonishment. If he'd received promotion on the spot he couldn't have been more surprised. "I've enjoyed seeing the case develop, sir. The Simpson boys have been to visit Mr Saunders, Inspector McInnis. They asked me to go with them." He offered an explanation where none was required.

"How did it go?"

Pretty allowed a smile to sneak onto his face, displacing the official blandness for a minute. "I'm invited on the next trip too. He's a fascinating gentleman. He knows so much about the history of the area, sir. He was telling the boys about the silver mine up in the hills."

McInnis gave a low groan.

"Sir?"

"Nothing, Constable. What was he telling you?"

"Well actually the boys already knew about it. One of the older boys in the school had been mates with their brother James and they'd talked of making their fortune from it." Pretty shook his head. "Mr Saunders said it would never work; there wasn't enough silver to make it commercially viable. But the mine had an interesting history." He relaxed, smiling, his official stance long since submerged by his enthusiasm.

Sandy's lips twitched. "Well I hope you enjoy yourself, Constable."

Pretty, recollecting his surroundings, slammed to attention; saluting and getting himself out with what dignity he could scrape up.

Oakes turned to the new file. "This is the forensics report. It's only a prelim'." He scanned over the page. "They've confirmed your opinion about the place of the fight in the mine." He handed over a sheet and then two photocopies of footprints. "These match; it was Eric Potts in there. That much is certain."

He continued flicking through the paperwork, passing over each sheet as he finished.

"So now we know how he got into the water, Sandy." Bob finished reading and waited patiently for Sandy to do the same. "Disappeared down a tunnel to wait for our suspect to go away and probably got lost down there. I wonder if he succumbed to CO_2 poisoning before he haemorrhaged out completely."

"No way to tell now, Bob." Sandy sighed. "It's a hell of a way to go for a youngster. For anyone for that matter."

Bob nodded agreement but he was frowning too. "Have we got a warrant to examine Paton's shoes?"

"Yeah, got one for the shoes, the shed, the van; if he's been up to the mine we'll know about it." Sandy rubbed his chin. "I'm ninety-nine percent certain he's our man. But we need solid proof of his presence. We've got means and lack of alibi, we still haven't got motive, Bob."

"Maybe he'll give us one."

15

It was a bigger room; there was plenty of space to accommodate the three detectives, their acolyte in the shape of Gareth looming by the door, and several uncomfortable chairs set around a very solid table.

Paton, seated next to a stern man in a pinstripe, was glancing nervously from one man to the next. They had taken his details explaining the need for a further interview to establish the timeline better. Now Bob was preparing to open the main line of questioning. Paton supplied him, unknowingly, with his feed line.

"I really shouldn't be away from my mother too long; she can be difficult with strangers."

Bob, all sympathy, nodded, "Yes I remember you saying you didn't leave her. In fact you said you hadn't had a break in three years. Is that correct, sir?"

"That would be about right. I moved in with her when it became obvious she needed full-time care. To tell the truth my wife threw me out of our home because I was spending so much time round at my mother's. It was convenient."

"And before you moved in with your mother, sir, what did you do?"

"What, do you mean where did I live or what work did I do?"

"Well work, and hobbies, sir."

Paton looked at them a bit blankly. "You want to know my hobbies?"

"Yes, sir."

He shrugged. "I worked in an office, organising tours of the Lake District. Sometimes I even acted as courier and guide myself."

"And your hobbies?"

The frown was gathering, "I biked, I fished, I walked the hills. You can't guide if you're not fit. I taught my son football too, when he was younger."

"You went caving too, didn't you?"

"Well yes, but not for a long while. My son's eighteen now, he used to go with me and…"

"And who, sir?"

"Just one of his school friends. I forget his name."

"Would it be Eric Potts, sir?"

"Potts, yeah I think that was his name." A slight film of sweat was sitting on his forehead and was duly noted by all three men.

"Did you know Eric Potts has been killed?"

"Has he? What was it, motor accident?"

"No, much worse than that, the poor lad, he bled internally, then suffocated. It would have taken him a long time to die according to our medical examiner. He'd been beaten up." Sandy smiled faintly. "It's lucky he got a scratch or two back. We've got some interesting stuff from under his nails; hopefully it will lead us back to his murderer."

They watched as Paton glanced at his own hands. "I thought you said he'd drowned. Wouldn't the water have washed away all that sort of evidence?"

"Who said he'd drowned, sir?"

"You did. You said he suffocated." The hunted look on his face said the hounds were closing in.

"No. I said he suffocated, that would be from loss of blood, but you're right, Mr Paton, he did drown. Not in water though, in his own body fluids. We'll still get some DNA evidence though. We've also got some fingerprints. Would you like to know where we found them?" Sandy was using a mailed fist without the velvet glove now.

Paton was shaking his head, partly in negation of the question but also in denial at what was happening to him.

"We found them on a bike outside your house. A trail bike with Eric Potts' name inside the upright." He mentally thanked Mark, who'd had the wits to look when he'd finished taking footprints and tyre treads.

"Don't you need a warrant for that?" Paton was fighting for his life as much as Doctor Sandman did.

"No, sir. Public domain, it was in plain view."

"Eric must have left it last time he visited then."

"And you just happened to borrow it in the recent rains and get it covered with lead dust?"

"He went up to that mine you were on about. He'd been investigating it for months, years even."

"Funny you didn't think to tell us about that when we asked you if you knew of an entrance."

"I'd forgotten." Paton was openly sweating now, his hands shaking slightly as he rested them on the tabletop.

Bob took over the questioning again, his gentle voice lulling Trevor Paton into relaxing as much as his question did. "You have an interesting vehicle to bring your mother to the hospital Mr Paton."

311

Paton looked at him, as grateful for the lifeline as Sandman would have been. "It's specially adapted for her wheelchair, Inspector; it has a lift at the back to raise and lower her."

"Yes, I was looking at it in the hospital car park. It not only goes up it looks as though it extends outwards a bit too."

"Goes out nearly three feet, it's instead of a ramp; it means I can get the wheelchair up steps easily. I got an engineer friend to design it for me."

"How's it stabilised then? Won't it tip with the weight when you extend?"

"No, there are extra weights that swing down when it swings out." Paton was obviously beginning to relax and swell with pride at the praise for his invention.

"So if you extended out over water, say at the harbour, it wouldn't tip up when you dropped the good Doctor in, would it?" The question slid silkily into the room, almost as silkily as the doctor had slid into the water, and with just as dire consequences, and Paton seemed to deflate.

Bob continued to look, a small part of him pitying the man in front of him. "You see we have nearly all the pieces, Mr Paton. We know that you drowned the Doctor in the harbour. We know that you used your adapted van to drop him out and over the water. We know you weighted him with a millstone that you'd been using to grind lead ore and that the combined weight caught on the Harbour Master's boat, which was filled with gravel, and tipped the boat over and into the harbour." McInnis ground down the man in front of him, leaving very little hope.

Relentlessly the evidence, small dusty particles of it, were being used to choke him as effectively as a noose would have in the past. "We know you could do all this because your mother was staying the night in Maryport Hospital, we even know that you

312

dumped his car up at the mine. You might have worn gloves before you took hold of the wheel, but you forgot about it when you fastened the seat-belt and you obviously didn't think about it when you hid the Doctor's number plates in that van of yours." He laid down the pen he'd been holding.

"We think Eric Potts and you had some sort of fight up there. We have matched footprints from you both in the mine entrance. What we don't have is a motive."

"All this is very circumstantial, Inspector. You'll have to do better if you want to get a conviction," said the sartorial vision from the law courts.

Both McInnis and Paton ignored him. McInnis was watching Paton's face. Paton was looking at his hands again.

McInnis asked, "Why the text messages to Mrs Sandman? Wasn't that rather cruel Mr Paton?" His voice had become stern.

Paton looked blankly at him for a moment. Then he lifted his head. He spoke to McInnis, ignoring everyone else. "He said it was my duty, my bloody duty. I lost contact with my kids, I lost my job, I lost my home, I lost my wife. And he said it was my bloody duty. More like a millstone, so I gave him one and watched him suffer as well; see how he liked losing his wife and child." He sighed.

"I used his phone to text her to delay things a bit. I didn't know you'd found his body until the constable came to question me." He shook his head. "Mother broke the TV." He sighed again.

"He was pretty tired when he came to call. He sat down and I offered to make him a cuppa. By the time I came back into the room he'd nodded off, sound asleep, man was shattered; he had something wrong with his heart you know." The last was said almost conversationally. "I tied him up nice and neat while he sat and snored." He stopped speaking and the silence filled the room like a dark aura, a conflation of guilt and self-pity surrounding the man in front of McInnis.

"Did you know he was arranging for you to have day care for your mother and respite for you? It was in his notes; he'd filled the forms out, they were among his papers at the surgery. They just needed your signature." He paused as Trevor Paton started to shake. "What brought things to a head Mr Paton? Why now? You've cared for your mother for three years."

"She had an infection. She's hard enough to deal with, but when she's sick she's unmanageable. Why didn't he let nature take its course instead of stuffing her full of antibiotics? Her mind's gone, or why couldn't he put her into hospital, just so I could have a break? All I wanted was a bloody break." He was almost whispering, "Was that too much to ask? But he insisted she stay at home; he said it was better; she wouldn't be so agitated in her own place with her own caring for her. But what about me? What about me?" He stopped speaking and sat staring at his hands.

Sandy nodded across at the lawyer, then at Bob McInnis. His voice was very gentle as he spoke but the words were a death knell to Paton's freedom. "Mr Paton, you have admitted murdering Doctor Sandman and will be formally charged with that offence. We are also cautioning you and will be charging you with the manslaughter of Eric Potts. You did fight with him didn't you?"

Paton sighed deeply. "Yeah. He was working the mine for bits of silver. I thought he was finally getting his act together, making something of himself and trying to finance his way. I showed him how to get the silver from the ore. We found the old mine years ago. I took Doctor Sandman's car up there after –" he swallowed "– after I'd been to the harbour. I was going to dump it inside but Eric was already there, camping out." He stopped. "Could I have a drink of water?"

McInnis looked at Gareth, who quietly left the room and returned with a plastic beaker of water. Paton sipped and set it down.

"Sandman never locked his car, it was outside the surgery. I took the car up and Potts recognised it. He was feeling aggrieved anyway; he couldn't find the top of his grindstone." Paton gave a small and crooked smile. "He started asking about the car, he recognised it; he said he'd report me and then we started arguing and we fought. He tripped and fell and I thought he'd knocked himself out, so I went outside to get the car and bring it into the mine. By the time I'd started it up and manoeuvred it round, he'd locked himself in."

He sipped more water before speaking to Sandy Bell. "I took his bike to get home. I should have gotten rid of it shouldn't I?"

Sandy said nothing; what could he say?

Bob McInnis took up the threads. "Would you like some time to talk to this lawyer, or would you prefer one of your own?"

"What does it matter? You write it down and I'll sign it, Inspector. At least I'll get a decent night's rest tonight and someone else will have to deal with my mother." He looked at the pity in Bob's eyes and sighed.

Sandy and Bob extracted details, as painlessly as dentists with degrees, and at the end of the day he went quietly to a cell without a backward glance.

The report came in later that afternoon. The streambed had indeed led to the top of a water blast. The child had paid its debt for being found; it had shown them the second entrance, and Jeff Lyell couldn't wait to abseil down into the cave from the top and explore some more. Mark was planning on going with him and taking the fascinating details back to Maureen Sandman. He figured it was the best excuse for maintaining contact he'd ever have.

McInnis was attending a funeral. It was his second that week, the first had been for Doctor Sandman. His wife Maureen looked ready to burst, and Mark had hovered solicitously around her. He had been calm and courteous and fiercely defensive, shielding her from journalist and the inquisitive alike, without making his feelings for her obvious. As far as anyone else was concerned he was her police protection, and he intended it to stay that way.

The second funeral only had four mourners and the coffin was tiny. McInnis stood bare-headed as the small child found on the hillside was laid in the angel's plot in the Catholic cemetery.

Beside him Jenny Lowther stood quietly waiting. He'd contacted her to give her the information about the child and she said she wanted to attend the funeral. McInnis turned away as the Father finished speaking and nodded at the gravedigger to cover the coffin with soil. He looked across to where Sandy and Sarah stood waiting at the entrance gate, his daughter in Sarah's arms. "I'm lucky to have her, and I intend to keep her safe." It was almost a vow.

"She's beautiful, Bob."

Bob McInnis turned as the sun glinted on the woman beside him. He offered her his gentle smile. "She is isn't she?"